RED NAILS

a novel

D.C. LEGENDRE

MUIR LIGHT
Publishing

Cover design, interior book design, and eBook design
by Blue Harvest Creative
www.blueharvestcreative.com

Published by
Muir Light Publishing

ISBN-13: 978-0615969336
ISBN-10: 061596933X

Visit the author at:
www.facebook.com/dclegendreauthor
www.twitter.com/DCLegendre

To the Pirates and Angels
who have come into my life,
bringing laughter, love and experiences
that I never dreamed possible.

one

THE END

DECEMBER 8

I sat on the floor looking through a book trying to find anything I could about divorce. I heard a key in the door and he walked in. He came over to me as I sat there. He hugged me and said that he forgave me. I didn't know what to say. What was he forgiving me for? He then said he was leaving, that he was moving into his sister's house. Then, he walked away. I couldn't speak.

I stood in the living room unable to move as he walked around the house taking things, packing things, and carrying them out to his truck. He was in a state of shock too. He carried shirts and pants out without packing them. I went to the closet and took out his backpack and a suitcase. I went into the bathroom and filled the backpack with things he hadn't taken yet, things he would need, things I wanted to make sure he had. I did this like a robot. I was moving and doing things without thinking. I didn't know why. Like when you have an accident and your survival instincts kick in and you do what needs to be done. You just do them. My heart lay in my gut dying. He filled the double-cab section of his truck and said that he would be back later to get the extra bed. I asked him when and he said that I didn't have to leave. I said that I couldn't be there when they came to take the bed. I just couldn't. He told me that his family didn't hate me. I didn't understand why they would hate me. I told him I wouldn't be in the house when they came.

I left before it was time for them to come. I drove around town for what seemed like forever, and then stopped at my sister's house. Anna's house was less than a mile from our house and his sister Portia's house. Good thing I stayed all afternoon because Jon and Ken never went to get the bed until long after he said they would be there. Anna and I watched as they backed the truck around to the basement entrance of Portia's house to unload the bed. I couldn't believe he was moving out of our home.

After a while, I went home to an empty house, empty only because Jon wasn't there. I couldn't eat. I couldn't sleep. I didn't call him. I stood in the tower windows and said goodnight to him out loud in the black dark but there was no one to hear me. I had never felt so alone and so sad all at once. My heart was broken and I cried tears of sadness so deep that I felt as though my heart was ripping into shreds.

The bed was so big for one person. I couldn't sleep so I went back downstairs and lay on the couch and cried. At 4:00 AM in the morning, I searched through the phone books for crisis hotlines but had no luck. At 6:00 AM, I called the man who married us who said he would talk to him. At 6:30 AM, Jon showed up to get his shoes. He looked like death. He couldn't talk to me and he left, but he asked for a hug before he did. I thought I would die. I wanted to die. I wanted him to stay. I wanted him to come home. Being at his sister Portia's house was a death warrant for our marriage. I felt it. I knew it. A friend told me that it was. How could someone who believed in divorce be good for our marriage? I had no control. I was in shock.

What had happened? He had stopped and talked to my sister, Anna, and her husband, Jackson, the night before for over two hours and had agreed that counseling would be the first step to figure out what was wrong. But on the way home he stopped at his sister Portia's house and it was over.

I remembered how Jon had threatened me and how I had begged him to change his mind as he sat in front of me on the sofa. I told him that I would do anything to make things right and his reply was that if he did he would look "stupid" to his family. He used the excuse that we had no children. He screamed at me. I yelled back at him. We had planned on having children but he had insisted on waiting. Then, he used it as an excuse against me in the end. Jon had a master plan in mind and I, Hunter, wasn't part of it. The reality was that if he had really wanted children in our life together, he would have pushed it with me years before this moment in time.

DECEMBER 12

At the counseling appointment that he agreed to go to with me a few days after he left, things didn't go well at all. Jon said, angrily, that it was through talking to his co-worker, Kristan, that he had decided to divorce me. What was I? Stupid? She was at the top of the pay scale at the school where they both worked and had a young daughter and was getting divorced. If he were with her, he could spend money like water and become a part of a child's life at an age where she wouldn't know the difference. In his mind, it was the perfect set-up. I found out shortly after he left that rumors were running like mad dogs at the school where he worked about Jon and Kristan being together. He took his anger out on me. It was then that Kristan had cut the string and Jon was left to fall off the cliff alone.

Two weeks before Christmas and I was alone. Later, I found out that Jon had had a tree and I didn't. I just couldn't forgive that—at least not now.

So I wrote a letter to his mother and never received a reply. I mailed a copy of it to the one sister-in-law I thought would understand and never heard anything. Spineless cactuses. That's what Sheryl and Michaela were.

I wrote a letter to Jon but couldn't give it to him or mail it to him. I asked him if he would read it and he refused. I wanted him to know that I could not willingly go through with what he wanted. I didn't believe that divorce was the answer. Running away wasn't the answer.

DECEMBER 24

Jon went to church with me on Christmas Eve and as I kneeled in the church I prayed that he would give us a chance. I begged God for our marriage. Jon just sat there and on the way back from communion, I found he wasn't behind me but three people back. It was so strange. He really wasn't there with me. He was gone. He was lost to me. At our house, we exchanged gifts. I had searched for the perfect briefcase for him before he had left. He gave me a watch. Was he trying to tell me that all we had left was time or that there was no time left for us?

JANUARY

When Jon found out I wouldn't go through with a "do-it-yourself divorce," when I wouldn't agree to sign the papers he had brought me from the courthouse, anger raged and the monsoon began.

I couldn't help thinking how it all started with him sitting in front of me on a ripped hassock telling me that I deserved the best in life. I guess I should have known his ego was talking even then.

I rifled through the letters we had written to each other. There had been so much love and now there was so much pain. There was one that just broke my heart.

Dear Hunter,

My life began the Fall of 1985. That was when I realized the woman I was talking to was just like me. From then on, we have been inseparable.

It's been almost nine years since our wedding day. I remember it as though it were yesterday. I remember my face being sore from smiling all day long. It was the happiest day of my life.

Something is lost in translation from feelings to words. I don't think anyone has the capability to describe how I truly feel about you. I can only try. You are my partner in life, my wife, my best friend, my lover. We wake each other up in the morning. On weekdays, we kiss each other goodbye for work and give each other a hug upon return. We laugh, talk, discuss, hug, and touch every day.

I don't know what I would do without you, without my wife, my partner, my best friend. Without you, my life would be empty.

We have worked so hard to get ahead. There are times when we have lost hope and we should never do that again because we will always have each other. There is nothing we can't do. We have made it through every problem that has come in front of us.

I just wanted to tell you how much I love you, my partner, my wife, my lover, my best friend. Happy Birthday.

Love, Jon

It broke my heart to see what he had written because I had not ever lost hope along the way. And, this was proof that he had lost hope once again. But, his solution this time had been to leave me and our life even after he had said in his letter that we had made it through everything and that we would always have each other. Guess he had forgotten his words. Like they said, action spoke louder than words and his were really talking.

JANUARY

As I sorted through everything over the next two months, I picked out pictures and made copies of letters and put them in places where he would find them eventually. I didn't want him to forget me or what we had had. But, then, when I found them I destroyed them. I didn't know what to do. I couldn't stop sorting through things and separating things and putting his things on the opposite side of the closet from mine. I did this with everything. It was the only way I could begin to separate myself from him emotionally. The hard part was finding the baby t-shirt we had bought on our honeymoon in Bermuda and the little shorts with the fish all over them. All I could think of was the pain—the pain that comes with losing the person you thought you would be with forever.

I couldn't stop watching James Bond movies and eating beets. It was a strange combination but I craved both every day.

I found his wedding ring and put it on a chain around my neck. I held onto it for my life. I couldn't breathe without it. It became my lifeline to him. I wore my love for him around my neck. My fairytale had become a nightmare.

I realized that I was in big trouble financially. I had managed to get cash out of the bank before he had cut me off completely but I needed to do something to protect myself. If this was really going to happen, I needed to find a place to be. He was determined to have me out of our house and I needed a place to go. I spent hours on the internet searching, feeling that I couldn't stay even in the same state because of the intense pain in my heart. I found an au-pair agency and created a profile—and hoped for the right thing to happen.

FEBRUARY

I received a response from a kind man who was looking for a housekeeper and for someone to look after his dogs when he traveled. I was surprised that someone would even consider someone who wasn't 20-something. But, it was too early for me to commit to anything. We exchanged information and it was left for future consideration. I also considered an ad for phone actresses. I was getting really desperate.

Valentine's Day was the worst day of my life, second only to the day he walked out on me. I cried all day but I pulled myself together and went to an opening for a local writer. I felt like it might be my only way to have my own home again.

Shoveling snow and pushing it around on the deck and off my car became my outlet for anger and pain. I had never shoveled before and it was an exhausting chore. But, it wore me out enough so I could at least sleep for a few hours at night. As I shoveled, I thought to myself that I would find a way to survive. I knew two things about myself—that I was resourceful and that I was a survivor.

MARCH

On the way to the first hearing, I forgot that I had to straighten the car out as I backed out of the garage. I had parked at an angle, I ran right into the metal rail that held the garage door. The door wouldn't shut and all of Jon's expensive tools were in the garage. I called my father who said he would come up and patch it and I left for the courthouse. I waited and waited at the courthouse. Finally, my lawyer came. His case had run late. Before that, I had had to witness Jon and his female lawyer talking about me, not knowing that I was sitting listening to everything they were saying. It was like watching two monsters scheming about what to do to the caged princess in a fairytale. As we sat in the conference room, the clerk came in and announced that the cases were behind and that the judge had ordered we attend mediation sessions.

The mediation sessions were a disaster. Jon wouldn't bend and announced that work had to be done on the last apartment building because the State had found it to be below standard. He was impossible. The mediator talked with us together and separately. I broke down alone in the room with the mediator. He would agree to nothing.

I continued to go to the counselor who gave me no feedback except that the reason Jon had left me wasn't about children, but about Kristan. He was right about that. Next came filling out the horrible court forms, which took hours, days and weeks to complete. After that, I was subjected to appraisers walking through my home assessing its value. How could anyone put a value on a "home," especially when it was "my home." I was heartbroken. I couldn't believe John was doing this to us. And, I remembered him insisting at being at our house during my appraisal and how he stood on the deck and kept staring at the roof. He kept insisting to me privately that there were so many cracks in the shingles that the entire roof had to be replaced. There was only one crack. He had replaced the few shingles that needed replacing several months before and had left one. To get a credit for the damaged shingles, I had to send in the cracked ones. Jon had insisted we would get nothing, but he was wrong again. I got a check in the mail for over $700. For some reason, he left one of the cracked shingles on the roof. And, now I knew why. He wanted proof. Maybe Jon had been thinking that he would leave me and he wanted to make sure that the appraisals would be lower so he could get the house for a lesser price.

In the middle of all the pain, I realized I didn't know myself and never had. I didn't have my own identity. I was him and he was he. There was no me. I had started to find me in previous months taking classes but the happier I was with this, the more miserable he became toward me and it finally led to him leaving. I missed the red flags of truth and I realized I needed to discover what the truth was. I had trusted him completely. I should have known all the talk about red nails and bleached hair in September when he returned to his job was trouble in disguise.

I needed to know the truth. I couldn't afford a private investigator, so I decided to be my own, somehow.

two

REVEALED

MARCH

I kept thinking that if I knew where Jon was spending his money, maybe I could figure out what he had been doing because we had some joint accounts. I came to the realization that I could access his credit cards on-line. The first credit card didn't really tell me anything. As I was talking to my mother, I realized that there was another credit card that I hadn't thought of before. I dug through a box of discarded papers in the storage room and found an old statement. Then, I accessed the account. There it was. What I had been looking for. I couldn't believe my eyes. Restaurant charges like crazy. Jon was spending money as if it was water but he couldn't give me anything for groceries. Then I saw it. A charge posted as "Hearts.com" for $49.95 on January 27. I couldn't believe it. No way. It couldn't be. Was it an internet dating service? I quickly typed in the web address on the computer and there it was. I typed in the age range and zip code and on the first page produced by my search there was an entry for a person from Doeville with the user name "Iflyinsky." As I read through the description, I knew it was him after reading the first line, even though he had listed himself as divorced with a Bachelor's

Degree. Even without a photograph, I knew it was him. I couldn't believe it. What was he—on drugs?? I was disgusted, devastated and sickened all in the same moment. I was speechless. Without words. I read through his online profile. How could he write that he would be supportive of someone else? He certainly had not been with me, at least in recent years. How could he advertise himself on a dating site? He was mine. I was his. No wonder he couldn't talk to me or look me straight in the eye. My mind reeled with thoughts of revenge. What if I contacted him as someone else? Quickly, I set up a new email account and returned to the site and signed up for one month's service. His would expire at the end of April and so would mine. I sent him an email asking him what his Bachelor's Degree was in. How could he possibly answer this lie? He had advertised himself as divorced and with a Bachelor's Degree. Just couldn't stop lying, could he? In real life and in his fantasy life. Would he reveal the truth?

The next morning, I checked out all of the credit card charges and found that Jon had been eating out all over the place—dates? Probably his sister, Portia, had fixed him up. Who knew. I decided I'd better set up a complete profile that matched his "requirements" for an ideal woman so the match setup would be unquestionable. I was to be 34, 5'5' and a resident of a nearby town. I decided I would get him but good. "Maria" was born. If he wouldn't talk to me and tell me the truth, I would get the information in any way that I had to. I knew that I might be setting myself up for more than I bargained but I knew it would be worth it or at least I hoped it would.

I checked the email account constantly throughout the day. Finally, there it was. A message from him. He had taken the bait. Desperation. Here he was corresponding with someone he didn't know. He had no idea it was me. Fool. I laughed so hard. My sister, Anna, laughed so hard. "...So wickedly mean, Hunter!" she said. I thought to myself—this is nothing compared to what he had done to me and to us. You just don't divorce someone for the stupid excuses he kept giving. This was just the start. Jon said in his message he would email pictures later that night. I would have my proof. How to string him along—that was the question. At the end of the month—my character would, hopefully, have him on a string and get him to correspond directly with her through her email address. The longer Maria could keep him occupied, the better. Maybe she could find out some information from him. Jon seemed to have sunk to such a level of stupidity that he would probably do just about anything.

He sent me a picture as an attachment to his second email. My husband, Jon. The photograph revealed what I already had known.

Maria was questioning and bitter and after only a week she had heard it all. All of his cruel comments and excuses had come out about his "tobeex." This was how he referred to me, his wife. Maria was dying. It was through Maria that I knew I had to return his ring. I couldn't keep it knowing how much he despised and resented me. I had to start letting go of him. I had to give him back his ring, the ring that had spent so little time on his finger. He never wore it because of his work. Or, maybe that was an excuse. It was Easter Sunday and I saw Jon walking out in the yard looking around again. He stalked the house as much as he could. I remember during the winter months when I would go out and see footprints in the driveway after a fresh snow the evening before and knew that it had been him walking around in the middle of the night. He had probably been watching me through the windows and I never knew it.

As Jon turned around and walked back toward his truck, I opened the door and told him that I had something for him. I held my hand out and put it into his hand. The tips of my fingers touched the palm of his hand. It was the first time I had been able to touch him in any way for months. He looked surprised when he saw what it was because I had refused to give it to him when he had asked where it was a few months earlier. I told him that I thought he should have it and said that I hoped he wouldn't flush it down the toilet. What a stupid comment. How could I go and give him any ideas. He had enough bad ideas of his own.

He quickly put the ring into his pocket. I had worn it around my neck during the day underneath my clothes and on my finger next to the ring he had given me at night for over three months hoping he would come home. Some nights it was the only thing that got me through. I felt the love that was in that ring. And now it was gone. I gave him the symbol of my love, again, to hold and to touch and to look at. But, he probably wouldn't. When I handed it back to him, I was giving him my heart all over again. He had hardly ever worn it, so maybe he never really cared about it. But, he certainly used my love for all it was worth. How could I have given fifteen years to someone who could turn around and dump me so easily? I was so afraid of what my future held.

In a phone call with a friend, my alter ego "Maria" was revealed. I told her about the Internet ad and the creation of Maria. She quickly transformed Maria into a "hot babe" thinking out loud to me. She asked if it was possible to change an existing online profile into someone else. I said I would check.

three
HALLEY

"Halley" was borne out of a combination of our minds. She was a "nice" girl, but "hot" on the side. If it weren't for my friend, the link would have been lost and so much truth would not have been revealed. From then on, I called her every day to read his emails to Halley, and my responses to them. Two heads were definitely better than one.

I tracked Jon's moves daily by printing out on-line credit card statements. There were so many restaurant charges that I knew he had to be seeing someone. I vowed to find out through Halley what he was doing. He was so predictable. He answered Halley even faster than he had Maria. By the time Halley came on the scene, he had changed his marital status to "Separated." What followed were many emails of discovery information that would never have been found by the courts or a private investigator.

APRIL 2

I like how you describe yourself and I also like the way you describe your ideal match. So, you're looking for someone who wants to have fun. Well, I have to say you e-mailed the right guy. I want to do things I've never done, go places I've never been, and experience things that I never have. I just want to live. I even drove to Salem last Thursday night by myself just so I could sing karaoke at "The Pounding Hammer." I've always wanted to sing in front of others and never had until now. I just let it out and it was so much fun. I even won a free t-shirt. I like how you said you're looking for someone who is "fairly" intelligent, hehe. It sounds like you're trying not to rule out half the guys before you even start looking, eh? You ski and bike, what's not to like? Do you have a picture available? I'll show you mine if you show me yours?

By the way, I'm not only looking for fun, I too am looking for love like you. Jon

APRIL 3

I'm impressed! I'm a virgin at this. Shouldn't we talk before we reveal "all?" Maybe you could give me some pointers with this dating game? H

APRIL 3

I've talked to maybe six or seven women online through "Hearts. com." I haven't met one of them yet. In most all cases, I've wanted to move very slowly too. You have to admit, though, that it would be a hoot to meet and have dinner solely because of "Hearts.com." Like I said, I want to do new things, meet new people and I want to live like I never have before. Isn't it exciting to have this whole new future? From the sound of your writing, I think you want and feel the same way.

From how you write, and your profile, I think you're the best match for me that I have found. We are both separated. Many women are hung up with the fact that I'm only separated. I would think that you would understand, being that you are separated yourself. I have two months remaining before being divorced. You say that you want to have fun and find love. That tells me that you may have been in the same type of relationship that I have been in—"life sucking."

We have so much in common, we're both teachers, we're both separated, want to live, enjoy life… The last thing I don't want to do is scare you off by asking for too much too soon. We can talk all you want, for as long as you want, okay?

It's funny that you say you're a "virgin" at this. There are so many things that I have never done, the singing for instance. I sometimes refer it to as being a virgin at this or that. For instance, I've never been out to dinner with a woman who is blonde. Isn't that pathetic! That's something I really want to do. You specified a tall, dark and handsome type in your profile. That's me! You have blue eyes and a slim/ slender body type. I can't help imagine that you're wonderful.

So, you say you want me to give you some pointers with this dating game, eh? Well, my advice to you is to stop emailing everyone else and stick with me. Hehehe I'm not a creep, or a stalker or anything. I'm a teacher for Christ sakes! I'm just a guy in the same position as you. It's the school year still so I'm kind of busy and limited on my free time. That doesn't mean that doing things is impossible, if that were to eventually happen for us. I think you should be cautious, but I also think that you should realize when it's okay to put a little trust in someone. I'll put a little trust in you right now. I'll trust you not to pass my photo all over to friends and coworkers. Please give me that courtesy, and I hope to talk to you later. Please tell me something about yourself in your replies. Jon

I couldn't believe he was asking someone to trust him. All I could think of was how he had destroyed my trust in him completely. And, if he hadn't met anyone through Hearts.com yet, who had all the mystery dinners listed on the credit card statement been with? And, two months? Where was he getting that from?

APRIL 4

Nice picture! But, don't you think we should get to know each other's minds? (Sorry, my camera is in Colorado with my brother who is on a ski trip—lucky guy!) So, what's this "Pounding Hammer?" Sounds like fun.

Two months?? Lucky you. How did you get that solid timing? As for the baggage of the past—let's just skip over it for now. What is this "hehehe?" Should I trust you? And, don't worry—your picture is safe with me!

So, as a teacher, you've got the summer off—what are YOUR plans? I have a seminar to go to but that is about it. The rest of the summer—fun! (and, hopefully, love?) H

Whew! I wondered how I was going to put the picture issue off!

APRIL 4

Yes, I agree. We should get to know each other's minds. I want to ask you lots of questions. I don't know if I have time right now to start. It's my free period and I only have about twenty minutes left. I've also read some information on the "Hearts.com" site that says to not wait too long to meet because your first meeting will be strange in that you will have already covered a lot of the subjects that should be covered when you meet, leaving little to talk about. Just thought I would mention that.

"The Pounding Hammer" is the closest decent nightclub that I have found nearby even though it is almost an hour away from where I live. It is a classy place with a good dance floor, high ceilings and good bands.

I don't have solid timing, but in two months it will be six months since I left. I'm hoping for this timing. As for the baggage of the past, I agree. I'm ready to look ahead, not behind.

Why, does "hehehe" sound kind of evil or something? I'm sorry. I'm just trying to keep things light. You can trust me. I don't tell anyone about "Hearts.com" stuff.

Oh, you're killing me! Yes, I have the summer off. I have a graphic design class that I've received a grant for, which is in Kansas. It lasts for about two weeks. Other than that, I have no plans. Our spring vacation is coming up. Do you have one at your school?

Questions: Do you ever wear a red coat? Do you have your nails done? Do you sing in your car to the radio? If you do sing, how do you sound? What do you drive? I'm out of time now but I'll ask more when I get the chance. Talk to you later. Jon

The grant for the graphic design class in Kansas. It had been me who had had the connections to his new career. Everything was paid for—grants, college classes, insurance....thanks to me.

I thought I would throw up as I read through his message. He was clearly still stuck on Kristan, the girl he worked with who he had intended to go to when he left me. But she had cut the string so he was obviously looking for a twin. It was all about her. Red nails, red coat, bleached hair!

APRIL 4

So, you are artistic, are you? So am I. A graphic design workshop—how great! I would love to go to something like that. "Do I ever wear a red coat?" Sometimes, but I won't tell you where! Nails done? Yeah and a lot of other things too! I love to sing in the car to the radio but how would I know how I sound?! I drive a Saab. How's that that for a start. Now, questions from me to you.

I am really hot on knowing about this nightclub. I've been to Salem a few times but have no idea where it is. How do you get there? And what song did you sing at "The Pounding Hammer?" Do you wear boxers or briefs? Hehehehe Do you sleep with them on or off? Just thought I would ask for the "bare" facts! H

Wow. There was no time to be wasted. My friend helped me to get jump started to get the "hot" truth that I wanted and needed to know.

APRIL 4

I like wooden silverware trays and knives that have big rounded ends so you can get lots of peanut butter on them. I prefer "Skippy" to "Peter Pan," for no particular reason. I made the big change a while ago from installing toilet paper so it would dispense from under, to preferring that it dispense from over the top of the roll. Just a sign of how diverse and acceptable to change I really am! I've used Crest toothpaste since my childhood and I have just one filling. I also have one front tooth capped because it was broken off in High School. I purchased my first new vehicle in August, a Chevy Silverado four door extra-cab pickup. I may end up selling it to purchase my house back, but I don't want to. I like all kinds of music and like to sing to it while driving down the road. My voice is kind of like George Michael or Elton John.

I like to put my cereal into bowls that have almost vertical sides so I can carry it into another room without spilling milk all over the place. I like big spoons and a lot of food. I like wine with dinner and candles, especially in the winter when it's dark out at night. "Wal-Mart" is the place to shop for a lot of different things. The quality is great and the price is always right. I enjoy going there and filling a couple of shopping carts with stuff. That's fun. I used to own a share of an airplane but I sold it because it was just so outrageously expensive to operate. Someday I will get back into flying again. My pilot's license is good for the rest of my life as long as I can pass the check ride and physical. My eyesight is not quite 20/20. I don't wear glasses but sometimes when I'm tired or if it's that funny time during the summer when there is lots of pollen in the air, I do wear them to drive at night or read. Sometimes I go a couple of years without ever needing them. I like going for walks in the forest just after the leaves come out, smelling the air with that fresh new smell. I have a Special-ized mountain bike that's a lot of fun. I need new ski equipment because mine is about ten years old. I love spring skiing. I buy beer in 30 packs and it takes me months to drink it. I have this huge desire to own a Harley and drive across the country and on dusty dirt roads in the heat of the summer. I love convertibles. I've been working on this email for about two hours being constantly interrupted. I was just talking to someone and I realized that I have never been in a boat in the ocean. That's something I'm going to have to do this summer.

Do you have lots of "firsts" to do? I like to have an impact on the thoughts of others. I hope I make you think about living more. I hope that in some small way, I influence you in a way that helps you do something that you never would have done. Would you ever sing out loud in a club full of strangers? Would you like to if you could let yourself do so? It's a great feeling.

Just so you know, I will be really upset if you respond to this email with a ten-word response. Talk to me. Tell me what you like and don't like. Tell me what you want to do with your life, the things you like to do. I'll talk to you later. Jon

I couldn't believe what a nerd I had been married to. What would anyone else think of a guy talking about how toilet paper was put on a roll? Skippy? Then why did he always let me buy Peter Pan? A Harley??? He had tried out a motorcycle before we were married and told me how he was shaking by the time he took it back to the used car dealership! Was I communicating with a drone or what? I had no idea how to respond to this one. I was rolling with sadness and laughter. Had I been married to such a boring person? I was surprised he didn't tell me what side of his pants he put his penis! Here was someone looking for excitement and he seemed pretty boring to me.

APRIL 4

The graphic design workshop is fifteen days, twelve to sixteen hours a day, including weekends. Kind of takes the fun out of it, but I'm sure I will learn tons of stuff.

Nails done? Yeah and a lot of other things too! Oooooooooooooooohhhhhhhhhh Please tell me more! Has anyone ever told you to stop singing in the car to the radio?

Just how hot are you? Do you plan on going to Salem without me? I'll tell you what, you don't need to know where it is because I'll take you there anytime you want to go. At "The Pounding Hammer," I sang "Don't Let The Sun Fall Down On Me" by George Michael. I wish I could find a place that offered "Drops of Jupiter" as an option.

So now you like the "hehehehe?" Good question. You made me laugh out loud. I've always worn briefs but since I moved I've switched to boxers. I've heard it keeps the "boys" a little cooler and a little more alive. Guess I want to be alive all over, don't I? Even better question. I sleep with them off. Most of the time I sleep with just a t-shirt on.

Well, seeing how you brought up all this naked stuff like boxers, briefs, etc., I would like to comment on something that I recently heard about. I've heard that whenever women are together talking about guys, the question that seems to always come up is, "Is he capable of doing it more than once?" Is this true and would you like to know my answer to that question? I promise I will tell you the truth. Just tell me that you want to know.

Do you sleep with anything on? Do you have any body piercings or tattoos? Would you dare to go parachute jumping? Saab 900 or 9000? Convertible or hardtop, standard or automatic? Jeez, I wish I knew what you look like. You're lots of fun to talk to. You seem to be a happy person and I like that. It was nice to get an email from you mid-day. Well, it's 10:45 PM and I need to get up earlier than usual tomorrow, so I guess I'll talk to you later. Jon

Was his brain dying on him or what? He had switched to boxers months before he left. I couldn't believe how he was talking to my "creation," Halley. And, this was my husband? Who knew!

24

APRIL 5

I can't keep up with you! I will try to answer questions from both your previous emails but it's going to be hard! Boy, are you detailed! I like whitening toothpaste. How white are your teeth? hehehe I love wine with dinner and candles and music. I love "Drops of Jupiter"—how did you know it was my favorite? Hehehe Instead of parachute jumping, what about parasailing or renting a plane and taking me flying? That would be so great! I love fallen leaves and the way they rustle in the woods. It's my favorite time of year. But a warm, tropical place is great too. Spring skiing—the best! Beer—maybe just a swig. Like wine better. What about driving a convertible across the country. There's nothing like the wind blowing through your hair and riding with cool shades on. That's one of my "dreams." What about Route 66? Right now, I have a hardtop, but my goal is a convertible. But, I do like things hard! Hehehe I have always wanted to go to France. Voulez-vous couchez avec moi????? As for "firsts" that I would like to do…I would love to be with someone who communicates deeply both verbally and with their bodies! Hehehehehe

I'm still stuck on this karaoke thing. How do you know that everyone there is a stranger? What if someone is there who knows who you are?? I would die!!

Whoaaaaaaa about the boxers! Silk is the greatest. But the ones with little pictures just can't be beat! How do you keep "things" under control all day long? Hehehehe What do I sleep in? Well, that's Victoria's Secret, isn't it? Hehehe How did you guess? I have a belly ring.

As for my looks, you wouldn't be disappointed! Another question for you. How did you ever come up with your "Hearts.com" username and what does it really mean?

"Firsts," huh? So many. Can you rent a plane with autopilot so I can become a member of the mile-high club? Hehehehehe Got to go. My break is almost over. Later. H

I felt like I was buttering my toast so thickly that the bread wouldn't show. My friend helped me with my response and from there I started running away with innuendos.

APRIL 5

I thought you were being selective in your responses. It's good that you want to answer all the questions. I'd like to know all about you.

I like whitening toothpaste too, but it makes my teeth sensitive. I want to try some of that bleaching stuff but I hear it is also bad for sensitive teeth. I'm going to try it anyway.

We could go parasailing instead of parachute jumping if you want.

Oh baby, now you're talking! I'd love to drive on Route 66! I used to have a convertible. It was a Pontiac GTO. There is nothing like riding around on a beautiful fall day with the top down and leaves swirling around the road. I would love to drive one across the country.

Speaking of hard, you didn't ask me the question in your email. I'll give you the answer anyway. My personal best is eight times in less than three hours. Just give me the chance and I will give you deep communication both verbally and with our bodies. That's the only way to have it.

I used to think the same thing (about singing karaoke in front of people you know) but now that I've done it, I don't think I'd care anymore if I did it in front of a room full of people I know.

Yes, silk is the greatest. I've got a pair of black silk ones with little Looney tune characters all over them. I'll let you see them if you want?

It's a little tough to keep things under control all day. I'm a right side hanger. I have a special shoe on my right foot that has a special pocket for the head to fit into. Hehehe Now that was the first untruth that I've told you. The right side thing is true, though.

I have to admit I absolutely love belly rings. They give off some kind of magnetic force that requires me to go down there and use my tongue to make little circles around them.

What do you mean "wouldn't?" That's kind of implying that "if" we meet. Can't we just say that we "will" meet and that I won't be disappointed?

"Iflyinsky" means that I am high on life and am flying above the ground, happy and living life as much as possible.

Now this is more like it—the "mile high club." No "ifs" or wouldn't here! I've thought about this myself and it would be kind of hard in many ways. Hehehe Do you realize how much ground you can cover in a half hour? We'd have to stay out of Class "C" airspace and watch for traffic but it sure would be worth a try!

It's been very nice talking to you. I just hope that our conversation doesn't embarrass you and make it impossible for us to meet. It doesn't mean that anything has to happen. I would just like to sit and be able to look you in the eyes and talk with you over dinner. How can that be a bad thing? If our conversation does not embarrass you, all the better. See you later, I hope. Jon

What a braggart! Eight times in three hours. I knew it was me. We had rented a motel room when we were engaged. It was like we had to get it out of our systems. The sex wasn't quality but it was necessary to release all the pent up sexual frustration. Looney tune characters? How disgusting. Who had bought those for him? Probably his mother. The belly ring comment really threw me off. I was getting into deep territory and I knew that it would be possible for me to get the information out of him if he would make a joke about being so long in the penis that it fit into his shoe. For someone who wouldn't talk to me while we were married, he was certainly making up for it on-line with a person he didn't know at all.

APRIL 5

I just can't keep up! I will try to answer your questions! I've heard those Crest whitening strips are great and maybe safer to use! *******8 times********* You have to tell me! Who was the lucky girl??? But, you know, quality is all that really counts! Looney tunes? I just wouldn't have guessed! I was thinking "trout!" Hehehe And, who was the lucky girl who got her belly ring licked? I just cannot get past this "Pounding Hammer" place. You have to tell me when the next karaoke night is! Maybe I'd even wear my red coat..........hehehe-hehehehe So, who's embarrassed? It's fun to flirt, isn't it? So, what's exciting this weekend????? Let me know...... H

APRIL 5

Yes, it is fun to flirt. Tomorrow, there is a snow-cross race up Bear Mountain that I want to go to. Then, I think it would be exciting if I drove down to White Haven to have dinner with you, what do you think? Let me know. Jon

So, he was going to avoid my question about the girl who got her belly ring licked but I wouldn't give up until I got an answer.

four

THE BELLY
RING GIRL

APRIL 5

You didn't answer my questions!!!!!!! So who was it? Tell all! So, who were they? Hehehehe And, when is the next karaoke night? I want to hear you sing! Then, I will reveal myself to you! Is this too "hard" on you? Hehehehehehehe   H

APRIL 6

The eight times in three hours was my "soontobeex." The "Belly Ring Girl" is someone I'm still just friends with.

How are you going to hear me sing? I suppose that could happen if you want it too. Sometimes there aren't many people there. You may be the only blonde in the bar. If that happened I would know who you are. I still couldn't talk to you until after I sang, I guess. "Karaoke Night" is Thursday night. There, you finally got it out of me. If you want to visit their website, it's www.thepoundinghammer. com. They don't keep it updated the way that they should. We could drive over separately the week after next. I have Friday off, the first day of my spring vacation. That way, there would be no need to rush

29

home or anything and we could stay up as late as we want. That's if you are not working the next day? As if you would divulge so much information as to let me know that! I am taking a class on Thursday nights, which runs from 6:00 to 9:00 PM and it's an hour drive to Salem for me, much longer for you. I was lucky the time I sang because the instructor was sick and canceled the class. Sometimes we get out early. I suppose I could even leave during class if we really decided to do this.

There must be a decent place somewhere between the two of us if you want to do that. Oh baby, I want to meet you so bad. I just want to give you a nice, long soft hug while I give you a kiss on the neck and all the while I inhale the smell of you and your hair. Then, if you want, you could show me your belly ring. We both know what would happen if you do that don't we? Hehehehehe If you like, I can e-talk to you like that more? What do you think, do you like it? Tell me what you think, talk to me. Maybe the true question is, is this too "hard" on YOU? Hehehehehe Jon

So, he had slept with someone else. My heart was in my stomach. I had to find out details. The "Belly Ring Girl?" Jon even had a name for her. But, he was really getting hot on me. How could he talk to someone like this without knowing who he was talking to? Was he crazy? All I could think of was how we had known each other's bodies so well, or at least I had thought so and the thought of him being in bed with someone else made me sick. How could he do this? How did he do it? We were still married. This was the truth I had been looking for and I couldn't swallow it. There were a lot of things I couldn't swallow and there were things that I would never be willing to swallow. Maybe, she was willing to swallow! How could there be any hope between us now after what he had done. I wondered if I was right in my assumptions about what he had done or about what he was doing. He was clearly trying to get into Halley's pants. I knew that.

APRIL 6

Lucky girls! So, why didn't anything work out with the "Belly Ring Girl?" Sounds like things got hot! Tell me tell me…. You say "still just friends" but do I have competition here? hehehehe So, you're saying I would have to wait until after your class is finished to hear you sing? I suppose I can wait a little longer! Can you??? When does your class end? Tell me where a decent place to stay is over there? So, you want a girl who kisses on the first date I suppose? Hehehehe   H

I couldn't believe myself. Our conversations were bringing out a part of me that I had never experienced. I had to know about his actions and who he was now, but in the process I was learning more about myself.

APRIL 6

Just wanted to tell you that I might have a surprise for you. Do you like surprises?

I never cheated on my wife while we were together and I would never do that. I met the "Belly Ring Girl," Ashley, about one month after I moved out of my home. We went out for about a month. Maybe I told you more than I should have. She has a ten-year-old daughter and it was getting very confusing for her having me around. I'll explain the rest after we meet but for now let's just say that things got very complicated and it was up to me to do the right thing.

Maybe you won't have to wait until after my class is finished to hear me sing…

The "Snowflake" is an excellent place. Our entire department stayed over there one night on retreat. We can get a room with a fireplace. Hehehehehe

Kissing is up to the moment, the situation and how we feel. Right? Depending on how long you make me wait until we meet, we may know each other pretty well by then and it won't be like a first date anyway.

I'm sorry I'm so anxious, it's just that it's part of the way I feel now, to not want to waste any time and to live as much as possible. I always think about what would happen if one of us were to die tomorrow. The other would just assume that the interest just dropped and would never know what happened. I don't want to miss any opportunity to spend time with someone that might make me happy. We don't know what will happen tomorrow, or even before then and it would be sad if we could have had a wonderful time together and then missed the opportunity forever. I'm sorry but that's just how I feel. You didn't answer my last question. Do you want me to write you a hot email sex note? Would you like that or is that more than you want to see? Jon

Nice to know that he didn't cheat on me before he left. But, I know he cheated on me in his mind with Kristan, that was for sure. One month. It only took him one month to sleep with someone else. I had little appetite for food and his comments just killed it completely. I still wondered what had happened at the Snowflake "retreat" that night. I was supposed to be there but he had told me he didn't want me there and with my class work I didn't fight it. What I should have done was drive over anyway and surprise him. I wondered if it would have helped. Sleeping with a girl who had a ten-year-old daughter. How nice. Instant family. Was that what he wanted? The desperation in his message was so apparent. And the angst for sexual innuendo was unbelievable.

April 6

Surprise me! But what is this "thing" you are trying to surprise me with? Hehehe Seriously, which we haven't been much, I really need you to give me pointers or it will be very difficult for us to meet. I have to know how you kept this "Belly Ring Girl" relationship under wraps for over a month without anyone ever knowing about it. I can't have anyone knowing about anything that I am doing or might do, seriously, because of our situations, in regard to both marital and work. And, there is nothing wrong with your honesty. You haven't told me too much. Now I know how honest you are. But, I just don't understand. Wouldn't it have been a great thing for this woman to have someone like you around for her daughter? I am confused why it was you thought it was complicated and it was the right thing to do to end it? And, how can you still be "just friends?" I can't imagine being just friends after a "relationship." How is it possible? Was it too complicated because she lived too close to where you live or because of her "ex?" Sorry for all the questions but I really need to understand this. I just can't have my "tobeex" to ever know and I need to know how to be completely "under the covers" with this. How did you keep it so no one knew?

As for the fireplace, sounds great. So, what's your hurry? Why do you feel like you have to rush everything? Sometimes things are better when they take a little longer? Hehe But, you shouldn't apologize for the way you feel. It's okay to say what you feel. As for the "hot message"—what do you think??? Hehehehe H

How could he not know it was me? I was asking too many questions! But, a man thinking with the head between his legs doesn't think clearly. He thinks like ejaculate looks! Cloudy!

APRIL 7

It's not much of a surprise if I tell you what it is now, is it? Ah, so here is the problem. You're afraid people will find out. I didn't exactly keep it under wraps. Sure, I didn't want my "future ex" to find out, but I did tell a few people at work and some friends. My situation may be a little different than your own in that my wife, Hunter, has no friends and sometimes doesn't leave the house for three or four days straight, but that's another issue altogether. I figure she is trying to screw me over about as badly as she can already financially. It couldn't make it any worse if she found out about me dating someone else. She does not know about it now, I'm sure. Remember, someone close to them has to have the balls to actually tell them. Most people would rather just talk about it or not even think it's a big deal anyway. Legally, it makes no difference and there is nothing wrong with seeing someone if you are separated. Without getting into the "ex" thing anymore than necessary, I'll just say that she listed on her asset allocation sheet that my electric toothbrush has a garage sale value of $50.00.

So, this is why I have to work so hard to see you—because you can't have anyone knowing. We have a problem here. You have to decide if you are truly ready to take the chance. I know I am because you seem so wonderful. Do you want to get on with your life?

I'm sorry, but I just don't want to reveal the main issues to do with Ashley with someone I haven't met yet. I'll explain it to you when and if we meet.

Well, we live a long distance apart. If we meet closer to my end, you can be sure that no one will know on your end unless you tell them. If I told no one, the only people that would have known would have been my sister, Portia, and her husband because I'm living with them. You say that you can't have your "tobeex" to ever know. To ever know? Surely, he will know at some point that you are getting on with your life. Do you mean he can't know that you "did it" with someone else before your divorce was final?

Again, if you don't tell anybody and we live so far apart, how is anyone to know?

We have a problem that we need to overcome if we are to meet. The truth is you joined "Hearts.com." You have been talking to me. You're afraid to take the step of meeting me but it sounds like you want to. This is a common problem that I've had with many women on "Hearts.com." Everyone is apprehensive. To me, it isn't that difficult to have a friend tell me about a woman, that friend then mentions my name to her, and then I give her a call. We go out totally not knowing each other. That's how I met Ashley. Maybe it's the only way I'll meet anyone. I think the Internet thing freaks women out. They have heard so many stories about freaks looking to kill them or something that they're afraid to meet someone.

I hope that you choose to reveal more about yourself to me. I hope that we can meet, but that's all I can do. It's your decision. It's you who has to decide if you want to take the chance with me on this. I think you know that I'm not some creep or something. Maybe you need to wait until your divorce is over before seeing anyone. I'll keep writing for a while and we'll try to work this out, okay?

I promise you that no one on my end will know. I'll keep it quiet for you if that's what you want. It just seems to me that we have so much in common and this might enable us to actually have someone to talk, share and do things with, through this tough time. I think that's a pretty good thing. Jon

So, Jon thought there was nothing wrong with sleeping with someone while he was still married. What a nice guy. Oh, if he only knew who he was communicating with! He had no idea what I was doing or how my life was going. He was basing all of his opinions on the time when I hadn't been able to leave the house because of an injury. He hadn't known me for a very long time. He was sure I didn't know anything! I wondered what his reaction would be if he knew he was telling his own wife of his sexual escapades! I had to know more about the "Belly Ring Girl," Ashley, and I would find a way to get it out of him. It drove me crazy to know who had introduced him to her, but I had an idea about that. The only other person who he confided in besides Kristan and his sister, Portia, was his hairdresser and I knew it had to be her. How could he go out with someone only a month after leaving me? What would his mentor, the "Great Deacon" who had married us, think of all this? He had given Jon all of his support after I had called asking him for help. To both the "Great Deacon" and his hairdresser, Jon was perfect. They were kindred souls—the "Great Deacon" and the hairdresser were as imperfect as Jon! Actually, I knew that they were. In fact, the whole town knew their stories and they were far from pretty!

APRIL 7

After all our detailed conversations, I'm sorry you don't feel you can confide in me. I just wonder if these same "complicated issues" will arise with us? Is it possible? I really need you to at least tell me your thoughts about this. I don't want to be another "complication."

Who knows what is wrong and what is right but my background requires me to think that maybe it is wrong to have an affair while you are still married??? I guess I have to get over this, right?! Part of the new plan.

Since I am still a "virgin" at this I have to ask questions and I hope that you don't mind answering. How can you be sure that some-one won't tell her? Or, how can you be sure that she hasn't figured it out? She just can't be that naïve, can she? And, how do you know that she can't see it on your face??? I don't know how I could hide it—tell me how, please?

And, yes, there does seem to be a lot of paperwork with all of this and she was probably just trying to do the best she could. Sorry, just a woman's point of view. We have this thing with details! Have you ever read the book "Men are from Mars, Women are from Venus?" It's all in there! And, you know, it must be pretty bad for her losing someone as great as you seem to be. I can't help but feel sorry for her as a woman. Don't be offended, it's just a woman thing!

Like I said before, I don't want to get into the baggage. Maybe, we will never have to! Sometimes, it's better to just "throw" it!

So, at what point do you tell them that you cheated (or is that the right word?) on them or do you ever???? Are you ever going to tell her?

So, I am dying to know what it was like to be with someone else for the first time? Are you willing to share that with me? (I want to know what to expect!) Hehehehe

Well, I do want you to know that I DEFINITELY want to meet you but am not sure when. Seems like both our schedules are booked solid. Maybe the week of your vacation? Or, after your class is over?

What do you think? I would definitely have to get a day off so I wouldn't have to drive back the same night and would I want to??? Hehehehe I also have the first Friday off in May so Thursday night karaoke is definitely a possibility!

P.S. Have you heard the new song by Darren Hayes *Insatiable*? Do you think you could sing that one for me? I would love it! H

APRIL 7

I'm testing the surprise right now!

Oh, I can see that you're not going to let this one go, so I guess I have to tell you at least part of what happened. Ashley is, like I said, a very nice person, but I just don't think that we are compatible. There were fundamental things that we just thought differently on. She has been on her own for a very long time and has grown very independent which is good, but is also very stubborn and unwilling to change certain things. These things I will tell you about when we meet. I don't want to make anyone have to change anyway. She also smoked and that was a huge turnoff for me. So, I had reservations going in. I think that we are still friends because we were very open and honest with each other and communicated these things from the moment we met. There were no surprises.

Oh man! This is why I would like to meet soon. I'm afraid if we continue like this for too long we won't meet at all. I'll try to answer your questions, though. I was married for a very long time. I was very foolish to wait as long as I did. I put work first and just thought that I would work through our problems at a later date. When I started looking at the problems, I realized that they could not be fixed. I cannot change her. Hunter needs to want to change herself and she sees no problems.

Complicated issues. You say that you wonder if these complicated issues will arise with us? You mean like what we are both currently going through? Like you said in your profile, no one is perfect. I can't say anything is going to work out for us any more than you can. I will say that I don't play head games and I won't tell you things that aren't true just to get what I want. I will be open and honest and, hopefully, whatever happens between us, we will at least always be friends. Isn't that the way it should be? It's not right to hurt someone by leading them on or lying. Going out with Ashley was a great experience for me. It was also a learning experience for me. I realized that I had not really dated women before I got married and that this was a completely new thing for me. I was in total awe as to what women can be like. Now I see that many women are like that. I also see that there is a huge variation between women and people in general. I just want to find the ideal match for me.

I feel that when it is right, I will know it. I just hope that when I feel it's right, so will the woman. It always seems that he likes her, but she likes someone else. I hate playing that game and that's why I took the easy way out when I got married. It just seemed to work with Hunter, so I thought it must be this is the way it should be and got married. I was young and stupid.

I want someone who is my other half. I want a true love type of relationship. I want a family. I want someone who works hard outside the home so as to have a life of her own. I don't want to think that if something happened to me, she and my children would be helpless to the world. She needs to be strong. Most of all I want someone to live life with and do things with. It would also be nice if that other person had a similar schedule as my own so that we could enjoy time off together. I realize this can't be a requirement, but it would be nice.

This is my second chance. I will not have a third. This is it for me. The next woman I marry, I'm spending the rest of my life with if she will have me. I don't want to rush into marriage and look out at the world and think, what would "she" have been like. There are few "firsts" in this area now for me. I can only think of one. I realized that all people are different regardless of how they look. I realized that blonde is only a color, but it is a color that I've never smelled or buried my face into. Blue eyes are eyes I've never looked deeply into. I need to experience these things. I know that it may sound stupid but it's how I feel. You can give this experience to me. I will never go through a divorce again. And the next person I marry I am going to be head over heels in love with when I do it, because I will know she is the perfect match for me. I need to experience what is out there to know that. Does this make sense?

We don't even have to have an "affair." First, I define an affair as two people who are having sex and then going back home to bed with their spouse. That's not the case here is it? It sounds like you really want to get into it and that may or may not be a good idea. Take Salem for instance, we could get a room with two beds. We can sleep in the same room, listen to each other sleep and wouldn't that be okay? I think we should take it slow with all these uncertainties. But, I think the place to start is by meeting each other. You might take one look at me and not want anything to do with me for all you know.

Yes, I am afraid that Hunter is that naïve. She doesn't know about my relationship with Ashley. Personally, I wish that she would start dating too. It would take some of the pressure off me and put her mind onto the future instead of the past.

Perhaps you shouldn't do anything that you would have to hide which I would think would be having sex with someone. Would you have to hide just being friends with me? Would you feel uncomfortable just with the communication we already have had? You sound like you are truly having a difficult time with this. This worries me a little bit.

Questions: Do you think there is any chance that you may end up getting back together with your "tobeex?" Can you tell me approximately where you are in the schedule of things with your divorce? I just hope that when we meet I don't fall for you and then you end up going back to your "tobeex" (but, that's the chance I am willing to take). Who's decision was it to separate?

I don't think it's any of Hunter's business what I am doing. No, I have no plans to tell her. I also don't think it's cheating on them. Maybe I feel that way because I feel my marriage has been over for years.

So, expect things to be different in ways that you didn't realize. I know that Ashley was taken by the way I purr when I'm close to a woman. I had never thought about it before. I have this kind of deep sound I make in my throat when faces are close to one another. My wife never mentioned it. Expect things to be mentioned that you never realized. Yes, I gave first experiences to her also. I wanted to make her happy in every way. Expect differences that are nice. I had such a sheltered life for so long, it was truly amazing for me. I don't know your situation. We went indoor rock climbing one day. That was a huge thing for me to do with a woman. Just the entire experience was truly amazing for me and she gave me many "firsts."

So, you definitely want to meet. Remember, we don't have to have sex, we don't have to kiss and I don't have to lick your belly ring the first time we meet. Hehehe There should be no pressure on our meeting, okay? We should meet for the experience of meeting and take it from there. We can come up with a time and a place together. Can we consider Thursday, the 18th in Salem?

I'll check out the song by Darren Hayes that you mentioned.

One last question. Can you tell me your first name? Please give me something. Jon

God, I couldn't believe the crap I was reading. He admitted to his working too much and putting it first which was a fact but couldn't see any hope for a fifteen-year marriage. I didn't know there were problems. I didn't see the red flags because I was too busy taking care of him. Stupid. It was clear in his message that he blamed me for everything, for the complete breakdown of our marriage even though he had not communicated anything directly to me in a way that would begin to attempt reconciliation. I couldn't believe the comment about "he likes her" and "she likes someone else." I remembered the night he had asked me out for his friend and I had made a similar comment because I liked Jon and not his friend. And, he wasn't even willing to take responsibility for falling in love with me and asking me to marry him. I remember how alike we were and how we wanted the same things and how much he loved that about us. We did have a true love. I did know that without a doubt. I wondered how he could be so flip about it. But, I suppose that was his way of talking about it and glossing over it with a complete stranger, a stranger he hoped to get into bed. I couldn't help remembering the first day I had worn my engagement ring and had hoped no one would see it. Was it because I had been unsure? Had it happened too fast? Had we really known each other long enough? Obviously not. From his message, I was getting that he wanted to have his cake, eat it and puke it up unchewed! I had gotten that feeling back in November before he had left but didn't know what to do about it so things completely fell apart and now, here I was writing to my own husband under an assumed name so I could seek the truth. So, there were few "firsts" left for him to achieve? Sounded to me like he had been around the block a few times since he left. I wondered what his list of "firsts" had consisted of and knew that I had to know. NEVER. How could he say never when he had run away from me for reasons that were not real. All of the excuses he had given me were in the hole with everyone. His actions were speaking louder than his words. Affair. My definition was very different from his own. My definition: sleeping with someone else while you are separated or married. His definition: sleeping with someone while you are living with your wife.

Calling me NAÏVE! Boy, he was more out of it than I thought. Yes, I had been but here he was calling me naïve and it was me he was spilling his guts to. And, wanting me to date so he wouldn't look like such a schmuck! I couldn't help thinking that he was so lost he was falling for anyone or anything! The line about our marriage being over for years sent me into tears. If he had felt that way, why hadn't he told me or tried to do something about whatever he thought the problems were? And, my biggest question for the day was what "firsts" had the "Belly Ring Girl," Ashley, given him and what "firsts" had Jon given to her?

April 7

How sweet! Do you think it would work if you only sent one line of the song? Could you try please?

I'm really glad to hear you don't smoke. I really don't like smoke. So, as far as this "other woman," do you still see her? I like my man to myself! Hehehe The way you talk she was much older than you or maybe it just sounds that way to me as I am younger than you are.

It's too bad that you didn't think the problems could be fixed. Did you try? I tried but Alan just wouldn't budge on some issues that are important to me so I made the decision. If he had said he would try, it would have made a big difference. So, I don't think that there is any chance of us being together again.

So, what do you mean that you were in "total awe" of what women can be like? How do I know if I will fit this criteria?

You say that it seemed to work with Hunter and that's why you got married. Didn't you love her? When I got married, I believed that I was marrying my "true love." Didn't you?

So, it sounds like you have almost filled your quota of "firsts?" What do you mean by that? Hehehe

I really worry that the next time around (if it happens) will be worst than the first. You say that the second time will be the last but how can we really be sure???

How could I take one look at you and not want anything to do with you—you sent me your picture!

My situation is that I just filed and I have to do all the awful paperwork with all the financial stuff. It's too much on top of work!

Well, that's a new one for me—you purr?? Sounds interesting! These "firsts" you talk about so generally are driving me crazy! What do you mean??? You gave her "firsts" and she gave you "firsts." This is code for what????????? It's sounds wild!

Where can you go indoor rock climbing! I have always wanted to try it and would love to do it!

The 18th huh? I thought you had classes on Thursday nights and it's pretty short notice for me to get that Friday off. And, don't you have to work the next day? So, when we can FINALLY decide on a date, how should we book the room or were you planning on driving home the same night and should I just get my own room? Let me know what you think. Halley

five

FANTASIES

APRIL 7

It's summer, and we just spent the day together having fun enjoying each other's company. We have a room out of town where we will spend the night. We're just talking and I look deeply into your eyes and want you so badly that I just can't stop myself. As you're talking and finishing what you are saying, I stand up from the bed, hold your face in my hands and give you a long kiss. I move my face to your neck where I begin kissing you. You smell so good. My hands lower to your waist and begin rising back up again under your shirt. They stop with each hand on one of your sides and my thumbs are firmly placed against the bottom of each of your ribs. I continue kissing your neck ever so softly and you enjoy it as we continue.

As you stand there, I lower myself down on my knees and begin kissing your belly button. I slide my hands so they are on your breasts and I begin using my tongue to firmly make circles around your belly ring as you unbutton your pants. We slide them down together. I lower my hands to your bottom softly feeling your curves in my hands. We move to the bed. How was that? Jon

APRIL 7

Thank you so much for telling me your name. I really needed that. What a beautiful name, I love it. I guess you're right, things are sweeter if you have to wait for them. I tried to send only the very first part of the song and it was 1.2 Megs, which was too big.

No, I'm not seeing the "other woman," Ashley, but we sometimes email each other. She was 29 when we first started going out and is 30 now.

I begged my wife to change. If they truly don't want the change for themselves, they are not going to. I'll have to explain my situation to you more eventually. Do you walk, get out and do things, live? If you do those things I will be in awe.

Yes, I did believe I was marrying my true love and, yes, I did love her, but I was so young and had no idea of what was out there that I just didn't know. And, use your imagination about what the "first's" are!

You can't be sure of anything, but don't you think that you will notice a problem and act on it much earlier now than you did the first time? I will never put a problem off again. It will be solved when it comes up. If I manage to marry someone who can communicate and who I can have an intelligent conversation with, the rest should be just fine.

We were going to do all the paperwork on our own without lawyers, but then Hunter decided that she could not trust me and got a lawyer. Consequently, I needed to get one too. It has made things much easier, though, because I don't have to deal with her daily and the lawyers handle all the paperwork.

It started with completely innocent things and progressed to a lot of other things (the "firsts"). Like I said, I lived a very secluded life and hadn't done a lot of things. I had never been rock climbing with a woman before. I had never gone snowshoeing with a woman before. I never had sushi before. Ashley introduced me to a lot of new things.

You can go indoor rock climbing in Stockwood. We had lunch at the Stockwood Inn. During that meal, I had buffalo meat for the first time.

No, the 19th is the first day of my vacation. The only thing I worry about is that it's putting a lot on the first date. I think that we should spend a lot of time together when we do meet but I don't know about the singing thing as a first meeting. If we did it on a Friday night, we could meet earlier, have dinner together and spend the night dancing and have a room to talk in without having to worry about getting up early the next day.

I certainly would never leave you over there and make you sleep alone. We can split it or I can get one next to yours. I can put it on my charge card if you don't want a record of it on your own card. Personally, I think I would prefer staying up all night and talking to you over sleeping anyway.

Jeez, I enjoy talking to you. I don't know what it is but I like it. Jon

I thought to myself—Hey Stupid! It's me, Hunter, your wife! Maybe that is why our conversation is clicking so well? The "Belly Ring Girl" was ten years younger than me. Perfect to use for a baby factory? And, me on the verge of menopause. He believed all the crap his sister told him about the big "40." And, he had never been there for me really. How could anyone expect him to be there, especially a child!

Change. He hadn't told me there was a problem and never gave me a chance to change what he perceived to be wrong. He was the problem. His lack of communication and his stubbornness. Maybe he belonged with Ashley. He described her as stubborn and he was stubborn. As for intelligent conversation, this exchange we were having was below intelligence. I felt like I was communicating with an imbecile.

APRIL 7

Nice seduction! But could I have a little more…. Maybe you could bring a tape of your song for me when we meet or even better you could just sing it for me privately?

Change. Such a hard thing. But you never know. How do we know they won't? Don't you wish sometimes that you could go back in time and pay more attention to what you should have done with your wife, Hunter? Sometimes I wonder about Alan… Do you wonder?

So, what is it that you like about my email "personality?"

The 19th sound great, but I think we should make our own reservations at the Snowflake. Could you give me directions to the Snowflake and the Pounding Hammer? I know where the McDonald's is—is it close by? (How pathetic!)

Where should we meet and what time? It will be after 7:00 PM before I can get there. I was thinking we should meet at the Pounding Hammer if they have dinner? 8:00 PM? Let me know.

I will be the one in red. Hehehehehe Halley

APRIL 7

I didn't know how far I should go with the seduction. It's your turn. Tell me your thoughts, your fantasy. I want to hear what you have to say.

I'll sing to you privately, I hope you don't think I suck.

Yes, I do wonder how it would be if we could go back in time and pay more attention. And, yes, I'm getting an idea as to the way you think and I like it.

Yes, we'll make our own reservations. It would be nice if we could get rooms either in close proximity or next to each other, though. The place is kind of spread out and it's a long distance from one side to the other. It's funny you use McDonald's as a reference point. The Pounding Hammer is the first place beyond McDonalds, right on the corner and the Snowflake is the last one before McDonald's. Fate or what?

The Pounding Hammer offers dinner. I'll check to see how late they serve.

I'll be looking forward to seeing you in red. Jon

The red obsession was getting to me. It was definitely linked to his infatuation for Kristan. Was she who he really wanted and was anyone else a substitute?

APRIL 8

My turn.

I open the door and look around through the crowd. There you stand. Tall, dark and handsome. You move toward me. I am dressed in an electric blue sheath, my blue eyes shining into yours. You reach out for me and hold me, burying your face in my soft, blonde tresses. We stare into each other's eyes for so long….. I imagine our time together after dinner. While we eat, I slip my shoe off searching for that warm soft spot between your legs. But what I find is not asleep but ready for an evening's fiery delight….. We go to my room and slowly remove our clothes. Fragrance fills my head. You are wearing "Higher" by Christian Dior. I wonder if you will take me "higher" than I have ever been…. I find soft, smooth skinned buttocks waiting for my tender touch, and everything else below so soft, smooth and silky. You cover me with soft, gentle kisses that take my breath away and rock me to the core of my very being as I stand before you in only a red sequined thong. I wait for you to lead me on a journey to the moon where I will fall off the edge of its perimeter and burst into millions of glorious pieces…..

Your turn! Continue on?

You'll sing to me privately! I am so excited!

Let me know what area of the Snowflake motel to ask for so I can try to get a room nearby. But, it doesn't really matter because it's so much fun to run through the halls late at night from room to room! At least, I think so! Halley

My friend, who had helped me bear Halley into being, had helped me with details of my fantasy writing but some of it began emerging from within me. I was shocked by the discovery of what lay hidden in my mind. I felt like I had removed one of the bars from the window of my prison. All these years of holding things in and it was finally leaking out....I wondered what was to come from it....

APRIL 8

Oh you're good! You write very well. Well, you've gotten us to the interesting part. This is also where I left off. We are both waiting for the other to continue aren't we? I'd like to know what would make you happy and that's what I want to do. Please, open up to me, Halley, and tell me what you would like to have happen on this special fantasy night of ours. You can tell me anything. Please continue.

Yes, you're right about how much fun it is to run through the halls. I guess if we make sure we're in the "non-smoking" section, that's all that matters. There is an old wing and a new wing. The new wing is better only if it includes non-smoking rooms. I'll try to give them a call this afternoon.

I like lunch break emails very much. It makes my day. Jon

So, he thought my writing was good. Or, was he just saying it to please my alter ego? He wanted me to open up. Yeah, right. I imagined how many different ways he wanted me to "open up!"

APRIL 8

It's your turn! But, here's just a sentence to start you off.......

"And happiness and bliss radiated from my heart to his and our souls intertwined and we knew in that moment that we were meant for each other.........and always had been......."

(Have you guessed that my degree is in English yet?) hehehe-hehehe Halley

Boy, was I pushing it! A degree in English?

APRIL 8

I can clearly see that you have me beat when it comes to writing. So, she is starting to show her true self to me. This is why I wanted to read more.

It's 11:31 PM and my alarm is set for 6:30 AM. I want desperately to say something witty, something that will make you feel good when you read it tomorrow. I just don't know what that is.

I keep imagining the moment when we meet, and what it will be like. I try to imagine what you look like. I think about it during the day. One of the things that I said in my profile is that I'm looking for someone who is strong in my weak areas and weak in my strong areas, or something like that. English certainly is not one of my strong areas. Like you said, no one's perfect right? I'm going to hold you to that comment. I don't know your weak areas yet. There are so many things to talk about, so many things to learn. I want to save so much of it until we meet. At the same time, I don't want to say anything at all when we meet. You say that I won't be disappointed when we meet and I believe you.

I'm looking at the world so differently over the last few months. I see things that I simply would not have in the past.

I took my black boxers out of the wash tonight—the ones with the Looney tune characters on them. They are ruined! The seams are all coming apart. I wanted to wear them on the 19th. Don't know—I'm so disappointed maybe I won't wear any underwear at all. Hehehehehe

I will try to expand on your fantasy sentence that you gave me but for now I think I should go to bed. Talk to you soon. Jon

And he seemed tired? I wondered why. And children and family are the only things that matter? Then why had he been so down on me for not making enough money or for not making any money at all while I

took classes so I could get a better job that would allow me to make more money? Admitting his own imperfection? Then, why was he blaming me for everything? There were just too many unanswered questions and I knew that getting the answers this way wasn't going to be easy and I wasn't going to get all of the truth, or was I?

APRIL 9

No one IS perfect! It makes me feel guilty when I make this statement because of what my situation is right now. My mind says that I can't stay with my husband, Alan, but my heart is telling me that I have been a failure. You know what I mean? I keep thinking about what you said. How you said that you didn't want to make anyone change, but what if they really wanted to change. Would you give them the chance? I really don't want to get into the negative baggage. I just want to know you as a person.

If there was something about me that you thought should be changed and I wanted to change, would you give me the time to change?

Do you wish that you had tried to be more communicative with your wife, Hunter? I mean, you can't deny that it must have started out that way? I know that I can't. But, you know we are responsible for ourselves and we must have really neglected things along the way. You did talk about that a little before. I will admit that I did. That is one of my imperfections. Too much work! And, if we want them to change, shouldn't we be willing to change first?

To me, the most important thing that matters in life is love and family and making a difference, which is what I think you are trying to convey. And, that we do the right thing. But, how do we really know we are doing the right thing? Sorry, I am getting too deep! It's the "philosophy" in me coming out.

It's okay about the boxers. You MUST have others! I really have this thing for little fish. Do you have any with fish? Hehehehehe

So, here I am, waiting for the fantasy to continue....... Halley

I was trying so hard to get through to him. The fish. I had bought several pair of boxers for him for Christmas and ended up having to wash and pack them up with the rest of his things after he left just so he would accept them. One of the pairs had tiny trout all over them and I wanted to know if he still had them. And, I wondered if he was capable of a fantasy... Yet, this was a fantasy for both of us and he didn't even know it. He was living in a cyber fantasy world and I was not who he thought I was. Hell, he didn't even know who I was. And, I was living a fantasy. I was communicating with my husband through a fake persona so I could get the truth about the real world. Living in a fantasy to get reality.... Could it work?

six

DELUSIONS

APRIL 9

I didn't mean to make you think about your situation when I reminded you of your comment, "no one is perfect." That's not how I meant it. You and I are doing something about our situations. We both tried. Everyone has some basic individual need that must be fulfilled and we are just trying to do that. I feel that my marriage will forever be the biggest failure of my life. That is not going to stop me from getting a divorce because I know it is necessary. I am already much happier than I was.

I have a co-worker who is about your age. She is also getting a divorce. Her situation seems so different than my own. My co-worker has a two-year-old child with her husband. She says that he is an excellent father. She has simply lost respect for him as a man. One of the reasons is because he can't run a chainsaw! For the sake of the child, you would think they should at least seek some counseling, but that's not going to happen. I don't know the best answer to the problem. It always seems that when someone gives their spouse a chance to change, within a couple of years they end up getting a divorce anyway because the same problems resurface.

I think it has worked well not talking about our "stuff."

The question here is whether or not you are a complete, whole-minded individual. If you are and you can recognize a problem, I would always give you the time to change.

I had the same imperfection of too much work. I'm not like that anymore. I worked ten to twelve hour days for ten to twelve years and most weekends too. I did it all for money and it was very foolish.

How do we really know we are doing the right thing? I ask myself the same question all the time. You have to think about the entire situation and the alternatives. When I look at my alternatives and the most likely outcome, I simply don't feel I have a choice.

Everyone deserves to have their needs filled. I think that an increase in divorce rates can be seen as a sign of improving times. In all humankind, we are one of the first generations to know the meaning of happiness. We want to remove ourselves from situations that make us unhappy. Fifty years ago people didn't have the life that we now enjoy. They stuck out bad situations and remained miserable their entire lives.

You wouldn't have made the decision you did if you were happy. Something in your life is not the way that you feel it should be. You deserve to have that happiness. You have just filed. You have lots of time to think about all of this and you will. I know that my life is going to be better than it was. I made the decision months ago that I would walk away with nothing if that was necessary.

I know that if I had not left, I would not be talking to you. I would have missed so many experiences. I have grown and become a better person. I understand things that I never did before. You will see this happen to you also. The day I moved out, I felt like I was eighteen again. I suddenly had this second chance at life that I never realized I had all along. This huge weight was lifted off my shoulders. I started my new hotmail account, flyinghigh@hotmail.com. Everyone has a different level of anxiety about leaving their spouse. I think you can tell that mine is pretty low. I'm just so glad to be where I am right now. I just want to get through the remaining time and get on with my life. I sometimes think about dying or that something terrible is going to happen to me. It's as though my mind is telling me I can't have this much of a second chance. I must pay for it somehow. I know this isn't true. I'm not superstitious but I think it anyway. I'm just so glad that you're willing to live a little too and meet me. It will be a good experience for both of us.

Yes, I have a pair of boxers with fish. I'll be sure to wear them.

I know, I know. I need to continue the fantasy writing but you've made me a little self conscious of my writing ability telling me you are an English major.

I think I'm creative enough to pull off a good "climax," but I'm going to need lots of rest and I'll need to be in the right mood to write it. Please be a little patient. Also, it seems that we need to have this happen in real life first. I've never talked about this with a woman before doing it with her, have you? That was worded a little strangely, I hope that you have never done it with a woman! Hehehehe I want to come up with something comical, bizarre and very nice all rolled into one. Jon

All I could think of was how Jon had run away from our marriage. He hadn't even tried. He had not communicated to me whatever he thought the problems were. Sure, he had threatened and screamed at me for the entire month of November after he returned from the department "retreat" in Salem, but no real communication. No caring. Just self. Himself. He said he was happier. Yet, whenever I saw Jon he seemed more depressed than I had ever seen him. Was this all a fake on his part? Counseling. He hadn't agreed to it either. Wasn't he calling the kettle black? I had spent the last fifteen years pulling him up by the bootstraps and I was so tired. Who was doing it for him now? I had spent fifteen years doing everything and anything for this person whom I loved and he had left me without any real explanation and he was telling a stranger that I would never be who he wanted me to be. Tears ran down my face. The truth was so painful. But, it was necessary.

I wondered who he was getting all of his advice from. The "woman in red" at work who left her husband because she had lost respect for him? They had only been married a few years. Here was a person who had been married for fifteen years taking the advice from a bleached blonde who couldn't hold her marriage of three or four years together. Where was the sanity in that? And both refusing to go to counseling. Whole minded? Who was whole minded? The person who ran away or the person who wanted to work things out? Was mid-life crisis an issue here? As for the ten to twelve hour days, I lived through every one and the money that came out of them was not worth it in the end.

We lived work. No wonder Jon ran away. Every time he looked at me he was reminded of how we crawled along the ground for so many years to get where we were. And we had accomplished so much. Here we were at the edge of the hole with one hand on the edge and he had decided to let go of my hand and let me drop back down into the dark abyss while he grasped onto the edge with both hands and leapt out into another kind of abyss—an abyss darker than could be imagined like the little creature in that movie I had just seen at the theatre who was stuck in a cursed body and didn't know who he was until someone told him—and even then he fought within himself as to who he really was.

So, I was left to pick up the pieces of my life. I had no identity. His life was my life. I had no life without him. And how could he say that divorce was a sign of "improving times?" Where was he living? On the frozen planet Pluto? If he was going to leave, why didn't he walk away without anything? If he was willing to run away, all I could think was that he didn't deserve to have anything that was a part of our lives together. A better person, huh? A person who screams at the person who loves him and runs away from commitment and responsibility and one who says he feels eighteen again? I felt like I had to be a victim of mid-life crisis—that deadly thing that ruins so many lives. The collateral damage was increasing every minute. All I could think of was how he had looked *the day after he left me. He looked like death. How could he say now that he had felt eighteen again? I was so confused. When I saw the email address, "flyinghigh@hotmail.com," my heart started beating so fast I thought I'd choke! He was handing information to me on a platter! Oh, he was going to pay for what he had done, at least a little.*

My hands shook. I thought how this email account might reveal a virtual treasure trove of truth. I quickly went to the sign-on screen and typed in the address name and clicked on "forgot password." The secret question. I waited for it to appear. And there it was. "The tail number of my first plane?" I thought how he had taken everything after he had left, all his papers. I rifled through the folders left in the drawer and couldn't believe my luck. Or, was it fate? The tail number of his first plane, plain as day right on the bill of sale in the folder with everything else. I typed it in and changed the password. I was in! My heart raced so fast as I waited for the account to come up that I saw stars. And there they were. Messages from my alter ego and something else I never expected to find. E-mails from the ex-girlfriend, Ashley. I thought I would faint as I accessed and printed every one that was there. There were only five that hadn't been deleted but they were like gold to me. And in them was proof of his violation.

As I read through them, it seemed like I was reading messages from a high school girl. And this person had a ten-year-old daughter? It was evident from the messages that they weren't currently having sex but that they had. I was in a state of shock. I couldn't breathe. I discovered she was a waitress at a local restaurant and that having fun was the most important part of her life. There was no evidence that she had any ambitions at all and her manner of speaking was very young, on the rough side and very childish. No brains here! I couldn't believe the message where she came right out and admitted to sleeping with him. She had many male friends, but she said he was the only one she had slept with! Yeah, right! She also believed that if his divorce was final that he would be with her. Cocky or what? The last email revealed why he had seemed so tired in one of his previous emails to Halley. He had been with her, talking to her the same night he had been emailing me. She told him how great his hug was and how she had wanted to kiss him. I thought I would be sick. My husband had slept with this brainless girl, he had kissed her and hugged her while he was married to me. I thought I would die. Instead, I sent him another email.

APRIL 9

Oh, I'm sorry. I didn't mean anything offensive by the "no one is perfect" comment. I was only trying to tell you that it's okay if you or I are not absolutely perfect!

I think you're right. We should skip the baggage for now and just have fun! I just have this imperfection of getting too deep sometimes!

So, would you "type" me as a whole-minded person from our conversations so far? What do you think of my mind? I would love to know! Do you think it is "whole?"

Not to get into the baggage, but why would you have to walk away without anything? Just one more question and I will completely get off the subject. How long did it take you to make the decision? It took me about six months. That's why I feel the guilt. I did not tell my husband, Alan, when I should have.

Back to the getting to know you questions……..Do you believe in fate and destiny? Do you like a woman with intellect or not?

And, I think your "fantasy" writing has been great so far. Don't be so hard on yourself!

No hurry on your end of the fantasy. I think you're right. We need to meet before we can finish "our story" (and lots of rest is VERY important!) and we need to look into each other's eyes and see if we can see each other's souls….And, I can't wait to see your fish! Hehehehehehe

Oh, and I love your email address. I might as well give you mine as my subscription is going to run out after next week and I don't see any point in renewing it at least for now….Do you???? It is: Whitehavenite@hotmail.com. Would it be okay if I emailed you directly at your email address? Let me know. Halley

I felt so devious. I had just gained access to his email account and here I was sending a message like nothing had happened and I was even asking if I could send messages directly to his "secret" email address. I wondered if he would figure it out.

seven

MEET ME

APRIL 9

Halley: For some reason I cannot enter my email account tonight. If you wrote to me tonight, I cannot access it. I called the Snowflake. Available rooms: Luxury $200/Club $240/Deluxe $170/ Standard $150. Luxury and Club rooms have fireplaces. All rooms should still be available this Friday, so I haven't booked one yet. I was told that usually a Friday booking requires a two-night stay, but they are willing to overlook it. Jon

I was scared that he would figure out who I really was. Who else would know the tail number of the plane? He was hot for me judging from this message and wanted to get me into bed. His brain was between his legs and the chance of him realizing the truth was pretty low.

APRIL 9

Halley: I realize that the rooms in Salem are a little pricey. I just checked on the cost of a room at the Sheraton in Burrington. A deluxe room with a king size bed is $125.00. I don't mind paying the

Salem cost. Whatever you would like to do is fine with me. I will try to contact the Pounding Hammer tomorrow afternoon. Sometimes it can be difficult to get someone to answer the phone. I've checked their web page and they still have not updated it past the month of February. I want to find out who is playing. I still cannot access my email. Jon

How could he be so stupid? He hadn't even figured out how to get back into his own account? I woke up at 1:00 AM in the morning just wanting him to come home, crying myself awake. I was so alone and so lonely. Why did I want him to come home after what he had done to me, to us?

APRIL 10

Halley: My hotmail account still is not working. My other email address is *jlogan@dover.us.net*. This is the only way I can get messages right now. Jon

He was giving me his school account? He was so desperate. I realized then how deep he was into our cyber relationship and I was afraid of his desperation.

APRIL 10

Halley: Whew! I'm finally able to access my hotmail account! I just got back in and its 12:48 PM. I was dying to hear from you. I think you're right. I haven't had any problems telling people about all the stuff that's going on in my life right now, but I've focused on it too much. It's been nice to not discuss it for a while.

I like the fact that not only have you flirted with me, but you are also open to new things and willing to take a little risk. It's not really a risk meeting me, but it seems that so many women are so guarded that they never manage to get past a "hello." So, yes, so far it looks like your mind is logical, realistic and certainly intelligent and you're not a prude so you're able to have a little fun. That's very important.

My wife, Hunter, is very upset with me because I told other people (my brothers Ken and Dave and my sister Portia) before talking to her. How can you possibly tell your spouse when you're contemplating and realizing that you are going to do such a thing? The walking away without anything came into play when I thought about the possibility of her fighting the whole thing and attorney's fees. It took me about a month to make the decision. In actuality, now that I've had the time to think about it, I've thought about it for about six years. You should not feel guilty about thinking. That's all you were doing.

I love women with intellect! I believe in fate and destiny only to a certain extent. I believe that when something is right, it always falls into place just the way it needs to and it is relatively easy. When something isn't right, it's like pounding your head against a wall.

If you mean your "Hearts.com" subscription? No, I don't see any need to renew it. Yes, you can email me at my address—it is mine alone. Jon

Oh, he was definitely hot for me. He must have been crazy all day trying to figure out how to get back into his account. But, I wondered why he wasn't mentioning anything. Wasn't he even suspicious that there might have been a link to his account being closed to him and him giving me the address? He really wasn't thinking straight, or maybe it was because the head between his legs was too straight and too hard so the brain in his head didn't have a chance! So, he said he loved women with intellect and he felt I was a "whole-minded" individual. Oh, that was great! Then, why had he dated someone who seemed to be at the other end of the spectrum? Maybe, just for the sex? I would find out. I couldn't believe he didn't see that what he was doing was like pounding his head against a wall. Wasn't divorce the ultimate "head banger?"

When I had found out that he had told everyone about what he was going to do to me, I had been livid. It brought me back to the beginning. Then, I remembered that he had told them all he was going to ask me to

marry him before he had asked me. It made perfect sense. He could make no decision on his own. He defiled them for their behavior but went to them for advice. It just didn't make sense.

I was on a fact-finding mission to discover who Ashley was and where she lived. When I went to return a movie to a local video rental shop, I talked with someone I knew who worked there. She immediately knew whom I was talking about when I mentioned the girl's employer and the age of her daughter. She also mentioned her ethnicity and other names that were connected to her in some way but didn't tell me why and I was too busy thinking how I could find out what she looked like. I just couldn't believe it. She said that she expected to see Ashley that afternoon because she always came about the same time to return movies before she went to work and that she drove a black car.

As I stood looking out of the arched window on the second floor in the children's library later that afternoon, I noticed a black car parked just outside. I watched as one of the girls who had been in the library just a few moments before got into the car while a woman of Asian descent waved boldly to people in the street as she walked around to the driver's side of the vehicle. She drove down the hill toward the video store.

Then, I remembered what had happened two days before. The librarian had directed one of the children to me and referred to me as "Mrs. Logan." The girl who had left with the Asian woman had stared at me constantly after hearing my name. I had been suspicious and she had turned out to be part of the truth.

APRIL 10

Halley: I just wanted to tell you that I realized who Darren Hayes was yesterday afternoon. He's from Savage Garden. I've got a couple of their CD's. I got his new CD yesterday and listened to "Insatiable" over and over. That is one of the best songs I've ever heard. It's put together so well and it's very well written. Should have known you would pick that song. I've got to say, though, that it's going to take me forever to remember the words because it's so complicated and it's next to impossible to sing. I hope you can open the MP3 and I hope you don't think I suck.

Question: I'm curious, what's your maiden name? Jon

Singing me a song? I couldn't wait to hear it.

APRIL 10

I can't open the song file :(I got an error message when I tried to download it. What am I doing wrong? I wanted to listen to it so badly!

I did get your messages about the Snowflake and the Sheraton. The rooms in Salem do seem expensive. Do they have any other rooms available that may be less expensive? The room does not have to have a fireplace. We probably won't even notice it anyway! I really do want to meet in Salem. It seems to be such a great place!

I loved your comments about how when things are right they fall into place and when they're not it's like pounding your head against the wall! I know the feeling so well!

My name? "Kingsley" is not really my last name.....hehehehehe Do you think I would reveal all?? :) It's sweeter when you have to wait.......isn't it? And, why would I tell you my "maiden" name?! :) Halley

It was getting harder to fake everything knowing the truth that I knew. I had turned into a flirt. Me, someone who had never known the definition of "flirt" had become a very devious and truth seeking online flirt.

APRIL 10

I forgot to ask! How and where do you sing these songs and create files so no one hears you! Or do they???? Halley

This had to be good!

APRIL 10

Portia and Mark get home after 5:00 PM. I have at least an hour and a half by myself if I hurry home. No, I couldn't do it if they were standing there listening to me. It's hard enough by myself! It took me forever to get something that seemed good enough to send. If you have a program that can play MP3's, you should be able to listen to it. Jon

I wanted to sneak over to his sister's where he was living, just around the corner from our house, and listen to him while he did this!

APRIL 10

I guess I'll have to try sending the file to myself just to see if I can open it.

The cheapest room is in the old section and it's $150.00. This is considered the off-season! I'm sure that it's nice enough looking and everything. To me, it's a question of who is playing that night at The Pounding Hammer. If the "Beat" is playing, it won't be much fun. If "Prime" is playing, it will be a blast. I don't really know of any other nightclub in the area, so if the band isn't good we're kind of out of luck.

If we went to Burrington we could almost stay two nights for the same price and we could "do" Burrington. We could do things during the day but there really aren't any good clubs in Burrington that I've seen for nighttime fun. It's not like I'm a party person and have always gone out to bars and clubs. I've only gone out for the last four months and checked things out. One night my sister and brother-in-law went with me over to Salem. It was a weekend that the "Beat" was playing and they were terrible. So, we went to Burrington and checked out the bars over there. They were even worse. Another problem in Burrington is that it's full of young college students. The bars look like they are full of teenagers. I'll try to find out who is playing in Salem. I just wanted you to know that I'm not a "bar fly" or something, because I'm not.

The Snowflake also has a restaurant and a nice bar that we could stay in if we wanted to.

"Kingsley" is not really your last name?.....hehehehehe   Sneaky! errrrrrhhhhhh! Jon

The Pounding Hammer. All I could think of was that the place was for people who had been around the block so many times that they were pounded nails. I kept thinking that he had some kind of obsession with the place and had really become a "bar fly." Just trying to be eighteen again. Mid-life crisisitis.

APRIL 10

Let me know about the reservations. But I can't let you pay for the room completely. That would not be fair. So, are we thinking one room, two beds or two rooms, two beds or one room, one bed????? What do you think? :) hehehehehe Halley

APRIL 10

I thought that you wanted two rooms? Well, it would be nice if we had one room with two beds, but I can understand if you don't want to do that. That would be a club room, wouldn't it? That would be $240.00. It would save a lot of money if we chose one room. We should decide by Friday morning so we can make reservations in time.

Talk to me, tell me what you think. Jon

Boy, did I want to tell Jon what I thought! That he was a pig. But, I had to admit to myself that it was getting very amusing. This was becoming quite a diversion for me.

APRIL 10

Halley (?)

Or is it really "Kingsley" and you're just covering yourself because you forgot that your last name would show on your emails?

I just did a check with a similar MP3 file to my own email address. A little box came up called "WINAMP" with a "play" arrow. It worked fine. Jon (Logan)

P.S. Jeez, I sing to you and you won't even give me your last name?): :(I was hoping for a picture. A little guilt works sometimes, right? hehehe

Guilt, huh? I wondered why he had none. Or, did he?

APRIL 10

I guess my computer is just not MP3 capable. Need a new one! Or, is there something I can get as an add-on to make it work? Tell me, tell me! I really want to hear what you have done :) I did a little Internet surfing tonight on Salem and I found a great place! But, I am not sure if this is okay with you? I really don't want to do the Burrington thing—not "romantic" enough......too noisy, too busy.... too many distractions!!!!

So, here goes, check out the Norac Nordic Lodge. The rooms in the Ice House are $129 per night and you can get two queen beds. Or, two separate rooms at that price would not be a problem. Instead of the Pounding Hammer, we could do the romantic restaurant and have a great view of the mountains! We would have more time to really get to know each other...... Well? Tell me what you think! Halley

I had to find a way to access the song! I couldn't believe that he had recorded himself singing for someone he didn't even know! I was really laying the mustard on the dog with all the talk of getting a room together.

How could he not be suspicious? That brain hanging between his legs—that was it!

APRIL 11

The Norac Nordic Lodge sounds great! I like that idea. So, we just need to decide on one room or two?

I would think that if you accessed your hotmail account on a newer or different computer, you might be able to hear the MP3. Jon

If Jon didn't figure out who I was now, there was something really wrong! I had forever wanted to go to the Norac Nordic Lodge for our anniversary and it just never happened. I should have made a reservation and told him he was going, I guess. Now, he was so eager to go with someone he didn't even know it was unbelievable. He didn't even know what my fake persona looked like!

APRIL 11

I am very confused by a few things. I just don't understand how you can be "just friends" as you said earlier with someone you have had a "relationship" with—how is it possible???

I am just trying to get inside of your mind!!!!!!! Is that possible? I just wonder, that's all.

Well, on to another subject! I figure when my situation is finalized, I will be able to trade in my Saab for something new and I wondered if you might be able to help! I know that people say that cars reflect a person's personality and I wondered what you thought mine might be!

Let me know what you think! Halley

APRIL 11

I'm at school so I only have a few minutes. I think that there are a lot of new smaller SUV's that are great. Maybe you would consider one of those? I'll think more about this and email you later when I have more time. Jon

Time to think. That was something. Then, why hadn't he taken the time to really think about what he was doing to us before he left?

eight

TRUTH, LIES
AND FEARS

April 11

Well, school is over so I have some time to talk.

Now, about the friendship thing. Ashley thinks that I need time to think. I didn't have the heart to tell her the truth. The truth about why I don't think we are completely compatible. We have some very basic differences in the way we think. I'll try not to sound like a snob, if that's possible.

I had a meeting with a student's parents. This particular student is having some major difficulties and it's easy to see that something is not right at home. Anyway, when I met the parents, the student's father was wearing sweatpants and was about eighty pounds over-weight. His belly was hanging out and he hadn't shaved in a couple weeks and, generally, looked like a complete slob. Imagine going into a meeting regarding your child while looking like that. I'm sorry, but I can't help it. Well, it wasn't a week after this meeting that I was having a conversation with Ashley when she said that she was talking to the very same man who happens to be a friend of hers. His wife was also present. The "Belly Ring Girl" and the "Sweat-pant Guy" were joking around and saying how nice their children would look and that they would have three. She also had names for them. This was just talk, which was meant to annoy the "Sweatpant Guy's" wife. After she told me this little story, I looked at her and said something like "You mean, Garand?" She said "yes" and what a nice looking man he was. I again said, "You mean, Garand?" "Oh yes," she said, "he is a very nice looking man." We then proceeded to talk about what matters and what doesn't matter. I discovered that she has some very basic rules regarding finding someone to spend the rest of her life with. Basically, everything I have strived so hard to accomplish meant very little in her eyes. As long as she can find a man who doesn't drink a case of beer a day and who doesn't cheat on her, Ashley said she would be content.

I've heard a lot of guys say that they want to marry someone who is easy to please, because it would make their lives simple. Well, I can understand what they're thinking to a certain extent but I also want to marry someone who wants the same level of success that I do. If you don't marry someone like that, wouldn't that mean that you would have to work toward that level of success alone? Does that explain the "Belly Ring Girl" situation to you?

I thought about your questions this afternoon and they are the reason why I told you the above information. I want you to know how I think. Would you like to know my biggest fear? I think my biggest fear is speaking in public. Isn't that pathetic? I recognize that I have difficulty in that area and am going to get over it. I've always wanted to sing in public. I thought that the desire to sing would get me to do it and perhaps alleviate some of my public speaking fears at the same time. I think it's working and I will continue. I have no trouble speaking in the classroom and keeping control. It's just that I know I would have a hard time speaking in front of the entire student body and faculty combined. I think most people would fear that. I would like to be able to speak in front of a large group and do it in relative calm.

My goal is to become the most complete person I can be. To do that I feel that I must conquer my fears. If I can become a complete person, then the money and lifestyle will follow.

What are your fears? What are some of your goals in life? I have always thought about running for some type of statewide office. I have a real desire to do this and know that with the right person in my life that I could accomplish this. Jon

I couldn't help but laugh at Jon's story even though I felt compassion for these people. Jon's description of the situation was outright hilarious and it made him somehow endearing to me. It was obvious to me that Ashley didn't exist on the same level as Jon or did she? If he had slept with her, maybe they were the same? Or, had he just used her? Or, was it a way of masking the pain of our breakup at least for a moment? Was it worth it to him to break all the vows he made to me for a moment's pleasure? I had to keep in mind that he was thinking with the "other head" as my friend kept reminding me. So, we were right about her. No ambitions but to be with someone who didn't drink excessively and who didn't cheat on her. But how can someone expect to find someone who doesn't cheat on them when they sleep with someone who is cheating? My mind was spinning. I was really confused by Jon's statements about needing the right person to accomplish the goals he wanted to achieve. I thought that he should really be able to do this on his own. But, he never had. I had helped him every step of the way and he had never helped me. That was why I was where I was. I remembered helping him with a speaking class he took. I worked so hard on it with him and he really did improve. I loved helping him and couldn't under-stand how he could turn away from someone who cared so much. In the last month we were together, I remembered him saying that I cared too much. And, I wondered now, how can anyone ever care too much?

Why was it after reading his message that I knew in my heart that we truly belonged together? I felt it with every thought. Even though I knew he had done what he did with the bimbo, I felt we belonged together and that we truly were soul mates. I wondered if this tragedy was necessary

to wake me from my dark sleep. How could I have not seen this coming? Maybe it couldn't have been any other way? I wondered how it would be possible for us to ever be together again. Why did my heart know what his heart would not admit? He was the best friend I had ever had or at least I had thought this to be true. Had I been wrong?

APRIL 11

I understand what you are saying. It's okay for people to want what they do but it seems you are not compatible with her. There is nothing wrong with the way she wants to live and there is nothing wrong with the way you want to live. Everyone has different levels of expectations and goals. It's all about happiness. Wouldn't it be better for you to be honest with her. I know that I would want the truth. Do you think it's fair to keep the truth from her?

SUV's? No, I don't think so. I was thinking red BMW! Wouldn't that be hot???

My fears? That I won't find someone to love me as I want to be loved....that I won't make a difference in the world...

My dreams? I want to write something that will inspire people to do great things and to really think about what they are doing with their lives. I want to contribute something to the world, to leave something behind that will never be forgotten.

You know, they say behind every great man there is a great woman. As a woman, I can see between the lines that your wife must have done something for you. She must have had a positive influence on your goals and dreams in some way?

Right now, all I can think of are those little fish! Hehehehe Halley

I was desperate to hear him say something good about me, Hunter, and I had to use a fake persona to ask the question. I just felt such an overwhelming sense of sadness because he couldn't talk to me in real life but he couldn't stop talking to Halley.

April 11

So, who should make the reservation??? And when should we make it. Would it be better to wait until next week?

I'll make it if you like and whenever you think we should. Just tell me what I need to know. Or you can do it. If you want to reserve the room I could send you the money now, but that would mean you would have to tell me WHO YOU ARE!

I can't believe you said BMW! I had written that down then deleted it because I didn't think you would be interested. I was looking at them before I bought my truck. I think the model was a 330i and it's all-wheel drive. Very nice car. If you take delivery in Europe, you can deduct something like 8% off of the price. They have this European package deal where you can take delivery and drive it on the Autobahn at speeds it was built for and take it all over Europe. Then, you drive it to the loading docks, fly home and pick it up at your BMW dealer in something like a month. The savings in costs pays for your vacation. Pretty neat huh? You also get a special sticker on one of the windows that acknowledges the European delivery. And you didn't think I was a snob! hehehe

Yes, Hunter did have some positive influences on my life. She was the one who came up with the idea of working where I work now. My job has really saved me. She also made my first flying lesson appointment. It was something that I always wanted to do but probably still would not have done, if she hadn't made that first appointment. I do think about the positive stuff. I think the negative things that are really irritating right now are things that will fade with time.

Very nice goals. I've always wanted to write something too. We could solve the travel aspect of your goals this summer by going to Europe and picking up your new "Bimmer." What do you think? hehehe

So far I like your mind very much, but you're not telling me enough to satisfy my interests. I want to be able to talk to you on the phone, to hear your voice and I want to be able to see your mannerisms. I want to know everything. I think I've told you a lot more about myself than you have revealed to me. We have less than a week now before meeting. I'm counting the days.

Do you ever look at my picture? Or, did you just file it away or do you look at it once in a while? I wish I had one to look at. It's okay for now, but it might add to the whole experience at this point. Once we meet and if things go well, you will tell me everything won't you? Things like phone numbers and where you work? Your NAME would be nice too. For all I know, you're a man. THAT WOULD NOT BE GOOD!

AND THERE IS NOTHING LITTLE ABOUT MY FISH! If you're a good girl, I might let you play with it. hehehehehe Personally, I've got red sequins on my mind. Jon

He was so eager I didn't know what to think. On the one hand, I was amazed at my ability to pull off such a farce. On the other hand, I worried that he might really get himself into trouble with the wrong person on the other end of an email connection! The BMW. I had suggested the European delivery plan as a trip for us. Then he went and bought that stupid truck. We could have had a great vacation and a lifetime experience and he could have had the car he said he had always wanted. I should have seen the signs. I couldn't believe he would even admit to me having any positive influences on his life. I'm sure he was admitting to it to make himself look good to my fake persona. I wondered if he really meant what he said about letting go of the negative someday because whenever I saw Jon all he focused on was the negative. He wouldn't even talk to me. But, I could hardly hold him off as "Halley." So, he wanted me to play with his "fish" and he was thinking about the red sequins. What was I going to do to hold him off and keep this going long enough to discover as much truth as possible?

nine

THE SONG

APRIL 11

I FINALLY got to hear your song! That is the sweetest thing that anyone has ever done for me! You have a wonderful voice! I absolutely loved it! (And, I will never erase the file!) Could you please sing me a few lines of Drops of Jupiter! Please? Halley

I cried when I finally was able to access the song file and listen to him singing to me. But he wasn't singing to me. He was singing to "Halley." And, I meant what "Halley" said. I would never erase the file. I even figured out how to copy it onto a disk! I wondered how I could use it or if I would just keep it and someday someone would find it and listen to it and wonder what the story was behind the song.

APRIL 12

I'm glad you liked the little MP3 thing. Can I send you a little Drops of Jupiter? I would love to, but I need some inspiration. Perhaps a picture? Jon

How was I going to keep holding him off on the picture? If Jon was as eager as he seemed to be, there was a way. I felt that I could probably go a while longer or at least I hoped I could.

APRIL 12

I still don't have my camera! My brother is still away! Would it help if I tried to describe myself?

I will call this weekend and get more information on reservations. So, do you want to stay in the Main Lodge or in the Ice House? I did find out that the Ice House is across the street from the Main Lodge. More privacy there??? I think that this time of year is considered the "slow season" in Vermont and New Hampshire because it is in between skiing and summer, so I'm sure there won't be a problem getting a room even if the reservation is not made until next week. I even thought I could use my sister's card to make the reservation so it won't show up as a charge for either of us! What if you paid for dinner and breakfast (and maybe lunch if we make it that far!)? :)

This BMW plan sounds like so much fun! But it will probably be next summer before I could do anything like that! I won't have the money by this summer!

I hope I didn't offend you in any way about the "Belly Ring Girl" situation. They were just my feelings.

Sounds like your wife really cared about you. I guess there is no way you can be a "creep" if someone cared so much to do so much for you. I'm ashamed to say that she has me beat! It's good that you think that the negative will fade over time. I believe the same for myself. Now, for some truth from my end—Alan couldn't be what or how I wanted him to be—do you think I was right in making the decision that I did? I know it was the work that got in the middle of everything and made this happen but everything seems so out there..... Too much talk about all of this!

Mannerisms? What mannerisms do you find annoying??? Tell me! If I satisfy all your interests now, you won't have anything to look forward to, will you? You are so demanding! Well, ask me questions and see if I answer! Hehe

I'm really looking forward to meeting you too. And, yes, I do look at your picture and I see someone very special...... And, I'm so sorry that I still don't have my camera but wouldn't you rather see the real me in person instead??? Remember, it is sweeter when you have to wait! And, noooooo I am not a man! Do I "sound" like a man?

Well, I can see you definitely have some confidence—"There is nothing little about my fish!" What about when it is cold outside? Hehehehe You know, I don't think you ever answered my question about whether or not you could keep it under control all day in those silky boxers. Well, I'm waiting for an answer. How does it react when you read my sexy messages? Hehe

Play with it, huh? You are so BAD!

So, are your buttocks soft and smooth? I want to imagine what they feel like..... (Am I getting myself into trouble yet?) hehehehehe And, what do you smell like? Hehehehehehe (How will you ever answer this one?)

I definitely have to go shopping this weekend—need some red sequins! Or, do you like red silk?? Halley

This was so much fun. I knew his butt was as hairy as a monkey and I wanted to see if he would admit it. In the midst of all the heartache, this was something to look forward to and be creative with even though it was deceitful. I figured that all was fair in love and war—right?

APRIL 12

The picture issue. Where there is a will, there is a way.

Main Lodge or in the Ice House? Wherever your heart desires. :)

Aren't you clever to think of using your sister's card. How else do you hide things?

I was thinking I could pay for dinner and breakfast. Perhaps I could pay for Saturday also? :)

I think you made the decision to leave for a reason. The bottom line is you need to be happy.

When I mentioned mannerisms, I was thinking along the lines of how you move when you speak, to get the true meaning of what you're saying. Mannerisms that I find annoying? I think it would depend who was doing it. I know one thing I don't like is when people smack their lips when chewing. I really don't like that.

I would like you to satisfy all my interests now. We have tomorrow to look forward to. Another day of being satisfied all over again. I'm demanding? Maybe a little bit. I just want to see the woman I have been writing to and singing to. No, you don't sound like a man. I think that you are a woman. I do have one question for you though. Did you tell the truth about yourself in your profile? Height, weight, etc.?

Yes, when it's cold outside it shrinks up a lot! It's very elastic. Can I keep it under control all day in silk boxers? I have to because it would really show if I stood up with only boxers on. So when I'm thinking about you and students are around, I have to start thinking about Hunter instead. hehehehehe

So, you ask me again what my buttocks feel like. I guess they're soft and smooth. There is something you need to know so you aren't taken by surprise. I'm pretty hairy. Mostly from the waist down. Not like ridiculously hairy, but hairy. I've been told that I smell good.

Being that your blonde with blue eyes, I'm guessing that you're kind of light skinned? Is that right? Tell me, do you have any moles in sexy places? Like on the bottom of a breast or buttock or even someplace more interesting. hehehe

Red sequins or red silk? I think you should buy yourself whatever will make you feel "oohhh so good." Then I can slowly, gently take it off you. Whoops, I have to start thinking about my wife again. hehehe (Not kidding!)

I wish we could do something this weekend. I have to work a school duty tonight from 6:00 PM until 11:00 PM. I just don't know what I'm going to do with myself all weekend. I've got some class work to do, but otherwise, nothing. What's your opinion? Do you think we could do something this weekend? Jon

Wish he had said that to me "wherever your heart desires," Hunter, instead of to "Halley." But, I knew when I started this that I would have to take whatever I got and deal with it. I couldn't believe he was talking about annoying personal things. He was the one who got spit strings hanging from his top lip to his bottom lip when he talked. Sometimes, they were like spiders webs! And, bad breath. He chewed gum all the time and it still didn't help. And, when I would tell him he would always be disgusted with himself. Shrinkage! Well, he was right. It was VERY elastic! You would never think that something so small at its coldest could get so big at its hottest! The comments about me hurt but I knew they were coming from a place of negativity and resentment and pain. And, that was only detrimental to him. And he admitted to being hairy! And his smell. I would never forget the way that he smelled. It would stay with me forever and I knew that it was me he was referring to. I told him how good he smelled all the time. I smelled his scent whenever we hugged or kissed. I just couldn't help myself. They say that if some of your senses are weak, the others are much stronger. And that is the truth. The moles. He was referring to mine. How could it be anybody else? Mine were on the bottom of my left breast and another in a very interesting place that always drove him crazy! How could a mole ever get there?

APRIL 12

What a beautiful day!

This is my phone call to you. I feel good and it's a nice day and I feel like talking to my new friend for no particular reason other than to say "Hi." I have some errands to do this afternoon before my duty starts tonight.

Do you think you could have a relationship with someone who you have revealed everything in your mind to? I would like that.

What is the main reason you haven't told me much about yourself? Is it because we're talking online and you feel you don't know me. Is it because you don't want anything getting back to your husband? Is it because you feel by keeping things unknown, it makes for more fun? Just a question.

What color is your Saab? How long is your hair?

I almost went over to Salem last night. My class got out early. I stayed home and did some school work instead.

I think it's great that we're going to do this Salem thing. Have you ever found that when you expect a lot from a situation, you usually end up being disappointed? I hope we're not doing that. Maybe it's like I said earlier, when it's right things just fall into place. We'll find out soon.

I'm happy that you have taken the chance to write to me and that you are willing to take the chance to meet me. I think we're going to have a good time. I have to go now and get ready for tonight. Talk to you later. Jon

He didn't have a clue what was coming his way. And, I wasn't sure what was going to happen either.

APRIL 12

Do you want a Polaroid??? But, then you would have to give me your address and I think it's too early for that! I'll bring one with me so you can have something to put under your pillow at night!

I found out that the rooms in the Main Lodge are $180. The Ice House rooms are $129. What's your preference?

And, why would you want to go over to Salem without ME? To sing karaoke without telling me?

"Clever?" What do you mean? Are you speaking of the female mind?

Saturday night too? Whoaaaaaa! Maybe?! I just can't keep up with you!

And, yes, my "dimensions" are all correct. Why? Do you have a problem with a certain size? And, my Saab is silver and my hair is past shoulder length.

Are you as nice as you seem or do you have a side you have not shown to me??? Do you feel like that about all your "ex's?" Will I be on that list too someday? Not a good thought!

And, WHAT do you smell like? And, what kind of perfume or fragrance do you like on a woman?

Hairy, huh??? Now, that would definitely be something new and exciting for me! Hehehehe Moles? Well, I guess you will have to locate them, won't you? :)

What is your thing with the color red? Tell me. What other colors do you like on a girl? Do you like makeup on a girl? What kind of clothes do you like on a girl? haha

I can't this weekend. Don't you have any PATIENCE! I have a family event to attend and I am so tired! Don't know how I will get through it but it will be fun. But remember, I will be checking my email…….. I'll be looking for more "deep" questions…….So, what is it you want to know about me—ask away.

So, you ask the main reason why I am so discreet and the answer is everything you said and isn't it more fun this way? Isn't it more exciting? I don't know everything about you. I expect to meet the person I have gotten to know but I'm thinking what are you hiding??? Maybe you are not what you seem? What is hiding behind that gorgeous smile? Should I be afraid??? Very afraid?????? :) Halley

I wondered just how much farther I could push the depth of the conversation. The more I pushed, the more he gave. But, I felt that Jon was starting to hold back a little and that couldn't happen at this point.

APRIL 12

I would like something to put under my pillow at night. You'll have to give me a picture on Friday.

Let's go for it and get the nice room. I didn't want to go to Salem without you. That's why I stayed home. Clever? I'm speaking of your mind. It's good you think from multiple angles.

If things go well, I wouldn't be able to see you for a whole week. Saturday night too would be nice wouldn't it? Maybe we should just think about Friday for now.

I don't have problem with a certain size. Just curious…. And, I think I am what I seem to be.

Feel like what about all my "ex's?" First of all there aren't many of them.

I don't know the names of the perfumes that I like.

I'm glad you are okay with how I am hairy. For a while, I thought I might have to start using the "NADS." That stuff hurts.

I'm not hiding anything. I am what I seem to be and I hope you're not afraid of me. I know I'm anxious, but it's because I just can't wait to meet you. I guess I'll just have to. Jon

I felt guilty after reading his message. But how could I? After what he had done to me leaving me an emotional ruin. I felt like this was part of the healing process to find out the truth and to find a way to accept it. How much more did I need to finally get that he didn't want me? And, how could he say that he was what he seemed to be and that he wasn't hiding anything when he had hidden the truth from me for who knows how long. And, the "NADS!" I had ordered it for him. We were constantly looking for some kind of hair removal system for him! He hated the hair on his butt and on his lower back. This was the third attempt to find something that wouldn't be painful but it was even worse! The hot wax had burned him, the power tool had hurt and the "NADS" was so powerful at ripping the hair out that the holes the hair came out of bled! He was right, it did hurt! Probably, we weren't doing it right! It worked great but we were probably pulling the strips off in the wrong direction. And, I remember how funny he was when we were doing it. I couldn't help but laugh with compassion—an inherited family trait. I remember begging to do his eyebrows either with tweezers or the "NADS." He laid on the floor and I sat on top of his chest and plucked. We would make deals. If he let me pluck his "third" eyebrow out, then we would do what he wanted to do! Plucking his eyebrows really turned me on!

APRIL 12

You just made me laugh so hard you wouldn't believe it! What in the world is "NADS?" "That stuff hurts" What do you MEAN? I can't wait to hear about this? Is it a way of removing hair??? Oh, baby, bring it with you—I think it would be so much fun! hehehehehehe Let's try it out! I'd love to try it on my legs! Would you do it for me? hehehe

What I meant about the ex-thing, you said that you had to think about your wife when you wanted to calm "it" down. So, I thought if I was on your ex-list, it would not be a nice place to be! So, how many "ex's" are there???

I can't believe I am going to ask you this, but it's so much easier to ask in an email rather than to your face! So, what about it. Do you have a problem with being "careful" if you know what I mean???????hehehehehe Or, do I have to be more specific with what I am trying to say? Do you let your horse run wild or do you make sure it has a saddle on it????hehehehehe And, you know, the way things are now how do I know where "it" has been? :) And, don't you want to know about where I've "been???????" I assume that you checked this out with your "Belly Ring Girl?" I hope I haven't embarrassed you! I've embarrassed myself!!!!!!!!

You don't know the name of a perfume that you like? Well, tell me what it smells like and maybe I will know what it is? What do you wear or do you just wear your natural wonderful self?

I know how you feel. I have been so happy to have someone to talk with and communicate with who seems to be what he says he is. It's been really lonely as Alan will not talk to me right now. It's understandable but it is still hard. It would be so much easier if we could have some sort of communication. But, what's a girl to do? So, thanks for being so "there." And, I can't wait to meet you too.

I'm still waiting for more questions......I am not sure what you want to know so if you ask questions, then I will know what you want to know! Halley

This had to be one of the most hilarious messages I had ever written and I really did mean what I said about communicating with him. I was becoming the self that had existed within me that I had never released to freedom. I was becoming "Halley" and leaving Hunter behind. How could he not know that it was me behind the façade? I was finally realizing that he had never taken the time to get to know me, the real me, or maybe I had never let him know me?

ten

QUESTIONS AND ANSWERS

APRIL 12

I just finished my night proctor thing. It's 11:00 PM and I'm in my classroom. I was going to just see if you replied and I wasn't going to respond if you did. I was thinking that I don't want to drive you crazy by talking too much. But, this email is the best one you have ever sent me so I just can't help myself.

"NADS" is a gel and you spoon it on, then you take a special piece of cloth, place it over it, then rip it off fast. It hurts like hell. I don't know if you can buy it over the counter or if it was something that I ordered on TV. It works, but it's not easy. But, you never know, I might be doing it wrong for all I know.

There is only one true "ex" and there will never be another.

I've had to use "rain gear" for longer than I care to admit. And good for you for bringing up the subject. I've thought about it too but didn't have the guts to bring up the subject. It just seems better if the woman initiates some subjects, don't you think? As far as I know, I don't have anything. If you like, I wouldn't mind getting tested first. I never have had any symptoms of anything. Ashley said that she was tested a while ago and had nothing and hadn't been with anyone for a year before me. She was with her previous boyfriend for five years. She didn't sleep around or anything.

Yes, I do want to know where you have been, will you tell me?

I've had time to think about the perfume thing. I would rather you didn't wear the same thing as anyone I have ever been close to. I want you to be you and I don't want you to remind me of someone else. Hunter had a little bottle of "Miss Balmain" when we were first married. The stuff smelled great and it took less than a drop to smell up everything, but I wouldn't want you to wear it. You can't get the spray stuff—it's a cheap version of the real thing in a bottle.

I just wear my natural wonderful self. But if you like I'll get some of the "Higher" stuff. Is it something someone who you were close to wore? If it is, I don't want it.

REMEMBER THAT IT WAS YOU WHO ASKED FOR QUESTIONS!

You say that "then you will know what I want to know," you didn't say "then you would answer all of them." Please do.

What does your husband do for work? Are you living alone or with someone? How long have you been separated? What are your parents like? Are they retired or still working? What was/is their occupations? Where do your parents live? How many siblings do you have? Where do you fit in the family—youngest—oldest? How many hearts have you broken? What's your nationality? Does your job have a traditional school year schedule? Spring vacation? What's your zodiac sign? Are you ticklish and, if so, where? Do you like massages? Do you wear a towel on your head after washing your hair? Would you mind if I watched you put on make-up? The last question. It's hard to explain. I love watching female hands and nails do things the way females do and I love to watch them primp themselves in the relaxing way they do. This is something new for me. I haven't always been like this. It also doesn't mean that I need different women. I would be perfectly happy to watch just one. I think it's more like I'm in awe of a beautiful woman who has a career, supports herself, is strong, intelligent, capable and also is a woman and treats herself that way. The thought of having someone like that in my life is something that I never thought I would experience. Now I realize that I can have that. If you're all those things, you might have a hard time getting rid of me. What do your parents think of your separation? Would you be willing to reveal "all" your secrets to that special someone? Do you truly want a family some day? Are you wondering what you have gotten yourself into yet? Jon

All I could think of was "Never say never." There would never be another "ex." How could he know? How can anyone know? Maybe he would be the one who would get dumped the next time or maybe he would run away again.... No guts. Now, that was the truth. I had had the guts for both of us. I was burned out because of his lack of spine. Birth control pills made me sick and he didn't seem to mind what we had to use. And, he never insisted that we go without.....As I read his message, I realized that the child issue had not been as important as he had told everyone as one of his excuses for leaving me. I told him I would do anything to make things right and he had left anyway. Instead of telling me, Jon had told his brothers, his sister, my sister... everyone but me. But the real truth was hidden far away from me. It was hidden in a classroom a mile away from our house and she liked to wear red. I remembered the "Miss Balmain" perfume—the perfume someone at work had given to me for Christmas. On our last anniversary, Jon had given me the spray bottle. And, here he was saying that the gift he had given me was the "cheap version." Nice. I couldn't believe all the questions he asked. I definitely had some inventing to do! I couldn't believe the tirade on women he gave. It was a description of the bleached blonde jock girl. What he didn't get was that she did all the things she did because she was so "unfemale." It was the only way she became the girl she wanted to be. So, what was I? I was almost the complete opposite of jock girl. I didn't have to do all of those things to be "female." And, I had known her first, before he had worked with her. I wondered if Kristan knew of her role in our divorce.

APRIL 13

So, you liked my message! I'm glad. It was so much fun writing it!

So, you didn't say if you would bring the "NADS" or not? You have to bring it with you baby! I really do want to do my legs! Unless you would rather I shave before???? Haha

Only one "ex?" What about ex-girlfriends? :)

Now another embarrassing question! How do you know that Ashley was telling you the truth???? So, I take it you let your horse run wild with her???? What if I need to ride with a saddle (just for now)? Would that be a problem for you? (I am so embarrassed!) :)

There have only been two for me and they were both completely "safe." So, that is why I feel the way I do. :)

Perfume, hmmmmmmm, I will have to pick something out that is truly "high!" And, your natural wonderful self sounds great to me!

Answers to your questions, here goes!

Alan is into investments so that means, hopefully, I will be able to buy that BMW! Right now, I am living with my sister who has a very big house (which she bought on her own) with lots of extra room, so it has not been a problem and the extra income really is great for her. And, as we have always been so close, it has been great to be with her. I have been separated about two months. My father, Hugh, is into law enforcement and my mother, Marie, is a retired nurse and they live in the White Haven area. I have one older sister, Laurie, and one younger brother, Joe. I am in the middle.

I have only broken one heart (my husband, Alan)—how about you????? As for my nationality of descent, my father is French and my mother is Scottish. My "school" does have vacations, but right now I have been assigned to a "special project" because of my major and my past performance in my field. Grants, ways to improve etc. My sign????? I'm a sexy Scorpio!

Ticklish?—well, I will let you figure that one out! Massages? They are so heaven! I think I read on the website that the Norac Nordic Lodge offers this service. Do you like them? We could have them when we are there! Or, would you rather be the one giving the massage??????

Towel on my head. Doesn't every woman do this? I love the ones that are just for hair. They really "suck" the water out so fast! I have one and it's great! Makeup watching? Ohhhhhh—maybe?

Your level of devotion is incredible! But, what do you mean by primping? Putting on makeup and doing nails? Is that what you mean? My husband hated the smell of nail polish. Do you?

So, have you only ever been with "beautiful" women? I hope that you mean inner beauty as well as outer attractiveness? But, I have to say that there are women out there that are so beautiful on the inside that their outer appearance should not be an indication of their beauty, don't you?

As for my separation, my parents are upset about it as they don't believe in divorce but they know it is my decision to make. They believe that reconciliation should at least be attempted.

All my secrets? Haven't I almost told you everything??? What are you hiding???? Haha

And, yes, I truly do want a family some day. I want to know that I have made a difference in this world and maybe that is just one way of doing it.

And, yes, I am wondering about what I am getting myself into but it seems so right and so good..........

I have to go now to get ready for the family "event." I hope to hear from you by tonight! Halley

I officially dubbed myself a writer after this email.

APRIL 13

I'll look for some "NADS" before Friday. Mine is back at my house. I think it would be nice if I did your legs. hehehe I also think it would be nice if I washed your hair and your entire body in the shower. You could then do mine. hehehehehe

I didn't really date much before I met my wife. I was too shy and things just never seemed to flow right.

I am sure Ashley was telling me the truth. One quality she had was that she was very honest and open about everything. No, I didn't let my horse run wild with her. I'm used to riding with a saddle, so it would be okay. Like I said before, I don't mind getting tested.

It sounds like you have a wonderful family.

I guess I have broken three hearts. One really doesn't count because it was puppy love in high school, my wife and the "Belly Ring Girl." I hate hurting people because I know what if feels like.

I would rather be the one giving the massage.

By primping I mean the whole scene—towel on the head, mirror, bathrobe, makeup.... I really don't like the smell of nail polish either but I deal with it.

Ashley was very attractive; she was half Japanese. I know what you mean by inner attractiveness though. I think if a woman feels good about the way she looks on the outside, it makes her a much happier person on the inside. Again, my particular situation is a little different. I'm used to someone who honestly thought that she was ugly. I could not convince her otherwise. It made for some very difficult inner emotions.

I can't possibly know all your inner secrets yet. The things you think and do that you have never told anyone about, like your personal thoughts. Is it wrong to be that close to someone?

I'm glad this seems right and good to you. It does to me too. How was I was able to come up with so many questions last night? I had to monitor students for five hours. I had lots of time to work and also lots of time to think and write down questions.

I hope that you don't think I'm strange in that I'm too intense with questions and email. I know it's because I've been starved for the sustenance I need for a very long time, so I just crave it more. A healthy, normal relationship. It all relates back to my decision to move out of my home, "iflyinsky," the way I feel inside, and the life that I can now see is possible. Does this make sense to you? Jon

How could he be so naïve as to believe what this bimbo told him. Essentially, she was a stranger to him. I couldn't believe it. And he broke her heart? Yeah, right. He was more concerned about her than me. I already knew she was half Japanese and I had also found out that I worked with her father years ago. Small town. Crazy family. Her mother used to hang out in the bars and was a waitress. Family occupation I guess. So, he also left me because I had self-confidence issues. It seemed he had a million reasons to blame me for everything. I was really taken off guard when I read how he had been starved for sustenance for a "very long time." I had no idea what kind of "sustenance" he was referring to. I had given him everything I had to give..... He had never told me he was "starving." I had done everything I could possibly do. How could I know? I couldn't read his mind. I wondered if this was a Jon thing or a man thing. Why was it so easy for him to tell a stranger, yet he never could tell his own wife? The truth was that he was a coward. That's why.

APRIL 13

Well, I just went out and got you your very first container of "NADS." It was available at the drugstore. So, you can do your legs Friday night if you like. Hehehehe I had this stupid smile on my face all the while I was holding it and paying for it. The woman behind the counter gave me this strange look like, "What's so funny?" :) Hehehe

Can you answer a question I've been thinking about for a while now? What exactly is it that your husband could not give you that you feel you need? I only ask so I will know if I have it and can give it. Is that okay? Jon

*I wondered if he truly realized how small the town was. Didn't he
even wonder if the woman behind the counter might know who he was
and wonder what the hell he was buying hair removal gel for?*

APRIL 13

Oh, I am so tired! But a good kind of tired! You must know
what I mean! It was a great afternoon and it was fun being with the
ENTIRE family (except for my brother, Joe, who is still on his trip).

I think you have me addicted to you and your emails! I just got
home and the first thing I did was run for the computer!

So, I don't understand. Why don't you just get your "NADS"
from home? Whenever I need something, I just let my husband
know. If you've used it before, there is nothing for her to suspect.
Why can't you just pick it up when she isn't there? Or, even when
she is? Ooooooooooo Do you have a look of guilt???? (Just joking!)
I don't want you to spend any extra money. If you don't feel you can
pick it up, I don't want you to go out and buy another! You are just
too good to be true!

Shower?????? Wow, you do move fast! Wait and see...............!

So HOW do you use a "saddle" with all the "firsts" that you
"received" that you told me about before? Please explain!!!!!

So, how long has it been since your horse has run wild????

So, now some questions from me and these are not all going to
be easy!

Has anyone ever broken YOUR heart???? Didn't your wife ever
primp as you describe it? So, WAS Hunter attractive? And, why would
she think she was ugly if she was attractive? Come on, there must have
been something that attracted you to her in the first place! I know that
there were many things that attracted me to my husband. Just being
honest! Explain this to me so I can better understand where you are
coming from.

And, what do you mean by difficult inner emotions? I just don't
understand this part of it. I know that if you communicated with

her the way you have communicated with me, I can't imagine how you got to this point. Or, did it take you leaving to be able to be like you are now? Did she know that you were "starving" inside? I just can't believe that anyone who would do the things for you that you told me about (the job, the pilot's license) would not want to do anything she could to make you happy? So, now you have me getting too personal!!!! Sorry!

Jon, don't you believe in leaving anything to the imagination???? Don't you want there to be some mystery between us at least for now??? We can't possibly know all each other's personal thoughts yet? You know what I mean? But, your intensity is a wonderful thing. I do want you to know that and it is unbelievably attractive.

Now, I really have to go and get some work done! Talk to you later! Halley

I was treading into deep water with the questions I was asking. But, really, I wanted to know how he felt about me, Hunter.

APRIL 13

I just got your message after I sent the message for you to not buy it if you couldn't get it at your house! But, you are so sweet! Halley April 13

I hope you don't take comments I make like taking a shower too seriously. I'm just having fun, no pressure.:)

It's been years since my horse has run wild!

The rest of your questions got me going into quite a bit of detail about my wife and "future ex." I took a second and third look at it and decided not to send it to you. I sent it to myself in case you want to see it at a later date. Don't worry it's not dark or anything. Please don't take my intensity the wrong way. For now, let's just say there is a perfectly logical and healthy reason I don't want to waste a moment of my life and for feeling the way I do. I'm sorry that I'm in too much of a hurry sometimes but I think you will understand why when you know the whole situation. Just slow me down when you need to. Jon

Who was normal and healthy? Was someone who engaged in an online relationship with a complete stranger normal? And, if he ran away, who could be called healthy and normal? And the intensity and desperation he was communicating—was that healthy and normal? He clearly wasn't dealing with the situation he had left, namely me, and was jumping into the fire head first. The only logic to the situation was that he didn't want to have to admit to not dealing with issues he needed to confront and was avoiding reality. If he couldn't even speak to me, what else was I supposed to think? And where was the logic is all of this???

APRIL 13

I'm sorry. I only wanted short answers to short questions! I didn't mean to send you into the "depths." But, I really wanted to know if anyone had broken YOUR heart? Has anyone ever? Was it Hunter that broke your heart?

And, if you feel comfortable with me reading what you wrote, I am open to it. I just don't want it to be too painful for you?

I woke up in the middle of the night and I just couldn't get this thought out of my head. I thought that maybe the one you should be telling all of this "stuff" to that you described about in the email you didn't send me is your wife. Wouldn't it help more to send it to her instead of telling me or anyone else?

I just want you to know that when my situation "came down" I told my husband everything and it really helped. I don't know—I'm so sorry to have hit a bad "nerve" for you. I hope this makes sense. Halley

APRIL 14

Now that you mention it, I guess that she really has broken my heart. With the broken promises and all the disappointment, not to mention fifteen years of struggling for the future only to have it taken away. Through a secondary business, I managed to pay off everything we own. The house is paid for and the vehicles—everything. The plan was to secure a stable base to raise a family. Now, I feel like I'm starting over. Was it all a mistake? I don't know. It's not like I didn't learn anything along the way and it won't be as difficult the second time around. I'm still optimistic towards the future. The money doesn't matter. Only happiness matters. Jon

I was so angry with the content of his message. I had broken his heart?? He was the one who left. I told him I would do anything to make things right for him. I wasn't even taking into consideration what would be good for me. Broken promises and disappointment? I had broken no promises and if he was disappointed that was his responsibility to explain what the problem was to me. Fifteen years of struggling. I crawled along with him and lived his life, not mine, and this is what he had to say about me? The secondary business. Apartment buildings that made both of us physically sick. I begged him to sell them for years and he would never listen to me. The second time around. Who did he think he was that he could say that it wouldn't be as difficult the next time? What if it was worse? On the last sentence, I almost choked. Out of our entire marriage, money was the only thing that mattered to him. For years, I pleaded the happiness case to him over and over and he never heard me. I couldn't make him happy. He had to find happiness within and he hadn't been capable of it. Maybe now he was because things were finally sinking in? I was devastated by his appraisal of me. And, how could he say his heart was broken when he was chasing after any woman he could find—even a cyber fantasy?

APRIL 14

Am I making you wake up in the middle of the night? I can only hope I'm on your mind that much! :)

I've tried to talk to her and she just doesn't get it. She is seeing a shrink right now. Maybe, that will help her understand.

I don't really have a problem telling you everything. I just think that it would take all the mystery away. That's why I don't want to tell you. I'll tell you soon after we meet. Isn't mystery a neat word? The way it's spelled and what it means? Jon

His approach to talking to me before he left was to threaten and scream. Like that was going to work because I only reacted to his behavior, which was wrong but it was the only defense that I had. Shrink. He had a real stigma in regard to psychiatrists, psychologists and counselors. He believed that only he could help himself and no one else. That was why we were in the mess we were in. His attitude was like a brick wall with no loose mortar.

APRIL 14

Well, let's get off that subject! And, I would like to make a suggestion. That we don't talk about any of our "stuff" on our weekend together. I think we should just focus on US. What do you think?

So, I don't think you have told me about your family and what sign of the zodiac you are? Let's have it! Maybe that will cheer you up?

And, I think that we should get that wild horse out of its saddle as soon as possible, don't you think? Hehehehe

Now, I have to go shopping!!!!!!!! I'll be looking for black silk boxers!!!! (Oh! What size are you?)

Oh, and I will also be looking for something red for me!

I just had to ask you another question.

Have you ever caught a glimpse of yourself in a mirror at a strange moment when you are thinking certain thoughts and frightened yourself in either a good or bad way? Have you ever thought you could see into your own soul at one of these moments? And, have you ever stood in front of a mirror with someone else and looked into their eyes through the image of the mirror? Did you think it was more intense this way and did you think that you could see their soul?

(Hope this isn't too intense!) Just wanted to know if your mind works like mine! :) Halley

APRIL 14

In my house I have a full-length mirror on a bathroom door. To see your entire body is very different. Sometimes I would just stand there and stare into my own eyes. Yes, it does give you a strange feeling. Maybe it is your soul you're looking at. Maybe it's your true self. I have stood with someone and looked at them in the mirror. It is more intense. I know what you mean about seeing yourself when you didn't realize what you were doing. Like when you're at a shopping mall and you happen to see something move out of the corner of your eye only to realize that it's a mirror and you're looking at yourself. It's kind of like listening to yourself on a recording. You don't always give the outward appearance that you think you do. Sometimes, it's very different than what you imagine. Jon

I can remember doing this with Jon so many times. Standing in front of the mirror together, holding each other. It was especially intense when we were both naked. I can remember looking away. Now I know that I looked away because I was afraid that too much of myself was being revealed. It felt as if my soul escaped my body in these moments... and I will never forget them. His skin was so dark compared to mine. He always said that we were a perfect fit and I loved it. What happened to him? Where did he go?

APRIL 14

I think you're right. We should focus on us during our weekend.

I'm a Pisces. I have two older brothers like I said before, Ken and Dave, and one older sister, Portia. That makes me the youngest. Don't worry about having to cheer me up. I refuse to stay down for long and just having you to write to is all I need.

Bless your big, beautiful heart for wanting to let my horse run wild! Now, see, that's what I mean by a good woman and being in awe.

I have a size 34 waist, but you don't have to buy me anything. As far as the "NADS" goes, isn't it worth it to have your own jar around and when you look at it, you can smile? Now, I can look at my jar and smile too. :)

You said that you bike ride? What do you have? Jon

I wondered what he considered me, Hunter, to be? A bad woman? As I sat reading his message, his truck drove into the yard. Not again. I just couldn't take it anymore. Every time he was here, it started the cycle all over again. He was feeding the ducks in the pond and all I could think about was why...why did he sleep with someone else? How could he sleep with someone else? Was his soul dead? Tears welled up in my eyes. Did he do it so I would never want him back, so he would have another excuse not to ever be with me again because he knew that I wouldn't allow myself to be with him if I knew? But he didn't even have the guts to admit to me what he had done, how he had broken our marriage vows.

APRIL 14

I mentioned the bike thing because Salem has a very nice bike path if you're interested. Maybe we could go for a ride Saturday? Just a thought. Jon

Biking, huh? My bike hung in the basement from the wheels. He had insisted on buying it for me even though I had an injury at the time. I tried riding it but with him standing there and staring at me, I just couldn't do it. I was afraid that I wouldn't live up to his standards so for the last six years it had just been hanging—just like me. It made me want to see if I could do it without him watching.

APRIL 14

Wait until you see what I got! I had a very successful shopping trip! And, I guessed right! Your ARE a medium, just like I thought!

Biking sounds great! But I don't have a rack on my car. It is on "his" car! I suppose there are rentals over there? I know I couldn't get my Cannondale inside my car! Maybe save it for a later date??? :)

So, you are a sensitive and dreamy "fish," are you????? :) Oooooooooo And, the baby of the family! Uh oh! So, what about your mother and father? What do they do?

You seem so "quiet" this weekend. I really miss your long emails. Is something wrong or are you all "talked" out? Are you okay out there???? :) Halley

He was definitely the baby of the family and I had paid the price for it.

APRIL 14

You really didn't have to buy me anything, but I'm glad your having fun. Did you have a little smile on your face while you were shopping? hehehe Yes, there are bike rentals. I've got a Specialized. Cannondale. Nothing but the best, eh?

My father is a building contractor and my mother does the bookwork for the business and volunteers at a nearby hospital.

So, I seem quiet and you miss the long e-mails? Nothing is wrong. I guess I'm just kind of holding my breath until this Friday. I have to say that I'm thinking about it all the time. I'm really looking forward to seeing you. Well, it's almost dark and I promised one of my nephews that I would go fishing with him so I have to go for now. I'll write again later tonight. Jon

All I could think was that he was obsessed and desperate. Had I accomplished what I wanted?

APRIL 14

Well, I didn't catch any fish. We fished in my sister's pond. I keep checking out the Pounding Hammer web site to see if it's been updated yet but it still isn't. I'll try their number this week and we should be able to find out who is playing if we decide to go there Friday night. It's been awhile since I've seen the Norac Nordic Lodge, but I do remember the separate building on the left side of the road.

It might be nice just to go for a walk on the bike path? I saw a silver BMW convertible today. Very nice. I have to get back into flying again. It's been a long time. I need a biennial flight review. It should only take two or three hours to get signed off to fly again. It consists of about an hour and a half in the air doing stalls, emergency maneuvers, communication and then an hour on the ground going over procedures. Have you ever been in a small plane, small as in four seats? I started taking lessons in Newbury. Then, I felt I needed more time learning communication skills so I switched to Burrington for about a year. Finally, someone started giving lessons in Lendon, so I was able to finish up close to home.

I'm trying to think of something to write and I have to admit I'm having a hard time and I don't know why. Maybe I'm just in a strange mood or something. I'm nervous. You know so much more about me than I know about you. You know what I look like and you know what I sound like. This really is going to be a different experience for you than it is for me. You know what to expect.

Meeting someone over the Internet is an experience that I want. This is something most people would never dare to do and that's why I want to do it. I won't ask you again for a picture before Friday night. I hope you bring one with you so I'll have it. It would be nice if you did surprise email me one, but I want you to do it "on your own" and because you trust me and want to give me that piece of you, not because I continually ask you for it. That is the last comment I will make about the subject. It's all up to you.

I can't wait to get back into my house again. It's been appraised and I just got approved for my loan on Friday. The house has always been off limits to the world because of the way my wife is. I want to have a gathering of friends and family as soon as I'm settled back into it. I'm just hoping it happens sooner rather than later. It seems that court dates get postponed all the time and nothing ever happens. Do you ever hear faculty members counting down the days until the end of the school year? I hope I never do that. It seems like you're wishing time away. They count only the school days, not the total days remaining. I would think that it would make time move very slowly. My thought is that I just want to be back in the house for the summer months so as to get things settled during my time off.

If I can be back in the house for the summer, this summer is going to be the best ever! I haven't overstayed my welcome at my Portia's house yet. She wants me to get a second phone line installed because of all the Internet time and the busy phone line. I wonder why? :)

Did you find yourself some red today? Sequins? :) Tell me, baby, what you got for yourself to make you feel "oohhhh so goood." I'd like to know. Jon

Didn't catch any fish, huh? But, I wonder if he had caught anything other than fish! I couldn't believe how he had just dropped the flying. He had completely let it go. Instead, he was fishing for fish and women. The flying had been such an effort. He had almost given up so many times and I had had to talk him "up" every time. But, he finally had gotten his license. What a relief it had been and how happy he had been. The first time he had attempted to get it, he had gotten caught in a storm. Thought I would lose him that day. Think I appreciated and loved him more that day than any other day I had ever loved him. I felt that "original" spark all over again. We went to a restaurant for dinner that night and I felt like I could see his soul when I looked into his eyes. I don't know if that was what it was but it was so surreal. I didn't remember it ever happening again after that night or before......except when we stood in front of the mirror together....

He was so hung up on new experiences. What about new experiences with the person you love? Why couldn't he see that option? So, he had gotten approved for a loan. Jumping the gun again. Maybe the reason we had never "lived" in the house was because we were always working. Off limits? Maybe in his brain? I had never told him not to bring his family into our home. So, he was saying he could have the best summer ever if he got me out of the house! Nice guy. I just couldn't believe the attitude I was reading. Still living at his sister's. He had never lived alone in his entire life. What would he do when he had to? Or would he ever? I figured he was planning to have someone ready and waiting to move in with him as soon as he got rid of me. How could you just dump fifteen years out of your brain and just take up with someone else virtually overnight? Red again. Was it his obsession with Kristan that was driving his obsession with the color red? This was "oh so strange" to me.

APRIL 14

I had a BIG smile on my face when I was shopping!!! I am holding my breath too........this is just too exciting!!!!

I would love to go flying with you! The smallest plane I have been in was a commuter plane—nothing as small as you are describing! I think it would be so unbelievable!

Oh, I think this will be almost the same type of experience for me as it is for you—you can't tell everything from one picture! My brother is still away so I guess you'll just have to bring a camera with you! And, I will bring a Polaroid too!

So, tell me, I was told that in my case there would be at least two appraisals required, if not more! How is it that you can get a loan approved based on your appraisal in a divorce case? It sounds like you got only one? Or, did they just give you approval for whatever amount you need? Do you have that much clout????? :)

And, it sounds like the court has already decided who gets the house? How did you do that? I was told that this was something we either had to agree to and if we couldn't agree to it, the court would decide at the final hearing. Please explain this to me! Must be each state has different laws?

So, if the court does have to decide and they decide she gets the house, what are you planning on doing? Moving in with me??? :)

Yeah, it does seem that faculty members do count down the days everywhere. Just the way it is. After so many years, the students seem to get to them.

Oh, and baby, did I find something red or what???? You just wouldn't believe it! But, it will have to be a surprise!!!!!!!!!!!! Got to go. Early morning meeting. Have a great day tomorrow! Halley

Oh, I had to know what he would say when I mentioned the fact that "she" (me!) might be awarded the house! I wondered if he would even reply to that comment!

APRIL 15

I'm glad you had fun shopping. Hunter didn't like the amount that the appraisal came back at so she has ordered her own appraisal. She would like to think that the house is worth more, but it isn't quite finished yet so she's being a little optimistic. I used my appraisal, then added to it for an estimate to get approved for my loan. Hopefully, that will cover any additional costs.

My house is located in very close proximity to three family members. My dad sold us the land. My lawyer advised that this would make it almost assured that I would get the house. She is packing her things and this is good. It hasn't been decided yet, but I have told her that I would fight for the house and she seems to want no part of that. If I don't get the house, moving in with you does sound like a good idea. :) And, if I do get the house, maybe you can move in with me :) hehehe

I think I'm in for a lot of surprises! hehehe I hope you have a chance to write at noon. Talk to you later. Jon

The stupid nerve of him. His lawyer advising him that he was "almost assured" of getting the house if three family members lived nearby. The truth was that two of his family members lived in the same neighborhood, as well as two of my relatives! His father had a garage in back of his sister Portia's house but didn't live there. And, yes, we bought the land from his father but immediately after he bought it from the seller and we purchased only half of what he had purchased. How pathetic—that was all I could think. He had the ability to duplicate the house and I didn't. I had no place to go and he did. Yeah, I had been packing up only because I was unsure about what to do and it kept me busy. And, my heart was aching for him so badly that I didn't want to take his house away from him. At other moments, I felt like unpacking and saying "to hell with you." I was on an emotional roller coaster and couldn't make up my mind. And all I could think of was that for years he had told me that it was my house and I would always reply that it was "our house."

APRIL 15

Jon, Oh, the shopping was great! Do you like shopping! Most men don't!

So, am I going to be one of the "friends" you invite to your party??? I'd love to see your house! Since your father is a contractor, I assume that you helped build it and in your profile you said something about construction being one of your strengths?

Sounds like you should give me some pointers in the legal area. It seems like you have covered all your bases. So, do you have any pointers for me? My attorney told me that we would have to split all the assets, whatever they are in addition to the house, cars, cash, etc. etc. Help!

So, it's tax day today! Ughhhhhhhhh Got to go mail them! I'm sure you have already mailed yours? How did you handle that in your situation?

Surprises????? You don't even know!!! I have surprises for you that you cannot even imagine! Just wait and see and make sure that horse is running wild!!!!! Halley

Surprises. He had no idea what was in store for him because I didn't even know yet! Surprises from both Halley and Hunter!

APRIL 15

Do I like shopping? Depends on what we're shopping for. I have a limited tolerance when shopping for clothes. I can last longer than most men can in this regard I think. I do like malls and just looking around.

Will you be one of the friends invited to the party? We'll have to wait and see, won't we? Maybe all you'll have to do is get out of bed and get dressed. :) hehehe

I had the crew help me do the rough framing and then return to help do the sheet rocking. Total time for them was about three weeks. The entire rest of the house I did myself. There is a lot of custom work like a free-form tile bathtub and tiled sinks, steam-bent wood arches and curves and the house also has a tower with a steeple roof.

Do I have any pointers for you? I'm getting a little burned. I was stupid and I trusted my "future ex" with three accounts. I told her to use the money as she needed for household expenses and that I would cover all major bills like heat and electricity. She hasn't worked for over six years. Within a month she had zero balanced all three accounts. That's a lot of toilet paper and toothpaste! I'm even paying her phone bill. We have gone through two sessions of mediation and now are waiting for May 3rd, which is the date set for temporary matters. This court date has been postponed three times and that's good for me. She still hasn't got a job and she is starting to look ridiculous. It will have been five months by then, she has no job and has drained all accounts to nothing. She wants me to cut her a check to settle the cash value of my life insurance policy and to equalize the assets. Vermont does not require equalizing of assets, so I don't think she can get that. The biggest thing that upsets me is that she cashed in her life insurance policy a couple of years ago and called that "her" money. Now, Hunter wants half of the cash value of my policy. That is a chunk that I really don't feel she deserves, but I think I have to pay it. So I'm willing to give her half the value of the house, half the cash value of the life insurance, and half the value of my school retirement account (I'm glad that's been losing money!) and that's it.

She has been a total pain when it comes to the personal assets. Who really cares what side is worth more? She believes my side is worth more than hers so I told her I would switch with her. She wanted no part of it and just wants a check instead. She's not going to get one. I want the contents of the garage, the lawn tractor and my truck. She can have the contents of the house, her car and the outdoor spa. Vermont requires that each person be able to maintain relatively the same quality of life. Why would she need a percentage of my truck and the garage contents to maintain the quality of her life? I'm going to walk into an empty house.

I just took out a ninety-day loan out for the exact amount of the taxes and preparation costs and she will have to pay half of that out of her proceeds from the house.

You will have to fill out a form and list all your assets and what you believe they are valued at—a total waste of time if you ask me. Hunter and I haven't even gotten to an agreement on our personal assets, how pathetic. I'm just glad we don't have any pieces of antique furniture, because it would be a real nightmare. I think it's so pathetic that she is going for every little penny of every little item. It's a part of the thing that should be decided in a matter of minutes between the two individuals. Just walk through the house and pick and choose as to who gets what. In the end, she is getting a thousand here and a thousand there. Will it really make a difference in my life in ten years? It's all really nickels and dimes and I think it's pathetic. The simple solution for her is to get a job and support herself.

Back to the interesting stuff. You say that I don't even have a clue as to what's in store for me on Friday night? I could take that a couple of different ways. A good way or a bad way. I'll take it the good way for now. Let my horse run wild and free? Jeez, I know he would really like to do that! You know what? I'm going to make you feel so good that you won't ever want to leave. :)   Jon

Oh God. I, Halley, could get out of bed and go to the party. If that wasn't delusional, I didn't know what was. It was amazing how he took full credit for the construction and design of the house. It was as if I, Hunter, had never existed. I was so angry. The bathtub had been my design, as well as most every other unique part of the house including the tower roof. He was a master woodworker, but I was the designer. For this, he gave me no credit. Penis brain. I couldn't believe he was saying that I had zero balanced all of the accounts. On Christmas night, he threatened me and told me he would be paying for nothing so I went to the bank and made sure I had some cash to survive on and when he realized that I wasn't as stupid as he thought, he went crazy. I did push it when I found an "emergency" credit card in the wall safe and withdrew $500.00! I felt like James Bond! But, I gave it back to him when he got the statement and yelled at me for doing it!

I had worked over the last several years. How quickly he forgot that every endeavor I attempted, he put down. My writing, my business, managing the apartment buildings, etc. Nothing was right for him. Then I started taking classes and all hell broke loose. Every time I got a grade or comments that were positive, he reacted silently. The resentment he felt inside showed on the outside. As for me not being able to get a "job," he hadn't told me I needed to until just before he left. And, it wasn't such an easy thing to do when you'd been out of the "normal" job market and you are still up at 11:00 at night doing book work for three apartment buildings. Wasn't he lucky that I had had such great "connections" for him. If things were truly "equalized," I'd be getting ascending alimony for years! Equalized. All I could think of was his first email address, "Equalizer"...... Had he had all of this in mind back then?????????

I had cashed in my life insurance policy so I could take classes. He knew that. He had become a "twister of truth." He twisted everything to make his leaving seem acceptable. I had no idea where he was getting his information but the state we lived in required "equitable distribution" meaning that if one partner had better prospects, the other got more from the settlement. He was comprehending this through his penis, I guess. As far as looking ridiculous, the only one who was doing this was him and he was completely oblivious to it. Of course, he didn't want the assets to be equalized, his were worth more! He was so certain I would be responsible for this and that. He didn't have a clue. His information must have been coming from the blonde bimbo who didn't have a clue either. And, no, he didn't have a clue as to what was in store for him and I was convinced that it had to be a real slap in the face. He was going to make me feel so good I wouldn't ever want to leave? Maybe, Halley wouldn't even show up!

APRIL 15

Just sneaking in a peak at my email while I work! Boy, are you full of it today????!!!!!

Like I said before, I like to focus on the positive but I hope it helped you to air everything out! :) But, I am sure she is hurting on her end, you know? I just hope things go easier on my end in my situation!

Just get out of bed and get dressed for the party! Ooooooooooo

Your house sounds like a dream! But, won't you feel her presence even after she's gone? My husband has said that to me.......that he is not sure he wants the house because he feels that he may always "feel" me there...... actually, a compliment I think? Oh well!

So, who knows, maybe we will agree to just sell it and split it. I think that would be best in our situation.

Oh, and I'd like to answer a question that you asked this weekend that I hadn't answered. I really needed to think about it. You had asked me what Alan had not been able to give me that I feel I need. Let's see: communication, fun, more time together, and children. So, tell me, what you were "starving" for? The same? :)

Oh! and I meant the surprise in a GOOD way! So, do you think I might be an "8-timer????" :) Halley

I wanted to get back to the good stuff. I wondered how he would answer the "8-timer" question!

APRIL 15

Oh God! Can't you please keep the spa??????   Just think how much fun we could have in that!!!!!! Oooooooooooooooooooooooooo oooooooooooooo Halley

If I could get him to keep it, I wouldn't have to sell it! I knew he was easily influenced at this point but I wondered just how far I could go?

APRIL 15

It's an 8 person, 550-gallon spa with a big geyser jet that comes straight out of the bottom shooting water two feet in the air and I've never even gotten laid in it! We could sneak down late at night while she sleeps. She'll never know. :) hehehehehe   Jon

I didn't ever remember him having a good attitude about the spa and I didn't ever remember him ever using it very much unless he had hurt his back and I didn't ever remember him asking to make love in it. I needed to remember that with Jon it was necessary to initiate everything because he gave up so easily or didn't even try. What was foreplay???

APRIL 15

Will I feel Hunter's presence even after she's gone? I don't think so, because my life will be completely different. The question is, will any woman be willing to join me and my life in that house? It's never been decorated, or really lived in for that matter and it's going to be empty so it can take on anyone's look. I don't need to spend the rest of my life there. It's just easier than having to build another house. I don't want to have to do that right now but maybe some day.

I was starving for someone to do things with and have fun. I've had to do things on my own for years. I want to do things that make me feel alive.

Simple things like a hug when coming through the door at night, someone who looks back at me when I look at them, going out to breakfast on the weekend, taking a day trip at the last moment just to do something different, giving a foot massage and pushing hard with my fingers, caressing a calf muscle that's both strong and soft, chasing someone around the house while laughing out loud. Going outside naked in the rain on a steamy hot summer night to run around in the wet grass, making love anywhere and everywhere just because we can, teaching her the little things that I know, while she teaches me the things she knows. Yes, I am starving for that.

I was hoping it was in a good way. Let's see, I don't know your last name. I don't know where you work. You could be from anywhere for all I know. I don't think I would let you tie me up on the bed. I'd be afraid that you might want to cut off and steal my "peepee." hehehehe.

Are you an "8 timer?" Oh baby, we'll just have to find out, won't we. I promise I'll give you as many "firsts" as I can. Jon

I was so pissed! Never been decorated? All of the permanent things in the house like the tiles, they could never be changed unless you ripped the house down! Never lived in? We were home more than the rest of his family combined! We lived in our house. It was our refuge from the world. It was our castle. Didn't want to build another house, eh? Didn't have to spend the rest of his life there, eh? His family redecorated and moved as often as people changed their clothes. I started thinking how I should be the one to stay in the house.

So Jon wanted someone to do things with? What about all the times that I made suggestions and got information on places to go and showed him brochures of where we could go on a vacation? Had someone removed part of his brain? No, Jon's penis had become his brain. So he felt that he had had to do things alone for years?! The only thing I could think of that he had done without me was take flying lessons, besides all the work, and I really couldn't do that with him! He wasn't telling the truth, but what did I expect from someone who was trying to get into a new girl's pants?

All of the things Jon said he wanted I had done. If everything wasn't just perfect, he believed something was wrong. If he walked in the door and I couldn't hug him immediately because my hands were stuck in a chicken, he thought something was wrong. I remember running around the house chasing each other and laughing. I remembered being outside naked in the steamy, summer rain and feeling the coolness on my skin. I remembered him running around the house naked with nothing but his shoes on. And his laugh. There was nothing like it. No one laughed like that. It was contagious. When Jon laughed, everyone laughed. And, I remember that I hadn't heard that laugh for a very long time. And I taught him everything I knew and he taught me what he knew. We had all of the things he wanted so why had he run away? The work. He couldn't deal with learning how to communicate with someone who he had been through things with. There had been difficult moments, just like everyone else had. Jon wanted to forget the hard work and the crawling and his solution was to find someone else. I knew it was a mistake but he didn't feel that way.

So he was wondering who I was. The "pee pee." How could he say this to someone he didn't know? The only "8-timer" he would ever have was me. I thought how it would not ever happen again. He had been 22 and now he was 38. Unless he wanted to get some Viagra? Promising me as many "firsts" as he could possibly pull off. His constant mention of "firsts" was really getting to me.

And, he said it all when he voiced the question as to whether or not any woman would be willing to join him and his life in that house. His life. Not their life. That was the way it had been from day one. His life.

APRIL 15

Maybe it's just a female thing. I know every time I walk into "my" house, I feel so much emotion. But my husband says the same. So, maybe you just have a different take on it? Oh well. If you don't think you want to stay there, why don't you just let her buy you out?

So, I take it you must have done SOME of the things you listed with SOMEONE before??? Outside naked in the rain. I love that one! :) You must live in a secluded spot! So, tell me what do you know that you can teach me? You've got me hot for this info! :)

Now, that's a new one for me! Now the wild horse is a "peepee?!!" Tell me MORE!!!!!

So, tell me, Jon, let's not be shy! We've pretty much covered EVERYTHING! What do you have to offer me in the way of "hot firsts??????????????" Give me details! Bet you are too shy to answer this question! I dare you!!!!!!!!!!!!!! Halley

I wondered if he had the nerve to answer my question about "firsts." But I had to know the truth. I was constantly reminded of this, especially when I had to take all of my emails and my legal paperwork with me everywhere I went. I was really getting tired of carrying around my briefcase. It was getting extremely heavy but I had no choice because he was coming into the house when I wasn't there and if he found my "paperwork," my secret would be out. I finally decided that if I didn't split up the papers, the briefcase was going to rip and my arm was going to fall off. So, every time I left the house, I packed my briefcase with my legal paperwork and a duffel bag that held a binder with all of the printed emails and writing in the trunk of my car. I had no choice.

I was so tired. I had gone through my first mammogram. It was a torture session that I hadn't imagined. Hurt like hell. Everyone who said it didn't hurt was on drugs or crazy. I had gone all alone. And, now, I was sitting in front of my computer trying to carry on a "fun" conversation

while I was feeling so alone and wounded. My heart was breaking that he didn't care about me. He only cared about finding someone new.

APRIL 15

So, have I done some of those things with someone before? Outside naked in the rain? I think that I might have gotten her to do it one time for only seconds and she didn't make it off the deck. Yes, the house is very secluded. You can't see it from the road so you can run around naked in daylight if you want. I think it would be nice to be out there for a while, get all wet then hold our two bodies together all slippery and moist and see what happens next. I can't remember a lot of the things that I said. You liked the sound of running naked in the rain? Would you like to do that? Do you think that would be fun? It's sad but none of those things I mentioned were possible anymore with my "ex."

You know, I'm still doing most of the talking here. Tell me some stuff about you and what you want to do.

What can I give you for "firsts?" I'm sorry but I don't really have an answer to that right now. The first thing I would do is ask you what your fantasy is. I would take little cues from you and find every possible first that you have never had no matter how insignificant, and immediately work to give them to you. This is very important to me. There is a need to live. I think I've already found one "first" that you never have had. It's been many years since I've done the "8 time" thing, but if that's what you want, that's what you'll get. I think if we end up getting that close, I'll discover other "firsts" you never have had. I'll give you those too. You're hot for the info on what I can teach you? I was thinking more on the lines of construction. Jeez, your mind's in the gutter. hehehehe I would like to think that we can teach each other some things in every aspect of life. :)

To be comical, I called it a "peepee." Did I make you smile? I hope so. I also call it "Henry," weiner, sausage and probably lots of other things too. The female equivalent is a "bunny." The two together are a sausage in a bun, a tuna boat in tuna town, hotdog in a roll and, again, probably lots of other things too. :) I hope you're not getting disgusted with me. Really, I'm just trying to make you smile. :) Tell me if it's working.

Condoms are called "jobes." That name came from the little mini beers that you can sometimes still find. The little five ounce size? The guys on the crew and I used to call those beers "jobes." When it came to condoms, I just transferred the word over to those as well. Don't ask me why, because I don't know.

What can I give you for "firsts?" We'll just have to see, won't we? Jon

After reading this, I wanted to give him a "first" like putting his penis in a vice! God, he didn't want to give me any credit at all. Not possible anymore with me, his "ex." First of all, I wasn't "ex" yet and second of all, they weren't possible because all he did was sit on the couch or work! I couldn't believe how he was so willing to spend so much time making a stranger happy. I wondered what had gone wrong between us. Was it all the work that had come between us and every time he looked at me, all he could see was all the struggling and all of the hard work? Maybe. Or, maybe his family's tendencies had finally eaten him alive. He wasn't strong enough to overpower his genes? He couldn't control what was in his blue jeans either. Now, why in the world would Halley want to know how to build something? Why? That's what he wanted to teach her?

I named it "Henry." For someone who didn't want anything to do with me, Hunter, he certainly brought up a lot of things that had to do with me and our life together—the good things, the funny things. I wondered where the name "jobes" had come from. He had never told me but, I guess I had never asked! It hurt me so deeply that he was so willing to communicate to a stranger in such depth and he wouldn't even speak to me on the phone without screaming at me. It was crazy or was I crazy to think that there was any hope for us?

APRIL 15

I was about to send you an e-mail with quite a bit of detail when I realized that I was at school and all Internet action can be monitored there. I'm safe at home now, but at school I should be a little more careful. The last e-mail I sent you was from school and that had too much stuff in it. Please don't bring up the monitoring thing in future emails just in case I open it at school. :)

Dare me eh! I'm going to give you a massage. I'm going to take my mouth and latch onto your lower "lips" like a suction cup. Then, I'm going to use my strong powerful tongue and its swirl ability to give your sweetest spot a warm wet massage in a way you never thought possible.

Now it's your turn. I dare you!!!!!!!!!! Give it to me baby! Jon

I needed a break. I just couldn't write anymore. I was so emotionally wrung out from the mammogram and all of his descriptions of what he was going to do to my character, Halley. I knew after reading his message that he had gone "down" on Ashley, the "Belly Ring Girl." I was getting the truth I had been seeking but it hurt like hell. I just sat and cried to make the words disappear. But, they didn't disappear. They were rooted in my brain forever. How could I ever forgive him? How could I ever forgive the person who I had given my heart, my body and my soul for what he had done to us, to our marriage, to our life together?

APRIL 16

The message I sent last night. Don't worry about the cyber patrol stuff. I checked into it this morning. Where are you? I'm sneaking this in now during my work because lunch is taken up with a meeting today! Jon

APRIL 16

Jon, you never answer all my questions! The spa idea was great but I am NOT into getting caught!!! If you are going to stay there, why don't you keep it!!!! So much fun! Or, why don't you let her buy you out and we can have matching BMW's!!!!!!!!!!!!!

You know, you keep saying things weren't possible "anymore." You just don't know that! You also keep saying that nothing is impossible! Think about it! I just want you to see the positive in your wife so I know that if I ever "hit" this list you won't speak badly of me! That is just the worst thought any woman can have in her mind! (I took a few psychology classes in college! Sorry!) So, now off that subject!!!

Naked in the rain. Love it. But, what about the wild animals in the bushes!!!!!

You saw that movie too????? Grumpy old men? Wasn't it funny? And, yes I am very familiar with the "bunny!" I wonder how that got started? You definitely made me laugh! :)

Now this "jobes" thing. That is a new one on me! Cute! Cute! Cute! You definitely have a "playful" imagination!

So you want to know what my fantasy is…..I dare to take the dare…………

I want to be made love to, the kind of love where you give your soul away and get one in return. I want trust, trust I never have to question no matter what. And a deep sense of understanding no matter what the circumstances. I want a hand to hold when I'm sad or afraid….. I want someone who loves me so much they'll be by my side no matter what…..and I want a list of what you consider to be "hot firsts!!!!!!!" hehehehehehe other than the powerful "suction cup" (That WAS good!)!!!!!!!!

And, about me, I like hot scented baths and candles everywhere and soft sheets with rose petals scattered on top of them. I like cheesecake and strawberries and sexy lingerie. I love autumn leaves and butterflies. I love the ocean and the sound of the pounding waves and the way the sunlight reflects off the water and the way the sand feels beneath my feet. I love to look through lingerie catalogs and read sexy novels. They turn me on! I love spas! (Keep it! Keep it!) I love Godiva chocolates and champagne. (Am I too expensive yet! Hehe) I love fast cars and dark haired men! I love painted toenails. I think they are even sexier than painted fingernails! Maybe because they are hidden most of the time? And when they are revealed, the mystery is revealed. I like the feeling you get after skiing and biking. I like sitting in bed and watching TV. (Do you have a TV in your bedroom at your house????) More in future installments......!!!!!!!!!!!!

Got to go back to work! Halley

If it killed me, I was going to get the truth. Halley was me and I was Halley. Everything I told him that I liked was me, Hunter. If he didn't know it was me writing to him, it would show me that he never knew me. I had focused on him exclusively. Had he listened to me? This message would tell me.

APRIL 16

About the spa, let's see if you can convince me to buy it.

I'm going to have to explain the situation to you so you can understand why I say that things weren't possible anymore. You just don't understand. You and I have a more normal relationship already than it has ever been with her. I'm totally serious. You can't possibly understand because you don't realize her mentality. I would never say these things about a person if it were not true. I don't talk badly towards Ashley, do I? She is a great woman, but just isn't compatible with me. My divorce is a totally different situation altogether. She has thrown things at me and thrown my shoes out into the driveway. I knew that something wasn't right with her before we were married. She has had an injury for over five years and it won't go away. I had to push her in a wheelchair through the airport when we went on our last vacation. I can't live this way. I can no longer stay. I have done everything for her. It's been fifteen years. Life is too short and I want someone I can live with and be happy with.

I just want to find a good woman who wants to come on the ride with me. I have "firsts" to fulfill that are so simple and basic that most people probably take them for granted. I will give them new light and open someone's eyes to what's real. I'll treat her better and appreciate her more than she has ever known. I'll give her the same feeling that I have and awaken her awareness as to how fortunate she is too. I'm looking forward to Friday. :) Jon

I was seeing Jon for the first time. The blinders were coming off. Underlying all his excuses was the belief that everyone else needed to change. But, not him. And, Jon believed that everyone was responsible. But, not him. He was clearly delusional about me as I was delusional about him. He believed me to be capable of only negative situations and I believed him to be capable of everything that was good in the world. I had been so naïve. He was living in a circle of lies and he was really putting it on to appeal to Halley's heart. And, how would a woman on the other end of this email he sent other than me react to his comments about my injury and how he had to push a wheelchair and how he couldn't stay???

What about the real men out there who stayed by their wife's side through a life threatening illness? He had never been able to handle any problems. If anything went wrong, he saw it as "the end." Everything had to be perfect or he lost it. He had no faith that things would get better and that was why he ran. But I wondered.

What would happen the next time something went wrong? Would he run again?

He believed he had done "everything" for me? What a joke. He had done nothing but create angst for me and it morphed into injuries that wouldn't go away.

It was all about blame—he blamed me for everything he thought of as negative in our situation. He wouldn't allow himself to see the truth of his withdrawal in our situation. I knew that I was partially responsible.

But, I had tried so hard to get him to communicate with me. Every time I had asked, he said he "didn't want to talk about it." He didn't know how to fix himself, so how could he even begin to be in a healthy relationship? I had thrown his shoes outside because it was the only way I could get his attention when he would run out the door to leave. Every time there was an issue that we needed to discuss, he would take off and I would be left alone wondering what to do with someone who would not talk to me on even a basic level.

I couldn't believe how he was praising the "Belly Ring Girl," Ashley, someone who he had said so many negative things about. He had said in so many words that she was a stubborn, classless Amazon and now she was a "good woman?" Just because she could climb a wall??? And, he categorized me as a "bad" woman because I couldn't get over an injury.

Jon had put so much pressure on me that all I did was run around trying to do everything he wanted me to do and kept everything as he wanted it to be twenty-four hours a day, even with my injury. Maybe it could have been this that caused me so much physical and emotional pain? I wasn't doing what I truly wanted to do in my heart. And, maybe it was the source of any anger and anxiety that I did have inside me? It was the same over and over. Jon would take no responsibility for anything and I let him blame me for everything.

His message was shallow and hurtful to me. How could he say that he had known that something was not "right" with me before we were married? Wasn't he the one who had been in the hospital for anxiety before I had even met him? So, why did he marry me? For my money? Because I would help him peel wallpaper and paint windowsills at his decrepit apartment building? Was it the shoes I wore? Yes, someone had told me that after he left—that he had married me because I had a good job and wore hot shoes! As soon as I could not wear those shoes anymore, I guess I was damaged goods and he wanted no part of something that was less than perfect, even if it was someone he had promised to love for the rest of his life in sickness and in health.

I had thought he made me happy because he had wanted me. The truth was that he had been a damn good actor. I gave him my heart and he threw it back at me. A desperate and delusional husband.

Why couldn't he have appreciated me? I guess he never had. He had told me that I cared too much. Red flag. I missed another one. How could anyone who had handled a relationship the way he had think he was capable of having another right off the bat? Jon wasn't dealing with our relationship and, yet, was desperately seeking to start a new one with someone he had never met. How could any new relationship survive with all of his distorted beliefs about us lurking inside of him? He was so "gone."

Jon was looking for someone perfect, something or someone who did not exist and never would exist. I knew that it was possible that he would spend the rest of his life searching for nothing. Yes, maybe he would have the material things he wanted with a new wife who made a good living, but would he ever be truly happy deep inside? All I could think of was what a sad little boy he really was and maybe his leaving might be the best thing in the end for me. But for him, I felt he was lost and had a rusty train for a brain!

I was so angry that I went down to the basement and lifted my bike down from the hooks that held it suspended from the rafters. I then pushed it up the basement stairs into the hall. The tires were flat but I would do something about that when I had the time—after answering all of his emails! His assessment of me drove me to start overcoming the limitations that had been imposed on me by his attitude toward me.

APRIL 16

You saw that movie too????? Grumpy old men? Wasn't it funny? Hilarious! hehehe, I'm a hack aren't I? "I want to be made love to, the kind of love where you give your soul away and get one in return. I want trust, trust I never have to question no matter what. And understanding, a deep sense of understanding no matter what the circumstances. I want a hand to hold when I'm sad or afraid….. I want someone who loves me so much they'll be by my side no matter what."

That sounds beautiful.

I have to agree. I love it when women paint their toenails. Talk to you later. Jon

How could he not know it was me? I felt that we had had those things when we were first married and where had they gone? He had destroyed the trust in our marriage and he had not even tried to understand me. And, he hated dealing with anyone who was sad or afraid including his own sister, Portia. I remembered him telling me how upset his sister had been when she had separated from her husband—and she had kicked him out of what she termed "her" house.

Had he never loved me as he said he did? His message only said that what I wanted sounded beautiful but didn't say that he was capable of doing what I wanted. And that was the key. He wasn't and all I could think was that he was sitting in front of his computer thinking the same. I knew that was what he was doing. For sure.

APRIL 16

I was just wondering if you reserved a room yet. Jon

It was obvious from this message that he was only thinking of getting into Halley's panties.

APRIL 16

I am so sorry for your pain and for hers. If I didn't feel her pain too I wouldn't be a person you would want to meet, now would I? I hope your wife comes out of this and I hope someday you can really talk to her about all of this so you can get some closure. Do you know what I mean? I really think that she wanted the best for you in her heart. She never would have supported your dreams like you said she did if she hadn't loved you. And, like I said before in a previous email, the only person that you really should be sharing these personal thoughts with should be her......even though I am grateful that you feel you can share it with me and it seems you really need to "get it out." I really hope my opinions don't offend you! That is the last thing that I want to do. But, sometimes an "outsider" can see things that the person in the middle of the situation cannot? Do you know what I mean? I hope this makes sense!

Enough of that subject! I really am looking forward to meeting you and I want you to really think about that SPA????!!!!! I can't imagine NOT wanting to keep it!!!! Think of the fun!!!

So, what color toenails do YOU like? Or, do I even have to guess??? Red, right?! But, the question is what shade of red? Pink red, dark red, bright red, orange red.........What's your favorite? Hurry up, tell me, not much time left!

Two and a half days!!!!!!!!!!!!!!! My bag is packed! Is yours????????????? I was thinking we could meet in the parking lot????? Or, I could get there first and be waiting in the room!!!!! :) But, then, you will probably get there first because you have the day off? But the room will be in my sister Laurie's name because I am using her card. Or, maybe I should go in first and get the key and you should come in a few minutes later? How mysterious! Let me know how you think we should do this! Halley

I amazed myself with my ability to compose the messages that I did while I was hurting so badly. Was I a consummate actress? Or a devious bitch? All I could think of was how I had spent the afternoon helping my sister baby-sit. Me, holding a baby. Anna was out of patience so I held the baby for the entire afternoon. It felt so good I had to die inside to hold back the tears. I wasn't nervous or apprehensive. It felt so natural. I wondered if the reason I had been so afraid of having a child in recent years was because of the pressure I felt from all of the responsibilities he inflicted on me. I had spent so much time on him because of all of his needs that I had nothing left for myself, much less another human being. There was no time for my family and no time for a baby. But, I realized in one afternoon that it would have been impossible to have one with him. I had thought about it over the last years and remembered something someone had said to me years before. My friend had told me that if she had married a different kind of person, she would have had a large family. With her husband at the time, she had had her tubes tied. I knew that afternoon if I had been with someone else, I would have had a family. Jon had put it off in the beginning and by the time he decided it was time, he used it as an excuse to leave and to justify his actions. That I had not had a child. How many times had I attempted conversations about it and he wouldn't talk. And, now he was using it against me when I knew in my heart that with a different husband it would have been so easy. Jon was so needy in every way and demanded all of his needs to be met in such a way that it would have been impossible. It had been impossible. How could anyone ever meet all of his expectations and demands? How?

eleven

OVER AND DONE

APRIL 16

Over and done. I think we have talked about my tobeex enough.

If you do have light skin, I like bright red toenails, but you should use the color that you like.

I keep thinking about how we are going to meet. I keep seeing myself sitting in a chair in a lounge by the front desk. I, too, think that I'm there first because I have the day off. My back is to the door and I don't turn around when you come in. You do the room stuff, key...I hear the conversation and know that it's you but I just continue reading a newspaper. You walk over and sit down in a chair facing me about three feet away. I still have the newspaper that I'm reading and you can't see my face but you know it's me. I put the paper down and we look at each other.

I think that one of your ideas sounds better. How about if I get there after you. I'd like to come into the parking lot and park next to a silver Saab. :) It might be neat if we did meet in the room. I can knock on the door, you can come to it and ask who it is. It will be the first time I hear your voice. We can just stand with the door closed for a second and think before you open it. It should be relatively private for us if we did it that way. What do you think? How does that sound?

Sorry, my bag isn't packed yet. Maybe it's a guy thing. How many days did you pack for? :) Jon

"Over and done." That was his comment to everything he didn't want to deal with. His message was all about a "fantasy." He was looking for someone who didn't exist and a situation that was "fantastical." You just meet someone, they are perfect and you have amazing sex and you don't get anything and they meet all of your demands and do everything you want them to do without asking and are everything you want them to be. I knew that he was looking for a "non-human" entity at this point. How could he believe in what he was looking for? How could he believe that it could exist? He scared me. I was afraid for him.

APRIL 16

Maybe we should just pick a time to meet there and leave the way it happens to chance? Jon

Now, that's the guy I had known for so long—"Mr. Boring."

APRIL 16

I'm just responding to your e-mail which describes things you love. Isn't there something special about the ocean? To walk along the shore and feel the sand between your toes is like heaven. So, must be you had an experience in a spa that was unforgettable. Can you tell me about it? It's 10:47 PM and it's so warm! I'm sitting here with the window open next to me listening to the bugs outside in the night. It's so nice.

My truck is "Sunrise Orange." Most women hate the color, but most guys like it. Jon

I remembered how he had to show me the truck he wanted to buy. It just couldn't get any more conspicuous. I had spent over a year dealing

with his indecision about a vehicle and it just didn't matter anymore. We finally had money in the bank and he spent most of it on a truck. I just couldn't believe it.

APRIL 16

I felt like I was reading a romance novel when I read your ideas of how to "meet!!!" And, I just got your message about leaving it to chance and I love that one the best...... So, I guess now we need to pick a time. If I bring everything with me to work and leave from there, I should be able to be there by 6:00 PM? Let me know what you think.

I hope you don't mind but because I had to use my sister's card and her name, she knows where I'll be. As I said before, we are very close and she is the only one that knows.

As for the packing, didn't your mother ever tell you to pack an extra pair of underwear (or boxers in your case!)?????? Hehehehehe Do you have any other interesting ones other than the fish? I always pack extra.......just in case! Oh, and don't forget to bring something to wear in the spa! (If we get that far!) I can't wait! And, no, I haven't had an "unforgettable" experience in a spa other than to actually enjoy them. I'm just HOPING!!!!!!! Maybe you could describe one for me???? :)

Sunset orange? I love orange sunsets, don't you? I love the color orange because it is so alive! Is that why you picked that color? And, it shouldn't be very hard to spot either! :) And, I just can't believe this weather! It's so great! You must live in a wonderful place to be able to listen to the bugs outside. I'm more in a neighborhood where there are more houses and less bugs! But, I bet at the Norac Nordic Lodge there are crickets "cricking" all night long!!!!!!! I can't wait! Halley

I thought I would throw up on my own words! But I had to keep him in tow.

APRIL 17

As I was laying in bed last night I kept thinking about all the things I haven't asked you (among other things)!!! :) And, I kept thinking about sand and the ocean and the waves......

I was thinking how great it was going to be to meet you and then I thought how mysterious it was that I was driving to Salem so that no one would know.....

Sunset orange. I kept thinking about such a "hot" color and how I don't think I have ever seen a truck this color. And, then I thought, how do you ever keep anyone from knowing where you are with a truck this color! My silver Saab blends in if you know what I mean. I'm just curious. How did you keep anyone from seeing your truck when you were visiting the "Belly Ring Girl???" Must be she didn't live in the same town, right? Just wondering. All of this is so intriguing to me!!!!!!!! You must be as clever as I am??????? hehehehe

Then, I wondered how you felt about women and the cars they drive. Do you somehow associate a woman by the car she drives? Tell me, what did your "ex's" drive and how would you describe how their personalities fit with their cars. I am so "hungry" to know how you think about this!

Oh, and I forgot to ask you if you like dogs and, if you do, what kind? I'd better go for now. I'm supposed to be working! Can't wait to see you! Halley

Oh boy. I knew I had to get all the information that I could before Friday because then it would be over unless I could come up with a way to delay our meeting. I just had to know how he was able to be with Ashley without people seeing him. I was pushing it but in a way that sucked him in. The more I talked "penis-style," the more information I was able to get out of him.

APRIL 17

I've sensed all along that you have a lot of anxiety about wanting to keep this a secret. Salem is a long way for you to travel. But, it's okay. Whatever it takes so that you feel comfortable and relaxed so you can enjoy yourself. How are you doing? Are you getting nervous yet? I'm anxious and nervous, but it's okay. You do feel it's okay if we were to, say, drive down the road together in Salem don't you? I've never been the "hideaway man" for anyone before, but this is different. I can totally understand where you're coming from though.

The main reason I chose "Sunrise Orange" is because I had never seen another truck that color before and I wanted something different. At a quick glance, it almost looks red so in passing it on the road some people might not realize who it is. I kept anyone from seeing my truck at Ashley's apartment because she lives on a not-too-traveled side street in town and also by parking behind the house so it was pretty much hidden. The tough part is the fact that my wife's sister, Anna, lives just up the road from my sister Portia's house so she could see if I didn't spend the night. I thought about this situation and I don't believe that Hunter's sister would tell her that I was not parked in the driveway overnight. She might if it became a regular occurrence, but it didn't. Ashley and I even went to the video store in town together to rent movies, and other things in town. The windows in the back of my truck are very dark so it makes looking into the truck difficult. I haven't heard anything about it from Hunter. She isn't the type to not say anything either. I wasn't throwing it around in everyone's face, but I didn't totally hide out either. Ashley knew that I wanted to keep things somewhat quiet and she could understand why. When we went out to dinner, it was almost always out of town. Only one time did we eat out in Doeville.

I saw my in-laws in the grocery store last night. It was strange. I can tell that my father-in-law is in this mood of wanting to kill me or something. What can you do? Things happen.

I think everyone wants to have a car that somehow fits their personality. Yes, I do associate a woman with the car she drives. I want to see your Saab. Just seeing the car isn't enough, though. I have to get inside and go for a ride with you. I look around at everything, what's hanging from the mirror, the music that you listen to, how you drive, what kind of mats you have…all of it is part of the person and understanding how they live. The "ex" drives a Volvo 850 sedan. Before that she had a Ford Taurus sedan. She likes the Volvo much more than the Ford.

I was going to ask you about dogs too. I like bigger dogs. My favorite is a golden retriever. I had one as a kid and it was the best dog ever. Very intelligent, friendly and didn't bark a lot. Do you have a dog? I'd like to have some kind of pet someday. Talk to you again later tonight. Jon

All I could feel when I read this message was that I wanted him to feel my pain. He even went to the video store in town with "her!" The one where we had always gone together. And, he stayed overnight with her! And I couldn't believe he was referring to me as his "ex." How could he do this? Was it that he already felt that we were divorced? What had happened to the vow of fidelity and the commitment to our marriage? And, why had he become a Catholic before we were married? Was it just for show like everything was in his family? Doeville. Eating out with another female in the town that we actually lived. I couldn't believe it. Why didn't he just shoot me and get it over with? And, yes, my father was very disgusted and hurt and felt as though he never knew Jon. He felt the same as I did. My parents had treated Jon as the son they never had and he turned around and threw it back in their faces. Jon seemed so flip with his comments. Was he really feeling this way? Had he stifled everything so deeply that he could actually believe what he was saying? I knew he had been a very sensitive person but he had become so unfeeling. Maybe that was the only thing he could do because of everything he had done.

APRIL 17

6:00 PM sounds great. It's still early enough for dinner and lots of talking.

My sister and her husband also know where I'll be. I hope you don't mind. It would be pretty hard to keep it a secret from those living in the same house. So, what does your sister, Laurie, think of this whole thing? Do you tell her about me at all? Do you let her read the e-mails or did you let her hear me sing? Hehehe, just curious. No one has read your emails other than myself. I don't mind if you showed mine to your sister.

As for the packing, I think I'll pack lots of extra things. :) Jon

While I was reading this message, I got a phone call. I had to go in for an ultrasound because my mammogram indicated a possible problem. I thought I would die. I didn't know what to do. I knew I had to stall with Halley so I could deal with the potential problem. I couldn't stop crying and felt so alone and didn't know what to do. As I sat there wondering how I would deal with my situation if it turned out badly, there was knocking at the door. I couldn't believe it was him. He came in and said he needed some clothes. How could he not notice that I had been crying my eyes out? He went upstairs and I went into the living room and sat facing away from his sight. I asked him to remove the insulation from one of the vents and he did. He never asked me how I was and I didn't tell him anything. I just sat facing away until he left. It was one of the saddest and loneliest moments of my life. Why didn't I tell him? Why didn't I ask him to talk to me? I knew that I couldn't confide in him because of the truth that I knew. I knew he didn't care. I didn't want someone who said just horrible things about me to have reason to resent me anymore than he already did. So, I dealt with it and did what I had to do.

APRIL 17

Jon, I can't believe this. My mother just called and told me that my grandfather has had a stroke and is in intensive care in New Jersey. I am so sorry but I will not be able to make it to Salem this weekend. My sister and I must go with my mother tonight and will be gone for the weekend. My father is going to fly in to meet us there on the way back from a conference. We are not sure what we are going to do as my grandmother was completely dependent on him as she has Alzheimer's disease and we may either have to bring her back with us or find a place for her to stay until my grandfather's prognosis is known.

I am so disappointed that I will not be able to make our meeting and hope that you can forgive me and make another date with me??? I just can't believe this is happening on top of everything else I am dealing with right now. I hope that this will not discourage you but I really do have to go as my mother needs me to be there and my grandparents are really very important to me.

My grandparent's relationship is one that I have always admired. No matter what their difficulties, they have always faced things together and worked through them. So, I kind of feel like a total failure when I think of all they've been through and how their love has always kept them together and here I am in my situation which does not even begin to compare with theirs.

I am not sure if I will have to stay into next week or not. For now, I want you to know that I still have the first Friday in May off and I know by then things will be resolved enough so I could meet you then. Please let me know if this is okay with you????

I will email you as soon as I get back. But, please email me in case I can get access to a computer while I am there!!!

Again, I am so sorry that the weekend is ruined! I have been looking forward to meeting you so much! Please be patient. I promise that we will meet soon. I already miss you! Halley

I couldn't believe what I had been forced to do. I couldn't believe my lies. I would find out soon enough how good a storyteller I really was! And I needed the time to deal with my real-life situation.

APRIL 17

Halley: I don't know what to say or where to begin. I'm very sorry about your grandfather. Of course, I can forgive you. I want to meet you so badly and I hope we will meet as soon as possible. We've already met, just not in the physical sense. I've told you many things about myself. You have told me things about yourself. We have talked and had conversations about almost everything. I know you, Halley. I know your personality and I'll be thinking about you all the time until we meet. I want to be able to hold you and give you a nice long hug, especially now. I want to be able to put your hand in mine and tell you that everything is going to be alright. Don't feel like a failure because of your situation. Don't feel guilty because of the decision you have made. You're a very caring person and you would not have made the decision you did if you felt it wasn't necessary. I promise you that things will get better with time. They have for me. I know myself so much more than I did just a few short months ago and am a better person for it. You will be too. I wish I could be there for you. Actually, I can be there for you in any way you would like me to be. Jon Logan, 666 West Drive, Doeville, Vermont, 05882, 208-784-2929. If you want, please give me a call. It would be nice just to talk to you. I have next week off so I'll probably be home most of the time or in my classroom. My classroom number is 208-715-9422. Both locations have answering machines. If there is anything I can do for you, let me know even if it's just to be there to talk. The first Friday in May sounds good. I just can't believe this happened. I'm so sorry. Jon

I had him hook, line and sinker. I couldn't believe it. How gullible could he be? If he was this gullible, what would happen to him out there in the real world? I felt guilty and angry at the same time. He was so willing

to comfort a stranger, but not his own wife. I really wondered if he was capable of comforting anyone. I felt like it was a lot of talk as it always had been. He thought that he was a better person? How could that be? He now had no morals. And, he had just given me all of his personal information on a platter. He wanted me, Halley, so badly that he divulged his true identity. Didn't he know that in the hands of the wrong person, he would be nailed to a wall? So, was I that person? I wondered.

APRIL 18

Halley: I miss your noon e-mail. I feel like I'm lost in space and that I'm calling out on the radio, but there is no one out there to hear me. Well, maybe it's not quite that extreme. :) I hope things are going okay with you. Take care. Jon

What I would have given for him to have been comforting me in this way at this very moment as I was dying inside knowing how I had to go for the ultrasound test the next day and I was scared to death. I knew I had to do something to keep myself distracted until then so I washed and waxed my car. And, when I was finished with that I got a phone call to help my sister baby-sit again. I hoped that somehow it would help me deal with the rest of the day.

As I held the baby and fed her, I had to choke back the tears. I had so many regrets. I would probably never have the opportunity to have a child of my own. How could I ever forgive myself or Jon for this? The baby was fussy. Maybe she could sense my unhappiness. I let her suck on the edge of a cool glass. She was teething and needed something to chew on. She wasn't the only one who was chewing—I was chewing over all of the truth in my head and didn't know how I could ever get past the destruction caused by Jon's words and actions. How could I ever forgive him for what he had done to us and for what he had not done for us? How could I forgive him leaving me standing alone in our house? How could I forgive him for robbing me of my husband and my best friend—the person whom I had given my life to on a silver tray? How could I ever forgive him for break-

ing the trust and fidelity of our marriage? How could I forgive myself for trusting him and not doubting him? How could I ever forgive the mess he had made of our lives? I wondered how he could ruin everything by breaking the vow of fidelity? I wondered if it was anger and resentment that had driven him to it? And, I hated his sister, Portia, and her husband, Mark, for supporting him. How could I ever forgive his family? I wondered if he had been drunk the first time he had slept with Ashley. I wondered how he could violate me in such a way. I was still his wife!

APRIL 18

This was sent to me today and it's so true to the way I feel. "TAKE HOLD OF EVERY MOMENT.....A friend of mine opened his wife's underwear drawer and picked up a silk paper wrapped package: "This,—he said—isn't any ordinary package." He unwrapped the box and stared at both the silk paper and the box. "She got this the first time we went to New York, eight or nine years ago. She has never put it on. Was saving it for a special occasion. Well, I guess this is it. He got near the bed and placed the gift box next to the other clothing he was taking to the funeral home. His wife had just died. He turned to me and said: "Never save something for a special occasion. Every day in your life is a special occasion." I still think those words changed my life. Now I read more and clean less. I sit on the porch without worrying about anything. I spend more time with my family, and less at work. I understood that life should be a source of experience to be lived up to, not survived through. I no longer keep anything. I use crystal glasses every day. I'll wear new clothes to go to the supermarket, if I feel like it. I don't save my special perfume for special occasions, I use it whenever I want to. The words "Someday..." and "One Day..." are fading away from my dictionary. If it's worth seeing, listening or doing, I want to see, listen or do it now. I don't know what my friend's wife would have done if she knew she wouldn't be there the next morning. This nobody can tell. I think she might have called her relatives and closest friends.

She might call old friends to make peace over past quarrels. I'd like to think she would go out for Chinese, her favorite food. It's these small things that I would regret not doing, if I knew my time had come. I would regret it, because I would no longer see the friends I would meet, letters... letters that I wanted to write "one of these days." I would regret and feel sad, because I didn't say to my brothers and sons, not times enough at least, how much I love them. Now, I try not to delay, postpone or keep anything that could bring laughter and joy into our lives. And, on each morning, I say to myself that this could be a special day. Each day, each hour, each minute, is special. If you got this, it's because someone cares for you and because, probably, there's someone you care about. If you're too busy to send this out to other people and you say to yourself that you will send it "one of these days," remember that "one day" is far away... or might never come..." Jon

I felt ashamed of myself and sorry for him. I was guilty of some of these things and he was too. He was guilty of more of them than I was. I was always the one who had said that we needed to do things now. And now he was doing what he wanted to do without me. It was as if he had never listened to anything I had ever said to him. It was as if he had never heard my words.

twelve

HELL

APRIL 19

I was scared to death. I knew that everything had to be okay. But, what if it wasn't? I felt so alone. I was alone. As I sat and waited for my name to be called, I felt a sense of peace. No matter what happened, there was nothing I could do about it. I watched the children play in the waiting room and I had to hold back tears for what I had been denied. His denial, my denial, our denial. The dreaded moment came. The nurse took me into the room. It was dark which made me feel safer. Bright lights would have made it so much harder. As I lay on the table with a towel over my chest waiting for the doctor, I had no thoughts. My mind was empty, like my heart. The doctor finally came. I had to admit it was much easier than the mammogram had been. The cold gel felt good. I closed my eyes and prayed that it was just an insurance moneymaker. The doctor said I was definitely like my mother and left the room. I nervously asked the nurse if I was okay and she was surprised. She confirmed that I was and I just started to cry tears of relief. As I walked out of the hospital, I felt reborn. I felt like I had been given another chance and decided that I would do something special.

When I got home from the hospital, I sent Jon an email asking if he ever intended to talk to me about everything that had happened, about his leaving. The only exchanges that I had gotten from him since his leaving had been screaming and loud radio noise in the driveway and then nothing at all. He couldn't even look me in the eyes and it broke my heart. I asked him if he intended to leave things without resolution forever....

After I sent the email, I drove to Salem to trace Jon's steps. I stopped at the Norac Nordic Lodge, The Pounding Hammer and the Snowflake. It was so surreal. None of the places I visited meant anything to me. But, they meant so much to him. I just couldn't understand. All that meant anything to me was him, the Jon I had married. The Jon who had left was a mystery to me.

That night, I received a response, one that blamed me for the breakdown of our entire relationship. He would take no responsibility whatsoever. In the response, Jon stated that I should have been able to figure out why he left on my own without him saying anything. He gave me crap for "living through him." So, I had given him everything I could give and this is what I got in return! Another excuse. So, one of the reasons for his leaving was that I had given him my all. He also accused me of not being there for him. The ungrateful bastard. The bottom line was that he had never communicated. He had never spoken. I was always asking him questions and not getting a response. I was supposed to read his mind. He accused me of not being happy. But, he was the one who walked around in a depressed stupor. None of his comments made sense to me. I had isolated myself in his world for him and now he was dumping on me for doing so. He was also dumping me for not having a forty-hour a week job. Money. That was another heavy issue. He accused me of having "imaginary injuries" and of needing counseling. This coming from someone who left with no attempt at reconciliation and no explanation. And who needed the counseling??? It was very obvious to me that he felt everyone, especially me, needed to change to his standards—whatever they were—

and that he was perfect just the way he was. He did admit to working too much and that was his excuse for ignoring me. His solution to the "problem" was to run away and start over. He was adamant that "we" could not be "fixed." Of course it couldn't be fixed if he wouldn't try!

He accused me of being controlling, yet he was the one who had controlled me for over fifteen years and who was still controlling my life. As I read on, he spoke of the requirements of the divorce and more issues related to money arose. Money, money, money. The core issue. He was mad at me because with a contested divorce I would get half of everything. He was mad because I would not go through with an uncontested divorce and it seemed from his words that he would hate and resent me forever for his own decision! His message defiled me and our marriage in every way possible and I cried out for his soul. His accusations were horrible. He was angry because I wasn't stupid. Another bottom line. He accused me of having the ability to keep him from his goals through the divorce and he had initiated it! I knew he needed help and knew that he would not seek it. The bottom line of his message was to blame me for everything, whatever everything was, and to accuse me of being the sole reason for us not being together. I was devastated by his appraisal of me and our marriage and knew that I didn't deserve what he had said. I always blamed myself for everything and now I knew it had been a mistake. It had allowed him to do the same to me. He was gone. He was lost to me and I knew it. But, I didn't want to believe it. And, I knew I had to find a way to stop him from continuing to control me.

APRIL 19

I wrote back to Jon that same night.

You seem to think you know me. You have no idea who I really am but, someday, you will come to realize just how strong I really am. And, I know why you cannot look at me—it is because of your tremendous guilt. Guilt in connection with the way you left and guilt in connection with anything else that has happened since you left and guilt because of your lack of attention in the years we were married. Suffice it to say that I would never conduct myself in the manner that you have in regard to this entire divorce situation. They call it "class" and you have proved you do not have it. You have sunk to a level at which I truly did not know you were capable but now I do. Over the years, you left me in the "box" and did not even attempt to help me out, and you know it. As far as physical abuse, there has been none and you know it. On my side, there has been much emotional abuse from you because of your distance and uncommunicativeness among many other things.

It is ironic how you say that people must be happy "on their own"; that is something I have been trying to communicate to you for several years. As for money, I have always tried to communicate to you that happiness was more important and you seem to be catching on to that one. However, you do not seem to understand that I had to have something to survive and the money I used was "ours," not just yours. I have nothing to fall back on and whatever I do receive at the end has to carry me through until I can find a job. And, there is the whole issue of our house.

As for the conditions and circumstances of divorce, it is all ruled by laws and courts. I have no control over this. As for whatever I will receive in the divorce settlement, it will never be enough to compensate for the pain I have had to endure because of your actions and attitudes.

What I have done for you over the last fifteen years, I will not ever do for anyone else again. I put your life on a pedestal and mine in a box. Please don't forget that you would still be a carpenter without a pilot's license if it weren't for all my help, support and encouragement and in return I get defamed and denounced by you. This is not meant to be taken in an offensive manner; it is just a reality check for you. My constant attention to your needs was my main "cause" in life and it was wrong for me to do this. I neglected myself to a terrible extreme. I gave you fifteen precious years of my life and you left in a manner that can truly be termed as "despicable"—even using me emotionally, physically and intimately while you were planning behind my back your final departure and telling me that we were going to work on our relationship. For this, I have had to search deep within my heart to find forgiveness. It is what you said to me one of these nights that has allowed me to forgive you. You told me that you loved making love to me and that you loved me. I shall always keep that within my heart, forever.

Perhaps, the constant "imprisonment" of all of the responsibilities associated with the house, the apartment buildings and your needs and negative attitudes were what prolonged my injury. Your choices caused me much weakness in many regards. I should not have lived according to your choices.

I do know that I have more dignity and self-respect than you or any member of your family will ever be capable of.

You have truly become "one of them." I have realized in recent weeks that it seems as though I made a terrible mistake fifteen years ago and have paid dearly for it for years, even though as far as the Catholic faith is concerned it is God who brings two people together—so, perhaps, it was all for a purpose and a reason and, perhaps, it is only your own "will" that is splitting us apart and for that a price will have to be paid. I have never been truly "welcomed" by your family and how many times did you tell me you felt the same way? Now, you are truly your father's son and it is with much sadness that I say this to you. I thought you were better than that. I had such hope for you but, sadly, your genetics have finally reared their "ugly heads." As you told me many years ago, you never wanted to behave like the rest of your family. In this one regard, I feel terribly sorry for you. The level at which you exist is far beneath what is acceptable to me. Running away and "feeling eighteen again" is not a solution to one's confused feelings.

You are right about one thing. I have come to realize and believe in recent weeks and days that you have not been good for me in many respects and that this divorce will enable me to have the success I have always been destined for and I WILL have that success. It is just very sad to me at the price that will have had to be paid in order for it to happen.

As for you, Jon, I do not believe you will ever find "exactly" what you are looking for because there will either be something you do not like about the person in some respect or, frankly, they may not be able to accept your attitudes unless you seek out counseling and work on your own imperfections. No one is perfect. And, that is something you cannot accept in your mind. Through counseling, I have realized that I am not responsible for your actions, nor are you for mine.

Even after reading all of your misdirected comments and thoughts about me and toward me, I do truly hope that someday you do find what you are looking for because I know deep down inside you are a good and loving person. From my perspective, you seem to be very confused and the justification you are receiving from those around you is only making matters worse for you. Again, I hope you find the life you are looking for, somehow, someday. Hunter

I had to admit my response was full of pain, hurt and longing, as well as indignance, but I was also intent on ending the communication positively even if the remainder of the message was like a drill boring a hole into cement.

APRIL 20

The war of words continued when I received another email from him the next day. His responses were pathetic. Only negativity, contempt and resentment. Nothing positive. It seemed he was afraid of my strength even though he accused me of being weak. I couldn't believe it when I read in his message that he had made our situation the least painful as he possibly could. I could not even begin to digest this statement. All he had done for months was scream at me, accuse me of things and treat me like crap after everything I had done for him. He had intimidated me for so long and I finally realized that it had not just been months but years. He finally admitted that it was me who was behind his career change and the attainment of his pilot's license. Finally. But then he accused me again of living my life through him. He couldn't be gracious. He had to use something I had done out of love to belittle me and put me down. Then he really did it. He accused me of being melodramatic. I wondered really who was being melodramatic at this point. His next statements made me want to throw up. That his family had class. What a joke. They were a group of misdirected cheaters. They lied, cheated on their wives, and dated married people. And that wasn't everything…. if I had known what they were, I might never have married Jon. His family lived by none of the morals or standards that my family embraced and I never knew until it was too late. And then I tried to swallow what I had gotten myself into and I choked on it. He was so confused and screwed up he didn't know that his genetics were destroying his life. They had finally caught up to him and they were eating him alive. They had destroyed our marriage and he didn't even know it. He was out there searching for something that would never measure up to what he had had. Not ever.

APRIL 20

Halley: 6:00 PM Friday afternoon came and went quietly by. For me, there was a stillness like something was going to happen, but it didn't. I woke this morning to the earth shaking beneath me at 6:56 AM. An earthquake. I check my email but all is silent. I accessed my account to see "0" new messages. I know you will write when you get the chance. I'm just talking because I feel the need to. It's Saturday morning and it's 10:25 AM. I hope when you have the chance to write, you will have some good news regarding your family. Talk to you soon. Jon

It sounded to me like he had just admitted that I was the only one writing to him. Zero new messages. What about all the others? I was still coming down from the week of torture, the mammogram and the ultrasound and I needed a break! As I looked out of the atrium door as I passed through the living room, I noticed a stray oak leaf leftover from last Fall stuck in the grass outside. It was almost as if it was waving "goodbye" to me or maybe it was waving "hi?" Maybe I was on the verge of a new beginning and I just didn't realize it yet?

APRIL 21

Jon, I have only a few minutes to write you. Someone was generous enough to let me use their computer to access my hotmail account in the waiting room at the hospital and they'll be back in a few minutes. I just wanted to let you know how beautiful and caring your emails were! They brought tears to my eyes…. I miss your emails so much. I hope you miss me.

My grandfather is out of intensive care but has a long road ahead of him with rehabilitation. We are taking turns staying at the hospital for now. My sister and I plan to be back by Monday or Tuesday at the latest. I will have so much work to catch up with! My mother and father will be staying for at least the remainder of the week. I think my mother may stay longer to take care of my grandmother until everything can be decided for the long term.

I am so grateful for your kind words and I hope you still want to keep our "date." I will make the new reservation as soon as I return. I will be there no matter what. I will talk to you soon. Halley

I hated lying. But what choice did I have? I had had to put off the meeting so I could keep our "thing" going. I needed as much information as I could get.

APRIL 21

I miss talking to you too. I'm glad your grandfather is doing better. Jon

APRIL 22

Halley: Last week I needed to do something to feel alive. I decided to go to Salem. I went up to the Norac Nordic Lodge and looked around. The place has changed considerably from what I remembered. It is huge! The Main Lodge is three or four stories high and very long. There is a nice sitting area and dining room and lots of halls to roam through. The building across the street looks like it has two levels and is even longer. Everything looks new. I think we are going to have a lot of fun. The Pounding Hammer must have changed its hours for the season because it was Thursday night and they were closed.

I have a confession to make and I hope you're okay with it. I know that we have never met or anything, but somehow I still feel a connection to you. I've never had anything like this happen before, have you? Is that okay?

I'm looking forward to you being back home so we can talk again. You know, May 3rd really isn't that far away. I have a meeting that I can't get out of set for 2:00 PM that day and it will probably last for at least an hour. We can work around it. I could take the day off? I'll have to get a substitute for the second half of the last block anyway to fill in for me during the meeting. Did you save my phone numbers?

I just wish that when you get into your familiar bed again for a nice comforting rest, I were in it to hold you and keep you warm. :) Jon

I couldn't believe it. He had gone to Salem just like I had. What if it had been on the same day and time!? What a trip that would have been! His confession. He felt a connection. It was me, his wife. He was feeling the connection and didn't even get it. How could he not know? How thick

could he be? My heart was in my throat where it generally resided these days. I wanted so much to tell him who I really was. I wanted to be like the couple in the "Pina Colada" song. One of them looks for someone else and finds whom they were with in the first place. I wanted that so badly. The meeting he spoke of was our temporary hearing. I was dreading it. I wanted to be the one who met him at the Norac Nordic Lodge but knew that he would only be meeting up with a ghost.

APRIL 22

Jon, I'm back! It's so good to be home. It was so comforting to see an email from you telling me that you went to Salem and checked everything out! I'm so glad you went!

So, you say you feel a connection to me and that you have NEVER felt this before??? I want you to know that I also feel a "special" connection to you.....

So, not to get off the subject but let me give you an update of my weekend. I hope you don't mind! My aunt, who lives a half hour away from my grandparents, and my mother are taking care of my grandmother and my grandfather is making progress every day. It is slow but it is progress. Something will have to be done, though, as my grandfather will not be able to care for my grandmother as he was doing. So, it is up to my mother and my aunt to decide what will be done but the crisis is over for now. They've hired a private duty nurse to be with her so they can take shifts at the hospital for now. It's such a relief to me that he is okay and it was so good to see both of them even considering the situation.

So, there's my weekend! And, I kept thinking about you all weekend and thought about how you said that it was so important not to miss any opportunities for happiness, and this weekend really helped me see that so clearly.

And, I do want you to know that I haven't shared any of your emails with anyone! My sister, Laurie, only knows that I was supposed to meet someone and that I wanted it to be discreet.

So, tell me about this earthquake! I couldn't believe it when I read this in your message. It sounds crazy! An earthquake in Vermont?

I have to go now. I have so much to catch up with and it looks like I'll be working straight through the weekend to catch up. But, I will be caught up and ready for our meeting next week! So, do you think you can get there by 6:00 PM? If you can't, I'll still be there waiting for you! :)

Hold onto that "NADS" and that wild horse (but not too tightly!!)

And, I do have your phone numbers but I really want to meet you face-to-face first….. I hope you don't mind! And, I want to feel your arms around me when we do meet and then I want to hear your sweet voice in person whispering into my ear and I want to smell your natural wonderful self.….Halley

I was digging down so deep that I was going to hit the sludge level in the septic tank! I was amazed at my own ability to keep going with this façade. Not that I didn't feel a little guilty, but there were so many confused feelings raging in my heart. I felt vengeance, love, betrayal and pain and didn't know which I felt at any given moment. I just wanted to keep him from anyone else I suppose.…and find out what I needed to know so I could fix things or let go…

APRIL 22

Halley: You have a very caring family.

So you're keeping me a secret even from your sister, Laurie? I've thought about my situation and I'm glad that Hunter never found out about Ashley. It just wouldn't be very nice to do that to her. I took your advice and communicated with her about the whole situation and how I feel. She asked me why I felt I needed to leave, so I told her. Does your sister know that I'm someone you met on "Hearts.com?"

The earthquake was pretty neat. I was half awake, half asleep and suddenly there was this snap and everything under me moved. Then the ground rumbled as if it was shifting after the snap to compensate for that original movement. It lasted for, maybe, ten seconds. The center was located in New York, just across the border.

I guess we're both busy. This class I'm in is taking up a lot of time. It really stinks to have this week off only to have to work most of it. I can definitely be in Salem by 6:00 PM. I'll bring the "NADS." :) And I'll try not to hang onto my wild horse too tightly before I get there. hehehe Jon

Was he really glad that he didn't think I knew about the "Belly Ring Girl." What would he think when he did find out that I knew? Because, in time, he would. It was inevitable. And the emails he had sent me, Hunter. They had been cruel and full of blame—only for me. He didn't even know his own feelings. He didn't leave. He ran away because of his true genetics that I thought he was strong enough to overcome. But I was wrong. I remember the earthquake that morning. The bed shook so badly it woke me up. It was a wake-up call in more than one way.

APRIL 22

I received one email from you and another asking if I had received another email. Did you try to send me another song? (Oh please say yes!) :)

And, yes, my sister does know that I met you through an online dating service but not which one! As for your wife, I hope you weren't too hard on her? I wouldn't want to think I'd be in that position someday with anyone! :)

So, tell me, what if she does find out about the Ashley? What do you think she would do? I can't imagine what Alan would do if he even found out about this! So, what is this class that is taking up all your vacation time?

I would have loved to feel the earth quake beneath my body! Ooooooooooooooooooooo (or on top of it or in it or ?????????) Back to work! (But, I want you to know that I love these email breaks!) Halley

I was so full of baloney! I wanted him to admit how cruel he had been—but like that would happen! He wouldn't want someone who he was trying to get into bed to know he was a jerk after all. And, I really wanted to know what he thought I would do if I knew about the "Belly Ring Girl"..... I was getting in deep again with any mention of sexual innuendo but I wanted to see where it would take the conversation and I was so preoccupied by having been in the same room with her that same afternoon. I knew that if I made a graphic comment he would overlook the short message.

I was so preoccupied by what I had seen that afternoon. There I was standing in the children's library talking with the librarian and up the stairs comes a big-boned, half-Japanese girl wearing a ski sweater and jeans. She looked as if she could take me and throw me like a toothpick! She hurriedly made her way over to a table where a young girl sat. I recognized the girl as the one who had stared at me continually for the last two weeks ever since she had heard the librarian call me by my married name and the one who had gotten in the black car. And then I knew. She was definitely Ashley's ten-year-old daughter! I confirmed her age with the librarian and told her how the mother was the girl my husband had been having an affair with. So, this was the "Belly Ring Girl," the daughter of the "wild" man I had worked with years ago. They left in a hurry and I looked out on the street and saw them leave in a black foreign car, the same car I had seen the girl get into two weeks earlier. I remember the mother standing out in the street in her fleece jacket waving to everyone and anyone before she got into her car and headed down the street, presumably to return a video. The girl at the video store was the one who had known who she was and what she looked like. It was how I was able to identify her. And she had a pug dog. My sister, Anna, had seen her walking down the street the entire week the restaurant where she worked was shut down walking this dog.

My nephew was at the library that day and before I took him home we went on an investigative spree and found where we thought she lived. But the next day, I found out I had been wrong and found her house two doors down. And, there was definitely a place to hide a bright orange truck. I was really beginning to wonder if I should be a PI!

APRIL 22

I was a little worried when I saw no subject in your e-mail. Last time that meant bad news. I am thinking of sending you another song but that wasn't it. It wasn't anything important.

I was not hard on Hunter. I tried to be as nice as possible and still say what needed to be said. She replied with a few comments, which I replied back to and explained my position on. I think things may be a little better now that she understands and you will never be in that position someday.

She might be upset if she found out about the Ashley, but I would say that we went out for a while and we are no longer doing so. She wouldn't do anything. What could she do? What do you mean?

Your "future ex" might really be upset about this? He's not hostile, is he? He wouldn't try to do something to you or anything would he?

My class is an experiential learning class.

I'm not completely sure about this but I think that I told you I would not ask you again for a picture before we met on Friday. That means the issue is wide open again.:) If you don't want to send me a picture, what if you sent me one of just your belly with its ring? Hehehe I'd really like to see it and I've waited very patiently, haven't I? Hehehe Please give me something of yourself?

Oh baby, there is nothing I'd rather do than make your whole body quake in ecstasy. I love our email breaks too. It's going to be hard to wait another two weeks to meet you. I have another present for you. Jon

All I could think was "What an asshole!" He wasn't hard on me!? *Everything had been blamed on me and it had been said in a cruel* *manner. He had been a real jerk. What a cover up. Better now? I don't* *think so. I wanted his ass and his head on a platter now more than ever!* *So, he wanted to make Halley's body "quake in ecstasy" and he had another* *gift. Buying gifts for a stranger. I was so angry I was "quaking" all right!* *It hurt me deeply that he hadn't given me anything out of caring or love* *for so long and it seemed to be so easy for him to run out and buy things* *for someone he hadn't even met. I couldn't help but remember the first* *Christmas we were together. He had come home to our little apartment* *with a giant stocking—so big that I could literally fit into it. And our* *first Easter. I remembered how he had bought a wicker laundry basket* *and had filled it just for me. What had happened? Was it really my fault?* *What had I done wrong?*

APRIL 22

Dear Jon: Sorry! I forgot the subject because I was in such a hurry to send you a message! What do you mean that it wasn't anything "important." What was it you were trying to send? Tell me, please!

Even if you think she understands what you said to her, she might still think you are doing the wrong thing just like my husband does. What do you think? Am I wrong or right? When I asked what she might do if she found out about the girlfriend, I just wondered how she usually reacted to "normal situations." You have to admit that we are in "unusual" situations! Actually, Alan wouldn't do anything to me. He would be looking for you!!! Hehehehe Uh oh!

Since you're into classes, I have a very, very special assignment for you that has to be done by next Friday before you meet me! Go to your library (I assume there is one where you live!) and get the book "Men are from Mars Women are from Venus" by John Gray. Then, every night before you go to sleep, while you are sitting in bed in just your t-shirt :), read a chapter and I will do the same! I want us to be able to completely "connect" in every way!!!!!!

So, I was thinking today about your horsey! Tell me, just how long has it been since it has been in the "canyon of love" and slid along soft, silky "butte-ocks???" hehehe Can you tell that it has been too long for me???? It has been almost three months! I think I may have to do something about it soon……"quake in ecstasy??????" Oh God!!!!!!!

So you want a picture of my belly ring???? How in the world am I supposed to get a picture of that??? There is no way I am going to ask anyone, not even my sister to take a picture of that! You'll just have to wait and see the real thing!!! I think I will even go out and get a very special "stud" to wear in it just for you!

My mind is just in "sex mode" tonight! Did you get any "good-bye" sex? I didn't! If you did, how was it? I really want to know because I didn't get to experience it! A few weeks ago, I overheard some of the other teachers talking about "divorce sex." Do you think either of us will get any????????? And, what do you think it would be like?

This is such a stress reliever to me after the weekend! Hope your horse isn't bucking too hard right now???!!!!! And, what is my "present?" What have you got for me now?????? Tell me, please?????????? Halley

I couldn't believe the words I wrote. I didn't know where they were coming from. I have never thought or spoken like this so how could I write like this. I was amazed at my ability to talk at what seemed to be the "penis" level. The language certainly seemed to get him going and I wanted to see how far I could push the "horsey" into the wild! And the book. A friend had told me about it and I wanted to see just how much I could get him to do. After all, I had been his puppet for over fifteen years and I wanted to see just how far I could string him along and just how much I could get him to do!

APRIL 22

I was sending you something about an interrogatory that I am doing for court right now. It has to be done tomorrow, so I have to work on that too. In it, I have to list all charge card accounts that I have had control over for the last twelve months and provide statements for twelve months. I also have to list my retirement accounts, their balances and statements for two years! It's a real pain. I hope that you don't have to do this.

Yes, I think that she thinks what I'm doing is wrong. Her reaction would be more extreme than the average person if she found out about the "ex-girlfriend." She might get really pissed. She can't fight me any harder in court than she already is, so what can I do? She's not going to shoot me or anything. At least I don't think she would. Your husband would be looking for me, would he? I'm not worried about it. I don't get it when guys get that way. Obviously, you have to be wanting to do it too.

Someone just mentioned that book to me the other day. I'll look for it tomorrow. It was highly recommended. I'll have to put on a t-shirt though. It's been so warm that I've been sleeping in the nude.

How long has it been since being in the "canyon of love?" It's been a while now, longer for you, but more than long enough for both of us I would think. It sounds like you need a release and, oh baby, I want to give you one so bad. I wish I could reach right through your monitor. I'm getting hard just thinking about it. You know here we are, both wanting it and instead all we're doing is talking about it. Here is something I want you to think about until May 3rd. WE COULD MEET ANYWHERE WE WANT, ANYTIME WE WANT, AND DO WHATEVER WE WANT! Think about that...... you have someone out there that wants to make love to you all night long and make you feel better than you have ever felt before and, oh baby, I would do anything and everything to make sure that you did. Just keep that in mind when you're working away this week and thinking about what you could be doing.

You may have to do something about it soon? Like, before the 3rd? :) What do you mean? Ohhh baby tell me what you mean. I want to hear what you might have to do. :) Tell me…

No, I didn't get any "goodbye sex." Hunter was never like that. I don't know what it is with me but whenever we had a fight I would get all wound up for it but she was always just the opposite. It would ruin her mood. Everything had to be just right for her. Just right for about two days or so. :(I for one will never go back for divorce sex. Now that I know what's out there. I would think it would have to be better than it was before though.

It wouldn't be much of a surprise if I told you what the surprise is now, would it? Good night, sleep well and I wish I were there …..Jon

All I could think was, "You pig!" What a pig he was. He took my words and literally ran into a forest of overtures with them. And he thought that I was fighting him hard in court? We hadn't even had a hearing yet! All I had done so far was give my lawyer a bunch of numbers and information. His "sex talk" was pathetic. I couldn't believe who I was married to. Some kind of guttersnipe or what! I was leading him on like a banshee so I had to expect that it would generate such a response. No goodbye sex, huh? Then, what was the three-day stint all about when he was telling me things were going to work out and then he left anyway? Rape? I was used at the very least. Three days in the row and he didn't consider it "goodbye sex???" I will never forget the second night and the beautiful things that he said to me. Later, I knew that it had been his convoluted way of saying goodbye and I couldn't get it out of my head. I knew the memories of that night would stay with me forever. Fighting. Whenever we fought, he left. How could I know he wanted to make love if he didn't communicate!? It was obvious to me more than ever that he pegged me as being a mind reader. So, he felt that what was "out there" was better than what we had had. The final insult or what. Then why had he always told me how wonderful it was between us? Was he degrading what he, Jon, and I, Hunter, had had together to impress my fake persona? To make her think that she was prob-

154

ably better than the "tobeex" (me)? And his comment about how it would be better than before……because of his new "experiences" and "knowledge?" Maybe he had learned what foreplay was? Or, because of the way it had been between us those three days before he left? He was still thinking about those nights—I knew that he was.

APRIL 23

Jon: I'm starting work late this morning and don't have to be there until this noon so I thought I'd get in a "morner" instead of a "nooner!!!!!!"

This interrogatory "stuff" sounds terrible but I think everyone has to do it. Just part of the whole process, isn't it??? Now, wasn't it me that mentioned that book to you when we first started talking??? Or, did someone else tell you about it too?

So you don't know how long it has been for you??? Must be it's just a female thing to count the days, weeks, months….????? But, I don't know, the way you "talk" it sounds like it's been too long for you!!!!!!!!!!!! Whoaaaaaaaaaaaaaaaaaaaaaaaa, Horsey!

What I might have to do???? Use your imagination! Isn't that what you told me when I asked you to tell me what the "hot firsts" were????? If you tell me what the "hot firsts" were (in detail!), I'll tell you what I might have to do to make it until next Friday! Tell me, baby, and you won't be disappointed! I'll give you details! Do you dare????

No goodbye sex, huh? Not even some love the week before you left? Nothing???? For me, it was about two weeks and it was "different." Maybe because of all the confused feelings I had spinning around in my head??? How were the "last times" for you???

Now, when you did fight with the "tobeex," did you TELL her that you were "wound up," Jon????? Jon, you NEED to read the book!!!!!!!! Library, library!!!! Mmmmmmmmm, divorce sex. And, how do you know that the "tobeex" would even do it?????? Can you answer this one???? :)

And, WHAT do you mean by "now that I know what's out there?" Tell me what you mean. Now, remember, I am a "virgin" at this. It seems that the "ex-girlfriend" made quite an impression on you! Is that what you mean by "now that I know what's out there???" And what in the WORLD do you mean that you think it would have to be better than "before???????????" You are confusing me!!!!!!!!!!!!!!

You know, from what you have said about Hunter, I think that you've put your heart in a freezer where she is concerned. Am I right? Is it easier to deal with all of it this way? Do you think that maybe the "Belly Ring Girl" was really the "rebound girl?" What do you think? Just asking! (Maybe I am getting too deep again!!!! Sorry!)

So, another surprise, huh! When do I find out about this one??????? Now, I'd better get ready for work! Talk later, baby! I'll be looking for your emails! Halley

I was heating it up. I couldn't believe my composure at being able to talk to my husband about his escapades about other women and I couldn't believe my "voice." I felt like being demanding and it seemed to be a turn-on for him. Wasn't Ashley just oozing with self-confidence from what he had said? Or, for me, was it a survival thing? I was going to try to get to the core of all of this if it completely broke my heart. I had to know where I went wrong.

APRIL 23

Halley: Oh, I like "morner's" even better than I like "nooner's." Maybe it was you who mentioned the book to me?

What I might have to do???? I knew you wouldn't tell me what you might have to do. hehe   I'm going to tell you some stuff and you better tell me "in detail" what you might have to do before the 3rd!

My hot "firsts." You have to realize that my wife didn't have a lot of freedom of expression and didn't experiment. For example, she would never talk the way we have been talking and was closed minded to a lot of things. Hunter just wasn't open-minded about "stuff."

She did not like it from behind. She said it hurt her. I never really got to do it from behind with her other than one time for a few seconds. I discovered that I like it that way very much indeed!

Another first that happened for me and this is embarrassing. She never, ever went down on me and I was never able to go down on her. Isn't that sad? So, I found out just how nice that could be and I discovered that I was also very good at it! So you see, I was like a virgin when I moved out of my house. I just wish that I found you to give me all these "firsts" before the "Belly Ring Girl" and, yes, Ashley made a big impression on me. She really opened my eyes to the world in a lot of ways. Just the way she introduced me to new things, like indoor rock climbing.

This whole thing with Hunter progressed so slowly that I didn't notice any big changes. It took fifteen years for it to get this bad. When I got out of the house and met a normal, healthy woman it was a slam in my face all at once. This is when I knew what I was missing! This is why I say that I won't go back. I now know that women can be open and think as freely as I can and it is so nice. It's not a matter of being cold; it's just the way it is.

I told my wife that I was seeing a lawyer. She said that she would change and for a few days I thought that, maybe, we could work it out. We had better sex during this time, but just how good could it be? If I told her that I was wound up after fighting, her reply was always, "How can you think about that right now?" It was like a sin or something. She had mentioned over the years about people who got divorced and how they would go back for sex until they found someone new. This seems to be on your mind a lot. It sounds like its something you would like to do?

I'll give you your surprise on the 3rd. Jon

His heart was a rock of ice and his mind was a bag of marbles. I was sure of it after reading this message. So, I didn't have a lot of freedom of expression. I knew that was a lie. I didn't know that he wanted me to talk "dirty." Perhaps, I was naïve in this area. I had to admit that. I did remember "doing it" in many different places. I guess, to me, that was "freedom of expression." But, if he had told me what he wanted.... I didn't seem to be having a problem now! From behind. I thought it was degrading and it was uncomfortable without foreplay! And, truthfully, I didn't like the idea because I couldn't see his face. I remembered this and I remembered feeling like he wanted to use me. Maybe that's why I wasn't willing to try harder. To Jon, foreplay was taking your clothes off. Well, it sounded to me like he got to use Ashley like a dog, a cow and in many other ways. Maybe it was an indication that he liked men rather than women? I was confused. Why would anyone want to make love in a position where they couldn't see each other's faces? Why? I felt dirty reading his message like I had been with a stranger for fifteen years. Going down. Maybe it was the "nice, Catholic girl" in me but he had never asked for it. He had never made it an issue. The bottom line was that he needed someone else to initiate everything and he never clearly communicated his sexual desires to me. I wondered if he knew how he had exposed himself to so many things in his search for cheap thrills. Fifteen years. He was so busy working and I was so busy working for him that I never noticed that things were terribly wrong and he knew things were wrong and didn't take the time to deal with them. As for the "ex-girlfriend" being "normal" and "healthy," I had to fall out of my chair on that one. What could be normal and healthy about a single mother having sex with a married man? And, doing it with him after only a week of spending time with him! She was as close to a whore as she could be! He bought her a few dinners and she repaid him with "extreme" sex. Real normal, eh? I wondered what kind of mother she could be to behave in this kind of manner with her ten-year-old daughter in the same apartment? I couldn't believe his comments about "divorce sex." He was clearly delusional from all of the sucking off he had gotten from his "normal and healthy woman." More like she was "pig girl" to me. And, the surprise. Sounded interesting.

APRIL 23

Halley: In my last e-mail, I gave you quite a bit of info. It's been a long time since we started talking. I want to know you. I am going to be totally honest with you about everything. That's why I say and reveal so much to you. Do you think you can trust me yet? You can trust me, you know. I know you are afraid of others finding out. I know you're afraid of anyone finding out about even our communication.

Do you think you can give me something about yourself? Remember the email I gave you about wanting to live every moment and to never miss an opportunity? Today is a special day and we don't know if we will be here tomorrow? Well, I believe that. That's why I gave you my phone number and address. I wasn't going to let it go beyond that Friday without telling you who I was. If I were to stop contacting you, wouldn't you wonder what happened? Would you call my number to see if I was okay? I would want you to. What if I was gone forever? I would never have had the opportunity to know you. This is how I feel and that's why I hate waiting to know you, because neither of us knows if we will have the chance again tomorrow. Tell me your whole name, tell me something, please. Tell me something that puts you out there just a little bit and do it for me and for yourself. Don't be afraid. Just be alive. What da ya say? Jon

The emails were coming so fast I couldn't keep up with them. He wanted to know too much and I had to figure out a way to keep him at bay.

APRIL 23

I'm sorry, I don't want to email you to death today. I just wanted to tell you that I have a copy of the book. I'll start reading tonight. Jon

thirteen

SEDUCTION

April 23

Yes! You got a copy of the book! I can't wait to hear what you think!

Wow! It sounds like you really were a "virgin!" But, you know, the "ex-girlfriend" did have a child and it might have loosened things up if you know what I mean! (At least, that's what I have heard!) So, she could probably do anything easily! My husband liked "tight," do you???? I have to warn you that it's been so long, I'm sure it's tight but I'll see if I can do something about that before next week!!!

You know, some people just aren't into the "going down" thing. I've heard lots of women don't get into it! People are different. Sounds like your "tobeex" was a "lady" in the bedroom and what you really wanted was a "whore" in the bedroom!!! Was that the problem?

"Normal." Who can ever say who is normal or not? Is anyone normal? Is Ashley really normal? (Just wanted to get into your mind again!!!)

And, no, I can't imagine being with my husband and having "divorce sex." I just wondered how you felt about it. I've heard it is unbelievably common! It is almost like it is a part of the whole deal.

Just what I heard! But, from what you have said, I don't think your wife would do it, especially if she finds out what you have been doing!!!

So, it was good with Hunter but how good did you want it to be??? Was it just that she didn't want to be a "whore in the bedroom" like I said before? Do you think she ever "got off" by herself??? Have you ever??? Do you think I have??? hehehehe

I have to wait until the 3rd for my surprise! You are killing me! So, now for my "details" about what I might have to do before the 3rd! Thinking about you, I find myself so wet and hard between my legs, so hard that I can't even stand! I go to my lingerie drawer and search for a red silk thong and matching bra. I undress until I am standing completely nude and slowly put them on, feeling with my hands the heat of my desire through the thinness of the silk. I walk to my bed and lay down between my silk sheets and think of you. I insert two of my fingers into my mouth until they are very wet.......and reach down beneath the edge of my silk thong and feel for my love canyon and reach deep inside probing for that special spot. I'll pretend that it is you, but knowing that you will be able to fill me as my fingers cannot.....(As I write this, I am throbbing with excitement!) Gently, I move my fingers in and out and against my outer warmth and slick wetness. It feels so good but not as good as I imagine you would feel! I feel myself reaching a point of no return and catch my breath…and I spread my legs wider......

With my other hand, I caress my breasts and feel myself reaching the point of climax…. Faster and faster I rub my fingers in and out of my love canyon and against my outer lips…..until I reach the point where I fall to pieces and lay there with my fingers still inside me and wetness between my thighs and my legs spread wide apart...…. My thong is wet with my own self and my bra is half off and I lay there and think of you………and know that this is nothing compared to what your wild horse can give me!!!!!!!! I feel the hardness coming on again…...I slip my thong off and remove my bra and turn onto my belly in between my silk sheets….. I spread my thighs open and slowly rub my outer lips against the silkiness of the sheets, fantasizing that it is your softness that I am caressing my lower lips against......The pace quickens and I move to the edge of the bed and straddle it with one foot touching the floor and one leg still spread out on the bed.....I sit up, naked, and rub myself harder and faster against those soft, silky sheets reaching a crescendo of desire and collapse onto the bed, my leg muscles aching from being spread so wide apart. I lay there sated with the rush of orgasm that envelops me in its wake.........(Would you like to watch me do this, Jon??????) :)

How was that???????????? How hard is "it" right now!!!!!!! Do you think you might have to go "get off???":)   Halley

I was appalled at my own self. Where had this come from? Was I finally waking to womanhood or slutdom? I had no idea where this was all coming from. I wanted to see the reaction on his face so badly when he read this. I wanted to know what he thought about me (his wife) and if he thought I had ever done anything like this. I was pushing it to the maximum level but he seemed to eat it up like a little boy with a Halloween bag full of candy. I knew that the email had to be a shock to him and make him wonder about the person on the other end.

And the lack of "divorce sex." I had to wonder if it was his attempt at "doing the right thing" that kept him from using me. I hoped that was the reason and not that he was completely repulsed by me. I couldn't stop thinking about what a liar he had become. Or, was it that he had always been a liar and was now a cheat too? Just like his sister. He had always said she was a consummate liar and we knew how much she cheated.

APRIL 23

Tight? I think its like you said, "everyone is different." But, it seems that when things get hot, they also get bigger.

So I want a whore in the bedroom? Is that it? I don't know if I would call it that. Please explain your thoughts on this a little more. If everyone has a different "normal," then....? I think you're right, everyone is different and I'm going to try to respect Hunter for what she wants to do and what she doesn't want to do. It's just that if you're married, you would think that you could at least be open minded enough to give something a try especially if the other person wants to do it.

"Normal." Who knows what normal is? No, I don't think Ashley is totally normal, but neither am I. I was a little worried about my last email to you. I didn't know how you would take it. I didn't know if you would be disgusted with me or something. I don't know exactly what you think is normal either.

I don't believe that Hunter has ever "sailed" alone. She never admitted to it anyway. I don't think she thinks that way. So, likewise what could I tell her about me? :) I could never tell her the truth.

Do I think you have? After reading your last email, yes I do, and I would most definitely like to watch you "sail" alone! How hard is it now? HARD! All because of you. See what you do to me? Thank you for giving me something of yourself. Jon

His email sounded tired. Sounded like I had tired him out! I bet he had "sailed alone" while he had read my email! I remembered asking him at times if he had ever done "it" alone and he would never answer me so I knew the answer. I would never answer him either. So, he admitted that the "Belly Ring Girl" wasn't normal. She certainly was strange from everything I had read about her. I wondered how he could have been with someone like that after being married to someone like me? Desperation. Wanting to squelch the pain or was it that he was into porn? I hated it that he kept making it sound like he had communicated with me. He really hadn't. Maybe he thought that his thoughts had been verbal? Who knew! So, he admitted to "sailing alone." I had known. Those extra long showers said it all. I remembered going into the bathroom to get something while he was in there and he would freak and I would run out the door before he started screaming. It had been strange... He seemed sublimely quiet in his response compared to the information I had given him. I expected so much more. But, maybe he was just in shock and wondered how he could keep it going long enough to meet me...or maybe he wondered who the hell was on the other end of the "line!"

APRIL 23

I agree, things do "stretch" as they get warmed up with hot friction!!!!!

I think what I meant by a "whore" in the bedroom was that it seems you want something more than what a "lady" will give??? From my end, I think the two of you had a definite communication problem in many areas! Did you ever REALLY tell her just how much you wanted what you wanted and how much it meant to you???

I think "normal" is whatever a loving or consenting couple is comfortable with doing, but I also think there has to be respect for the other on both "ends." That came out strange, didn't it??????? :)

So, you think she never "sailed" alone? What is this "sailing" thing??? Hehehe Did you ever ASK her??? So, I take it you did "sail" alone??? Come on, tell me! Did you do it in the shower???? So, would you ever dare ask her if she did??? Maybe you really don't know everything you think you do about her???? (Sorry! There I go again with my psych class background!) You know, Jon, you just never know......
I DARE you to ask her! Dare to take my dare??????? :)

And, I'm so glad you enjoyed my "show" and was able to give you a "piece" of myself (many more pieces to go!!!!)! And, yes, I have "sailed" alone!!!!!!!!! If things go well, I'll take you for a sail...................! Have a nice shower! Halley

Oooooh, it was getting crazy. All of the sex talk was making me uncomfortable but I was getting the chance to say what I really thought.

APRIL 23

Yes, I told her what I wanted and tried to get it many times!

Of course, there should be respect. I don't look at it any other way. I'll give you the answer to your question about the shower after we meet and I know your whole name. Yes, I did dare to ask her if she did, many times. It was always answered with an instant "no." I would love to go "sailing" with you. Tell me more. Jon

How could he not pick up on that question? "Have a nice shower!" He was so blinded by his hard penis, he couldn't even think straight—even though it was his penis that he was thinking with and that was straight at the moment! There he went again saying that he had told me what he wanted and how he had tried so many times. Was he trying to convince my persona that he could communicate? And, as for asking me, I only remembered him asking me the few times that I tried to get the information out of him! And, if he wouldn't admit to anything, why should I? But, I should have and maybe all of this wouldn't have happened.... "Sailing" together? What a thought. I wondered what that would be like? My mind was swimming with so much "newness" to a whole new range of possibilities that I couldn't even understand. The porn talk was getting to me in ways that I hadn't imagined. I was actually starting to think like he was talking. Scary! I had to cool it down or we would burn out soon!

APRIL 23

If you could see any band in concert, who would it be? What do you think we'll talk about during dinner May 3rd? Did you ever "solo" for your "ex?" I'm going to start reading Chapter One now.

Talk to you tomorrow. Jon

Strange questions. I felt like I was being interrogated on a constant basis and on some weird level that existed in his mind. Was it some kind of test? But, what I couldn't believe was that I had him reading the book. I

was amazed at my ability to suggest and convince. Had I done this to him when we were married? Did everyone do this? Was I guilty?

I had mulled over his last message to me, Hunter, of a few days before and finally decided that I needed to respond to it or I would think about it forever and never be able to put it behind me. So, that afternoon, I responded to his last email.

Dear Jon: I felt that your last email did not deserve the dignity of a response but if I don't clarify your comments from my view, I will always think about it and I want to move ahead. So, here goes everything and I hope you will just accept my comments as clarification to your mindset of misunderstanding. It seems the passing of time allows a more positive and clearer response.

How strong I am. When your husband walks out of the house (after fifteen years) and leaves you alone standing in the house you built together, you had better have some strength stored up because there are certainly going to be rough days ahead. While he is out having a good time, you are going to be walking around the house crying and wondering what the hell you are going to do with your life.

A job. I have a job search list that is almost three pages long. Would you like to see it? I also have other "prospects" that are pending.

Guilt. Again, you left me. I only feel guilty that I did not recognize the "warning signs." I should have known when you were talking about the "red nails" etc. that something wasn't right. Also, I should also have known when you sat on the couch and said that your mother "deserved" your father having an affair that something wasn't right. (Remember, two weeks after you called him a liar, you said this.) But, you probably don't remember. You seem to only remember what you choose to remember.

Physical and verbal abuse. Throwing objects is not physical abuse. And, I seem to remember that you threw a few, especially the time you threw a stool into the closet and made a gaping hole. Verbal abuse? When people fight, they swear. It's what they call "normal!"

This is not "verbal abuse." I know, when your family fights, they walk out the door and leave. Instead of fighting, they ignore, don't communicate and turn to others in their pain. This is called cheating or infidelity.

Six years not working. You know this is not true. I have tried several things and even had my own business while managing the financial, administrative and tenant end of the apartment buildings. And, you didn't like anything I did. You couldn't find anything good with anything I did in regard to my work efforts in the last few years. The problem was that I was trying to please you and not myself. I did make more money than you for several years of our marriage and if you add everything up you will see there is very little difference in the end numbers for a period of fifteen years. So, all your complaining in this regard was very unfair.

Divorce. The lawyers come up with the questions. The clients don't tell the lawyers what to ask.

What I have had to endure??? I have lost my best friend, my husband and my life. How can you even ask that question?

You have made this painless??? What about all the screaming in the past months and the fact that you did not even try to work through our communication problems with me? You did not even attempt reconciliation. We will both have to live with that fact forever.

You never wanted me to care for you in the way that I did? By the way, I wasn't standing behind you or beside you. I was standing in front of you pulling on you. This is why I had no energy left for myself.

The "imprisonment." Yes, the imprisonment of your choices has had negative effects on my health and deep down you know it. The problem is that women speak up and men hold it in and therein lies the root of this entire situation.

Melodramatic. No, I don't think so. Just truthful.

Where do I get off? I was simply trying to state that my family believes in fidelity. We do have moral standards in this regard that your family does not. Truth again.

My reactions to your family. "Measure up" consisted of their attitudes and how they looked. The lack of "fitting in" feeling on my part consisted of the superficial and physical only. Also, I never fit in morally. Thank God.

Class. Oh, I guess you could say they have superficial class but that is all.

And, no, I did not forget about children. I wanted children when we were first married and later but you kept saying we had to wait until we had a house and it was finished. In the midst of all of this, life happened. And, our lack of communication drove us apart and you expect the person you are with to do everything plus take care of a child with no help from you. It has to be a shared experience. And, you wait until now to really speak up. You told others more about your feelings in this regard than you ever told me. So, I guess you will have to find someone younger to have what you want. Good luck.

No apparent reason that I could live my own life. Jon, you had many needs and wants and I wanted to fill all of them because I loved you so much. That is why I neglected myself.

Health. I'm glad you finally see that it is all that is important. I had something happen to me last week that made me realize that this divorce is nothing compared to health.

My mind. My mind helped get you where you are today and it will take me where I need to go and I will make it and I will meet my goals with it.

The way I live my life. I have never lived my life the way I intended to live my life. But, now I will find a way. I only thought it would be with you and not without you. But, the way you want to live your life is certainly different than the way I choose to live. I want to be with someone who loves me for who I really am and communicates with me and is someone who I can trust. I thought I had that but found out that I didn't.

Oh, and I want to thank you for telling me that I was beautiful this summer. Because I now have days when I almost think that I am.

I always knew that my body was beautiful (because you told me so many times) but now when I look at my face I see something that I never saw before. Hunter"

APRIL 24

I never received a response to my final message. How could he respond to anything factual and positive when he was living in a world of lies and darkness? He was even lying to himself....

APRIL 24

I can't believe I am now sending emails before I brush my teeth! I am so addicted to you.....

There are so many bands I'd like to see....hmmmmmm What about Darren Hayes? You know, "Insatiable!"

What do YOU want to talk about over dinner? Do you really think we will get as far as the restaurant???? Hehe Maybe something non-sex oriented???? hehe :)

And NO, I did not "solo" for Alan! YOU have a way of discovering all my wild secrets! He still doesn't know! Unless he has guessed??? He's asked me before just like you say you have asked Hunter and I always answer very fast and avoid the subject! So, an instant NO is what you got? It probably means "YES!!!!!!" Women know these things!!!! So, what do you mean when you say "tell me more?" More "solo" stories??? How about one from you??? :)

So, tell me what you think about the book?????? Got to go brush my teeth! Later! Halley

I didn't know how much longer I could keep up the pace. I was even sending messages first thing in the morning. I had to make it look like I really was going to a job or he might be suspicious of my identity. I wondered if I could get him to give me a "solo." Maybe that was pushing it!

APRIL 24

Addicted to me? That's got to be a good thing isn't it?

Darren Hayes would be good. I've heard that AC/DC is the best band in concert from a number of people. Their music isn't exactly what I like to listen to all the time though.

During dinner (if we make it to dinner:), I would like to find out all your secrets. Your name would be a good place to start, phone number, your sister's name, your mom and dad's names, where you live, what school you teach at..... Do you think you could give me that?

You never "soloed" for your husband and he doesn't even know! We are communicating better than we have with them!

I THINK I JUST FOUND A FIRST FOR YOU THAT YOU CAN DO! hehehe

What I mean by "tell me more" isn't necessarily about sex. It's about you. I want to know all about you. Tell me something about you personally. I want to know all the stuff I listed that I want to talk about over dinner. I want to know all your wild and not-so-wild "secrets" too. This is what I meant earlier about being so close to someone and knowing everything about them. Halley, it makes me feel so good that you shared something so intimate about yourself with me. Isn't it nice? Have you ever told anyone before (maybe another woman) or am I the only one?

I'm beginning Chapter Three. It's good but I don't know how much it applies to me. I'm used to dealing with someone who had ALL the female traits. I know that I do some of the things it says males do like always trying to solve women's problems instead of just listening. I'll try to be aware of the things I do.

More secrets please:) hehehe Jon

More secrets, huh? Boy, could I blow his mind if I just came right out with the truth! "Jon, guess what! It's me, Hunter!" I wondered if it would be worth giving the truth away to hear his reaction. My gut instinct was that I would never hear from him again. The truth might have to wait forever

since he seemed insatiable for information about me. It was amazing how he could exaggerate negativity. Did he think it made him seem desirable or was he using it to make women feel sorry for him? I had to admit that he had always done this with anyone he knew. There was always something to complain about with him. It really made me wonder why he had to constantly demean people. He wasn't happy. Had he ever been happy? How was he ever going to find someone to fit his "perfect ideal?"

Well, if she made a lot of money that would be the ticket for him to get on the ride!

APRIL 24

Well, I guess we have hit on something we don't agree on! Not into AC/DC! Hehehe And, who are these people who recommended them? Students???? And, yes, I will definitely give you my name and address if everything goes well......but, remember, this has to stay between us and I mean NO ONE else!!!

Yes, you are the only one who knows I have flown "solo!" You have to understand it's a "silent" thing that women keep to themselves. You know, it's a "bad girl" thing!!! That's why you got an instant NO from your wife! So, do you believe me or not about the fact that she probably did do it???? Well???? Is it so hard for a man to take that they might not really know their "significant other" like you think you know yours??? Mine doesn't know!

Keep reading the book, Baby! (Maybe, you should get her a copy????) More secrets???? Shouldn't we save some of them for next week???? And, where's my "solo" from you??? Hehehe Oh, and one more very important question. Do you think my "solo" was so good it could be part of a book????? Tell me the truth! Halley

I liked being right to the point with him. I had never been allowed to do this before. Maybe I had never allowed myself to be this way or maybe he gave off the feeling that I couldn't be me. I felt so free. I wondered if I could get him to buy me a copy of the book. Just how far could I push it?

And, I wanted to know what he thought of my writing. But, could I really trust his opinion? He was trying to get into my pants so how honest was he going to be?

APRIL 24

Not into AC/DC? Well, like I said, I'm not really into them either. I like Jude Cole, Darren Hayes, the old Savage Garden and I like listening to just about anything that I can sing to. I can't sing to AC/DC.

I promise you, anything you tell me will remain between us. You gave me something of yourself that you've given to no one else. It is a gift of trust and no one else will ever see it or hear it from me no matter what. If we are going to build a trust like neither of us has ever had, we both need to respect it and I always will.

I've learned a great deal going through this divorce. It is that people talk and spread untruths terribly fast and it doesn't feel good being on the receiving end of it. I've learned the value of friendship and the need to remain silent for the sake of myself and for others. Right now, there are three faculty members in my department who are in the process of divorce. It seems so extreme that it makes for great gossip among others. The three of us are all friends and talk amongst ourselves to hear the latest about each other. It's mean what people do and say.

I don't know if I believe my wife has gone "solo." If she really did, she kept a lot of herself hidden from me because she seems so far removed from it. If it's true that she did go "solo" and she kept me that removed from it, that's kind of sad isn't it? I know that she really didn't completely know me sexually. What about your husband? Did he ever admit to you that he went "solo?"

The first thing I thought of when I started reading the book was that Hunter should read it too. I received a reply to my e-mail from her yesterday. She is very hostile. She attacked my family and I. I don't know if I should reply to her or not. Maybe the best thing to do is to let it go? She will never change her point of view and I probably won't change mine, so what's the use?

I agree that we should save some secrets for next week. You want a solo from me? Would you like to watch me solo? Would you like that?

I went shopping today. I found some clothes, but what I was really looking for was a pair of boxers with trout on them. No luck. I have a pair with fish but they aren't silk. I'll keep looking. :)

I absolutely loved your solo! It's the best thing you have given me. It would make a great addition to a book. What if you wrote something that you let everything out in? Let out all your fantasies, experiences and thoughts? Everyone would read it and everyone would totally get off reading it and most could never admit it. Hehe Jeez, I'm just wondering what you can top it with? Can you give it a try? Fantasy or truth, it doesn't matter. Just try to top it. Jon

So, the truth was hard to take. It wasn't "mean" as he described it. It was just the truth and he couldn't accept what his own actions had been. I had told him long before how "people talk" and he had ignored my advice. He should have listened. So I didn't know him completely in a sexual manner? I wondered what that meant?! Was it that he had "sailed" alone and that he wanted to be "orally pleasured?" I couldn't believe his comments about my return email being "hostile." It had been blunt and completely truthful. To him, truth was "mean" and "hostile." He just didn't get it. Jon wanted to exist in a fantasy world and he was looking for a fantasy woman and he was searching for something that didn't exist. He didn't understand that all marriages had their difficult times and that it was necessary to work through them. But, I guess he thought all the time and effort he was putting into a "cyber babe" was time better spent? Oh God! Watch him "solo?" What would anyone else think of this? I was his wife reading this message, but what if I was a stranger as he thought me to be? What would a stranger think of all this? I'm sure the cyber relationship wouldn't have gotten this far. So, he wanted more. Jon was addicted to me, his fantasy woman. I didn't know what to think so I just kept on writing.

APRIL 24

I love the Savage Garden CD's too! I can't believe the band broke up, can you? But the new single by Darren Hayes is so good!

Thanks for saying that you would keep my secret! Three of you in the same department! Wow! I have never heard of that before! All of you probably can't wait for the summer break! How have the other teachers in other departments acted toward the three of you?

Well, Jon, please don't be offended but I have to say it again. It does seem that you and your wife did not communicate enough. It sounds like it was all work and no play, like you said in one of your earlier emails. So, what do you mean that she didn't know you sexually? That you were into the "going down" thing like you said the other day and she wasn't interested? And, no, my husband never admitted to "soloing" but I just assumed he did as it is a "natural" urge kind of thing, right? And, there are times when women aren't able and what's a guy to do????

You know, if you think Hunter should read the book, why don't you send her a copy anonymously? I did! Then, I admitted it was from me and Alan was okay with it. Don't you want to somehow "help" her, especially since it has been fifteen years? (I hope this doesn't sound stupid!)

As far as her reply to your email, which was more hostile? Now, let's be honest! I have two questions to ask here that will help you decide what to do. Was there any real truth to what she was saying? And, did she say anything positive to you? If your wife did both these things in her email, then you probably got something "good," and that helped her deal with your original email and was meant to help you understand her views. If you do think you need to respond, I'd have something positive to say. If you say something positive, it can only help make things easier between the two of you. It sounds like there's been enough hurt already, you know? That's just my opinion!

Actually, I was looking for a "written" solo???? (Just for now!) Maybe a real one later????

You went shopping! I am so jealous! Where did you go? Did you come down my way???? What did you buy for clothes? I love shopping for men's clothes! I have so missed it (except for the day I bought the boxers for you!) And, don't worry about the fish not being silk! It doesn't matter. I just wanted you to have boxers with fish!

So, you really mean that about my "solo????" You don't even know how happy that makes me! (I just hope you are telling me the truth!) How could I improve it? What do you think? I'd like to write a story (fiction, of course!) that it is just a part of. I assume it would be a "chic book?" Or, do you think that men would like it too???? I'll try to come up with something new and exciting for next Friday!!!! Halley

I knew about the three teachers and who they were. It disgusted me. I called them the "runaways." Too afraid to deal with reality so they ran away. Because they didn't know how to communicate, they figured that starting over was the answer. If they couldn't communicate now, how did they think it would work with someone else? I felt sorry for them and saw them as pathetic at the same time. Shopping. I really did miss shopping for men's clothes. It sucked not going into the men's department any more looking for bargains. Once in a while, I would walk through just to look but it only made me feel terrible knowing I had no one to shop for and I kept wishing that he would come home so I could iron his shirts again, the shirts I had bought for him.

APRIL 24

Hi Halley Who? The other teachers in other departments, for the most part, have been very kind. Most everyone seems to understand that it's tough.

I know that I come across as uncaring and that everything is her fault. I know that you don't like that. I admit to being partially to blame. I was working all the time. I assumed that she could do things for herself, you know, improve herself. She needed direct support or something. Believe me, I tried to help her. I just didn't do it the right way, I guess. The last email from her was really out there and held little or no true information.

I would rather talk about you and I. I just can't wait to meet you, Halley. I want to just hold you so bad. I want to see your belly ring. I want to see your red sequins. :) I want to see your painted toenails and fingernails and hold your hands. I want to stay up with you talking all night. It's been so long communicating without seeing you that I'm not going to be able to get enough of you. You know that, don't you? I want to look into your blue eyes.

You want a written "solo?" I don't think that would be as good as your own. Its sort of like two women kissing is hot but two guys kissing are disgusting. :) Maybe I'll give it a try in the morning. I don't know. It's not that I don't want to give it to you, okay? It's just that I don't think it would be the same.

I went shopping up to the local shopping mall and JC Penny. Not much of a road trip. Believe me if I came down your way I would be checking out the driver of every silver Saab I met! What year is your Saab anyway?

I got a few short-sleeve, casual-type button down collar shirts, and a couple pairs of shorts. Everything was on sale and I saved about $60.00. If you miss shopping, maybe we can do some? I'd love to go shopping with you.

Yes, your "solo" was very good and I loved it. Whatever the story line, men would certainly enjoy that section of the book! Jon

I didn't understand the changing and seemingly hypocritical comments. First, he had said that everyone was talking behind his back at the school and now he was saying that "everyone" understood the "three runaways" and their situations. His mind was definitely spinning. Mine was. I was devastated and angry at his comment that my last email had held "little or no true information." He was in denial, that was for sure. Where was he? On Saturn with the rings of ice spinning in his brain?

Everything I had written had been the absolute truth as both of us knew it and I knew that he knew it. He was so desperate for pity or sympathy that he would write anything. As for me needing what he termed as "direct support," what did he think I had given him for over fifteen years??? After all of the years I had dealt with his depressed attitude, this was what I got? I felt so stupid. He was so desperate for someone to be with and to love. But, would it be love or just a way to be comforted? He was definitely looking for someone or something to squelch the pain. I wondered when he would ever deal with the pain or if he ever would.

APRIL 24

I'm sorry. It's just that women have this thing with trying to help! I'm trying to pull you out of your "cave" and that's not good! (Have you gotten to that part in the book yet?) You'd think I'd learn!!!

It's just that if I know you've done something kind for her like send a copy of the book to her, I won't have to feel any guilt. I just have to know that she will be able to find someone.....like we have found each other..... and be able to communicate with them better than she did with you. So, I still think it would be a wonderful thing if you could do this, but that is your decision to make.

I guess you may be right about the "male solo" thing! So, I will leave the "balls" in your court!!!!

Hey, JC Penney is a great place to shop! It's really the best place to buy men's clothes. Is shopping for your own clothes a new thing for you? And, I'd love to go shopping with you but I'd want to make sure we hit a Victoria's Secret store and you'd have to be willing to go into the dressing room with me!!!! Oooooooooo

So, do you think it's okay for an English major to write this "type" of book???? And, how do you think I could improve on what I wrote??? What else do men want to know???? And, it's only been since the beginning of April since we've been talking! But, I understand what you are saying. And, your words are so sweet! I can't wait to meet you too!!! I've already repacked my bag (a week early!)!!!!

I hope you sleep well and dream of me............Halley

My will was beginning to falter. The only thing keeping me going was the adrenalin rush that I got each time I signed in to get his messages. They got me through writing the return messages. Sometimes I cried, sometimes I laughed. It was a roller coaster of emotion that I was riding and I was heading myself straight off the tracks. I wanted a copy of that book so badly. I had borrowed a copy from the library and didn't feel I had enough money to buy a copy of my own. I needed whatever money I had to buy food and pay bills. So, if I could get him to mail me a copy, it would be great. Tricking him into it gave me a little guilt, but if he could spend all that money on dinners for strange women, what was one little book. It was keeping him at arms length while talking all the "sex talk" that was the hard part!

APRIL 24

Yes, I reached the part about the "cave." There is so much I need to know about you. How you communicate, etc. I need to read more of the book. You seem to be busy, which is good. It seems like you work hard and are advancing in your job? That's also good. Usually that type of person doesn't get bogged down on small things that can upset some people. Do you usually get over problems quickly? What I mean is that I like to communicate with a woman. I enjoy it, but I like to progress with conversation and exchange information and thoughts and reach some kind of point. Do you know what I mean? Am I being the "solution guy" from Mars?

I'll send her a copy of the book.

Shopping for myself is a relatively new thing for me. I've done a little bit in the past. It doesn't seem that difficult and it is kind of fun. I would love to go into the dressing room with you! I would love to do it in a public place. Hehehe   Laundry is a real pain though. I hate ironing! It takes me forever. I'm really slow at it, but I'm getting better.

This afternoon I did a lot of thinking. I'm thinking about what I want for the rest of my life. I want to make sure that I don't make another bad decision. I'm trying to consider every possibility and analyze the whole situation. I even thought about if I want to remain alone. I realized that I don't. I definitely want a woman in my life and I want to be totally open with her about everything like I never have been before. More than anything, I want someone I can fully communicate with and do things with because I've never had that.

I think it's more than okay for an English major to write that type of book. You can always be a "ghost writer?" Or change your name so no one knows. I don't think you can improve what you wrote. All you have to do for the reader is create the character so that when they get to that point in the book, they know her. When she is someone they know, it makes the whole thing much more erotic, real, and deep. It makes the character real.

What else do men want to know?????? I think that you gave me the big one. Maybe if you used tools and toys? Perhaps even with batteries? That would be erotic! Hehehe What do you think?

There has been something I've been thinking about. Should I give you advice as to what you should do? It's pretty obvious that I don't want you to go back to your husband and that's not giving you an unbiased opinion. I don't really know how you feel about him? I don't know what kind of guy he is or if he has been good to you or anything. I'll never be able to look at the situation without being biased. I would think that your sister is probably helping you a lot with the whole thing. What does she say? I think that you're having a hard time with it in your mind and you're feeling a lot of guilt. I think that it's the type of person you are, that you're very caring and don't want to hurt others. If this is the reason and you still left anyway, I think you probably have thought about this a long time and there is a true reason behind it all. You made the right decision for your own well being. I can't really think of any other reason??? We don't need to talk about it. I'm just saying things that are on my mind.

I will dream of you (after I do a little reading) :) Jon

Jon was definitely a twisted cave man of sorts. He wanted the woman to go out and kill the supper for him. He definitely wanted to know that he was conversing with someone who could bring home the bacon, fry it and make him a man. Bad decision, huh? Was that what our marriage seemed to him now? It had been his idea. Maybe he should have discussed it with me? I was lost on how his mind was working. Maybe I had never known his mind at all. I couldn't believe he was saying that he was going to send me a copy of the book. Great, I thought. I get to have my own copy! But, what a price I was paying. To be tortured by his comments and to have to communicate with my own husband as a fake persona so that I could know the truth or whatever he said the truth was. I had moments where I wanted a second chance, where I wanted to go back and share with him everything that he said he wanted to know—even though he had never made any attempt to communicate with me as we were communicating with one another in our cyber world. I wanted to "do it" in a public place. I wanted to know what it was like to "solo" together even though it made me cringe at the thought. I wanted to be with him so badly, even knowing what I knew. I loved him still and I had to painfully admit to myself that he didn't care about me or was doing a great job of saying that he didn't. I wanted for him to communicate with me as he described. I wanted it so bad that it hurt. Well, the character in my book would definitely be real. If that is what he thought would be good, it would be great. Tools and toys? Where had that come from? Was he into porn now? Where had he picked up that idea? From his friends at work? He seemed so concerned about my fake marriage and my fake husband. He wanted to know that he was more important. He was insecure. He was afraid he would never know me, Halley, like he had never known his own wife.....

APRIL 25

I am so glad you are reading the book. Problems? Well, everyone has their weak moments but I see things very differently since this separation thing and I try to see the blue sky instead of the rain clouds as much as possible. You know, it may be true that there is a reason for everything…..but, I remember you saying that you aren't a big believer in fate, are you? You have to admit that it's some kind of fate that helped us to "find" each other, don't you? And, yes, it does seem you are the "solution guy from Mars!" But, that isn't always a bad thing! I understand what you are trying to say. Don't you think that a lot of the time it is easier to communicate in writing than face to face? But, I think just maybe your wife didn't get any of this communication that I am getting from you. And, I wonder if she had where you would be right now. I just can't help thinking about this. I just feel sad for her that you couldn't do this with her. Like in the book, women have to talk and talk and talk to feel better! And, that's what I'm doing right now! Sorry!

I think it would be really nice for you to send her a copy of the book, but I hope there is some kindness behind the effort. :)

You think shopping is fun! Wow! Dressing room, here we come! And, ironing, I try NOT to do it! I find it's such a waste of time! But, with dress shirts, you really don't have a choice!

Alone? That would be sad, wouldn't it? How would you have children? Or, have you changed your mind about children? I think it's so wonderful how you want to be so communicative. You know, I know what you mean though. Rushing into anything "permanent" after you get through all of this is probably not a good idea. What do you think of living with someone (without marriage)? I've thought about this and I know it would be a problem for my parents. Guess I will have to figure it out if I get to that point, right? (Can you imagine if they knew about my "solo" flights????)

My sister, Laurie, and I have talked a lot about my situation. I do know that I don't want to feel negatively toward him. I really know I don't want to feel the way you seem to feel about your wife. Please don't take this the wrong way! I just want us to find a way to be friends or acquaintances somehow no matter what has happened between us. I was married eight years which is nothing compared to your fifteen and I know that this is too much time to invest and not at least be able to be friends. Right now, I know he is hurting and I don't know exactly how he feels about this but we do have a limited line of communication between us. That is very important to me. And, I find it's so important to acknowledge the truth how each of us made mistakes and the truth about influences around us that affected our marriage. I hope you don't mind that I feel this way but I just don't feel it's right to have nothing after eight years. And, maybe I'm wrong. Maybe I'm just dreaming......

So, do you think it would make my story more interesting if the character was someone who you would never expect a "solo" from???? Tools???? Batteries???? Oh my God! Really???? I thought that might be pushing it too far???? But, would women like this???? Or, I suppose this is for the male reader, right????

I just want you to know how I think it's so great that we've been able to talk on so many levels. I just hope the "serious" level hasn't been too hard for you. I know the "fun" levels are much better! Have a great day! Off to work! Halley

I wanted him to realize that no "quality" communication between us was not a good thing. I wanted this so badly. Halley was trying to tell him that he needed to communicate with Hunter, but he seemed so closed to anything. After fifteen years, he was closed to anything and everything. He had run away and didn't want to even consider that he might have made the worst mistake of his life. I tried to stay positive and continually stroked him with comments that would lessen any suspicions that might arise out of the conversations.

fourteen

FALLING INTO PLACE

APRIL 25

Halley: It is amazing how things sometimes seem to coincide and fall into place. For me, it's been fifteen years. I could have done what I'm doing now at any time, but I chose now. This is the only time that I would have had the opportunity to meet you!

Yes, a lot of the time it's easier to communicate in writing than face to face. I'm a better writer sometimes than speaker anyway. I'm glad you feel that way. But, I do have to say that I really tried to communicate with her. Sometimes even in writing. You have to understand how differently she thinks. I'm pretty creative. I can completely change the mood in a classroom, or most anywhere by making a completely unrelated, sort of comical comment. Something like, "wouldn't it be neat if we could build a flapping wing aircraft?" I do it to progress things along in stalled situations. She simply never came along with me to that new location, you know what I mean? She would just stay in the stalled location. She always saw the cup half empty and everything was a complete failure and panic situation. She had issues with some of her family members and couldn't communicate with them effectively. Halley, I have truly tried helping her and I have given up. When I tried to reason with her or have an in-depth conversation, she always got very mad at me. I just want you to know that I don't have this effect on anyone else.

I'm sending her a copy of the book because I truly do want her to understand.

The kind of shopping that I can get pulled into is when you go into a nicely constructed high-end mall and it smells good inside and they are playing classical music. I can really make some spur of the moment purchases because it makes me want to spend money.

I want children. I continually watch my sister, Portia, and her husband, Mark, with their three year old. I can only imagine what that would feel like. I busy myself with work and classes. I can't imagine what it would be like to actually have something that is so far beyond that in importance. It must feel wonderful. I've thought about living with someone for a while before getting married too. I'm so afraid of making another bad decision. I think when you have done it once it takes away some of your confidence in regard to making good decisions. For me, it makes me question everything about my future and what I should do. As far as having a woman in my life and children, I really don't have to think about it long to realize that's what I want. As far as taking the plunge, I don't know. I think it might be a good idea to live together for a while. I know some people need five years or more before they are willing, but not me. I think I would know in a lot less time than that, maybe a year, regardless if living together or not.

I understand what you mean about wanting to maintain communication with your "ex." But, consider the fact that at some point you both will be with other people. Do you think that his "future woman" is going to want him speaking to you, ever? I guess if I were your "new guy" it wouldn't really bother me too much but I'm sure it would a lot of other guys. Some guys are really possessive. They would want no part of you communicating with him. It would be good to be able to continue talking throughout the year and go your separate ways still communicating. I know you think that I should do the same and

I really would like to, but it has been very difficult trying to communicate with her about any of this. She focuses on things that bother her with situations and cannot get beyond them. She talks and talks but never seems to feel better by talking about them.

I know I should be able to communicate with her and I know it makes me sound like I'm arrogant or stubborn or something to say that it's her fault. I know some of it is my fault too. But, I also know how patient I am. I am a very patient person and I always try to consider everyone's point of view in every situation. Halley, I just can't get to that place with her. I feel bad about it and I don't know what she is going to do with her future. I do know that she has one if she chooses to see that she does. She needs to move on with her life. She has needed to do that for many years already. I truly believe that this divorce will probably help her out in the end because it is going to force her to start living again. I think it's the only way that she ever would. I just have to get through it the way it has to be. Maybe in time she will understand and we could then actually communicate. You know what I mean?

I'm just going to say what I'm thinking okay? I think my situation worries you. I think that you wonder what kind of person I am and that maybe I'm not a nice person if I can treat her this way. This is why you want to talk about it and I think that's great. That tells me you're looking for someone long term and I'm glad you're looking at me. I'm also looking for someone long term and that's why I also want to talk about your situation, too, at some point so I can understand more about you. I want to know if you communicated with your husband and told him what bothered you and if you tried to get him to change. If you didn't, would you the next time? Would we both do things differently the next time to prevent things from reaching the point they have? I know the kind of woman I'm looking for. I know that I want to raise any issue that I don't think is right immediately when it happens. She just has to be able to listen to what I'm saying, that's all I need. What do you need? We're both feeling unsure about our abilities to make a wise decision. That's why we ask these questions. I wish that I could have my sister talk to you about what my life has been like for the last fifteen years and she would tell you. My entire family has been very supportive during this because they have seen what it has been like and they know it's necessary. I guess, for now, we need to just start at the beginning and communicate and tell each other everything. I will try to do that for you.

"Tools" and batteries, I don't think that's pushing it too far. I do think that women would like this even if it's just for the shock of it all. Give them everything you've got! I think it would be more interesting if it were someone who you would never expect a "solo" from. Boy, that was a long one! Jon

I was so angry by the time I got through this message that I wanted to throw something at the monitor and have it reach him on the other side. Oh, how he was able to twist and turn everything to make himself look like angel cake. All I could think of was his uncommunicativeness with me for fifteen years! The bottom line was that he blamed everything on me so that he could do what he was doing without guilt. Move on, eh? How the hell could I move on when I had been stuck in his life for fifteen years. I had done everything he had wanted and cheated myself out of anything I wanted for so long. Then, when I began to recapture my independence and do something for myself, it angered him. He was getting the attention he wanted. How could he say all of the things he was saying when he knew it was crap—total crap. As for his sister, she was the sneakiest, most conniving slut there was and he was the one who had told me this about her. He had been so ashamed of his family. Neither one of us had any idea how many men she had had relationships with and she had ended up with someone she worked with as her second husband—someone who had watched her various escapades for over ten years—someone whom she hadn't even loved when she married him. What kind of a judge did he think Portia was in my case? How could he even suggest her as a source of information to a stranger? Anyone would see right through this if they had a brain. It frightened me to realize how distorted his mind had become. And, how his family had "seen" what "it's" been like???? What was that? Whenever we had been at family "events," it was me who had carried the conversation. He had sat in a corner and said nothing as usual. All he ever said to me what how he couldn't stand to be around them, never wanted to be like them, and here he was glorifying them. I felt sick. As for the story's character being someone you would never expect a "solo" from, that was a definite. Nobody would ever expect it from me.

APRIL 25

Halley: Wow, I had to click on every shot to get a larger image! Very nice lovemaking. It all looked soooooo gooooood. They have workshops? What do they do—have couples sit in a room and try these things out? :) hehe   Maybe we should go to one. :) Jon

In my research for "divorce sex" on the Internet, I had found a very tasteful website that illustrated various Kama Sutra lovemaking positions and had sent a link to him to keep him "hot." I had to admit it was definitely a turn on. And, from the message I got from him—he thought so too. But, of course, he was obsessed with it!

APRIL 25

I suppose you have a point about the fifteen year thing. It is like fate, isn't it? I just wish you had found me before the "Belly Ring Girl" like you said the other day! That was really sweet for you to say that!

So, with communication between you and your wife, maybe there was just some "bad" chemistry between the two of you? Or, maybe, she really needed somebody else to talk to? Or, maybe she was "starving" to get out there and do something for herself??? I'm just guessing. I really hope the book helps her and I think it is great that you are going to send her one. How are you going to do it? I sent mine to him via an Internet order.

So, you like to spend money???? Well, I suppose we can find something for you to buy!

I totally understand what you are saying about decisions, especially with one like this. And, especially, in the situations we are in. I think that you have to have no doubts in your heart and in your mind. Is that possible?

As far as who I would be with in the future, I would definitely NOT want the possessive type. I would want them to respect me and trust me enough to not be like that. But, I understand your point. I suppose it would be communication on a more periodic basis, like when you run into the person or if you have a specific question for them, etc., especially after you are "permanently" involved with someone else. And, when there are children, it's a totally different ballgame. There has to be constant communication whether you like it or not. But in cases without children, it is totally different. But, it would be really hard for me to not remember them on their birthday or our "old" anniversary....you know what I mean? Or, is this just a "Venusian" thing?

You say that you would really like to communicate with her but from all of your emails it seems like you wouldn't have anything good to say to her, whether it is what she deserves or not and I certainly can't be a judge of that. But, if you want to communicate with her, you should. You know, it has been over four months like you said and maybe after what you've emailed each other in the last week, there is a chance that you could talk to her in a rational way? I don't know. It is probably still too soon seeing how hard things have been between the two of you. And, you know, time and circumstance REALLY change people. Like you said, this is forcing her to do something about her life and how do you know that she hasn't been communicating with others, made friends and forgiven people??? I am not sure she has probably forgiven you but who knows what has happened since you left, you know? You never know!

And, I love it when you talk about what you are thinking. It really helps me to gain a perspective on my own situation and I hope that I have been of some help with yours. You know what bothers me the most about both our situations? I wonder why we didn't communicate when we should have with our "significant others?" I keep stumbling on this. Why didn't we do it? We had to be blind in a sense. I am sure of that. If we had had this book before, would it have been possible to save our marriages??? I think this book is so great at explaining the communication problem and I feel like it completely applies to my situation. Now that you have read more of the book, can you see the reality of your situation more clearly?

And, as for talking to your sister, that would not be a good thing. I want to know you the way I get to know you from your thoughts and from meeting you. Anything your sister would have to say would be justifiably biased (because she is your sister!) and I wouldn't get the "picture" that I need for me. And, I wouldn't want to hear any negative things she had to say about your wife because I MIGHT think that she was not being the sister-in-law that she should be or should have been and then I would think that if I was somehow someday in your wife's position that I might be at the mercy of your sister's opinion! You know, the person I would really like to talk to is your wife! (Gave you a heart attack, didn't I????) hehehe (Just joking!)

I do think that it is important that we not be negative towards them. It will only affect us if we do.

So, back to the fun stuff! Okay, now you've got me. I've never done the "tools" and batteries so I guess we could call this a potential "first" for me! Does that make you happy!!!! And, I agree, I think the story should be told from the viewpoint of a character who would never be expected to "solo!" So, do you have any ideas what my "ghost" name should be???

Can you believe that I found that website! I was trying to find information on "sex with your ex" (because of our conversation from the other day!) and I got this!!!! But, I wondered about the workshops too!!!! What were your favorite positions??? I am definitely into the "Andromaque" and the "Tiger," but the "Courtesan" really turned me on (another potential "first")! It has been too long!!!!!!! I wonder if I should send this link to Alan???? Hehehehe You have to wonder, both of our "tobeex's" must be going crazy (like I am!)! I'm sure mine hasn't been with anyone and it sounds like your wife hasn't, so it must be really "hard" for her! You said you had been apart for over four months!!!!!!!!!!! So, do you think she might have flown "solo" by now??? I'm sure mine has! And, what about you???? Hehe Later! Halley

Oh, I just couldn't believe myself! How was I able to write like this? Because I was writing to my husband! Even then, how was I able to write like this to someone who had left me and hurt me so badly. Revenge was definitely in my mind but, truly, I wanted to help him and I wanted to help myself to understand what had happened and what was happening. I was amazed at my own nerve.

APRIL 25

Halley: You're too much, you know that?:) Hehe

I had to go back to the Kama Sutra page and take a look at the names of the positions. We like all the same things! Ooooooooooohh The "Andromaque" and the "Tiger" Ooooohh. I love both of those! I thought the same thing when I saw the "Courtesan," I've never done that either and I would love to! A "first" for both of us. I've asked my wife to do that before and she wouldn't. I also, of course, like the "Cow." :)

Looks like we're finding some "firsts," for you, aren't we? Never had batteries or "toys." The "Courtesan"—didn't we find another one too????

You know, it's much easier to write about something if you have actually experienced it. :) Halley, do I have to go out and get you one more present for Friday? :) hehehe I'll try to find one with D size batteries! Hehehehehe

And, yes, I do wish we had met before I met Ashley. Just think of all the "firsts" you could have given me. I think it would have been more difficult for us to communicate, though, because I wouldn't have known about a lot of stuff. It looks like we'll do just fine finding "firsts" of our own.

I do think there was bad chemistry between my wife and I. It's so much easier to talk to you. We have covered things that I never talked about with her. Why didn't we talk and communicate with them? Is it time for me to put on my "Mr. Fix It" hat? hehehe Maybe it's like I said earlier, when it's right, things just go the way they need to, and when it's wrong it's like pounding your head against the wall. I know that was what my marriage felt like in the end.

Halley, I'm telling you, you will never be in the position that my wife is in, okay? If things were to work with us, you would probably have to kill me to get rid of me, okay? I would try to make a point of asking you every day if you were happy. If you ever said "no," we would talk about it. I'm only doing this one more time and, whomever it's with, I'm in it for good. I truly believe that the next time I will be going into it with much more knowledge and understanding and that I won't make the same mistakes again. Jeez, you have us getting a divorce already! Let's at least not skip over all the good times ahead, okay?:) Like all the "firsts"—the batteries and the "Courtesan."

Have I gone solo in the last four months! With all your e-mails with wet fingers, silk sheets and "love canyons," yes, I've had to do some "sailing." I'm beginning to associate the computer to getting a "hard on." hehehe

For your ghost name, you could reverse your name, but that wouldn't help much would it. :) It should be something with lots of meaning. I'll give it some thought. Right now, I'm thinking of Whitehaven Jobe. :) Talk to you later. Jon

He was definitely obsessed with sex. Bad chemistry? Oh yeah, right. What a load of baloney. If bad chemistry meant having orgasms, then we

had bad chemistry. As far non-physical chemistry, I supposed if he had spoken more it would have helped. It was all work with him until now, of course. I couldn't believe I finally had an answer to a question I had wondered about for over fifteen years. I suspected. Of course, I should have known knowing what I knew about myself!

"....in it for good" He was admitting without even knowing it that he would only be in it for the good. And what about the bad.......?

APRIL 25

I am too much! I have been told that before and I wasn't sure if it was good or bad!

I can't believe that Kama Sutra page. Did you look at the section that had more positions done as "illustrations???" Of course, the actual photographs are much better! And, you are right, I am getting "hard" every time I sit at my computer now!!!!!!!!! (I can't stop throbbing!) You know, I really think we should email the link to your wife and my husband! I will if you will!!! :)

Now, as for the "Cow," I have to be honest. I think you may have to go back to Ashley to get that one!!!!!!!!!! Hehehehe I just can't help but think "dog" when I look at it, even though they make it look good at the same time!!! Hehehehehehe (Please don't be offended!) This is so much fun I can't help myself! And, what do you mean that if you hadn't been with Ashley you wouldn't have known a "lot of stuff????" Which brings me to something that has been really getting to me and it's easier to ask through email! I wonder REALLY just where she has "been," you know what I mean? How can you be so sure that she was "okay?????" From what you told me the other day, the horse went wild at least for some of his "rides!!" I mean, I have been "out of circulation" for eight years! How do you really know if someone is "okay????" Did you look at it before you performed "suction?????" Oh God, I can't believe I am asking you this????????? (I hope you are laughing!)

I think we should wait on the batteries and "toys!!!" That's definitely something I would buy online like "saddles" and astroglide!!! Now my real secret is out! I am a closet "hot girl!" Who wants to stand in line in a drugstore and buy these things!!!! I am always afraid I'm going to turn around to leave and run into my mother!

I think it was wrong of me to say "bad chemistry" because there must have been some good chemistry if you even got married! You know, I've noticed that you focus on only the negative things. I want you to tell me something positive. Do you think you could say something positive about your wife so I can sleep tonight???? :)

I don't know. I still feel like a failure. How do you get beyond this feeling???? Reading the book helps, but it also points out things we should have done and shouldn't have done, right?

I guess you have probably guessed I have it in for sister-in-laws!!!! (Just don't tell your sister!) Have had my own problems there!!! I think everyone does. Haven't you? Or, did she have any sisters or brothers?

So, now a very important question. What do you want your next wedding to be like? Me, I want it to just be me and my husband-to-be on the beach in the sand with no one other than the person who is marrying us (and witnesses if it's required!), with a beautiful sunset shining across the ocean…. (Did the church the first time!) So, what's your idea of what your second wedding should be like and where would you want it to be? And, how do you know it will be your last???? Never say never!!!! Today, somebody told me about this husband and wife who got divorced and remarried a few years later. I didn't know what to think!!!!

Now, I think I will go take a bath and think about you….Halley

The cow. I wanted to throw up knowing that he had done this with the bimbo. How disgusting. The girl barely knew him and was willing to "do it" in such a fashion. Pig. That's all I could think of when the reference to her came up. I was laughing so hard as I wrote the message. I was asking him questions that were so unbelievable and so intense. Suction???

And, I wanted to see if he could say anything positive about me. I didn't expect much but it would be interesting to be sure. I wanted to stir up his mind, find out what he was thinking about anything and everything. I wondered what he wanted his next wedding to be like, if it ever happened. At the rate he was going, it was never going to happen. I doubted that anyone else would put up with his strange comments!

APRIL 25

Halley: Something positive about the wife. She's a good cook, she's very organized, she's a good writer and, in her own way, she is very strong.

I know that the "Belly Ring Girl" thing bothers you. I was reading an article in the newspaper tonight about STD's. The only thing that I could possibly have is HPV. Over 80% of the American population has it. I'm going to find out what I need to do in order to get tested and make an appointment if I can tomorrow. I think for guys it's more difficult. I think they might need to stick a BIG q-tip up inside. I don't know if that's true. It's just something I heard years ago from guys being guys. It doesn't sound like much fun but I think it's worth it in order to put it to "bed." I've read some articles on the Internet that say there are many strains of HPV and some are stronger than others. Some are harmless. They will possibly have a vaccine for it in the not-to-distant future. (I'm just telling you everything.)

What do you mean that the horse went wild for some of his rides? Not with Ashley. Did I look at it? Yes, I did. Yes, I was laughing but if you're concerned, it's really not funny. You should be safe.

You like astroglide? I thought that you would probably want to wait on the "toys." Hehehe I just wanted to put it out there to see what your reaction would be. I hate going to the drugstore and standing at the rear counter. I always get the big box so they will last a long time just so I won't have to go back for a while.

What I mean when I say that I wouldn't have known a lot of stuff without knowing Ashley is that I wouldn't have even known that women think the way that you do. You just can't understand how extremely different this is for me. That women are open and able to talk about sex and "solo's" and are able to be so physically active doing things and other stuff and how it's just so far removed from what I'm used to. I just don't know if I could have kept up with you without a little background knowledge beforehand.

Going through a divorce is the biggest failure of my life. Have you cried about how bad your marriage was and how you don't know what to do? I have, Halley. I was so unhappy. I hate the whole process and I hate what I'm doing but I know that I have to.

My next wedding. Your idea sounds nice. No, I don't think I need to do the big church wedding thing again. I have already talked with a deacon who says I could get an annulment if I wanted to easily with my situation being the way it is. I really don't see the point in it though. I was thinking a Vegas wedding but that's not as good as being on the sandy beach. Where? Well, if you're talking a sandy beach that pretty much opens the whole thing up to tropical locations and other nice places. The Virgin Islands would be nice.

You know, just about all your questions require me to include my "ex" in the reply in one form or another. How do I know my next marriage will be my last? That question tells me that we should be discussing your marriage more than my own because you left with less defined reasons than I did. My reply to that question is that I know how much I can withstand. I may not look it but I am the strongest man I know. I'm not kidding. I honestly believe that to be true. If I find someone who is compatible, the everyday life issues will be a cake-walk for me.

I understand your need to talk about my wife, but I kind of need a break from it. It's tiring for me and doesn't bring back many happy thoughts to my mind. You don't need to apologize about it. It's okay and we need to talk about it sometime. Just, possibly, a little break from it that's all? Can you tell me a little bit about your own "ex" and your situation? It's okay if you don't want to do that too.

I don't know if this email is going to make you feel very good or make you sleep any better and I'm sorry. I'm not going to lie to you and I'm going to tell you everything I feel and think and anything that I feel you would want to know because I care about you.

In your case, being "too much" is definitely a good thing! Jon

I couldn't believe he had anything good to say about me—not much—but at least something! It was as if he was straining himself to the edge to say what he did. Good writer, eh? He didn't even have a clue about that one!

I couldn't believe how stupid he was about STD's. If he had any unprotected contact with the "Belly Ring Girl" like oral sex, for example, which he had—he could still get something! He thought as long as his penis was covered he couldn't get anything. And, if he wanted to talk dirty with me, his own wife, why hadn't he spoken up. Was there a problem here with porn? He kept everything to himself. Sounded to me like Ashley was a slut. Anyone who would speak with a separated man the way that she evidently had in such a short time after meeting them was a pig. There was no doubt in my mind. Especially one with a young, impressionable daughter. Couldn't he see the connection between her and the people he used to say were disgusting? Or, had he conveniently shelved that in his mind?

I started to cry when I read about how he had cried himself to sleep. Why hadn't he ever told me that there was a problem? Was it something inside of him? I remembered his periods of depression, but it was always about his work or his job or his father—or at least that was what he had always told me. Why didn't I know it was about me? Why didn't he tell me? I remembered holding him when he was upset. His crying was so violent it scared me and I vowed to myself that I would do anything to make him happy. But it still wasn't enough. He had so much unhappiness inside of him at these times and it was apparent that he hadn't shared all of it with me. There was more, though. He had a lot of unhappiness bottled up inside from his childhood that he said had to stay there and be ignored. I think part of his unhappiness, at least, was from this place. He had never really let me know him.

The Virgin Islands. Sounded great. I wished there was a way that we could go there together and work out everything between us. His next comments were hypocritical. He made the statement that he was the strongest man that he knew after he had just said he had cried about the divorce. He didn't have the guts to be honest with the person that cared for him more than anyone else. Then he went on and said he couldn't take talking about his wife—that he needed a break from it. I was beginning to believe that he was plagued with delusion.

APRIL 26

Wow! She writes? Sorry, no more questions!

Well, I don't think anyone has ever given me so much truth all at once ever! And, please don't feel you have to go for "the test" because of our conversations. The vaccine sounds interesting but what if someone already has HPV? Then, probably it wouldn't do any good? And, yes, I have heard how common this all is. I wonder if there is info on the internet about all of this. You might want to check it out?

And, I don't have to use astroglide. It just adds to the experience, you know? So, why don't you order over the internet? It's so much easier and much more private!

So, you wouldn't have known that women think the way that they do if not for Ashley and me? Maybe you just never asked "her?" But, sorry, we will not go there again!

I still don't understand why you didn't tell your wife how unhappy you were. This just doesn't make sense to me. This has come up so many times over the last weeks. So, please don't take this the wrong way, but it seems maybe you didn't speak up the way you should have? But, I am not trying to make you feel bad. I am just trying to understand. It helps me put my own situation in perspective and I want you to know just how much it has helped me to do this.

I do want to apologize for asking so many questions. It's just that I want to be sure about myself and my own reasons and about your reasons and I want to focus on the positive. It sort of "scares" me how negative you are about your situation. It makes me feel that Alan may feel the same about me. I will try to define my reasons for you so you can get an idea of where I am coming from. We definitely had similarities in our situation. There was a communication problem and an overload and "over love" of our work. There was also a lot of confusion about children. He wanted them, but wanted to wait. Then he decided we should do it when I am at a critical point in my career and I wanted to wait. So, the scenario came around full circle. And, you know I think we have probably ALL cried about this (all FOUR of us!). Your admitting all of this to me just really took my breath away. But, I'm going to be really honest with you and hope that you don't take it the wrong way. I am concerned for you. Do you think it is really a good idea to get involved with someone when you haven't dealt with all the pain? It's just a question and I hope that you are not offended by it. I just wonder.

And, now the big one for me! I'm glad you say that you don't see the point in annulment because I don't believe in it. No matter what the circumstances of any marriage, it DID exist! Our marriages do exist! I have a real problem when I hear about people talking about annulment and how they are doing it so they can get married in the church again or for whatever reason they come up with. It's like they are trying to absolve themselves of something or pretending that they haven't failed. Maybe, in some cases, it is justified but I feel in most it is not. I hope this does not offend you but this is the truth of how I feel. And, since you have been so truthful, I felt it was okay for me to be. And, I can't help but feel disrespect for your deacon and anyone else affiliated with a church or any church that would advise anyone in this regard. So, another secret is out! I have strong opinions! You might not want to meet me after reading this!!!!

I am going to say it again and you won't like it. But, Jon, you really have to find a way to see the positive in your marriage that did exist or the negative will weigh you down for the rest of your life! I know it doesn't seem like it right now, but I really believe this.

So, I hope this email doesn't discourage you. I think it's really important to face all of this especially in our situations. Well, I certainly have a lot to think about and I think you do too.

So, for now, I'll leave you to think...later! Halley

I had to admit I couldn't believe he had even checked out the consequences of unprotected sex. That was mind boggling to me. It hadn't seemed like he cared. I so wanted him to admit that he hadn't communicated with me the way that he should have. I knew that he had never really tried. I had told him that if he ever had something that he had to say, especially something that was important to him—to sit me down and tell me so and not let me go gushing off at the mouth about something else and not listen to him. He just didn't have the drive to even bother it seemed. Sometimes he would tell me that he had told me something but he hadn't. It seemed as though he thought so hard about some things that he believed in his mind that he had actually said them—when he had not. It was so confusing to me. I really wanted him to think about what he was doing and what he had done and not done. How could he get involved with someone else when he was so clearly painting over the wallpaper on the wall. When he should have peeled away the wallpaper first, he took the shortcut and painted over it and it just didn't look pretty and it definitely wouldn't last. Time would reveal the feelings that had been hidden beneath and it would be even more of a mess then to clean up.

Oh, how I wanted to have the "Great Deacon" ousted from his post! How dare he tell Jon that he could get an annulment. Over my dead body! It was the only thing that Jon could use as an excuse to mask the real truth. The real truth being that he had left me for a bleached blonde teacher who ended up not wanting anything to do with him. I would never agree to an annulment and would fight it if he tried because there was no bearing to it. And, I was trying to get him to see some positive in his marriage and he seemed to be in such denial. How could he want to be weighed down by displaced anger for the rest of his life?

APRIL 26

Halley: I just came online to write to you. I'm sitting here working on my homework and I had checked my email this morning and you hadn't written yet. I was worried about all the stuff I said to you and I was afraid you were really having second thoughts about me. I couldn't think or study, so I was going to write you.

I was going to say something along the lines of how I've really put myself out there in that you know who I am, where I am, and what I look like. Through my wanting to give you everything, I've set myself up terribly for disappointment. I don't know your name, where you live, or what you look like. You can stop emailing me whenever you want to and I have nothing. I don't even know what you look like. All you would have to do is put a block on your email to stop my messages. I could be at a school-related meeting somewhere and you could recognize me and I would be totally oblivious to the fact. I've given you all the power and that's a mistake. But, I think this giving too much is a mistake that I keep making. I want to give women all of me. I think there is a better way that I could have handled this whole situation that would have made you want to give me more of yourself and we would have had more of an equal relationship right now, if that's what you want to call this. I don't know what else to say.

Yes, I am a little negative, but I'll get over it. Yesterday she emailed me because she needed salt for the water softener. I went into town and got a couple of bags and put it in the softener. I ordered her a copy of "our" book through "Amazon.com." I can deal with this. I will hold up my end of the relationship with her as long as there is one. I'm still paying for everything house-related including her telephone bill and car insurance. Can't it be possible for perfectly good people to be upset about this type of situation? It doesn't mean that I'm a bad person or that it will affect me for the rest of my life. In fact, if it does affect me for the rest of my life I think it will be in a good way. I don't hate her. I wish her well, but I want to put it behind me. This may be a "guy thing" or perhaps it's the way my mind works but I have always been able to put the past behind me. Regardless of the loss, difficulty or time lost, I forget about it because there isn't a thing I can do about the past to change it; it's over. I know that I can move on. I'm strong and I will be just fine on my own. I have learned a great deal from this experience and it will help me in the future. I know that any pain I have can easily be forgotten with the relationship I long for. I just keep watching my little nephew. I was watching him this morning and I just wanted to cry. I wanted to tell my sister and her husband how lucky they are but they already know it because they have had similar difficulties of their own. They have only been married about five years and have had difficult relationships in their pasts.

My sister was married before, about seventeen years ago, to a man that she left. Combined with the bad relationships of my brother-in-law, it has made their marriage stronger. They care more for each other because they know what they have. They don't take it for granted and they know how lucky they are now. I've never seen two people have what they have together with their child. Bad experiences can be as beneficial to your well being as good ones. I think the only way it can harm me is if I cannot find what I want—if I'm alone for the rest of my life thinking about the missed opportunities and the time wasted.

Questions for you: Have you made the reservation yet? Or, do you have reservations of your own?

You asked me once about what I thought of your personality. What do you think of mine? Am I getting too intense yet? Jon

Forget about it? He wasn't forgetting anything. He was stifling everything so deeply that it was going to erupt. How could he think himself as strong when he had done the weakest and most cowardly thing possible —he ran away from me. How could that be termed as "strong?" And, how could he say that any pain he had in regard to our relationship could be "easily forgotten" by a new one? He was so wrong. And terming his sister's relationship as being better and stronger, what a load of crap. I knew the only reason their relationship was working was because they both made so much money. And, what if he was alone for the rest of his life. I felt so sad for him as I read this. He was out there looking for a "perfect" person who just didn't exist and, perhaps, someone whom he would never find — imperfect or not. Wasn't it that you were supposed to work through the trials of a relationship to make it better? And, not run away? He was using his sister as his model for what he was looking for and that was at a level of existence that I had no desire at which to live.

As I was working on my reply to him, he stopped. He wanted me to help him with his degree plan. I explained that it was all in the notebook I had given to him. Here he had been dating other people and he was communicating with me—thinking I was someone else, of course, and he had the nerve to stop and ask me, Hunter, for help—the only person he could depend on—but also the one he was treating so badly and the one he had run away from. How could he speak of so many things in a positive way to Halley about his next relationship when he was screaming at me, Hunter, in real life? And, how could he dare ask me for my help when he was treating me so badly.

APRIL 26

Did you get my message from this morning? Halley

APRIL 26

Yes, I got your message. Didn't you receive my reply? Jon

I couldn't believe he kept asking me, his wife, for help. He called me to ask where his resumes were—the ones that I had composed and typed for him. It was so hard to deal with him in reality and in fiction at the same time.

APRIL 26

Halley: It sounds like you didn't receive my reply to this e-mail. I agree with you, totally, about the annulment thing, and why would I not want to see you?

You didn't receive my reply this morning? I wonder what I did wrong? It seemed to send okay. I think I'll wait on some of the things I replied about just to see if I get a returned e-mail from hotmail. Jon

APRIL 26

Sorry I haven't gotten back to you sooner. I have been so busy today!

You wouldn't believe what I had to do so I could hear your song! I had to buy extra hotmail storage space! I got this message that said I was over my limit! It cost me $19.95! But it was totally worth it! What is this anyway? Are you trying to "woo" me????

Jon, I know you are not a bad person. You are just in a lot of pain and the pain is coming out in negativity, that's all. I think you are a very sensitive, caring, devoted person who did not speak up when he should have and I think you held everything in, much more than you are willing to admit! Don't you wonder what would have been if you had? It is driving me crazy in my own situation! Why can't we appreciate what we have now? Or, could have if we would give it a chance? I know you see the up side from looking at your sister, but I just feel like it shouldn't take so many "wrongs" to make it "right." I am not trying to be offensive toward anyone who has had to go through multiple relationships to get to where they understand that they need to appreciate what they have but think about it! Why can't we make it work the first time? Why can't we feel "lucky" with what we have? Why can't we put that extra effort into admitting our mistakes and communicating like hell with the person we are trying to get rid of? I am so confused! Why do we focus on the bad instead of the good?

One thing that I am fully intent on is to remember the good things. And, that I am told is a female "thing." I just wish men could feel this way. I don't want my husband remembering only the bad things. And, I wish for you that you will be able to think of the good things.

I just think that the whole thing behind our situations is a lack of communication. Don't you think this should be so easy to fix???? How do we really know they are not capable of it? I just don't understand what I am even thinking at the moment!

And, as for your intensity, I love it. I love to hear communication from the "depths."

I think I should wait until the beginning of the week to make the reservation. It's the slow season so it's okay. Just make sure you really do want to meet me as for the last few days I have been VERY opinionated and VERY confused! Later! Halley

I didn't know how much more convincing I could get. If he didn't get what I was trying to get across to him, he never would. I felt my argument was so positive and he refused to have hope and believe. It was so evident to me at this point. There seemed to be no spirituality within him. He wanted so much to be happy but there was something very important missing. His soul?

APRIL 26

And she thinks...... Jon

I hadn't replied to him because I had been helping my sister baby-sit our cousin's baby again. It was surreal to me. After all the pressure and threats he had given me in regard to children before he had left, I didn't know how I would react to a baby the first time I had helped her. I couldn't believe how much I liked it. I wanted him to know but he would only have been degrading in his attitude. I was so surprised by my feelings. They had been stifled for so long and now it was too late. Too late.

APRIL 26

Halley: I'm sorry you had to buy storage space, the file was quite a bit smaller than the amount hotmail gives for free space. I don't quite understand it. Do you have a lot of messages in your box?

I know what you mean by the lack of communication. Yes, I'm guilty of all the things you said about me. I have to say that I wonder if you will go through with your divorce? If you think you can work it out, perhaps you should give it a try? Just don't put too much stock into any book. Yes, it may have some very good suggestions and it may work in some cases, but not all. It is just information that can help in some instances. It sounds to me that you are not sure about meeting "me" next week? I think that the whole thing is still very fresh to you. You haven't been separated for very long and I think you have a very caring personality and because of that you are feeling very guilty. Perhaps, so much so that you can't go through with it.

I'm trying to understand your question as to why can't we make it work the first time? Why do we focus on the bad instead of the good? Really think about that for a moment. Think about some of the situations out there. It's necessary sometimes.

I don't know your situation. You've told me a little about it. If my situation were just a matter of communication, I would be home and not talking to you right now. It is far more than communication. I had to make the decision as to whether or not I was ever going to have a life or not. You have helped me to calm down a little bit and not be so resentful toward her. I really do wish her the best and I hope she does become everything she wants. I just can't stay and live with her anymore.

Opinionated? Tell me what you're thinking. That's what I want. Confused? Who isn't?

I just want to say that you should give your thoughts some time. Don't rush back into a situation that only two months ago you had decided you could no longer accept. You have months to make a permanent decision. I think it's good for both of us to be communicating right now. I think it may help even more for us to meet and talk about all of this too. Talk to you soon. Jon

Was he just saying that he was guilty to get on my good side or did the real Jon feel this way? And he just couldn't stay and live with me anymore because he knew that he needed to learn how to communicate and that I needed someone to talk to. He had said that it was "too much work." So, what did he think all of this emailing was? It was work. It was communication. He did not want to admit that he felt that anyone who needed counseling was "weak," when the truth was that people who would not admit they needed help were the "weak" ones—and he was one of them.

APRIL 27

It's late, or early depending on how you want to look at it. I just had to get out tonight so I went on a road trip. It's 1:50 AM right now. I'm not really tired and I don't know why. It's beautiful outside. The sky is clear, the moon is bright and it's so still and quiet. I just had to do a spin in the driveway and take a deep breath. You know, the head back, arms out spin.

Well, Halley, what do you think will become of our situations anyway? I'm thinking about your question of fate. Maybe nothing matters and we're just tiny little beings traveling through space and our actions mean nothing in the scheme of things. What then?

You asked me about dogs one time. What was that all about? What kind of dog do you like? Do you have one?

I finally took the time to find and figure out how to use the spell check feature on "hotmail" yesterday. It's so easy and I've gone all this time without it. I think if I continue, it's just going to be gibberish so I'm going to go to bed now. Good night, or morning... Jon

I knew he had been on vacation all week. So, he had been on one of his famous "road trips." When we argued, that is how he handled it. By leaving and going for a "ride." Instead of dealing with the issue, he ran away. I

should have known it would come to this. That if he couldn't resolve a simple
difference of opinion how could he ever be capable of making a marriage
work? What did he think life and marriage were? All tits and champagne?
Yes—he lived in a dream world where there were no roots to reality.

APRIL 27

I loved reading about your "night" this morning. It was beautiful last night. Did you know that tonight is the "official" full moon? I love full moons. They are so mysterious. Road trip? So, where did you go or is it a secret? Wish I could have been there! Spinning, huh? I would have loved to see that! :)

Your question is a big one. I have no idea what will become of us, or our situations. I wish that I could predict the future. Maybe I should find someone who can? What if we meet and don't like each other? And, what if we don't find anyone and are alone forever?

And, yes, I think you are on the right track. We are just tiny little beings running around in circles trying to do things that don't really matter in the greater scheme of things. What we need to do is care about each other and love each other and get past all the resentments we have and all the pain that we carry around in our hearts. I think I am getting too deep again! (It's all in Chapter Seven!) I was so caught up in the part that talked about how if we suppress our feelings, divorce can happen. And, how when we are in these cycles our childhood issues come up and we need to feel unconditional love and how when we (females) are in a certain time of our cycles (PMS!), it's just really bad!

Dogs? Oh, I don't know. I don't have one. I just wondered what you thought. Where I live I couldn't have one unless it was an "inside" dog.

It sounds like you probably slept better than I did last night. I stayed up too late working and thinking.

And, I know that I want to meet you next week (so badly!). That's why I'm so confused! With all the talking we have done this week, my mind is spinning! I think if we had lived according to Chapter Seven, we would not even be talking to each other. What do you think or have you read it yet? And, I think it is more about communication than we realize or want to admit. And, it's not anyone's fault but our own if we do not "have a life" as you said in your email. It shouldn't depend on anyone else, you know?

But, I am so glad that I said something that helped you let go of some of your resentment. It gives me a sense of relief that you can't imagine. I seem to have this "thing" inside of me that wants to help people (like the book says!). Maybe, my writing is an expression of that need? Or, just a female thing? Or, maybe it is just because I can so totally relate because we are both in the same sort of situation.

Last week, when I was away, I had the chance to see my cousin who just had a baby last year. It was the first time I had held a baby for years. I can't explain the feelings that I felt and I think that is why I am so confused right now. I had been suppressing my feelings about all of that for so long. And, they just came rushing back from nowhere. And, I don't know what to think. I'm not sure if it was because I was in a situation of not being pressured or what. But, I really just wanted to hold onto that baby and take it home! So, another secret revealed! So, that makes for double confusion!

Now, I'd better get to work! Later! Halley

I wasn't sure, at this point, whether I was a master writer or a master deviant. I wasn't sure what I was going to do about the scheduled "meeting" but I had some ideas. It was the truth. What I said about the baby. I couldn't believe my feelings in regard to the baby and I wanted him to know even if it was coming from someone else that he thought had no connection to me.

APRIL 27

After all our talking the other day about a "certain subject," I was really interested in finding more info. I found this website that has so much information in question form. It is: *www.goaskshelley.columbus. edu.* Click on "sexual health" and you won't believe all the categories and the subjects are in alphabetical order! Let me know what you think! Halley

Was I opening up a can of worms or what?

APRIL 27

Do you ever do spins of your own?

I don't believe that we won't find anyone and that we'll be alone forever. I just don't believe that will happen. I haven't made it to Chapter Seven yet. Last night I was up so late that I didn't do any reading. I think I'm on Chapter Five. I did sleep well last night but it's almost 9:00 AM and I just got up!

So your mind is spinning and you're confused? Try to relax. I have to read between the lines a little bit but I think you feel about the same way as I regarding what you want for the future. So, you really felt something holding onto a baby? There's nothing like it is there? So, what I mean about having a life is having someone I can go on vacations with as a family and do outside activities with like skiing, biking, hiking.....someone to have a life with. With her injury, my "tobeex" can't do that. I can do outside things on my own and have for many years, but it's just not the same as doing it with that "someone."

Just in the last few days you have gotten me to let go of some of my resentment—actually a lot of it. I realize that I'm making a very big decision and how can I possibly hate her when I was with her for so long?

I'm wondering if you have ever been in a management-type situation and had to give someone the axe? Have you, and would you feel guilty if you did that to someone even though it was necessary? Jon

He wanted unconditional love so badly. It was clear in his words about children. He didn't want to have to work at a relationship and with children he thought it would be no work. But, that was a delusion. All relationships were work and he didn't get it. As for having a life, all he had done when we were together was work. In the beginning, we had done a lot of things together but then work became his "god." And, it seemed part of the reason he had left was because of my "injury" and the fact that I couldn't do some of those things he felt he had to be able to do with his "special" someone. So, now he wanted what I had wanted for years but not with me. I reminded him of all the work? I wondered if he was telling the truth about letting go of the resentment... So, he thought running away from fifteen years of marriage was like firing someone. Incredible. To me, it was like the worst kind of death possible.

APRIL 27

Halley: I checked the site out. It looks like there is no test available for males as far as HPV is concerned. It also looks like virtually anyone could have it or multiple strains of it. I just don't know what to think. I know I've never had any symptoms whatsoever of having anything. What am I supposed to do or think? Did you find anything that says otherwise? I'm thinking that I've put way too much thought on this subject and I shouldn't worry about it? What do you think? Tell me the truth. I want your "opinion." Jon

How could he just flip over this subject? This was serious business. This was life. This could be a matter a life or death in some cases. And it was... And, another lie. He had been with someone years before me who had given him a virus and he was straight-out lying to my façade!

APRIL 27

I also found another website www.allofmetech.com. It seems kind of weird but it had some info on the test that you had mentioned. Only thing is it says that the test is not always conclusive! It also says some negative things about "going down," if you know what I mean! So, what are people to do????

I was really freaked out about the "oral sex" answers on the "goaskshelley" website! It's like you can't do anything with anyone (without a "saddle") unless you have been married to them for several years or you are a virgin with a virgin????

Maybe a better place to look for info would be something like a medical website. There must be more information out there. Maybe try that?

And, as for being into information, this is a female thing too!!!! Sorry!!!! :)

Let me know what you find out and think about it! Halley

I really wanted him to think. Jon and I had had a similar discussion the week before he left. And, I had done some research. And, the answers were not pretty. And, it gave him another excuse, in his mind, to leave me. I wanted him to know that it wasn't just me that was concerned about their health. Sex wasn't worth dying for. But, his obsession overrode his rational thought. Was he even capable of rational thought? And, how could he expect me to "go for it" with him when he was threatening me. I had no idea if he had been with anyone else at that point. It was obvious that he cared nothing about anyone but himself and even that was doubtful.

APRIL 27

The site mentioned that HPV can be transferred during child-birth. This sucks. We took a perfectly good subject that we were having a lot of fun talking about and turned it into something serious that's no fun anymore. I don't want to sound negative again about my wife, but she always did this, and I'm sure everyone has done this at one point or another. To find a health related subject and research it on the internet is to scare the crap out of you. I've been with very few women. To find someone who has been with fewer, I think would be impossible. Does this make you want to stay with your husband so as to be safe?

Bottom line: At best, it looks like it's inconclusive for me to be tested. Another question. I knew I was taking a chance telling you about this but I am not going to be untruthful with you about anything. The next guy, who knows? Does this make you not even want to meet me? That last question is very important to me and I want you to consider everything that I'm saying before you answer it. AND, I want you to answer it. This question is important to me because it will tell me something about your ability to weigh facts and come up with a logical, rational thought. Most importantly, it will tell me how timid you are to the world you live in and the limits you will go to be safe. This is the area that my wife has the most difficulty with and why I am talking to you right now and not her. Out of all the things that any woman could have, this is one that I fear—limitations.

Facts: I have never had any symptoms of anything. I've had one encounter (one time) with another woman before my wife in high school. I've had a month with another woman a little while ago who was tested about two years ago for all STD's and found to have nothing and she has not slept around.

My question again: Does this make you not even want to meet me? The question I ask is if you want to meet me, not have unprotected sex with me.

I'm sorry, but when I find the woman I'm going to spend the rest of my life with I'll be damned if I'm going to use dental dams or condoms cut down the middle to have oral sex. I'll be more careful from now on and maybe have protected sex until I'm married again or close to it. But I also think that I'm just fine. I think that condoms should be used with new sexual partners, which I have already done.

I'm not going to be afraid to do anything with that someone who I will spend the rest of my life with.

This is exactly what I meant about living. Come on! Give it to me—your opinion, I mean. :) Take until Friday to answer if you need to. Jon

All I could think about was the "Belly Ring Girl" and maybe what he could have contracted from her....He had slept with her for over a month's time and at least the oral sex had been unprotected and I knew from my information that it was possible to get "things" doing this. How could he be so naïve as to think that she hadn't slept around? He was so willing to believe her over his own wife. There was definitely an addiction some-where in the mix. His statement about being more careful from now on was a dead giveaway. He had had unprotected sex with Ashley in some form and it scared me. Didn't he know that it took several years sometimes to know if someone was infected? It sounded like he had a death wish and that all he cared about was satisfying his physical urges. Anyone other than Halley would never have continued talking to him long before this message. He was emailing me like crazy and in desperation because he couldn't get anyone else to feed his sexual mindset. And, lying again about never having anything!

APRIL 27

I just can't keep up. I'll start first by replying to your email of this morning and then I'll get to your really "serious" one of this afternoon!

You said you like to spin around. I actually tried this the other day and got kind of dizzy! Usually I stretch my shoulders back and stretch my arms out to the sides. Try it. It feels really good!

So I take it your road trip of last night is a secret destination???

But, when you talk about having someone to do something with it doesn't sound to me from all our "talking" that there was much time to do anything but work?

So, do you look at marriage as a "corporate partnership?" Is that what you meant by your description of giving someone the axe? And, yes, I would not want to be in a position of doing this unless I could do it in a way that made the other person feel okay in some way. I like being in a position of "lone" authority. I essentially report to someone but have free reign to do my job. I guess you could say that we are both doing this in our personal lives, though! I hadn't thought about it that way. That must be why I am having such a hard time with it!

So, now for the serious email. I read something about that childbirth thing and it didn't sound so serious. It sounded like the woman gets tested before she actually has the baby and if the virus is present, they can take the baby by Cesarean and it also said that symptoms can be treated? Or did you see that part? Also, I read that you can have HPV and have no symptoms at all and never show any. Who knows if I have it? Just because I have never shown any symptoms doesn't mean I don't have anything either? Right? And, there are so many types of it, how can you ever know? And, anyone who has been with more than one person must have something, right? What about your sister and your brother-in-law? Assuming they have been with more than one person, which you said they have, what might they have that they don't know about? Since you seem so close to them, have you asked them if they have ever been tested for anything? Maybe that would help for you to know what to do (and for me too)! That's what is so hard! No one really knows anything! And, you have to be really careful how you take all the information you read and I agree, it is enough to scare you into keeping your pants on, instead of off!!!!

And, no, this is something that will not be the deciding factor and has not been the deciding factor for me in my situation but I do intend to be careful to a point, like you said.

This is probably going to be a lot harder for her than for you. Just like it is harder for me than it will probably be for my husband.

Since we are being so open and honest, I still wonder about the "ex-girlfriend." How do you know she didn't sleep around. If she was so willing to be so intimate with you in such a short amount of time, what can anyone think? Oh God, did it to myself again! And, listen to me the way I have been talking to you about all of the things we have talked about and our meeting and everything else!!!!

And, this does not make me not want to meet you! But, I am concerned about her and if she told you the truth or not. But, that is my problem to deal with.

And, I totally agree with you about the "dental dam" thing. It doesn't sound like fun!

So, it sounds to me like this was a BIG issue (oral sex) for you in your decision to leave your wife. Or, am I just taking it the wrong way? You know, it is not for everyone and it's usually something that would come later when you are seriously involved with someone you truly care about and after getting tested.

Now, let's take this and make it "better!" Last night I couldn't help myself but look up "tools" with batteries. And, I found one that looked REALLY good! I think I might order it! How's that sound for a "first!" It's called "The Ultima." It really turned me on! If you go to a search engine and type it in, a list of places will come up. Look at it and tell me what you think!!!! I'd really like your opinion!!!!

I just want to thank you for being so honest with me and I understand completely where you are coming from. Just tell me, why does everything have to be so complicated!!!! Halley

He just kept skipping over the truth about everything. It was all work and no play and he knew it. He just wanted to blame everything on me so he could forget about the guilt he was hiding inside. I also wanted to make sure he knew that the tests the "ex-girlfriend" had supposedly had were a load of crap. Even though nothing showed up, she could still be a carrier. I wondered how he felt after reading my email. I wondered that, perhaps, he looked his penis over every night after he took a shower after reading this! Actually, I had actually witnessed him doing this many times and thought it hilarious! And, I was admitting that I hadn't known everything. Boy, was I pushing it with the question that he should ask his family what they had! I was sure they had all the strains of HPV combined amongst them! I had to also admit to myself that I would probably never find someone so "clean" as Jon had been when we had been first together. What was the chance of that? And, I remembered him telling me that he had been with two girls—one who had been raped by her father and one who had slept with most of the high school and who was at our wedding as his brother's girlfriend! Who knew which one gave him the virus. He was lying again. There was also another who he had performed oral sex on—he had told me. Perhaps, he couldn't add? I really was concerned for him in regard to his relationship with the "Belly Ring Girl." If she was willing to sleep with him after only one week, give me a break! She had slept around. And, then to get the conversation off this, mention of the tools....... I knew I would lose him if I didn't get off the subject of protection.

fifteen

SPINNING

APRIL 27

Halley: The spinning around with your head back does make me a little dizzy too, but it just feels so free. :) I'll give your way a try.

My road trip last night was down your way, that's why I didn't want to tell you. I don't want you to think I'm a stalker or something. I just needed a ride and thought I would go that way.

There was a lot of work over the years, but there was always time for a walk, day skiing, or a hike. But, it wasn't possible anymore.

Marriage is a financial partnership, but it's also much more than that. Giving the axe? I do think that's why you're having a hard time with the guilt. No one wants to hurt others but for some their personality is much stronger in this regard. Or you could turn it around—some people don't like the idea of "anyone" thinking ill thoughts of them.

She was afraid of conceiving because she might die, the child might die or any other complication. The child might not be healthy or it could be sick...... She was afraid to pass a truck on the interstate because it might jackknife while we were beside it. She was afraid that I would bring germs home from school and make her sick. She was afraid to fly in my plane and only did so one time with me. The list goes on and on. What it essentially did was make it impossible to live. So the oral sex thing wasn't a big issue with me leaving home. It was the whole encompassing refusal to live that was.

I'm so happy with your answer to my difficult question. You think and you refuse to stop living. That's a huge thing to me! I'm sorry but I just couldn't ask my sister or her husband if they have anything.

The thing with Ashley was in many ways new to her too. She hadn't been with anyone for over a year. During that time she changed how she thought about sex and said that she would not waste any time the next time around in regard to being open about asking them what they liked and telling them what she liked. I really think that is where I'm getting some of my openness from. She just told it like she saw it and, in many ways, that was a very good thing. She was totally open about everything and I believe her. I know that she didn't sleep around. As far as you and I and how we haven't met yet and sex, I think that I know you better than I knew Ashley the first time we did it. That doesn't mean anything more than what I just said, okay? :)

The Ultima. I'll have to look that up. WHAT A WOMAN! Hehehe Why does everything have to be so complicated? I don't know. Maybe it happens when we think too much. Jon

He was so obsessed with me that he had driven to where he thought I lived. I was impressed with my ability and, at the same time, felt sorry for him. And, he was a stalker of sorts. He had stalked me like crazy when we were dating. He made it impossible for me to spend any time with friends. And, here I was stalking him on-line...

We did walk together, talk together, ski together and hike together. It was only after my injury that this stopped. I had to think back to before Jon and how active I had been. Maybe it was all of the work that had caused my injury to last so long.... Maybe I felt boxed in and "crippled" by the way he wanted us to live? It wasn't possible for me to do these things because, physically, I couldn't do them and I didn't see him trying to help me—all I did was work to make his life better while ignoring trying to find a solution to my own problems.

As for me being afraid that the child would not be healthy, that was the biggest load of crap I had read yet. I drilled him on this question and he would not answer the month before he left. He finally told me that he could not handle it if something were wrong with the child, so how was I to agree with having a child—when he was threatening me—knowing that if something went wrong I would be blamed fully for it and he would leave me as he had done anyway. Maybe the reason I was anxious when I was riding with him be it in a plane or a car was because he was so erratic in his behavior and I could sense so much anxiety and tension. Of course, in his eyes, it was all on me and continued to be. I couldn't win in his eyes no matter what. The truth was that I had not ever been afraid to drive at mach speeds or fly. It was only when I was with him. After too many near misses, wouldn't anyone be afraid?

I was so hurt by his statements, especially about my refusal to live. He had been the one who had refused to live for so many years. All he would do was work. I wanted to go on vacations and do things together and have children and he refused it all based on building a perfect haven for children and having a certain amount of money in the bank. He continued to make excuses so he could blame me. And, I was the one who was going to have to live with his mistakes and his refusal to live for the rest of my life.

And there was the answer to my question. He was incapable of intimate communication. He didn't even have the balls to ask people he had been living with for months a serious question that might have an affect on his life forever. What was so wrong with asking a question if you were truly close to them. But the truth was, he wasn't. And, he didn't know how to communicate. The only form of communication he was capable of was what he had with Halley—something shallow and meaningless where he could place blame and feel like a man doing it. It was as if he thought he was impressing Halley with his attitude and all I felt was anger and disbelief at the same time.

It sounded to me like I was right. Ashley was a very easy target and one with very limited brain function. Openness, huh? She was vulgar, crass and crude in my opinion and I hadn't even met her. I wondered what would happen if I ever did come face to face with her?

April 27

I just took a look at that "bad boy" you're thinking of getting. Quite a unique looking tool. You think it'll do the job? hehehehe Jon

I couldn't believe myself. He was bringing out a side of myself that I didn't know existed. For me to even be looking at vibrators. I was horrified at myself. But, I wanted to "live" in some way because of everything he kept saying. And, I was intrigued by my own openness to something new.

April 27

So, you drove down my way??? So, do you like it down here?

Well, since you brought it up I have to say something! It sounds as though your wife has some anxiety. Was she like this when you met her? Or, maybe it is something that she came to have over the years while you were together? Everyone has some level of anxiety in life and I wonder what has caused you to think that it is only her problem? And, have you thought about what you might have said or done that might have made it worse?

And, sorry, to ask you if you asked your family if they had "anything!!!!!" It just seems logical, doesn't it? As for living, people live in different ways and that doesn't make them better or worse, you know? It's really wrong to judge others and the way they live. I hope this makes sense without offending you.

So, I was just wondering if you would even answer this question. How many dates did you go on with Ashley before it got "serious" if you know what I mean????? Just wondering as I have been out of circulation for a "while." Which brings me to another question! How long was it before you and your wife "did it" when you were dating? For me, it was when I knew things were "really" serious. All this talk makes me "hard!" Wish I had that "Ultima" right now!!!! (Or, better, you!) And, you think it's a "bad boy!!!!" I thought it was very mild compared to everything else???? (Or, did you go into the same website that I did????) Later. Halley

I knew that my email time was at a premium because the game was almost over. I had to get answers to questions that I had in my mind and I wasn't going to be timid about it. And, I was going to make him think about the things he was saying to me, Hunter.

APRIL 27

White Haven is very nice. Lot's of open space.

Yes, she has anxiety. I never noticed before when we were dating. I don't know how to respond to your statements. I don't know if I should take any blame for it.

I don't mind you asking me to ask my family. It's a good idea. I just couldn't do it. Your words in regards to people living in different ways—I said almost the exact words to my tobeex in my email to her. There is nothing wrong with her wishing to live the way she wants to. I just cannot live that way too.

Ashley and I went out for only a week, but we were seeing each other every night and even for one day.

My wife and I went out for over three months before we "did it." It was around the same time that I asked her to marry me. Within a year from the time we met, we were married.

So, you're "hard" right now? I wish you had me right now too.

Yeah, you're right, it does look kind of mild. I bet that curve adds a lot to it though. How could any tool that is used for such a purpose not be a "bad boy?" What about your sister? Are you going to show it to her or are you going to keep it a secret? Hehehehe I didn't see the others. I guess I will have to go back into the site and take a look. So, is this something that you would never have considered a couple of months ago? Jon

I was meeting with a counselor and all that came out of that was me questioning over and over why he had left. As for any anxiety I had, it was always when he was around. He gave off this feeling of angst and tension and a lack of confidence I could not explain. Fifteen years with him was enough to kill anyone—even someone with as strong a will as I had! And, his reference to the way he wanted to live just made me convulse with disgust. So, going out and emailing strangers was what he wanted in life, as well as sleeping with someone after one week? He wanted casual sex and sexual innuendo. Unbelievable. A whole week before they had sex! Wow! I couldn't believe my eyes. And, we were engaged to be married and had been going out for almost five months before we were intimate and it was on his birthday AND he couldn't get it up because he was so nervous! He was only right about when we got married. Too soon. That was for sure. It was a definite that I would never have considered a "tool" before this email relationship—that was for sure.

APRIL 27

I really hate having to respond to your comments but I really feel strongly about some of the subjects that have come up and I hope you don't mind! :)

You know I really don't want to offend you, but anxiety is not a sickness. Like I said, the majority of people out there suffer from some level. It's just that some people have a much harder time dealing with things, but that doesn't make them crazy. I'm getting the feeling like you are trying to alleviate some of the blame or pain of this whole situation by making her out to be worse than she really is. Just my opinion. I really don't want to offend you. I think you might have to acknowledge that this might be harder for her than you as you made the decision to leave. That has to have made whatever anxiety she had before even worse. Hopefully, your wife will get to a place where it is much better when she starts accepting all of this. Do you think she has? I know that me being the one making the decision has made it harder on my husband. It has been hard on both of us, but especially on him. I don't think he has really begun to accept it yet. Sorry to be so serious, but I think it's important to acknowledge our actions even if we feel we made the right decision.

So, the "ex-girlfriend" definitely wasn't shy about what she wanted! And, you weren't either! One week! At least, I can say that we have "talked" and gotten to know each other for almost a month and I feel good about that and I hope that you do.

So, tell me. You know my body type and height and hair and eye color from my profile. Compare me to the two "ex's." Tell me where I fit in! Were they short or tall or small or big???? Give it to me, baby! How do I compare at least in the physical?

And the answer to your question—it is something I would not have considered doing two months ago but a girl has to do what she has to do! All your talk of "firsts" has been very "motivating" to me! I can't believe I ordered it! And, no! I am not telling anyone about it but you! But, I don't know. My sister might get a good laugh out of it! I can't wait to get it to see what it's like! It says that it is 1" in diameter but I'm so tight right now I wonder if I'll even be able to use it until after I've had the REAL thing!!!! If I get it before Friday, I will bring it with me!!!! Hehehehehehe

To bed! Good night! Dream of me! Halley

All I could think of was how I knew he had been hospitalized before I met him for anxiety and panic attacks. And, he had condemned me for having anxiety—talk about calling the kettle blacker than night! I wanted to make sure that he knew that I knew he was being a jerk. And, I wanted to know how he would describe us all. I wanted to know how he would describe me in the physical sense. I had heard enough of Jon's descriptions of me in every other sense and I wanted more. And, the sexual innuendo was meant to keep him off track—to keep him from being suspicious of my intent. I could say whatever I wanted to as long as in the end I turned the conversation to sex. At the same time, all I could think of was how the two of us had been spending a great deal of time sitting in front of computers communicating with one another most of the day! It was the most communication I had ever had with him and it was a farce—he didn't know it was me. Only I knew.

I felt so much anger at this point at myself, at him, at everything and how I never knew any part of the real me until now. I had been living in a box that had been created by other's opinions of me that was sealed with fear. I knew that I was going to have to face all of my fears somehow even in the midst of all of the turmoil I was having to deal with. I was most afraid of being a failure and my anxiety was based in this. Because of this fear, it was evident from everything he had spoken of—I had lost my husband—the only thing that had meant anything to me. I didn't know how to get out of the box and he hadn't known how to help me because he didn't know how to help himself—he just wasn't capable. Why did such a tragedy have to happen for things to change? Why couldn't he have held his hand out to me instead of running out the door? Why? At this point, I was starting to see that, maybe, he had done me a favor by walking out on me.

APRIL 28

Halley: I just tried to send you an email with "What, no good night?" in the subject line. Just as I was sending it, I got booted off-line. When I came back, there you were with "Good Night."

The email I lost explained what I'm thinking about, as well as anything I have said to date. I said something about the intelligence of my wife. She is very intelligent and somehow I think it makes things worse for her. This afternoon I've come the closest I ever have to fully understanding how she thinks. I don't have it figured out yet, though. Yes, she has anxiety, but it's almost like there is something else underlying it that causes it. I think if she could control it and get power from it, she could do wonderful things and I hope she does. She will have to figure it out and understand it first. I feel very bad about the pain that I must be causing her and I'm sure it's worse than my own. I think she is accepting it now because she has a fighting spirit where I'm concerned and I suppose that's a good thing. Her appraisal on the house came in yesterday and it's a little higher than my own.

I feel very good about talking to you as long as we have. It's been very nice. I feel like I know you so well and we have never met. It's something I have never done before.

To compare you to the two ex's!

Well, my first "ex" is about 5'3" and 105 lbs. She has what I would say is a very well-proportioned, attractive body. Light brown hair, shoulder length. She has almost transparent skin, very light and her eyes are sort of hazel and are very big and round. I can't really put a color on them and that's strange? She is very petite and almost childlike in size.

The second "ex" is 5'8" and weighs 160lbs. Without knowing what she actually looked like, I would say that's overweight but she really wasn't. She liked to wear shoes that have a 2" heel which made her almost as tall as me. She had short little legs and a long body. Riding in a vehicle, her head stuck up higher than my own which was a little weird for me. I'm not used to that. She is very attractive and I almost got in a fight in a bar because this guy kept hitting on her right in front of me. She said it happens all the time. Compared to her, she is BIG. She is very strong, has black hair almost to her elbows, is half-Japanese with big, brown Asian eyes. She has very dark and tough skin.

So, I would think that in some ways you fall between them and in others you're left or right of them. Like I said before, your hair color and eyes are a totally new experience for me. I have never been out to dinner or done anything with a blonde or blue-eyed woman before. :) Are you a true blonde? How light is your hair? I don't know how much you weigh, so I don't know where you fit in there. Can you tell me?

I'm glad if I have had an affect on your creativity. Is it affect or effect? Anyway, you actually ordered it! I'm proud of you! Your giving me a) and that's not a smile. Oh, I hope you get it before Friday!

I will definitely be dreaming of you.....Jon

So Jon thought I was intelligent and mental, huh? And, he thought he had me "figured" out, almost. What an idiot! I still wondered if he meant any of the nice things he said such as feeling bad for the pain he was causing me. I just couldn't believe anything he was saying because, of course, he was trying to impress my façade. Fighting spirit? He didn't know the half of it. More like vengeful spirit! So he felt like he knew me so well—well, I was his wife after all! But, then he hadn't known me, his wife, when we were together. He was getting to know me without knowing it was me. His comments about how he thought me capable of wonderful things made me cry even though I wondered afterwards if there was any truth or sincerity in his words. I just couldn't trust anything he said. Maybe he was just using these comments to get on Halley's good "side."

His comparison of me versus the "Belly Ring Girl" was entertaining to say the least. Tinkerbell and the Amazon Woman. That was what it seemed to me. He had spent time with someone who was the complete opposite of me in every way. Sounded like the only thing the Amazon had going for her were her supposed looks and how she liked to brag about them. Jon had been used to someone who had never had the confidence to think she even looked good or at least good enough and here he had dated someone who bragged about it. And, boy, he didn't even know the effect he was having on my creativity! Dreaming of me, huh? Yeah, right. He was dreaming of getting into my pants.

APRIL 28

Halley: Well, I did dream of you last night. No, not sexually. Actually I didn't sleep very well. I was in and out for half the night. I guess you were in my mind.

I just wanted to comment further on where you fit in compared to the two "ex's." I don't know about the physical. I don't really know what you look like. It's your mind that I like so much. You're funny, you flirt, and you can be serious when you need to be, you care deeply about others feelings and you're not afraid to ask the important but difficult questions. You certainly know how to keep a secret. I'm guessing that you are very professional on the job and you work very hard. I know that you're intelligent. I find something very attractive about you in that I'm thinking about what you must be like on the job and then how you can be and how you talk with me. I like the idea of a woman who saves something special just for me. :) It has given me the feeling of intimacy with you even though we haven't met and I like that very much—something that no one else gets to see. I like your mind and I think that's a very good place to start, don't you? Have a nice Sunday. Jon

He just couldn't get enough of me. I was so flattered by his comments and I had to believe he meant them. He seemed so sincere.... But how was I to really know. What he was admitting, if he was sincere, was that he liked and loved his wife. Hunter. It had taken all this for me to be me. I was pretending to be someone else but in the process, the real me had emerged. And he liked it. And, I liked it. But if he knew I was the person he had left behind, he would never believe it and would resent me into infinity. I wondered what would have happened if I had emailed him like this when were still together. It would have worked. He would have gotten to know me, I would have gotten to know me and maybe this tragedy would never have happened. Both of us seemed only to be able to communicate effectively through writing! But, he had such a preconceived notion of his wife (me) that, at this point, how could it work? If he did find out it was me, why wouldn't he want to find out if I was really the person I had been in the emails? Would pride keep him from discovering the real me?

APRIL 28

So, you think you might have your "tobeex" "figured out?" How do you do this because I would really like to know so I can apply it my situation! And, do you think you ever will really figure her out? This sounds really interesting. I guess I have a "special" interest in all of this because of the psych classes I took in college (like I said before!). So, there is something that causes her anxiety. Maybe something from her childhood? That was always a subject that came up in my classes. That things that happen to you in your childhood can have negative (and positive) effects on your life. It is just incredible how the mind works! Isn't it? If we could just figure out what those things are and erase them from our minds (or at least deal with them), we would be "free" from any dysfunctional behavior that exists within us. You know? I think you might be onto something.

I would really like to have a conversation with my husband like some of the "deep" conversations we have had at some point. I don't know if it would have to wait until after everything is over or if it could happen before or I don't know if it would be too difficult and maybe it would be years before it could happen. Do you think you would like to do this at any point or do you think it is pointless?

So, a fighting spirit, huh? Uh oh! But maybe that is what will pull her out of all of this, you never know.

You must be happy with the appraisal since it didn't come in too much higher than the first? Do you think you will have to get a third appraisal? We haven't even gotten to that point yet. And, they are so expensive when all you get is a package of papers that detail a house and give no value to the "home" that existed.

I loved your comparison of the "ex's!" I have to say that ex #2 sounds like an Amazon, as you described her before! And, I think I might be afraid of her! So, it seems like there is no specific type that you go for? That is really different! Most people tend to go for specific types. I suppose it's good that you feel that way. And, yes, I definitely fall between them. And, yes, I am a "true blonde!" And, my weight! I am about 110.

My husband has dark hair and a medium body type so I guess you could say I go in a specific "direction!" But, you definitely don't look the same. You are much more "intriguing!"

And, yes, my "creativity" is so "tight" right now I can hardly "stand!" And, it has been through talking to you!!!!! It's so funny and great how people can have such an affect on each other (as long as it is good!).

So, tell me, are you saying positive things now just so I won't think you are "mean??????"hehehehe Are you trying to "butter me up?" Tell me the truth!!!!!

Now for my responses to your email of this morning! I woke up this morning and felt cold. Then, I realized that I was only half covered with the blankets! The bed was a complete mess! I think I dreamt but can't remember what about? Maybe, you? And, maybe ordering that "Ultima" was really on my mind!

I absolutely love your appraisal of me! And, you know, it is more important to know someone's mind than anything else. This experience has made it so apparent to me! It has also made me realize how sad it is that this kind of communication did not exist for either one of us before. It just scares me a little to think about how devoted we are to our work. What if our work were to get in the way? It did for me before and you said that it did in your case. How do people keep it from causing a problem and a breakdown in communication? We or anyone can say that they won't let it be a problem, but what if it does?

See! I'm off to go work, again! So, I've got to go for now! I will take care of the reservation this week unless you think we should get separate rooms???? Oh God, I'm "throbbing" again! I can't imagine what the people I work with would think if they knew about my "secret" writings!!!! I don't want to know! Halley

How I was able to keep up the banter I didn't have a clue. My will was driving me forward. I was running out of adrenalin. Every time I checked my email account and found a new message, my heart raced. I loved questioning him and getting him to spill his thoughts out to me. I had never had this opportunity before and it wasn't going to last for much longer so I needed the river to flood as fast as possible.

APRIL 28

It might be possible to have a "deep" conversation with her. I think the timing would depend on the individual case. I don't think that I want to do it though. If I can come up with anything that may help her in regard to her mind or explain the situation to her so she understands, sure I'll tell her, but otherwise I don't have the desire to communicate deeply with her.

She might want to get a third appraisal. I hope not. Mine came in lower than hers did, but the difference isn't really that much when the two are averaged and then divided by two.

I told the second "ex" that she was an Amazon woman and she really didn't get it. She kind of took it as an insult and I said, "No that's not what I mean." I meant it in a good way. No specific type? I've thought about this and I guess that I just love all women. Don't get me wrong, I only need one, but there are special qualities in all types that I appreciate in different ways.

110 lbs, 5' 6" blonde with blue eyes. Oooohhhh, you must be such a honey! I just can't wait to meet you. I'm getting stiff again.

Am I saying positive things to, well, get into your pants? You have had an affect on my attitude towards my "tobeex." I am no longer as hostile as I was. I don't think that I'm mean regardless of anything. I know that it bothers you to think that I have ill thoughts towards her. I'll just say it... Yes, I want to make you happy and I want to make love to you so badly. I just can't wait to see you, to talk to you, to watch you walk across a room and so many other things. Is it a subconscious thing as to me not being so upset about Hunter just to please you? I really don't know. I think I have taken the words you have said and considered them logically and made up my own mind. Does it matter? I'm not sure of that either. Women have been getting men to do things they want for thousands of years, haven't they? If good effects come of it, it's okay isn't it?

I work hard, but I will never devote my life to it as I did in the past. It's just too important to live.

Separate rooms! Ooooohhh nooooo! Like I said a long time ago, even if nothing happens I want to hear you sleep, hear you move under your covers and it would be nice to see you in the morning. I'd like to see you with a towel on your head walking around the room and I would like to talk to you through most of the night as we lay there. If it's in separate beds, that's okay too, but please no separate rooms. Jon

He didn't want to talk to me, his wife, deeply because he didn't have the balls. It was as simple as that. He couldn't face the guilt of the pain he had caused me. He couldn't face his feelings because he didn't know what they really were... What a red flag—the comment about loving all women. He had said that for quite a while and I wondered about it but because we were so busy, it just went over my head. I should have known there was a problem when it got so he would stare every time the Britney Spears commercial would come on. It was to a point of obsession with him. So, he was admitting that he didn't know if he was saying nice things just to get on my good side. He didn't even know or did he....

And the towel-on-the-head syndrome. I always had done this. Was it because of me or someone else that he had such an obsession with this? I remembered one night we had spent in Maine and all that was left were bath towels so I had to use a full-size towel on my head. It piled up on my head about two feet and he couldn't stop laughing. Why did I have to keep remembering the happy moments in the midst of all the hurt. I couldn't help wondering how he could think that any girl in her right mind would get a room with someone she had only communicated with via email! He was delusional! And, it was so easy to keep him going. Was it a talent I had not been aware of that I had?

APRIL 28

I had to really think about the "deep communication" thing again. I don't think I could do it right now. I would be too afraid. Afraid because it is too soon. Does this make sense? You had said something before about waiting years before this could happen and maybe you are right. But, on the other hand, I agree with you that if it was something that would help them it would be a good idea to do it now, rather than later.

Are you sure you need only ONE woman?????? It sounds like you'd like more than that! Hehehe

I'm glad I have had a positive effect on you. You have definitely had a positive effect on me and have helped me to understand things so much more clearly. And, I hope that you have "listened" to my comments and made up your own mind about things because you chose to do so for yourself. So, you think that women can get men to do anything and have been doing it for thousands of years??????? Yeah! I think you may be right! And, if good things happen because of it, there is nothing better!!!!!!!! You ARE a woman-lover, aren't you??? Hehehehe

You know, I think that all four of us are going to live completely differently than we ever thought we could or would, don't you? I find myself thinking so differently than I ever have. My basic values are the same; it's just that I am thinking even more openly than I ever thought I would. And, talking to you has even made me think on an even higher level. I just want you to know that.

And, okay! One room with two beds just in case you roll around all night! Do you want to be in the Main Lodge or in the Ice House building across the road? I have only seen the Main Lodge building on the website and you actually went there so you need to tell me where I should make the reservation.

So, do you move around when you sleep? I never thought to ask that! So, what's the deal with the towel on the head? You had mentioned that before! Is it a turn-on for you??? Tell me! Later! Halley

It was true. He was getting me to think on a different level. But much lower. And I hoped that my life would not be too difficult to deal with after losing him, financially or otherwise. I was really concerned about it and it was on my mind a great deal. I hadn't been able to find any work and I was living off the money from one of the accounts. It was scary. I was hoping to get some maintenance support when we had our temporary hearing, but there were no guarantees. I was also so afraid that I would get kicked out of my home. But, how could they make me leave when I had no employment and no place to go? When I thought about this, I got angry thinking how he was spending all of his free time conversing with a stranger and spending money on gifts, dinners and hotel rooms while I was struggling to figure out what I was going to do with the rest of my life—as well as how I was going to pay for food.

APRIL 28

Halley: I can only imagine having more than one woman! Have you ever thought about having more than one man? Hehehe I would try my "hardest" to make sure they all were satisfied! hehehehe

I'm glad that I've had a positive effect on you. I think we will live completely different lives than in the past too. That's one of the things that makes me feel so good. Dreams and things that I had forgotten or considered impossible are now possible again. It's not just that, it's everything else about life. I'm discovering so many things that I never knew about myself and others. I'm becoming a better and wiser person.

Where to stay? The Main Lodge is huge! It might be four stories high. There are lots of halls, stairs and an elevator. There are two stories across the street in the Ice House. It all looks new. I really don't know which side we should be on. It might be easier in the Ice

House because you can park right in front of each unit. I don't know where you park if you have a room in the main building. Maybe there is parking behind? Wherever you would like to be is okay with me.

Whichever side we pick for this week, we could always stay in the opposite side next weekend. :) Hehehe

No, I don't think I move around in my sleep. I've been known to snore just a little, but if you nudge me I'll stop. :) Hehehe

I think a woman just looks so beautiful in two towels, one around them and another on their head. I just don't know what it is. Hehehe   It's not really a turn on thing—it's like an admiring thing. Like I said, I love women. :)   Jon

He was definitely obsessed with women in general. Dreams and things that he had forgotten? Had he not told me about these? Because every dream I knew about happened for him. I plucked them out of the air and planted them for him. Better and wiser? I really wondered about that. Worse and more stupid, maybe? I couldn't believe the lies. All he did was move around in his sleep. The entire bed would shake and his legs would jump and twitch. Sleeping with him was like sleeping with a bucking bronco! And as for the snoring! I would stay up late at night reading or writing and would have to yell several times to get him to roll over. The next morning he wouldn't remember anything. Were all the girls out there in for a treat!

APRIL 28

Do you know where to find the Norac Nordic Lodge in Salem? I'm going to do some reading. :) Good night....Jon

I couldn't believe I didn't get an email telling me he had to go to the bathroom! It was as though he wanted me to know his every move to feel the connection.

APRIL 29

Sorry I missed our good night! I fell asleep in front of the TV!!! And, no, I am a "one man at a time" girl!

So, tell me, what are the dreams and things that you had forgotten until now? I guess one of mine is that I'd really like to write a book but never thought it would be what I am considering!!!!! (You know, the one that includes the "solo!") Never would have thought that before!

I think we should stay in the Main Lodge. Let's go for it! And, yes, they told me to turn left onto a paved road after the Snowflake Resort and follow the signs. It sounds like it is some sort of mountain road.

The opposite side next weekend?????? "Jeez!" This could get expensive! And, I was told by my lawyer that at some point you have to produce all your statements etc. What if you had a charge on them (like a motel or restaurant!) that they questioned!!!! That's why I am using my sister's card!

So, how much do you snore, really??

Yeah, it's so great wearing towels! You know, a man in a towel isn't a bad thing either! This "I love women" thing is making me wonder about you!!!!!!!?????

So, you are still reading the book! I thought you might have given up on it! Got to go for now! Halley

I was running out of conversation. There were so many emails every day. But, I knew I still had questions.

APRIL 29

Jon: I just had the strangest and wild thought and had to do a quick email to ask you if you have ever felt the same!

Have you ever felt "chemistry" for someone you worked with? A few years ago, I worked with someone who I had the strongest "chemistry" for. I did not really acknowledge it because we were both married and I had no idea if he felt the same "wild feeling." Every time he would get next to me, I felt this inner "pull" that I cannot even describe! Do you think it is possible to have physical chemistry with someone else other than who you "think" you are supposed to be with or who you are married to????????????

And, I wonder what would have happened if I had told him!!!!!!!!!!!!!!!

I know you could compare it to what we have, but ours is an "emotional chemistry." But, on Friday, we may find it is also a "physical chemistry!!!!!!!!!" So, what do you think? Halley

I remembered feeling chemistry for a man I worked with several years before but nothing would ever have happened. I knew the boundaries. Jon didn't. I wondered if I had felt this kind of chemistry for Jon or had it been that he had so overwhelmed me with his constant and needy presence and his demanding nature that it was something else? I know that I hadn't cared about getting married. I had just wanted to have someone to be with and do things with. And, I wanted someone to care about me and even love me. But I know that I had had no immediate thoughts of marriage. I was sure of that. Was I the one who had made the mistake of going along with what he wanted because he carried himself off as being such a caring person? I remember not liking the limitations that I thought marriage imposed. I wanted to be free and to be loved at the same time. So, how had I ended up here? I had hated the limitations that had been imposed on me soon after marriage in the form of so many responsibilities—the apartment buildings, the drudgery of keeping an apartment like the laundry and the dishes, the constant work that Jon was always tied up with…… He dragged me into his box with allure—I could not resist whatever he wanted. Everything became for him and about him with nothing for me or about me. Maybe, I had made a mistake—one that ended up costing me over fifteen precious years of my life. Had my prison been of my own making?

I knew I had to try to get information about the real reason I suspected he left me and my revelation of an attraction to another man was a way that it could be approached. This was the only way I would know the truth and I had him opened up like a dead frog and it was time to go for the guts.

APRIL 29

Halley: So you just had this strange and wild feeling for someone at work or you had it a few years ago? Lucky guy. Yes, I have to admit that I had strong feelings for someone I worked with before. I wouldn't really call them wild though.

I think that we can possibly have a physical chemistry. I'm looking forward to meeting you just for the moment when we see each other for the first time. I just don't know what to expect at all. What will it feel like? It's a totally new experience for me. Will it be awkward or will it be very easy? I don't know. I try not to be too optimistic but we seem to be able to communicate so easily, don't you agree? It seems that the work environment adds a little something to the situation. It's a forbidden thing. Maybe that heightens the atmosphere a little.

Can you answer a question for me? Why have you not wanted to meet over a cup of coffee in, say, Bradford or somewhere, just to meet? Isn't that far enough away from your home? Can you tell me the reasons why you don't want to do that? I'm just curious. Jon

So he was admitting his attraction to Kristan. I needed more and I was going to get it out of him, somehow.

APRIL 29

Halley: Dreams and things I had forgotten. I am still realizing just how long I have wanted a different life. It's been many years and I simply had given up hope of having someone to do things with and to raise a family with. There are just so many little things that everyone just takes for granted that I am amazed by. The ability to just hop in a car at the last minute and do something, the ability to go skiing with someone, to go hiking, even just to go for a walk. All these things just make me so happy.

Yes, it is on a mountain road and go slow. There are at least two extremely sharp corners that really creep up on you in a hurry.

Producing all your statements. Yes, I just did that and my charge to "Hearts.com" was on it. I didn't have any charges other than that though. I have plenty of restaurant charges on them. You must mean restaurant charges in Salem and then your husband would have a clue as to where you spent some time? I've been driving and charging gas and things in every direction, so I don't think it looks like anything other than checking things out and having some fun.

Most of the time I don't snore at all. Sometimes if I have a cold or I've had dairy products or beer late at night I may snore a little, but it stops in a short while.

I'm a guy, how can I possibly not love women? When I look at a woman, almost all the time my mind is just admiring and not thinking, "Let me jump your bones."

I finished Chapter Five in the book last night. I'm going to finish it, but I am having difficulty in retention of the material. Chapter Five was the best so far I thought. I have so many questions for you. Jon

If he wanted a "life" as he termed it, why hadn't he spoken up or stopped working all the time? I had constantly pleaded with him that there was too much work and he ignored me. I was so sick of being blamed for him not having the "life" he was saying he had to have. As for the mountain road, I could imagine that he had been going too fast. I had to laugh at that one. Why didn't he remember the times we had driven up there to look around? It was like he had taken the last fifteen years and ripped them out of his brain and his heart.

No snoring? What a joke that statement was. It would go on for hours. I was up to Chapter 8 with the "Knight in Shining Armor" and

I realized it was us all over the place. I wondered what he would think when he got to that point.

APRIL 29

No, it was several YEARS ago!!! But, I don't think it had anything to do with the work scenario; it was the guy himself. When he stood next to me explaining something, I felt this feeling I still can't explain! Now, the only one I am having "wild" feelings for is you! So, tell me, when was YOUR experience and did anything happen?????? I can't imagine not having a physical chemistry if we have such a great emotional chemistry, can you??????

As for coffee, I don't drink it! Do you???? And, I have been so busy!!!!

Like I said before, it seems that there was a real loss of communication going on between you and your wife and that is not meant to be offensive. I think I'm probably right about the "all work and no play" thing, right again?

The road sounds so exciting! I love sharp corners! Thanks for the warning, though!

As long as you are not a "mover and a shaker" in your sleep, right? Alan actually has kicked me in his sleep before! But, that is why there will be two beds in the room! Hehehehehehe

I can't believe you are still reading the book! That's so great! Wait until you get to Chapter 8. I just finished that one. It was a mind blower!!!!!!!!!

So, do you want to save the questions for Friday or do you want to start asking now?!

I just want you to know that I've packed a lot of red "things!" Hehehehe Doing my nails Thursday night so they will be "fresh" and shiny just for you! Wait until you see what I've got! Hehehehehe Later! Halley

I had to keep him coming and pushing him back at the same time. I felt like I was in a push and shove situation. Only a few more days and it would be over. Mixed feelings. How would I go on not knowing what he was doing and what he would do after "me?" After my cyber demise......?

APRIL 29

Halley: In my experience with a coworker, nothing happened and it was about three or four months ago. We actually talked about going out and, well, it just didn't seem to work and we both kind of just let it go. We both were interested, but now that I look back on it, it would not have been a good idea. I think it was a wise decision.

No, I can't imagine that we will not have a physical chemistry after having such a lot of emotional chemistry!!

Wow, you don't drink coffee either? I thought I was the only one on the planet. I said coffee because everyone needs five cups of the stuff a day. If I were to have even one cup after 12:00 PM, I wouldn't be able to sleep half the night. Same goes with certain kinds of chocolate and I really hate that because I'm a chocoholic. I love the stuff. With chocolate, it mainly is the kind that is in certain cakes, the really good tasting ones. But, I can't help myself and I eat it anyway. As long as I don't have a huge piece, I'm alright.

Ohh baby, you seem so worried about my sleep patterns. Don't worry, I'll just cuddle up ooohhhh soooo close to you and we'll sleep just fine. :)hehe I would like to start asking questions now. I would love a full name?

And you're doing your nails just for me? "Wait until I see what you've got?!" In what context do you say that? :) hehehe Jon

I was so sad for myself that he had had feelings for someone else so easily. Had it been my fault or was it that he just never got "it" out of his system or was it his genetics? What happened?

But, I had my proof. He was admitting the Kristan "thing." I wondered what had happened. I could tell he was getting a little worried

about me. He wanted to know what I looked like and he wanted a name and he was worried about what I "had" for him... He wanted to know that he wasn't going to be matched up with "Godzilla" or worse yet—his wife!

APRIL 30

Wow! How do you work with someone after talking to them about dating and having "strong feelings" for them!!!! It must be "strange?" And, I'm hoping she has a boyfriend now!!!!

Oh God! I am a chocoholic too! Must be that's our replacement for coffee! But, the same thing happens to me. If I eat too much, I might as well stay up all night!! (Maybe we should have something like Black Forest Cake for dessert Friday night!!!! hehehehehe)

Okay, Okay! I won't worry about your sleep pattern!!!! What about a "spoon!!!!" A full name, huh!!!! Well, you will just have to wait until Friday for that one!!!!

What I've got for you............! What do you think???? I meant in the context of "red!!!!" Halley

My cleverness was overwhelming me. I had never thought myself capable of what I was attempting to do and was doing. I was going for more information. I wanted to know if Kristan still had the boyfriend that he had told me she had before he left me to be with her himself!

APRIL 30

Yes, she does have a boyfriend now and we get along fine.

You still won't give me a name! What, you still don't trust me? Do you know that's my number one primary need? Page 133. I started Chapter Eight last night. A "spoon" sounds so nice. Jon

He wanted to know more and was thinking more than he was writing.

APRIL 30

Well, it sounds like you've been a really busy boy!!!! Hehehehe It makes me wonder if you have someone else lined up to take my place if I don't work out!!!!

So, my last name is your number one primary need, huh? I'm sure you can think of something better than that!!!! Hehehehe And, yes, I trust you but I just want to be very careful!!!

And, Chapter Eight is my story in a nutshell. Except how the book says that sometimes we can see roles as being reversed. My husband is definitely the princess in this story! After you read it, tell me if you see any of your situation in it! Later! Halley

I wondered if he would admit to being the "princess" in the story?

APRIL 30

Halley: Someone lined up to take your place? No one could ever take your place. Your last name is not my number one primary need. Your trust is. You say you trust me, but.....? I suppose I can wait until Friday, but it just hurts my feelings deeply that you won't tell me. Being a guy, I interpret your refusal to give me a name as a refusal to trust me enough to get that close to you. I'm just trying to communicate my thoughts in a way that a beautiful, caring woman like you would understand instead of getting upset with you. I'm not upset because I also understand your needs. We have shared so much together, but without a name you are not allowing me to have a person attached to it all and I don't have a photo to at least give me a face to attach it to. Can you tell me where you are on your "wave?" It's just that I'm out of my "cave" and I want lots of intimacy with you. I want to be so close to you right now, but if you have to wait to give me that, I'll try not to get frustrated and I'll try to understand.

I bet right now you wish you'd never told me to start reading! hehehehe I'll try to do Chapter Eight tonight. Jon

Boy, was he desperate to make it work with my façade! And he was using my own ammunition against me in the process! I couldn't believe how he was going on......

APRIL 30

Please don't be hurt! Honestly, I think I am at the bottom of my "wave" today and feeling very vulnerable. Please try to understand! I just need to be so careful right now! Just remember, it's just three more days!

So, tell me, how long do you think you have been living in your "cave" before everything happened? And, has anyone ever told you that you have the potential to be an incredible writer??? The more you "talk" to me, the more I think about this! Got to go for now! Halley

The messages were just piling up on me and I had to make them shorter. I was tired and spent from hearing and speaking of so many feelings.

APRIL 30

Halley: Poor thing, I'm sorry you're at the bottom of your wave. Here's a big e-mail hug. I will listen to you for hours, okay?

Can you tell me why such secrecy? Is there more to your story than I know? I'm counting the hours, less than seventy-two to go.

How long have I been living in my "cave?" I'll have to think about that one. My first thought is that I bounce back from anything within a day or so but now that I'm thinking about it, how long has it been since I really talked to her? I guess I gave up.

I could be an incredible writer? Wow, and coming from an English major! My wife thought that I was good at it, but no one ever thought I could be "incredible." :) I hope I don't disappoint you too much with my verbal skills. Now, you're probably thinking that I stutter or something. No, I speak well, but not as good as I know I can. I strive to always improve, but it has been a long process.

I feel like we're holding our breath again. Our conversations have reduced a little. Have you noticed? Jon

No shit! He had given up, huh? He had never even tried to communicate with me. He was too busy thinking up his strange inventions like the three-wheeled vehicle or the "butter-cutter," which I actually encouraged or he was too busy working. He had given up before he had started. And, yes, his written communications blew away his verbal communications. His verbal communications were worthless most of the time as evidenced by the position I was now in. And, yeah, I was holding my breath alright!

APRIL 30

Maybe, it's the weather that is getting to me and trying to get all my work done! Right now, I really need a hug, more than you will ever know! I'll just have to save up for it until Friday! Is there more to my story? No, it's nothing to do with my husband or you. It's just me, nothing major. I'll tell you about it on Friday. But don't worry, nothing is wrong!

So, you're telling me that you don't know when the last time was that you "really" talked to her??? So, you gave up. You probably felt like she wouldn't listen? Is there no love left at all for her in your heart? I am only asking because I'm not sure how I feel for my husband. There is a part of my heart that just feels numb. Does this make any sense?

From now on in your life, promise me that you'll never give up again......that you will find a way to communicate no matter how impossible it may seem.

I'm sure you are too hard on yourself about your speaking ability! And, everything is hard, so hard! Life is hard! But the good moments are worth all the bad moments you have to go through to get to them. It just doesn't seem that way at the time!

And, I think that the emails are shorter because we ARE holding our breath and not much "talking" can come out when you are doing this! I'm just trying to get totally caught up so I can have only one thing on my mind when I meet you! YOU! Later. Halley

I was overwhelmed and didn't know how I was going to keep this up much longer. While I was in the middle of my email, Jon stopped and let himself into the house. I had to run to the bathroom for a towel because I was half dressed sitting in front of the computer. He wanted some of his books. To make matters worse, he dropped them back off when I was in the shower and called me after 9:00 PM and asked me to borrow the type-writer that night. I was so nervous. Here I was showing him how to use it knowing so much about what he had been doing with my alter ego, Halley, and with other women. It was so hard to pretend to be other than I was when I had to face him. And, to top it off, I had a towel on my head!

APRIL 30

Halley: Boy, I could really use a hug too. I'm working so hard on my class that I'm starting to feel sorry for myself. I've been on the computer for so many days that I can see myself wasting away. My arms look smaller! I'm getting so close to being finished but I just have that last hurdle to get over. I need my documentation letters so I can put things in proper order and number the rest of my pages but I won't get some of them until next week. This thing is like a book of my life. Right now, it's seventy-six pages long and it'll probably be about ninety pages long when it's done. I'm supposed to hand it in this Thursday, but I'm not going to be done. The drop dead date is next Thursday and I may have to take a day off from work in order to even make that date. I will finish it no matter what.

You sound tired. You sound like I feel. I think we're both working too hard.

Is there love in my heart for her? I just feel bad for her. No, I will not ever give up again. I will never let things progress even remotely to this level. I'm not the type to give up on anything. I stick with things much longer than most people do. Jon

I felt badly for him. I was supposed to be the one doing his report for him but he had refused my help. I couldn't believe he was doing it himself. My heart ached when I read that he just felt bad for me. How could he be so cold? He said he wasn't the type to give up but he had!

MAY 1

Oh no! Did I pick a bad weekend for you? Now I feel so guilty if you have all this work to do! Would you rather wait until after the report is done?

But, it sounds like when you get your report done that you will feel a major sense of accomplishment and relief! And, yes, we are both working too hard! Sound familiar? Doesn't look like either of us has slowed down like we said we would!

So, what do you mean that you feel "bad" for her? I can say that I feel this way but I also feel other things too about Alan, like numb, confused, etc. Don't you feel anything else for her after fifteen years? And, don't you ever wonder if you should have hung in there just a little while longer and really tried to figure things out?

I know that you said that you stick with things longer than most people but, in your case, maybe it was that it would just take longer because the problems had been avoided for so long? I'm just trying to comprehend what you are saying so I can really understand where you are coming from. It's just hard for me because from everything you have said, there really was no time given to really try to work through the problems? Sorry to get into this especially now when you are tired! I think it's my mood or something. I just want to really understand what drives people apart.

And, I wonder, what if we somehow get into worse situations than we thought we were in the first time and remember that we told ourselves that we would never give up again????? Can you tell? I want to know the future!

Well, I hope today goes well for you and don't get discouraged. You are almost done with the report! Just take it one step at a time and it won't be as bad as you think. What a thought! Maybe if we had approached our problems in our marriages that way, who knows what would have happened!!!!!!!! So, I'm sending you a very big hug across the internet! Can you feel it? I hope so! Later! Halley

I couldn't believe I was giving encouragement to the person who had deserted me. My mind was reeling at my own actions and words. But, I wanted information and answers and I knew I could only get them with "candy."

MAY 1

Halley: I have this thing where it seems whenever I want to get away, things pile up around me for a final climax just when I want to leave. Don't feel guilty in the least. If documentation letters don't come by Friday, I won't be able to do any work on it over the weekend anyway. I'm going to have plenty of time to finish it and I wouldn't miss this weekend for anything.

I feel bad for her because of what I've done. I feel in a way that I've abandoned her. She has no job and no way to support herself. I wish she would just get up on her own two feet and start doing something. I'm also numb and confused. I don't wonder about whether or not I should have hung in there. I just wish things could have been different. I have no idea how they could have been but, perhaps, there was a way. The whole thing really stinks. I've noticed something. Since you have gotten me to not be so hostile towards her, I have a different outlook on things. I think you gave me a reality check in that I see how I have hurt her and I'm taking all of the blame for that part of it. Before, I had just totally shut off any and all feelings for her and all I was looking at was how she was trying to take as much from me as she could.

I just got a phone call. My meeting for Friday has been cancelled! I didn't tell you what the meeting was about but now I can. It was a court hearing, a temporary maintenance hearing. That's why I wasn't looking forward to it and it's also why I needed to meet with my lawyer on Thursday. I'm so glad I don't have to deal with it now!

I read Chapter Eight last night. She was definitely the princess!

Please don't worry so much about the future. Did you try to work things out before you left or did you just tell him it was over? In my case, I did tell her some of the problems and how I just couldn't stand it any more. She seemed to listen, but really didn't change a great deal. It was just too late. She changes at a snail's pace and I'm not willing to wait. I don't second guess my decision to leave. I think about what I could have done differently and about the situation as a whole. I consider the possibility of any chance of having a happy life with her and I just cannot see how it could have been possible. Thanks for the hug. It felt so relaxing and nice. Did you feel mine too? Jon

So, he was finally getting it. He had abandoned me. He should have stayed. No kidding—there was a way. He could have talked to me—not threatened me! So, he hadn't even realized that he had hurt me??? How could he shut all of his feelings off for me—how could he numb himself to fifteen years of love?

I couldn't believe he was saying that I had been the "princess" when I thought he had been. As for telling me anything, when he finally had in the form of threats—he would not even give me one day to change what he felt needed changing. Second guessing. He really should have thought about what he was doing. He had only been thinking he was moving on to someone else—it was a simple as that. And, how could we have a happy life together if he wasn't happy inside? And, how could he be happy inside if he was hiding all his feelings? It was the truth and he had no idea.

MAY 1

Halley: If we were both treated like the "Knight in Shining Armor," I think we can safely say that we won't be repeating those mistakes with each other and that we have a great deal in common. Maybe we should try to get the two of them together! Jon

Yeah, sounded about right. He wanted me to be with someone else so he could rid himself of some of his guilt.

MAY 1

Two princesses together!!!! I think that might be a disaster! But, I think two knights together would be a dream, wouldn't it? But, does it really ever happen that way????

I'm so glad we don't have to postpone again! So, your hearing was canceled? So, what happens now??

I think in our own way, we are each guilty of abandonment. If she's been out of the job market for a while, it might be hard to get one now. Does she have a degree? That would really help.

In my case, I did not really give him a chance either. I also think that we may both be guilty of not giving them any time. Think about it. If things came on gradually as you said they did, how could all the changes happen overnight? It just isn't realistic. And, I did sort of the same thing. Maybe, we didn't want to face the work and the time that it would take to make things right? But is that really the right thing to do? I don't know.

As a Venusian, I cannot believe that it is ever too late even though I did what I did! It is just part of the biology of being a female being. For Martians, they always think it is too late! So, I have to feel bad for her as well as my husband and hope that you are not offended. Think about this. So, we walk (or run!) out the door and they are left standing there. In my case, my husband has a great job. In your case, what does she have? Nothing, just like you said. You say that "perhaps there was a way." That's such a positive statement. But, then you say that you can't see any possibility of a happy life with her and that you weren't willing to wait. Those are really negative statements. I think you are right when you say you are confused and I think that it is perfectly normal given the circumstances at the moment. I just hope we both have made the right decision!

I am glad I had one last Christmas with him and our families even though I had all the thoughts I had spinning around in my head. Since you said June was your sixth month, does that mean you were apart for Christmas? If you were, that must have been terrible!

I'm so glad that you don't feel as angry now. It makes me feel that I've helped you and, you know, Venusians just thrive on that! And, it isn't good to shut your feelings off. It just makes things so much harder. And, yes, the hug felt so good! Later! Halley

I wanted the reality of my statements to sink into his thick, dark, beautiful head. Even if it was filled with too much ignorance. I was secretly hoping that he would come to me, somehow, through another loss—one that involved only a façade.

MAY 1

Halley: You sound much happier tonight. Don't get too far up your "wave" before we meet. I want to ride it with you. I can't believe that we really will meet in forty-four hours. For me at least, it seems like the wait has been so long.

Why can't two knights together happen? I think it does. There are a lot of very happy people out there.

My hearing will be rescheduled for a later date. If it's late enough, my lawyer will try to just get it turned into a final hearing. I might be able to have the court stuff done in a matter of weeks.

Is leaving the right thing to do? We have one chance at this life. It's not a movie that we can watch over and over again. It's for real. I want to be happy. I was amazed at how I felt when I read you were giving me an internet hug. It felt great!

I noticed that I have an email from "Hearts.com." I haven't looked at it yet but it looks like something from billing. Do you think I need to be a member any longer or should I let it run out? :) What's your "opinion?" Tell me, baby, what you think. :) Jon

I was horrified by his statement that his lawyer was going to try to get the temporary hearing transformed into a final hearing. What was I going to do? Where was I going to go? And, happiness. He wanted to believe that happiness was all in the person you were "with." What about inside of our hearts? He just didn't get it. You had to be happy inside to be happy with someone else and he was so far from that point. So, he wanted me to tell him to give up his "Hearts.com" account. Yeah, right?

MAY 1

It's only been since the beginning of April that we've been talking!!!! You Martians are so impatient!!!!

So, wouldn't that be unfair to your wife if the hearing was changed to a final without even having the temporary one? I don't understand this.

So, it sounds like you are completely convinced that the only way you can be happy is without her. But, won't you always wonder?

And, you didn't answer all my questions! I know I ask too many, but it is the Venusian in me!! Is it that you didn't want to face the work and the time that it might take to make things right between you??? And, what is she going to do without a job? Does she have a degree to fall back on? And, what about Christmas? Were you apart??? I just can't imagine that. Sorry! I think I should have been a Psychology Major instead of an English Major in college!

So, do you think she got the book yet? And, I have not received my "tool" yet!

Hearts.com!?!? I can't make that decision for you! :) Then, I would be the "princess!" So, you'll have to make that decision for yourself!!!!!!!!!!! :)

Got to go now! Halley

I wanted him to question himself over and over and I was having a very difficult time with this. He clearly didn't want to face the questions

I posed because he would have to think of me, his wife, Hunter. He didn't want to have to admit more pain and more guilt.

When I went to the mailbox that day, I found the book. I couldn't believe I had been able to manipulate it out of him. I felt a surge of guilt thinking that, maybe, I had done this before? But, then, I thought of how he had lied to me and used me.

MAY 1

The temporary hearing is only to establish a way for her to live while we wait for the six-month waiting period to be over. It's been five now and I have continued to pay all of her major expenses since "Day One."

I suppose a very small part of me will wonder, but I am convinced that I have to leave her. No, I didn't want to face the work or the time it would take. There are no guarantees that it ever would have worked and I had only seen a gradual progression in the wrong direction, nothing else.

She will find a job as soon as she is no longer as picky as she is currently being. She won't be destitute. She doesn't have a degree, but is working on a Bachelor's Degree. She consistently made more money than I did while she worked. She can type over a 100 words a minute.

We were apart for Christmas. I didn't want to leave before that but I thought it was worse to stay through such a holiday and pretend. I just couldn't fake it. I'm sorry to admit it but Christmas for me was better than it had been for a long time. She always made me nervous and I couldn't relax when we were at my family's Christmas celebration. This past Christmas, I was able to relax. I had to cater to her every need. It was like taking care of a little old lady.

She got the book a couple of days ago. I had it sent to me and I left it in our mailbox. She asked me about it in an e-mail last night and I told her I gave it to her.

I hope you can bring your tool. What's taking so long? Jon

I could sense indignation in the tone of his email. So, he didn't want to work at a relationship. How could he expect to ever have one last if he wasn't willing to put time into it? This gradual progression he spoke of—I had no idea what he was talking about. If he wasn't willing to tell me things weren't okay for him, how was I to know that they were going in the wrong direction? I hoped that somewhere out there, a girl existed who could read his mind because that was the only way a relationship with him would work. Wow! Was I supposed to be able to get a job based on the fact that I was a fast typist? Now, that was a pathetic statement. I remembered Christmas. And, I knew I would never forget what he had done so close to Christmas. What a heel to take someone's heart and throw it in their face at the most beautiful and loving season of the year. How could he write this off in his mind? He never had had to cater to me when we were with his family. I carried the conversation and I definitely did not dress or act like a "little old lady." The negativity and resentment were leaking out. This was when he could lose the battle. Anyone else would have dumped him at this point, but I had a reason to hold on if even for only a few more days.

MAY 1

I am not sure what I wonder at this moment. It's just one of those moments in life that you never thought you would have to experience, don't you think? And, I am the odd one out. Hardly anyone in my entire family has ever been in this situation. In some families, marital problems are like walking the dog! And, I don't want to have to wonder. I want to know for sure. And I am sure I will figure it out.

Do you think that it's right to leave because you don't want to face the work and time it would take, especially after years of marriage in either of our situations? I agree that there are no guarantees but there are also no guarantees that we will ever find that "perfect" someone else???? You know what I mean?

Like I said, if she has been out of the job market for a while, it is going to be difficult and without a degree it is even going to be harder. Typing over one hundred words a minute is a good skill but, Jon, where do you think that will get her?

I'm feeling a lot of negativity today!!!!!! But, the positive is that you gave her the book and you say you don't feel as hostile toward her but I wonder……..

No tool yet!!!!!!!!!!! (I just ordered it a few days ago!) Looks like it isn't going to make it for this time, but maybe for next time???????

So, are you ready for tomorrow!!!!!!!!!!! If you don't hear from me (which you probably will!), I'll meet you in the lobby at 6:00 PM!!!!! Halley

I was blunt and I didn't care. He wanted to meet me so bad that he would deal with my comments. I wanted to see just how far I could push him, always remembering the positive "bait" at the end. This time, it being the promise of meeting him.

MAY 1

My sister is the only one in my family who has been through a divorce also. I thought that out of anyone, I would be the last to ever get one. You are really consumed by all the wonder and self-questioning aren't you? I think anyone who goes through this should give it a lot of deep thought. I think you will eventually figure out what you need to do. I was feeling so optimistic today. I just feel like I'm going to do something wonderful in the future. I don't know what it is yet. I was just in a good mood.

Do you think that I have helped you or do you think I'm confusing you more?

I think it's right to leave if I don't want to face the time or the work. Right now, my wife would be absolutely terrible with children. She could not provide good caring parenting. It would be an extremely unhealthy situation for children, for her and for me. She has never wanted to even hold a child. I thought that would change but I was wrong. I don't want to bring children into a world like that and I want to have at least one child. What am I supposed to do? I just cannot take the chance with my own child, to bring it into a world that could potentially be so bad. I'm not willing to give her the chance when it comes to the third party of the equation. That is the bottom line for me. I think I just realized that to the point of being able to write it down.

It seems that for you, the whole thing is pretty gray. For me, it's much more black and white and it is much easier for me to define, at least in my mind. I know my situation. Yes, I've been married for many years. What does it mean? I think a marriage is much more than two people living in the same house. For the most part, that's all my marriage has been for years. She wanted it to continue the same way with no child and just the two of us doing separate things for the rest of our lives. I'm not willing to coast the rest of my life. I want to live.

Part of living to me is being woken up in the night by a child. Taking it to the doctors. Hearing it cry. I want to live all the bad along with the good. Hearing it scream "Daddy" when I come home from work. Watching it grow and teaching it everything I know. Providing a wonderful loving home and life. If there is a chance that I can do that, I'm going to try. The thing that I kept imagining before I left home was being sixty-five and looking back on that missed opportunity. No way!!! I just can't do that.

I hope that you're able to have fun this weekend? I can't wait to be able to talk about all your thoughts face-to-face. Twenty two hours to go! I'll "SEE" you at six. :) Jon

I couldn't hold back the tears. He was so cold. He neglected to tell Halley that his entire family was plagued with marital problems. I felt sorry for the person who might have been on the other end of this conversation if I wasn't faking this relationship because they would have been getting quite a load of crap and a lot of lies to build upon. Not good. So he thought it was "right" to run away like a coward instead of investing some time in a relationship that had existed for over fifteen years. I was mortified. And, his appraisal of me. A potentially terrible mother. I was hurt so deeply I could do nothing but sob. My tears covered the keyboard of my computer. The negativity within him was bursting forth. And, not two weeks before, I had held a baby on two days in recent weeks for hours and enjoyed it. I was even brought to tears as I held the baby knowing that there was a slim chance I would ever be able to have my own. And what about all of the times I had held my sister's children? How could he forget that? Maybe it was because I wasn't being threatened, I had the opportunity to feel things out for myself two weeks before? There was no black and white to our situation. It was so foggy, you couldn't see one foot in front of you. All the bad with the good. Jon couldn't handle any "bad" as he termed it and had shown that side of himself to me for fifteen years. I doubted that he would even be able to deal with a child. I knew that his sister couldn't. If her child even had a cold and she had to stay home with him, she was a complete bitch. Jon had openly admitted to me when I asked him during the time he was threatening me that he could not deal with a child who might be sick or who might have something wrong with him or her. Even then, I told him I would do anything that he wanted me to do to save our marriage even knowing his inability to deal with adversity. I think it was this that caused me so much anxiety—his inability to deal with things and his constant states of depression when he could not come up with a solution to even the simplest problems. His talk didn't reflect his walk, that was for sure.

MAY 2

I'm confused because I'm not sure if you have given this all enough deep thought because of some of the things that you have said. Sometimes you say that you wonder a little and then you say that you know absolutely that you are doing the "right" thing. That is why I wonder.

I really don't want to offend you, but is it right for you to judge what someone would be like with children if they have never had any and when you don't really know her anymore? Almost six months is a long time and a lot of things might have changed for her that you have no idea about. And, if you really think about it, there must have been some time during your marriage that she held a child. And, how do you know that her heart isn't breaking over this, that she should have had one because now she is all alone. Does this make any sense? I think maybe it is easier for you to focus on the negative and maybe it is necessary so you can go through with this? Just wondering.

I just keep thinking about the part of the marriage ceremony when they say the part about taking each other for better or worse and it bothers me that you say that it is right to leave because of the time and effort it would take to make things right. I feel guilty because, maybe, this is how my leaving Alan is being interpreted by my family and his family.

And, how can you say that you want to live the bad along with the good when you have left behind what you say is "bad?" Or, at least that is how I am understanding your feelings about your wife? It's hard to say it right with email. I guess I could probably do a better job in person. I think we really need to talk about everything in person. I am sure it will make more sense then. And, yes, I intend to have fun!

And, I will see you at 6:00 PM in the lobby of the Norac Nordic Lodge! Can't wait to drive through the sharp corners! Look for the hot girl in red! Halley

I was pissed. That afternoon, I had been able to hack into his email account again and see what was really going on. He was still in contact with Ashley, the "Belly Ring Girl" while he had been talking to me! I didn't hold back on my message to him. I was going to push him as far as I could—even if it meant losing out on the meeting. I wanted him to know he was an idiot in regard to his marriage. I wanted him to know that it was wrong what he had done even if he wouldn't acknowledge it. How could he ignore what I was saying? How could he?

MAY 3

Halley: I really don't know how to reply to your morning e-mail.

I say I wonder because it's in my nature to always try to assess all possibilities, regardless of how unlikely. I don't want to sound negative towards Hunter, but isn't it true that some people should not have children? I really feel that she is one.

The bad along with the good, for better or worse. I don't know what to say. I think we will be able to talk more about this when we meet and I have to tell you, Halley, I am so looking forward to this afternoon! I will be looking for the hot girl in red and I can't wait to see her. Jon

Disappointment was hanging over his head and he didn't even know it. I felt sick. It was a good thing the hearing had been cancelled because I came down with a cold that morning. And the thought of what I was doing made my heart feel sick. I had wanted revenge so badly and now that I was at the crucial point of getting some, I wasn't sure I wanted it even though he was breaking my heart with his ignorance. I wanted so badly to walk into that hotel lobby dressed in my new red trench coat and see the look on his face...

sixteen

SEEING RED

MAY 3

Halley: It's 7:00 PM and I'm at the Lodge on their computer. Where are you? I wait and I worry. This is too difficult. Please, if you're home and you couldn't come, please respond to at least let me know you're all right. You could also call so I could at least talk to you. I'm going to stay here for a while longer. I just don't know what to think or how long I should wait. Please. I'll be here for probably another hour. Jon

I cried uncontrollably and my heart broke all over again when I read his email. He was alone. I was alone. We were apart. All I wanted was him. I wanted to be with him and for him to hold me in his arms and I wanted for the pain we both felt to disappear......

MAY 3

Halley: It's 7:47 PM. I sit here waiting like an idiot hoping that there is a good reason you are not here. I'm going into the restaurant for dinner. Jon

I sat and waited to send the final email or what I thought would be the last. I was getting my revenge for being abandoned by him even if it wasn't really enough. I kept thinking of him sitting there in the lobby of the place I had always wanted for us to go together. And, he was sitting there waiting for someone else. I hated him and loved him at the same moment. He was waiting for a woman dressed in red to walk through the door and I knew it wasn't going to happen. I wanted him to feel the pain I felt when he walked out on me, but at most he would only be pissed. But, he had only been trying to get into my facade's pants. At the same time he had been conversing with me, he had been communicating with Ashley and who knows who else! What was I supposed to think??? I could only cry.

MAY 3

Dear Jon, Please forgive me Jon and please don't hate me! I had to go back to my sister's house to get something I had forgotten after I left for Salem and my husband was there waiting for me. He wanted to talk. I thought it would be only for a few minutes but it turned into hours and there was no way that I could call you or the hotel to let you know that I couldn't leave. So, here I am emailing you so late at night and my emotions are spinning in my head. He just left. I hope that you didn't wait too long. I am so sorry!

He said that he didn't want to lose me and that he would do everything and anything in his power so we would be happy together. He said we could spend more time together and that he would wait until I was ready for a child. I think it may have been wrong for me to file for divorce based on the reasons I had in my mind. I am not sure what will happen, if it will work or not but I feel I need to give him a chance. It has been eight years and I feel I can't turn my back on at least giving him a chance. My grandfather's illness made me realize how important it is to find a way to honor my commitment to him as he was there in New Jersey through that whole weekend with my family and I. That is why it has been so difficult for me to understand all of this, especially in the last week. What I was going to tell you tonight was that he drove down to be with us that weekend.

Talking to you has made me realize so many things about how important it is to be alive and happy. I've also realized this week through talking to you that I can't just run away without trying and giving him a real chance.

He told me how my leaving really opened his eyes to the reality of our situation and how we needed to communicate with each other, no matter how hard it might be to start. He asked that I give him one month to see if we could figure things out. I am not moving out of my sister's house yet, but I will be seeing him to talk and see if we can figure all of this out. I am not sure it will work but my heart tells me that I need to do this so that I will know for sure that I am doing the right thing if I go through with the divorce.

Please forgive me but know that it was through talking to you that I know I need to give him a chance. I don't know what will happen but that's life, isn't it and sometimes you have to take chances that you never thought you would and not turn away from something that might bring you back where you should be and where you might find more happiness than where you thought it was…out there some-where. I know that deep down you must understand what I am trying to say, but words really aren't enough. I hope that I really have helped you to see more of the positive than the negative, and hope that some-day you will be able to let go of all the pain in your heart.

I just want you to know how much you have helped me through all of this. I am so sorry and hope that you will forgive me and wish that you would continue writing to me. I am here waiting to hear from you if you do want to "talk." I really do want to be there for you and don't want to lose what we have together. But, I want you to know that if I never hear from you again, I will never reveal your identity to anyone. I will keep it as a special secret in my heart. But, I hope that doesn't happen. I hope, with all of me, that I do hear from you again. Love, Halley

I thought I was going to die. I couldn't believe I had done it. Such little revenge for the pain I was feeling. Had it been worth it? It didn't feel like it. But, I had had the opportunity to communicate with him for over a month and find out truths I needed to know and hear. But it hurt so much. I wanted him to come home so badly. Perhaps, I had hoped without thinking about it that he would realize he needed to give us a chance?

MAY 5

I just want to tell you again how sorry I am for disappointing you and hope that you will be able to find it in your heart to forgive me. Halley

I needed for him to respond to me, no matter how negative his response might be.

MAY 5

I just can't believe that you would do what you did to me. Fine if you want to go back to your husband. I even suggested to you that you should possibly try working it out, but to have me drive an hour in the anticipation of meeting you, the nervousness of walking through the door at 6:00 PM, only to stand in an empty lobby holding your presents for two hours is mean.

I don't want to meet you now, Halley. I've been treated this way for fifteen years and don't intend to continue it. I'm not the one who is confused. I know what I want—someone who is totally honest and open with me about every facet of their life. It's not entirely your fault. I should have seen the warning signs, like the fact that to this day I don't even know who the hell you are! You're unsure about who you are and what you want and have protected yourself from others finding out about who you really are. I think I had a glimpse of the real you and I liked it very much, but you could show me that part of you because I didn't know your name right? Read my next sentence many times, because it is very important to your future happiness. I hope you can work things out with your "ex," or with someone else, but if you can't respect him for who he is and be totally open about the real you, like you were with me, you will never be truly happy.

There is only one way you could possibly redeem yourself with me and that would be to tell me your name. At least give me the dignity of knowing so if I'm ever in the same room with you, I'm not a complete ass for being so damn stupid. If you can't do that, if you can't give your name, you're not a very nice person, Halley. Jon

Oh my God! He had brought presents for me. I felt so badly. I couldn't stop crying. I felt so badly for hurting him as he had hurt me. Revenge was not the answer and I knew that now. I couldn't stop crying thinking about how he had abandoned me and how I had felt, but doing it to him had not been the answer. I realized that inside of me I had hoped he would know it was me, Hunter, and want to be with me. I wanted him to know it was me but I couldn't tell him. I didn't have the courage to tell him because everything he wrote was so negative about me and I feared that he would hate me more if he knew of my façade to know the truth.

MAY 5

Jon: I deserve all of your comments but there was no way I could get away to communicate with you. It's like you said to me in one of your emails that when things are right they fall into place and when they're not it's like banging your head against a brick wall.

There is one last thing that I need to say to you that will affect your happiness for the rest of your life. If you are never completely open with your wife and never give her the chance to be completely open with you, you will never know if that is where true happiness was for you. I wish for you that you could show your true self to her the way you did with me.

I am so sorry and please do not feel stupid. That was never my intention. Halley

All I could think was that Jon couldn't show his true self to me, Hunter, because he didn't know who he was.

I felt like I had to make a plea for myself as Hunter and sent him an email thanking him for the book that he had left in the mailbox at the request of my Internet façade and told him how I had realized my mistakes and how I was capable of change even though I was not sure that he was capable of being who he had been in the beginning. I placed no blame on him hoping that it would make him more willing to see things how they really could be and had been. I had come to realize that I had been forceful at times, even though without this behavior, I wondered where we would have been if I hadn't used my inner resources. He always seemed to climb into a hole when he didn't want to face life and things that had to be done and my behavior had been the only way I knew to push him out of the hole.....

seventeen

HOPING

MAY 5

Dear Jon: I wanted to thank you again for the book. I also wanted to apologize for pushing you into your "cave" so far that you couldn't even begin to come out. I am very sorry that I was the "princess" with the "noose and the poison" telling you what to do and how to do it until you could no longer breathe. I've come to truly realize my mistakes and I am sorry that I wasn't open to all of your needs the way a loving wife should be. I have been so blind and deaf. I have come to realize things I never knew about myself until now. I've realized things that I never knew I was capable of and the reasons why I reacted the way I did. I have realized things I would never have imagined I would want as part of my life. I truly didn't know myself until now and I discover new things every day and wish that I could share them with you. I know that I want to be alive and happy and healthy in every way. In life, all that matters is that we live and are loved and leave a part of ourselves behind in some way. I will always know in my heart that I have been loved and, if I never do again, I will always remember that I was once loved by you and that it was you who woke me from my dark sleep. Love, Hunter

I so wanted him to want me and I felt if anything could bring us back together, my admitting my part of the mistakes and the blame might help him to see the "light" in all of the darkness that was surrounding our situation. Hope was all I had to hang onto and it was dwindling... I received no response to my email.

MAY 8

I thought that I would love him forever and that he nor anyone else would ever be able to take that away from me. I thought that I would never stop loving him and that, someday, we would be together again, even if I had to wait until the end. I couldn't stop crying at this thought. To have wasted so much precious time already was unbearable to me. I loved him and my heart was breaking for the thousandth time. I wanted him to open up to me, and acknowledge his feelings toward me so they could be healed.

At the same time I was so anxious about what would become of me. Would I be allowed to stay in my home until the final hearing or until he changed his mind? I didn't know how I was going to pay the bills and I didn't know how I was going to find a job that I was capable of in my weakened state of mind. I wanted him to come back to me. But I didn't know if I could forget what he had done. I wanted him to have so many doubts that he would at least talk to me. I wanted him to stop ignoring how wonderful I felt our relationship had been. I wanted him to come back to me and for us to go away together, away from the past. I wanted him to know that I loved him and how I always would. And, I wanted to know that it was alright for me to love him forever as I had pledged that I would—forever.

MAY 9

As I sat in the hallway on the day of the Temporary Order Hearing waiting for my lawyer to return with my file, I noticed Jon walking through the metal scanner with his lawyer. Always together. Why didn't they ever come in separately? She always went for the corner table. Then I noticed him saunter over to the column post to see the breakdown of cases for the afternoon. Cocky. That was all I could think. I leaned over again to review my answers to possible questions I would be asked, hoping that I wouldn't forget what I needed to say or that I wouldn't say the wrong thing or the right thing in the wrong way.

My attorney walked through and motioned me over and we walked slowly up the stairs to the upper courtroom. Seems like it was the "main" courtroom. It was overwhelming and cold. I shivered with cold and trepidation. I looked over and noticed the blonde bimbo who was Jon's lawyer and thought she must color her own hair! Jon looked pale and had bags under his eyes but, again, held that cocky look. Then I looked straight ahead. That was where I would have to sit and spill my guts. Microphones on the tables and "the stand." Too bad Halley didn't still exist. The lawyers motioned each other outside the courtroom for a moment and I could feel his eyes on me. I looked out of the corner of my eye and he was looking at me. I decided not to give him the satisfaction of looking at him, the cocky bastard. But all I wanted to do was hug him and hit him at the same time. The bleached blonde deputy clerk came in and asked if everyone was ready. All I could think of was the note I had sent him the Sunday before thanking him for the book and for loving me and thinking he must have laughed at it.

The judge entered and I was called to the stand. I slowly walked over and took the oath to tell the whole truth and nothing but the truth and sat down. At one point, I realized that my hands were wet with sweat as my attorney questioned me in order to establish the basis of the case. Then, it was the viper's turn to question me. I had witnessed her snipped comments before in the hallways below with Jon and noticed it again. She badgered me with questions regarding various checking account statements and balances. As she stood next to me, I looked down and noticed her shoes and thought how ugly they were and I had to bite my lip from saying something about them. I was confused and looked over at my lawyer who had the same look on his face. Apparently, this was not something that was to be brought up, but she had decided to do so anyway. Then, onto my job search and the constant impinging comment as to why I hadn't sought employment at various grocery stores. I responded with the fact that I was seeking employment equal to my skills and experience. At one point, I could not answer her question and turned to the judge. She insisted I answer all of her questions with yes or no responses and it was impossible to do this. He explained that I could respond with the response "I cannot answer that question with a yes or no answer." At this critical moment when I was the most confused, the Judge announced that there was someone who needed to be arraigned immediately and we were shuffled out of the courtroom. My attorney and I went into a small conference area and the first words out of my mouth were in regard to her being a "bitch." He quickly reviewed notes and we came up with a response in regard to dignity—that I should be allowed the same sort of job that afforded the dignity of Jon's job. Since I was responsible for him having the job he did, there was no question here. If it weren't for me, he would still be a carpenter. At that moment, I wished he still were a carpenter. If he were, maybe this wouldn't have happened. She had no response to my reply when I was asked the question again on the stand.

All the time she questioned the monies I had had access to all I could think of were all of the charges that I knew about that he had made that were completely self-indulgent. Clothes, restaurant expenses, expensive birthday gifts for our nephew, new mud flaps that really weren't needed, and how he used the majority of the funds in the account she was questioning me about prior to leaving to buy a new vehicle. Her questioning was completely ridiculous. Various exhibits were introduced such as my job search list, checking statements, and my breakdown of what I had used the monies for to which she said she hadn't seen. My attorney said that she had received it but in a different format. She snipped on and on.

After more than an hour of me being on the stand, Jon was finally called to the stand and questioned about some of my responses to which he lied under oath. He said he never told me on Christmas night that he would not pay my expenses—LIE. He said he never said that he would not like it if I worked at Video King—LIE. With every response, he smirked. He was also asked by his lawyer about his AGI certification and he said he could not teach ground school classes because he was not current with his private pilot's license. He said he took the checkbooks out of the house because he had discovered that I was spending money. I was paying bills! The reason he removed the checkbooks was because I would not do an uncontested divorce! LIE again!

Finally, my lawyer got to question him about various things. Jon said it was my choice as to whether I was upset or not about his leaving me. God! He also made a statement that my anxiety was in my head....... This was one of the reasons he gave me for leaving!!!! It was the comment my lawyer made about the possibility of the court making the decision that the property be sold was when I noticed his face go a shade lighter than pale death. He didn't know what to say! My attorney also made comments and questions in regard to Jon not realizing how divorce would be costly and Jon replied that he had no idea it would be as it was. He left without thought about anything but the object hanging between his legs! With every answer, he smirked. His lawyer questioned him again as to whether he would continue paying the oil, electricity and phone bills and he replied that he would. He replied that he would not agree to paying me money for food. She asked him if he would agree to my staying in the house until the divorce was final and he did not answer. She continued to question him trying to pull the obviously previously rehearsed answer out of him. He finally answered that he guessed that he would agree to it. At that point, I nearly broke down. And at that point, the time was up. My lawyer had said it would take less than an hour and we had gone past the two-hour mark and his attorney complained to the judge that she had requested more than two hours for the hearing! Jon's attorney requested additional time to review the breakdown I had done and he gave her a week at which time she would notify the court as to whether or not she needed an additional session.

My attorney was angry as we walked out of the courthouse and said that he had no idea she was going to get into the checking account statements as she had. In a word, she wasted time so she could make more money off Jon. It also seemed as if she had attempted to turn the temporary hearing into a final hearing but without success. He told me that there was no doubt in his mind that this would take until September at least before a final hearing would be scheduled. I read between the lines and knew it was because of the way that she kept delaying things. Jon was so stupid. He wanted it over now and his lawyer was trying to stretch it out so she could make more money off him. I wondered if I should tell him this or if he would get more angry. No mortgage, no car payments, she could see $ signs and all he was thinking of was women and how he could get one for the weekend. My attorney told me to revise my breakdown once again to include everything from the date of separation to April. I dropped it off the next morning. But I couldn't give a breakdown of the checks written from the main joint account because Jon had them and still had not produced them. Then I thought about it. My credit cards were used to purchase the majority of everything we BOTH needed. So, a breakdown wouldn't even show what she wanted to see. She had copies of the credit card statements. She was only trying to make things harder for no reason.

I called my sister's business looking for her and talked to my brother-in-law who said Jon had just been there to pick up his new mud flaps and how he looked like death warmed over. I said that in the courtroom it had almost been like he was on the verge of laughing as he had smirked through every answer he gave on the stand. I was completely drained.

Friday afternoon he showed up to change his mud flaps and all I could think when I saw his truck was if he had spent the time on us that he spent on washing and taking care of that truck—that we wouldn't be in this mess. He brought my typewriter back and said he still hadn't looked for the checks. I went out and fed the ducks. He came in after he was done and asked me without civility why the phones were unplugged in the garage. I said I had unplugged them because no one was out there to use them. (I had unplugged them so I could talk in the house without thinking he was out there listening to my conversations.) He came back in again and yelled at me and said that the phones would stay plugged in if he was paying the electricity and the phone bills. I asked him—"So, you are back to being ugly again!" I then sent an email later and asked if he would refrain from going back to this behavior and never received a response.

MAY 9

My direct link to his brain was gone. He was desperately seeking a fire that would burn him. Out of the frying pan and into the flames. That's where he was. In the fire. I knew that doubts existed in his mind but his pride admonished them and quelled them and they caused him to act desperately. He was leaping from one woman to the next searching for a perfect life that would never exist. He was running from reality, from mortality to "eighteenitis." I wanted to save him from his path of self-destruction but knew that I had no power to do so. I knew he was headed for a black hole and I felt so sad that I might be forever without his love in my life. But, I was grateful for the love he had given me. At least I had been loved until the stresses and strains of life took his breath and mine away..... If only he had listened in the beginning and if only I had listened near the end. I hated the weakness within me that wished him home with me holding me close in love. I missed him physically and emotionally. I missed his scent and his body. I wanted to be held in his warm monkey arms so badly. I couldn't imagine how he had done what he had done but for the reason of desperation of closeness with anyone or anything. My friend had told me that men found love through sex and for women love came first, then sex. I wondered how two so very different creations could ever mate for life? I wanted him with me so badly holding me close and telling me that he had made a terrible mistake and that all of the rumors were not true and that he had not had an affair. But, I knew I was wishing to wake from a nightmare that had not been a dream. It really had happened. He really had cheated on me—even if it had been after he had left me and there was no turning back from that and no wishing it away and no hoping that I would wake from the dark place that I felt I was in.

MAY 11

I knew that I had to gain access again to his email account to stay up on what he was doing. But, if I "broke" in again, he would know or at least be very suspicious of who had gained access. But, I couldn't wait any longer and decided to take the chance. What I found was unbelievable to me. What I hadn't known after my link was severed through Halley was that all the time he had been coming onto my internet-self, he had been playing the field with other internet babes, as well as communicating with his ex-girlfriend, Ashley. The night he had returned from Salem after Halley's kiss-off, he had immediately started looking for women via his internet façade. And, he had been successful to a point. His communication with one of them in particular made me sick. Turned out he had gotten her to agree to a date three days after being dumped by Halley. But, the day after his date with her, she had told him she only wanted to be "friends" and he had communicated with another of his internet women that he had felt he could have done anything if he could have had her in his life. And, I knew then why he had looked so gaunt and tired in the court-room. Besides the obvious, he had been dumped not once but twice in the same week. I felt so hurt in regard to his comment about the "other woman" being someone who could have gotten him to where he wanted to be in life—wherever that was.

What about all the things I had enabled him to accomplish? Had it been time for him to move on to the next woman who could supply him with the energy to meet the rest of his "goals?" Was it because I was finally devoting some time to myself that he had seen he couldn't get undivided attention and giving from me, plus the fact that I was providing no income? He had left me on the premise that he was going to someone who made the top pay at the institution he worked for.....and he still had no one.

From the emails that I had been able to access and print out, it was clear he was only concerned with all of his "Internet women" and he was not interested in giving me any time to show him the "real" me.

I had free access to the credit card accounts via the internet and from this I had proof of all the expensive dinners and places that he had been. How I handled all of this, I really didn't know. I was so obsessed with knowing what he was doing that I didn't feel the pain all at once, only a sense of numbness.

Well, even though "she" only wanted to be "friends, they had decided that they would go skydiving together. I was floored by this. I remembered him mentioning it once or twice years before but never thought it was something he wanted to do? Wasn't the pilot's license enough? He was definitely on a tour of self-destruction and looking to feel alive. Only by cheating death, he could feel alive. It just didn't make any sense to me. My mind was spinning.

As I read through all the messages that I had been able to print out, it was so obvious to me that he couldn't stand to be alone. He seemed desperate for female companionship, especially in regard to dinner. He repeatedly asked them all to have dinner with him. It didn't matter to him that he was spending all of his money on gas and food. There was so much desperation. It just didn't make much sense to me. I remembered when I had first met him and asked him where he disappeared to one night after seeing him in a local pizza house. He replied that he had gone to the cemetery to eat because it was quiet there. His actions and disposition were so hypocritical. How could he go from wanting to be so alone to wanting so desperately to be with anyone?

274

It was also apparent that the demise of his relationship with Halley had brought his resentment to a head again. She had tamed him and brought him to realize that he needed to see the good in his relationship with me, Hunter. But, now, all hell broke loose again and in his correspondence with one of the women, he made very cruel comments about me once again as he had done with my first Internet babe, Maria. I couldn't stand to read his hateful comments. I knew that the girl receiving these messages would probably wonder about his mental state, rather than that of the person whom he had left. He spoke of his many accomplishments but failed to mention my part in them. He also spoke of his many "friends" and the activities they had done together. How could this be inviting to a new "friend?" Wouldn't they think that he had some sort of commitment "phobia" and just wanted to play the field to see what he could get out of it?

It was obvious from one of his communications with one of his "friends" that she wasn't into his blatant comments and gave it right back to him and let him have it. He came back in his return mail that there was truth to what she had said but he continued to try to get her to see his side by lying. And the only one who would know that was me.

MAY 11

The emails between us as separated husband and wife became scathing at best. He accused me and blamed me. I defended and cajoled. But, I always ended with statements that he had no argument for because he would not allow himself to admit any feelings for me. I only wanted to speak to him in person. But, he could not look me in the eyes. And, he could not be civil when we were physically standing in the same area. It was so hurtful to me that he could treat me so terribly after so many years. It just didn't make any sense to me and I could find no justification in his behavior. Weren't we supposed to talk things through and work things out—not run away?

eighteen

BIRTHDAY BLUES

MAY 15

He didn't even send me a birthday e-mail, but why should he? Forty and no husband. I couldn't believe it was my 40th birthday and I was alone. All I had ever wished for was someone to be with and someone to love me and he had left me two weeks before Christmas. Valentine's Day was ruined. And, now my birthday. I decided to try to hack into his e-mail account again as a gift to myself.. What I got was an unbelievable surprise. When I went in to change the password via the secret question, I found he had altered it. The question read, "My new name for you Hunter." I almost fell off my chair. He was guessing because he had no proof, but I couldn't believe it. I immediately took copies of all the disks I had copied the day before and hid them in a safe place and went immediately to the department store to buy a shredder. I got home and called the library where I had been volunteering after school hours and said I didn't feel well and wouldn't be able to come in that afternoon. I printed all the documents that I had finished transferring and typing the night before and went through all of the email copies looking for notes that needed to be transferred. Then, I shredded for hours. Then, I realized I had shredded e-mails

I didn't have copies of! I made notations so they would be recreated and, luckily, the important ones were intact. I sifted through miscellaneous notes and inserted them where they belonged within the e-mails until I had a stack of papers that was four inches thick.

At this point, I needed a break and accepted an invitation from my sister to go out to dinner for my birthday. It was better than nothing; better than what I had done the year before. I held up until I got home and then the tears fell like a flood as I continued to shred the evidence of our cyber relationship.

I heard from my mother and then my friend who had been helping me with my e-mails. She said there was a part-time job opening at her office and set me up for an interview. I also received an email from the person who had been looking for a housekeeper in Wisconsin a few months before and I was set for an interview with him. Everything seemed to be happening in a weird way.

Then, I noticed that Jon was out in the garage. Who knew what he was doing. No birthday wish. No birthday knock. No birthday card. Nothing. And, he left and was gone again. I got my piece of cheesecake out of the fridge that I had brought home and lit the singing birthday candle and made a wish—a wish that was a fairytale. Sadness couldn't even begin to describe the way that I felt. So, I took a shower and gave myself a birthday gift—one that Halley had introduced to me....

I had lost another link to him. But, I would find another way....

MAY 17

The court's decision on the temporary hearing finally came back. I would get $500.00 a month from him to pay bills but would have to find at least a part-time job to cover groceries and personal things. At least I would be able to stay in my home until the end, if not longer.

Then, I received another insulting email from Jon. He was taking our phone number for his own and cutting off the electricity. I had never known that my name was not on the telephone account, so he could do whatever he wanted to do. And, instead of telling me to change the electrical service over, he issued a cut-off. I was at a point of thinking he was totally beyond help. He was apparently very angry at the court's decision and was going to take it out on me.

MAY 19

I received an email that the interview for the Wisconsin job was canceled as he had found the "Englishwoman" he had been searching for. Evidently, I didn't fit anyone's "bill" for the perfect match! I knew I still had the interview scheduled for the part-time job, so at least there was still some hope.

MAY 20

I got the job I interviewed for but I didn't know how I was going to do it. I didn't know how I got through the interview. Sheer determination and will. At least I would have money for food. I also realized that I didn't know who I was at this point. Surrounded by these people, I was taken by surprise at my own lack of knowledge of myself and who I was.

MAY 22

I kept thinking about the harshness of the winter I had spent alone, all alone except for fleeting visits from Jon at strange and varying times. The loneliness of all the snow shoveling and pushing and all of the times I had had to clean off the spa cover—one time with a butter knife to get the ice off. It had been horrible and maddening and had taken me hours. How could he live with himself knowing that I was having to do everything myself. Because, he was mad that I was in "his" house. But he had left and he couldn't face the truth.

I remembered the disbelief and shock the first time I had found him on the internet staring back at me with his million-dollar smile. And, I remembered the beauty of the moon surrounded by glorious, hazy midnight clouds. Why was there always beauty and ugliness, good and bad, at the same time in one's life?

I repeatedly asked myself questions. How could I have ever married a person who would end up advertising himself to the world on the Internet? Had I ever known him, really? Was the real Jon the person who existed now? I remembered how I had stooped to a level I never thought myself capable of—how I had begged him not to leave me on my knees. And, all he could say to me at this low moment in my life was that his family would think him stupid if he changed his mind! How could I have missed the desperation and the warning "signs?" Was it because of my complete trust in him or myself? I couldn't believe that he had allowed his sister, Portia, to give him the justification to believe that he was doing the right thing in leaving me. He had never had anything good to say about her and he had gone to live with her. I knew that if he hadn't gone there the first night, we would have been able to work things out. Jon admitted to me that he wanted to come home that night. And, I knew right where she had been all that night—sitting in front of his face telling him he would have a better life without me. That bitch. I would never forget her part in all of this and I wasn't sure I would ever be able to forgive her. I might only be able to forgive her because I felt sorry for such a sad excuse for a human being. And, she would pay in all of this. Perhaps, her "picture perfect" marriage would fall apart or, perhaps, someday Jon would realize he should have listened to me and not to her. Hadn't I done more for him than all of his family? Yes. And I knew that without a doubt.

MAY 26

I kept thinking about how our relationship had begun. Everything had been a mad, devoted, crazy rush. No real dates. Just together. He made me feel so wanted. He was so kind and so caring. Then, suddenly he backed off. When he backed off, I went out as usual and he came running to isolate me away. He wanted me to himself. It was an almost selfish need. I gave up my friends, my classes and going out so that I could be only with him. When I started taking classes again fifteen years later, for real credit, he became a mutinous partner. He could take classes and be with people and meet people but it wasn't okay for me to. He jumped ship by the plank of his own accord. I had to wonder if my intelligence was a threat? He was financially and woman-desperate and became unfaithful to our marriage. I was so thankful that it didn't seem that he had been unfaithful until after he had left. But, still, we were married so it was infidelity. There had to be a reason he couldn't look directly at me, nor that of my relatives. Was it guilt or a lack of conviction in regard to his actions? He believed himself happy but he didn't look happy. He looked gaunt and thin and wasted away. He had always made himself busy but he was in a desperately busy mode. Now, instead of it being work, it was play. I was hoping that when school was out for the summer, he would take the time to think and realize that he had made a mistake. I worried that when he was away for his graphic design course, he would meet someone. I also hoped he would have to time to realize that he should be with me. Or, I wondered if he would bury his feelings even deeper. I knew he was running away from the truth. And, he felt he was running into it. Somewhere and somehow, I knew that his emotions had exploded and he could only blame me for everything. I didn't know how he could live with the fact that he had abandoned our marriage, our responsibilities, our life.….. a life that needed nurturing. He hadn't allowed me to be me and I had allowed him to take me away to a far cloud in his sky—a cloud that only a strong wind of fate could push back to where it belonged. But why did it have to happen this way? Why was so much pain necessary? Was it because I was so lost and it was the only way I could be found?

He wanted me to be doing the same things he was doing. The schmuck. So he wouldn't look so bad? But, he still would. And, I had no intention or interest in anyone else. I wanted to be given the chance to face him—for him to look me in the eye and speak to me as a man would speak to his wife. I thought to myself that, perhaps, the only time this had happened was on our wedding day. Did I really believe this? What would the "Great Deacon" think of Jon's infidelities if he knew of them? Or, perhaps, he had done the same thing in his lifetime? I wanted to ask Jon what sex without love was like because I would not ever know and I wanted him to have to tell me. But, I knew he didn't have the guts. He was a coward. He was a savage. Like the savage who cut a tree to get its fruit, Jon was so eager and impatient for pleasure that he was slitting his own throat.

MAY 29

The lawn was getting out of hand. I asked to use the lawn mower and he refused. Because I wanted him to approve of me and to come home, I let the lawn grow and wondered what I would do about it. I was so busy dealing with everything else, I put it off for later.

MAY 30

I couldn't believe my luck. My new phone number was only one digit off from the old. I knew that would be another thorn in his brain....

nineteen

WONDERING

JUNE 1

I contemplated my job options. I had five pages of places that I had submitted resumes to looking for employment. It was pathetic. At the same time, I didn't know how I could handle a full time job feeling as I did. I knew the right thing would happen at the right time but it was so difficult waiting for the right time—whenever that was supposed to be.

JUNE 2

I watched the ducks in the pond and how the male watched over the female. I knew that ducks mated for life and I wanted it to be that way for me too. I watched as the male duck watched over his lover as she ate. It was so beautiful. Tears streamed down my face as I watched their happy moment. And, I wondered where their babies were or if they had any yet. I wanted to stay. I didn't want to leave. I wondered why he should even be given the chance to come back after how he had left. I knew that I didn't have the money to stay, but maybe I could find a way. I wished that he would love me again like he loved me in the beginning. I wanted him to want our marriage. And, I knew he hated me for it. I wished he could come back to me. I was so lonely for my best friend, but was he? I wanted to be with him and I wanted him to want to be with me. We had been two peas in a pod in so many ways. Two odd ducks. We were like the two ducks in the driveway. We had been the two ducks in the driveway sitting next to their food.

I remembered the summer a turtle dug a hole in the driveway and laid her eggs and then buried them. But, no little turtles ever emerged. It was so sad to me. Like me—no little turtles. No babies. I would never be remembered. I was so confused by everything. I regretted not insisting that we have children when we were first married and letting him decide that we needed to wait. I knew that I should not have listened but that wouldn't have been right. It had to be a joint decision. But if it had happened, he would have been happy. We would have been happy. So, I let him decide and we floated along waiting for the perfect time. What we didn't know then was that there would never be a "perfect" time and that time would get away from us and then it would be too late—at least for him.

I kept hoping that this was all a bad dream and that I would soon wake up and find him lying next to me breathing gently and holding me in his arms. I missed him so much that it hurt. I had to believe that moving away would have been a good thing—away from the all the responsibilities that plagued us and took away from the quality of our life. I had been so naïve. I hadn't been aware of the warnings and he didn't even care enough to try.

I received an email from him about several things and I responded. One of the things it seemed he felt a failure for was that he couldn't "make" me happy. How could he not know that he had been my happiness. I replied that he was not responsible for my happiness but that I didn't understand how he could think he was happy living the life he was leading. How could someone be happy if they were searching for something that didn't exist? And, how could they be happy if they wouldn't deal with their feelings?

JUNE 3

I wondered why his internet-self had disappeared from the limelight. I guessed at his password and gained access to his account. I just couldn't believe my resourcefulness. I changed his username and password and waited to see what would happen. It was like magic but nothing happened. Then, when I went into the account information, I found that he had resigned his account. I thought this so strange. Dumped too many times or had someone he worked with found him out?

JUNE 4

The scathing emails continued. Whatever issue was brought up, it turned into an email war. But, this time, I really let him have it. I let him know and feel my pain in regard to his infidelity. And, no reply again. He could never reply to a dose of reality. It happened every time.

JUNE 5

I had heard that his sister and her husband had insisted that he move out of their house after six months. I also heard that they had nothing good to say about him. That hurt me. I knew they were assholes. And, I wondered how he could ever have moved in with them in the first place. I heard that he was going to move into his sister's apartment building. How convenient for her. She would have a paying tenant who would do free work. She was a user and would use any situation to her advantage. That was a sure thing.

Then, I received an oil delivery from his brother that I had not authorized. What else was Jon going to pull? So, I filed the bill away for the final hearing.

JUNE 10

I was losing patience. I had to know what he was doing. I wanted that connection back and the only way I could get it was to revive my alter ego no matter how she might be treated by him.

That morning I had come face to face with his mother in front of the post office and she had completely blown me off. I was shaking with rage and hurt feelings at her thoughtlessness and her lack of guts. After hearing everything I had heard about my father-in-law and his girlfriend, I supposed she was a coward in her own right, just like her son.

JUNE 12

I've been thinking about you. I hope you're doing well and that you have a great summer. Halley

I had no idea how he would respond, but I had to try.

JUNE 12

Yes, things are going well. I truly feel like I'm getting my act together. I'm not back in my home yet but, hopefully, I will be by the end of summer. How about you? Jon

JUNE 12

Things are going okay. I'm getting ready for a seminar. And, I thought you had your act together before? I do want you to know that I really miss our conversations. They were so much fun. But, that's over! Right? I'm sure you have moved on to "other things" by now! I'm so glad you responded. It was nice to hear your "voice." I'm glad things are going well for you. Halley

Well, no negativity yet. I was batting 1000.

JUNE 13

I'm curious. I've just got to ask you how things with your husband are going? It's none of my business and you haven't readily told me but, I just had to ask. You don't have to say anything.

P.S. You're right. Godiva chocolates are very good. Your "NADS" went back to the store. I still think you suck but, whatever. I learn from my experiences. Who's wearing the boxers? Is Halley just a name you chose to use? That's it for now. Jon

So, I "sucked." He had bought Godiva chocolates and ate all of them. Didn't he remember that we had eaten these on our honeymoon in Bermuda? How could he have forgotten? He was definitely hurt and resentful toward Halley and me, Hunter.....

JUNE 14

I understand your hurt feelings. I never meant what happened to happen. It just happened. I am sure there is someone out there who thinks we all suck in one way or another. It sucks. Things are going well between us. It's amazing what counseling can do for a relationship. It really helps to understand each other's side.

My husband rented a movie the other night called "Dinner with Friends." Was that an eye opener or what????? I could relate to both sides but in the end......well, you will just have to watch it to see what I mean......

So, it was Godiva chocolates? You are a sweetheart. Haven't you ever had them before??? I actually went and bought myself some "NADS" and it's great. I never would have known about it if you hadn't talked about it. But, it does hurt if you pull the strips in the wrong direction!

Who's wearing the boxers? I am. Halley is my name. Have a great weekend, Jon. Halley

All of these white lies were getting to me but I needed the connection to him in any way that I could get it. I was obsessed with him and with knowing what he was doing and with knowing the truth. How could anyone fault me for that? It was harder on me doing this. But, some would fault me for it. Obsessive or what?

That morning I had walked out into the driveway in my bathrobe to ask him "the question" to his face. I was tired of just getting lies. He denied everything in regard to his infidelity and to my statement that we were still married, he replied "only on paper." In his mind, this was truth but not for me. I felt like I was looking into the face of a stranger and it was frightening to me.

JUNE 20

Back from my seminar! Now, I can enjoy the summer. You didn't say before how your summer was going? And, I hope you have met someone to enjoy it with. So, did you ever do any of the things that you said you wanted to do in your profile? Rock climbing? Skydiving? Wondered if you could recommend anything for me to do? Halley

I wondered if he would tell me anything. I knew he had been skydiving from the credit card information but I wanted to know how it had been. I knew he must have been scared and I wanted to hear him lie. I was so used to the lying, I was addicted to it.

JUNE 20

Asking him for the truth again in person……. The second time he came into the driveway he came over and knocked on the door but didn't wait. He used his key to let himself in, but I opened the door for him before he could open it. I asked him if he had received the exclusivity paperwork and he replied that it was just for the house. I explained to him that it was for the property. He was more than mad. I said I would not make it hard for him if he would do me a favor. I needed him to tell me the truth to my face. I said how hard it was for me and I needed him to tell me the truth to my face so I could let go. Tears streamed down my face. He said it was hard for him too. BULLSHIT! So hard that he went out and spent all his money on women and expensive meals and skydiving and whatever else.... He wouldn't tell me the truth. He wasn't man enough to tell me the truth. I asked him how he could sleep around on me while we were still married. He said we weren't. I replied that we were still married. He went a little crazy with that one and turned away and I asked him not to leave. He said he could leave whenever he wanted and I replied that that was true. For sure. I raised my voice and continued to ask how he could sleep around on me while we were still married and he left....... He replied that he had not slept around—LIE! I couldn't believe that he was seeing the "Belly Ring Girl" again and thought how pathetic he must be to go out with someone whom he had said was not right for him months before. It was all out on the street... But, he hadn't admitted this to Halley....yet.

It was clear to everyone that he had no respect for himself, for me or for anyone or anything..... He looked terrible. His hair was turning gray and white in the front. He had to wear a belt to hold his pants up.... He couldn't be happy........... I couldn't help but feel sorry for him..... He had chosen this path and it was a terrible path to choose. I feared he would end up trapped in a life that would take his life away from him rather than give him one............more than he ever envisioned............ I knew that I couldn't keep warring with this .... I had to find a way to let go.. ... I couldn't do this anymore........ I didn't want this divorce but I didn't know if I could forgive the infidelity if I was given the chance.

The good in him was hidden. If he let his guard down—his fight against me would be over. He told me that I had been screwing him over from the beginning..........that was so untrue. He went to a lawyer first and he ran away...........

I wrote him a letter after this but never sent it. I thought after what happened that morning there was no point.

Jon: I need for you to tell me the truth so I can move on, even though I know what the truth is. Without hearing it directly from you, I will keep hoping no matter what because I was born with this tremendous ability to hope for the impossible. Please tell me the truth so that I can stop searching for the truth and start letting go. I know that you feel it is none of my business but it is my business because I am married to you. I need you to find the strength to tell me the truth to my face so I can face my reality and attempt to have a life. Please stop by soon and do this for me. I don't expect you to understand but I do think that it is the least you can do after all the years we were together. It's so hard for me because I keep thinking how wonderful everything was in the beginning and how it could be and know that you are thinking the opposite. I need the truth from you. Hunter

JUNE 20

Jon and Mark were both in the yard with trucks fully loaded with a sofa, the bed and a myriad of boxes. I knew that it must be moving day for Jon to the apartment building that his sister owned. I knew that he had spent three weeks doing renovations so he could move into it.

I thought to myself, "Big mistake, Jon." You don't ever want to scorn me. As I left the video store that afternoon, I couldn't believe my eyes. The black car. The girlfriend. I quickly turned and there she was. I said her name and she replied with sarcasm laced with trepidation. "I'm Hunter Logan, How are you." She replied, "So you are Jon's "soon to be ex-wife" and laughed. I replied, "Well, we'll see about that won't we?" and I turned and walked off. I was shaking with anger.

I called the Video Store and found out that I had completely taken her off guard and found out that she didn't tell my friend what she had said to me. My friend told me that she warned her. "You know, if he will do what he did to her, what do you think he will do to you?" "Watch your back, Ashley." That's right, I thought to myself, watch your back where Jon is concerned! There is nothing like a confused man or a scorned wife. And, to myself, I thought that

Jon had better watch his back too! Neither of them knew what was in store.......

I still believed that there was some good in him, but it was so hidden that only I could see it in my mind and, perhaps, my mind was deceiving me.

I called my attorney and asked if I could have the locks changed and he said it was no problem and asked via Jon's lawyer that Jon not come to the house or the garage at all without calling for permission. I called the locksmith and left a message. I was thinking that, hopefully, the locks could be changed within the week. I couldn't live with the thought that he might bring her into the house when I wasn't there.

I already had evidence that he was coming in and out when I was gone. I had put an automatic cassette recorder in the pocket of a bathrobe that he had left behind which hung on the backside of the bathroom door. When I returned home one day, I found that he had been there. All I could hear on the tape were "burps" and I knew that he must be stressed out. The only time he burped like that was when he was upset. It sounded from the tape like his stomach was going to come up out of his throat!

I wondered what his reaction would be to my introducing myself to his on and off again girl-friend. Would he freak or would he think it was a joke? The next day I received a message from him to Halley.

JUNE 21

I've done indoor rock climbing. I think you knew that. I've also done skydiving. It was the most extreme rush I have ever had and if you want to know you are alive, I would recommend you give it a try. I was in a free fall for about 45 seconds and jumped from 11,500 feet. You leave the place with a real sense of accomplishment. I'd like to go for a balloon ride and I have tickets for a glider ride.

I'm living more than I ever have my entire life. I'm learning so much and I'm not the same person I was just a few short months ago. I suspect I won't be the same in another few months either.

Ashley and I have started doing things together again. We are moving very slowly this time and are communicating about everything and just being totally honest with each other. We are friends and I do care very much about her. I'm much less critical of others now and I realize that sometimes people are the way they are because of the situations they are in and the difficulties in their lives. It's very early for me and she understands that it is much too soon for me for anything more than communication. Jon

I couldn't believe he was seeing the Amazon again like I had heard. The Internet babe thing must not have worked out for him. But, to resort back to her??? He was desperate. I was sure of that. And, to say that he needed to be more understanding of people's imperfections!!! But, he had left me because he felt I wasn't perfect! So, he cared about her? Was it that he needed to have someone to care for or he couldn't survive? What a load of crap he was giving out. I didn't think at this moment that he knew where the lies ended and truth began.

JUNE 21

Wow! Over 11,000 feet! Weren't you scared??? I think I might be more willing to try parasailing in the Bahamas like I said before!

So, the "Hearts.com" scene didn't work out? I am so surprised at you giving the "ex-girlfriend" another try after how you talked about her before. Be careful, Jon, that you are not acting out of loneliness or you could end up in a worse place. But, that's your decision and your life! You have to decide what you want and what makes you happy. I hope you are happy. Halley

I so wanted to save him from himself. What was my problem? I should let him get burned. I cared too much. He had told me that when he had left and he was right.

JUNE 25

My overgrown lawn became a thing of beauty. As I walked out to get the mail, I noticed that part of the lawn was a meadow of wild-flowers. I couldn't resist walking through them and feeling them with the tips of my fingers and smelling in the beauty of them....

The only problem was that the grass was so long I couldn't make my way down to the pond.

I remembered before the pond had been there. It had been a wooded, swampy place. Jon had cut most of the big trees himself. In their place was a hug brush pile of logs and limbs. The day he decided to burn it was windy. He couldn't get it to burn. As I watched him pour gasoline on the branches, I wondered what he was thinking. It wasn't long before the fire was completely out of control. I yelled out the door and asked if he wanted me to call the Fire Department. As he ran around the brush pile spraying it with a garden hose, he yelled back that he had it under control. Later, I realized that if I hadn't been so afraid that the house was going to burn down I could have gotten a tape that could have won a prize for being one of the funniest videos ever! Imagine thinking that the force of a garden hose could keep the roaring fire under wraps! Afterwards, we laughed until we cried. And, the neighbor was clearly not amused!

The pond—the heart-shaped pond where the fish swam and where we had rowed ourselves around in a rubber boat each summer looking for them. The water grass had grown so long it was difficult to see if any fish even lived there any longer. I remembered when the pond was new and the first time Jon had bought baby trout and thrown them into the clear water. And, I remembered how we had watched them each summer as they jumped around and out of the water. It had been so amazing. Then, I remembered when they had grown large enough to be fished out. The first time he had caught a giant trout he had had to jump back in to grab it because it had flopped its way back in after he had gotten it off the hook! With sadness, I remembered how few fish were left, if any, and how murky the water had become—just like our marriage.

JUNE 26

Jon came to the house without calling even with the exclusivity order hanging over his head. He wanted the wiring book. It was getting ridiculous the way he wouldn't comply with the orders.

That afternoon, my niece and I went shopping. As we walked into a local boutique, we came face to face with the "Belly Ring Girl's" mother. She quickly turned away and by the time we made it around the store, she had gone. Gutless wonder. They were all cowards. Jon's mother, Ashley's mother, Ashley and all the others. Where were the heroes in the world?

JUNE 27

I decided that I couldn't let the bike sit in the hall any longer. I had to see if I could ride it like I never had been able to before. The tires were flat. I carried it out to the garage and started to try to figure out how to use the air compressor. I called my sister's husband and he explained to me what to look for. I searched and searched and finally found the switch. It started with a loud crack and ran. I had air in the compressor. All I needed now was the attachment for the hose. Getting the attachment to fit into the hose was another story. I finally had to call my father and he came and got it in place and filled my tires. I was ready to go. I got my bike helmet and gloves on and sat on the seat with the tips of my toes touching the ground. It was either do it or die, or do it and die! I circled the yard. It was hard but I did it. I finally got the feel of it and ventured down the driveway and out onto the dirt road. I knew that at any moment I could go over the handlebars, but with each trip up the road and back my confidence grew. On the last trip, I was feeling free! I was drenched in sweat. Of course, I had picked the most humid day of the summer to try to ride a bike that had been held upside down in the basement for over five years. And, I had done it. I couldn't believe that I had done it..... He was wrong about me. I was capable and I wasn't a "little old lady!"

JUNE 28

Halley: I can't help wonder what type of woman you are. I can't help but imagine the situation the night that we were supposed to meet and what truly transpired.

I imagine that you were feeling totally in control. You were looking fine in all your red and feeling good. You thought it was a good time to tell your husband exactly where you stood. After all, you had this guy waiting to meet you and spend the night with you if things didn't work out. You held the conversation and totally overpowered him. He succumbed to your wants and luckily for him, said the exact magical words that you needed to hear in order for you to stay where you were for the night. Perhaps, he doesn't even know what was to transpire that night? So, you try to work things out. Hopefully, for you they will.

The way in which we were to meet was quite a production after all, wasn't it? I mean, who in their right mind would spend the night in a hotel room with a complete stranger?

Something else that I can't help wonder about is how you and I will feel in a couple of years. Will I be alone? If I'm not alone, I surely want to be "oh so happy" with the one I'm with. I remember this girl that I knew from high school and how I was so totally in love with her, in a puppy love sort of way. I would have done anything for her. I wanted to give her the world. When I met my wife, I just ripped this girl's name, face and personality from my mind. Now, when I think of what I want, her name somehow has returned to my mind and I never even expected it to. Ingrid. Such a weird, sort of ugly name but a magical time in my life and a magical feeling of that perfect woman, even though I truly knew little about her. I know that she knew how I felt about her and I do believe she would remember me, but that's about it. She has lived her life far away. The last I heard she had three kids and a husband. Oh well.

I wonder who's name will be in my mind in two years? I hope it's the name of the one I'm with and not Ingrid or any other woman's name.

During moments of personal thought, those thoughts that your partner can't begin to guess, I wonder what name you will be thinking of. I doubt it will be me, but I do wish we could have at least met.

I'm not stupid. I think you know that. I have changed. I see that the faults I saw in Ashley have another side also, a good side. She is stubborn and so pig headed. I tell her so to her face. She is that way because she has had to raise a child on her own and has done so without help from anyone. She refuses help from anyone. Yes, she is a little rough around the edges but, I also see someone who has never had anyone to lean on and help her. I see and know how she could blossom with the right person. She is so beautiful. She is totally open and honest about everything with me. I am the same with her. I've never had that before. It's a scary position for me. I don't want to think about changing anyone, yet I can see how she will change over the next few years. I have learned that changing someone doesn't work. I'm taking it very slow. We are friends. She needs to trust me and make changes on her own. That's where it should stay for now.

I've told you so much about me, yet you remain a ghostwriter with no face. Do you even exist? Are you alive? If you're alive, are you living? Answer this question for yourself—are you living the life that you truly want? Do you wonder about where you're going in your life? Where you should be? Do you even, perhaps, wonder about me? I would still meet you if you like?

Yes, I'm still not happy with what you did, but who's totally happy with anyone anyway?

I know someone just like you. You like the thought of someone waiting in the wings for your messages. It makes you feel good. I know it makes me feel good too to have someone looking at my messages. I don't mind telling you. I'm willing to do that for now, but I also wait and have others waiting for me. I will end up being with the one who finally decides to take a plunge like they never have before. The one who is willing to be open, honest and who decides that the time for games is over. I'll be with the one who also wants something REAL. There are many who seem willing to do this, but I also need to have the same feeling for them. I've never met you so I don't know if you could even do that for me. There is only one way to find out. I would never propose a meeting similar to the last fiasco. It would be lunch or, possibly, dinner. What harm could it do? In the least, it would be a meeting of minds and possibly good conversation. Jon

Well, it seemed he was only involved with Ashley because he couldn't get anyone else. Why else would he suggest a meeting after everything that had conspired between us. As for the "production" leading up to our original meeting, he had seemed to be totally into it and now he was trying to downplay his interest. His pride still had a hole in it. Ingrid. How I hated that name. I had heard of her before we had dated from him. I knew she was an idiot but thought it better not to say anything that would make him think badly of me. He seemed so stupid about women. He had had a good one and he had dumped her (me). He just seemed to want a bimbo and it seemed that eventually he would get what he deserved if he was willing to spend time with a bimbo such as Ashley. A little rough? The girl was a barfly with an eleven-year-old daughter who slept with men after only a few days of knowing them or, maybe, in payment for an expensive dinner! Was she supposed to be termed as a "nice" girl? So, there were "many" waiting in the wings for him? I doubted that.

JUNE 28

Jon, I explained to you how my husband came to me that night and I couldn't leave. And, we are still working on things as anyone should try to do when they are in the situation that we both are in. Then, you really know that you gave it your all. I will know, without a doubt, in the end that I made the right decision, whether it is to go back to him or to stay away and move on. I think too many people run away too fast without thinking and regret it later on.

It is confusing to me how you can say that Ashley is "beautiful" and capable of changing but you didn't want to think or believe that about someone you've been married to for years. And, how can you ask me out to dinner after telling me your feelings about Ashley and how you believe she will change in the next few years. What if she doesn't????

Why would you still want to meet me if you have such a "thing" going for her? Or, is your mind full of doubts about her? Maybe this will help. Someone told me the other day that if I wanted to really "know" my husband, I should look at his father and decide how I felt about him. Have you met her mother? If you haven't, maybe you should. That should either reinforce any doubts you may have or dispel them. Like they say, "the nut doesn't fall very far from the tree." Check it out!

Oh, yes, I am real, very real and I know I can overshadow and outdo her and all the other "many" women in every REAL way imaginable....but with whom—that is the question!!!!! :)

I am so intrigued that you think you know someone just like me. Tell me more. Who is this mystery person?

I'll think LONG and HARD about lunch or dinner......but what would the "Belly Ring Girl" and all the other women in your life think??? Aren't you playing with FIRE???? :) Halley

It blew my mind how he could be so willing to wait years for someone to change and he wouldn't even give me, his wife, just one week much less one day!

JUNE 29

Halley: I can tell that you have as many doubts about the future as I. I can tell that you're as curious as I am. You should try to work things out if that's how you feel. I simply don't feel that way in my case. I know you explained things to me in regards to how things happened that night. I just have my own thoughts and imagination as to what happened. I don't have a face or anything else to put on that night.

You wrote: It is confusing to me how you can say that Ashley is "beautiful" and capable of changing but you didn't want to think or believe that about someone you've been married to for years.

My reply: There are fundamental differences that apply to this situation. I would rather not get into the discussion about Hunter in this regard. Ashley is physically beautiful to me. I am, though, very apprehensive towards her and her totally unproven abilities. I don't know if I can move beyond that point. I admit that. No one is perfect. I'm learning this and I'm much more accepting towards others and their differences than I used to be. Others are very accepting of my abilities and weaknesses, so I should do the same. This area is our stumbling block and is what I talk about with her.

You wrote: "And, how can you ask me out to dinner after telling me your feelings about Ashley and how you believe she will change in the next few years. What if she doesn't?????"

My reply: I'm not married or going out with anyone. Good question, "What if she doesn't?." I imagine myself riding my lawn mower around during a summer in the distant future with my personal thoughts of this subject thinking about Ingrid. I don't want this. I simply want to make the right decision. I met this amazing woman through "Hearts.com." We went out to dinner and I just felt like she was the ideal woman. I felt like a better man just being near her. I asked her out again and got a reply to my email that she only wanted to be friends. Does it ever work out? I don't know. Why is it always he likes her but she likes someone else or she likes him but he likes someone else?

I have met Ashley's mother. She is a nice woman, but not exactly what I was thinking of. I ask that you not look at my father to judge me. I'm not the same person as my father. He is a good man, but I'm not the same as he.

My reply: The person I know who I feel is like you may not actually be like you at all. This is just how I perceive you right now and please don't be offended. This woman is a co-worker. She is a professional. She is very detail-oriented and is quite good at her job. She's going through a divorce and has a small child. She's really quite beautiful. She's kind of a jock type, blonde and looks great in red. She's very womanly and likes to have her nails done. She is divorcing her husband because she has lost respect for him. One thing that I don't think the two of you have in common is that she is kind of dingy. That part worried me a little bit about her. Her husband is great with their child and is a terrific father and she admits this. The problem is, she likes to wear the pants, but has lost respect for her husband because he does not. I'm not the only one who thinks this at school. Most everyone else does too. What I think is that she will never be happy because the perfect man for her does not exist. She wants the strong, take-control type, but would refuse to release that control to him. So, she is incapable of seeing anyone who is like that. I look at the man she is dating and I just want to say to her, "Why don't you just stay with your husband?." She has a very difficult time talking one-on-one with someone about important things. She can sing in front of two hundred people, but to sit down one-on-one and discuss things like this is very difficult for her. We talked about going out and now I see just how impossible the situation really was. I'm so glad that nothing ever happened between us. It was mutually agreed, in a very strange way, that we should not. I know that she enjoyed the attention I gave her. She liked having me around and even admitted she felt something for me. Now, it's very difficult for us. There is this tension in the air. I don't really know what it is. She has so many thoughts that she refuses to admit to. I think she just wishes that I would fall off the face of the earth so she wouldn't have to look at me anymore. I wouldn't be a constant reminder to her then. I know that she is confused as hell, just like everyone else, and refuses to admit it. She refuses to let me, or anyone else "in." I don't think she has ever let anyone in. No one has ever truly known her. She will never be happy until she can. She will never be happy until she can just be herself with someone and tell them all her thoughts and let "it" go. What does it take for a man to make a woman like this happy? I don't know.

How do I think you are like this woman? Well, the obvious physical likeness and a few others. You're not happy. You see good qualities in your partner, but have difficulty with some things about him. At least you are talking and trying to work it out. I don't know what you have for problems. In regard to your husband, it doesn't need to be you who is wearing the pants. Anyway, it really doesn't matter. Something is wrong and it needs fixing. I think when a child is involved you need to make some type of effort. My friend has not. This does not seem too appropriate for her or her common sense. The main likeness, though, is that you haven't let anyone in. Am I wrong? Perhaps through written words, I've come close? But, because we have not met and you have not let me put a face on you, you still haven't let me in either. You keep your personal secrets to yourself that way. I hope I'm wrong about this. I hope I'm way off. If I'm not, it's sad. If what I've said is true and you have never let anyone truly into your thoughts, please meet me. It would be good for you. It might be a turning point in your life. How can you know who you should be with if you have never let anyone into your world? It's a personal discovery. You may find out new things about yourself that you never knew, new things that make you see what you need to do more clearly. I know this has happened to me.

You wrote: "I'll think LONG and HARD about lunch or dinner......but what would the BRG and all the other women in your life think??? Aren't you playing with FIRE???? :)"

My reply: Yes, I am but this a serious game that deserves serious, difficult decisions. I am only seeing her right now. I've decided that no one will make me happy other than myself and that no one else will decide my future but myself. I will decide my future. As far as I know, I have only one life to live. I need to make the most of it and I desperately want to make the right choice of who I am going to spend the rest of my life with. I'm not going to go out with women that are obviously not for me....? Perhaps I'm actually doing this? Anyway, I've decided that when the opportunity to meet a unique woman that has many of the things I'm looking for comes along, I want to meet her.

Everyone I have met has shaped and contoured my thoughts in regard to the woman I want to be with. At the minimum, you can put your hands on my thoughts and shape a small part of it. If we were to meet, it doesn't mean that we need to get married. :) Lunch is a pretty innocent thing, you know.

I'm not going to repeatedly ask you to meet me. Although, I'm thinking that you're the type that needs constant prodding in order to do so. I want you to "tell" me that you would like to meet. "Tell" me what you are thinking. I don't want to pull it out of you or put things into your head. I want it to come from you. Let me into your thoughts. I want that type of relationship. I think you do too, but may be scared. I think many things could come from us meeting. You may see that you should stay with your husband and would be able to communicate with him more freely. You may think that I'm nothing like I seem to be in my emails and you have no interest at all. There is only one way to find out. Maybe I'm way off on everything I've said. It's just how I see it. I tell it like I see it. I hope you do the same. Jon

So, he was unsure about Ashley. And, the part about Kristan made me sick. He was telling me the "story" all over again but with more details. So, now I knew the truth of him leaving me. He really had left me thinking he was going to her. That had been the real reason or, perhaps, the main reason. I wanted to hit him. Boy, was he getting wordy or what? If he spent any more time trying to convince Halley to meet him, it would have been the length of the "Gettysburg Address!"

JUNE 29

So, Jon, you want to know what I "really" think. I have some "strong" doubts about where you are in your life right now. One of them is that no matter what your situation was with your wife (as you already explained to me in-depth previously) that you didn't attempt to work through things. That is a huge factor for me, maybe even more now because of my own situation. I don't think you want to really "feel" anything towards your wife (and that is what she still is unless your divorce is final yet?), so you have turned your head and your mind to any real possibilities that may exist because it is too difficult to face. And, it really is difficult but sometimes it is worth it. You seem almost willing to wait a few years for Ashley to change but your wife gets nothing. It just doesn't makes sense to me. And, I've heard all of your explanations and it still does not make sense. I think you felt that you had to run away. You said you didn't want to take the time to "fix" things but that is what you are attempting to do with Ashley, isn't it? It seems to me the chances that things would work out would be better with your wife. Just being honest from what I know that you have told me.

Is it just because of Ashley's confidence in the way she looks that you spend time with her? It seems that the two of you are on two completely different levels, if I am comprehending what you are saying. And, I remember how you said your wife did not think she was beautiful and it was a major block for you. I don't know if this will help you or not but I do know, in my case and in my mind, that I would not ever get involved with someone where I did not think I could "move beyond the point." To me, that is an indication of serious doubt and something that might lead to a serious mistake. But, that is for you to decide. It is just how I see things. Maybe you need to ask yourself a question—are you spending time with her because there is no one else now? If the answer is yes, then you are going in the wrong direction.

On the other hand, I want you to know there are so many things I don't have any doubts about, such as your willingness to communicate. And, I know you don't want to hear this but wouldn't it be a real "test" of your new abilities and new mindset to try this willingness to communicate out on your wife? Sometimes, you have to face the hurt to get through it. I just want you to think about all of this. You seem so willing to give everyone a chance, but of all the women out there she should be the one who gets the first chance. That is just my opinion.

And, I want you to know that it is possible to "grow" a relationship that you had given up on and make it better. Yes, it does take work but it sounds like a lot of effort is going into your relationship with the "Belly Ring Girl" and you have serious doubts at the same time. Wouldn't your time be better spent on your wife? You wanted to know what I really think and I am telling you and I hope you will not be offended.

You said in your email that "I'm not going to go out with women that are obviously not for me..." and say that "perhaps, I'm actually doing this?" I'm going to be completely honest with you. I think you answered your own question. Why would you go out with someone whom you had decided was too fundamentally different from you for things to be as you wanted them to be? I know that I want to be with someone who accepts me for who I am right now and someone who will grow with me so our relationship will become better as the years go by. That doesn't mean that there won't be "valleys" or seasons in a relationship—it means that we will always be there for each other and will be accepting of each other and work with each other and not run away from the difficult times. It's all about commitment. You say that you left Ingrid behind you when you met your wife and that is the right thing to do. And, right now, it is natural to wonder about anyone you ever were attracted to. I have done this myself. And you are right, it is a VERY confusing time—going through all of this!

And, it seems you are better off without the person you worked with. I want you to know she is very different from me. I would not leave my husband for the reasons she has given; her reasons seem very shallow. And, it seems almost as if she used you in a way for attention that she needed and now resents you for knowing what you know about her. I've also discovered some new things about myself. While I like to do certain things for myself, such as my nails etc., I have realized there are people out there that cannot feel good about themselves unless they do certain things for themselves on an excessive level. She sounds like someone I know. Unless this person gets their nails done every two weeks and their hair done every four weeks and goes to acupuncture and massage treatments and who knows what else every few weeks, she does not feel good about herself inside. It's kind of sad. I agree with you that you have to find a way to be happy on the inside without the outer "bandages" being what makes you happy. It seems there are a lot of people out there that disguise their unhappiness with material things. Not just nails but vehicles, houses, etc. etc. etc. Oh, there are great "benefits," but it isn't what is truly "real." To me, all that matters is that you believe in the power of love so that it can carry you through anything for as long as it takes to get through that difficult "moment."

I hope that I have given you something to think about. And I will think about all of this too. I'm not sure when your class is that you had told me about, but maybe if it is coming up you can think about all of this while you are away and you will get the perspective you need to make the right decision in your life for what you need to do right now. And, I will think very hard about all of this too. Your friend, Halley

I wanted so badly for him to give me, Hunter, a chance and my only chance was through Halley. But, he was so dead set against his own wife (me) that, perhaps, not even Halley could get through to him. When had I last been kissed by him? Christmas Eve. And, it had been the coldest, most unwelcome kiss I had ever experienced....

JUNE 29

Halley: You make some very good points. Almost all of what you said is true. I went to my niece's birthday party last night. I sat there alone just looking around, watching my niece and my nephew play. I have a great family. It was such a wonderful sight, just watching. I thought about what it was like with my wife when we went to family gatherings. Again, I'm not going to get into it, but I will say that I know for a fact that it could never be the way it was last night with her there.

It was very hard for me last night. I had a difficult time just trying to not look too upset and holding back tears. My brother is a very lucky man. His daughter was fifteen yesterday and she is so beautiful. I remember looking at her in the hospital the day she was born and thinking how beautiful she was then. She hasn't changed from that day.

I know you think that I should try to work it out with my wife. My situation is not like your own. You don't know what it's been like for me. I can't turn back and I refuse to. I have tried everything with her over the years and have gotten nothing in return. She simply was not there with me in her mind to understand and grow. I understand your position in regard to how you wonder about me and my unwillingness to try to work it out with her. Halley, I'm tired. I don't need to explain my actions and my position to anyone. I want my life back and I want something real. I'm losing so much and I have worked so hard for it. My new insult from her this week was that she changed the locks on the doors of the house so now I don't have a key. I don't know if I can do it all again. I certainly can't do it the way I did the first time with the apartment houses and all. I need to do it a different way and, somehow, if I end up having a family, I will find a way. You must know that I have thought about going back. Every time I do, I think about what it was like. All the things I had to do just to survive around her and I will not go back to that. Your difficulty with me not giving her another chance is not my problem. It is your own.

If it prevents you from wanting to know me better, there is nothing I can do about that because I will not go back and try to work things out. It is just so far beyond that point.

I know there is a woman out there for me. There are many things about Ashley that I'm unsure about. Does this make her an unwise choice? The truth is, I've messed up one time already. I'm not sure what it's supposed to be like. I need experience with people to find that out. Maybe she is totally wrong for me like you said and I'm only communicating with her because the right person hasn't come along yet. I don't know who that right person is. I know how capable I am. How much I can do. I feel like I can do anything. I have unproven talents. I would like to think that whoever I end up with can help me bring these talents out. I'm also unsure if she can do that. I think that you would probably have a better chance of accomplishing that. I do know that I have learned more from her than from any other woman I've met since December 8th. There are so many women out there, but so few willing to take a chance—so few to learn from. I don't need sex from ten different women. I want communication and I want to learn from different people, but I need the opportunity to meet them first.

In regard to where I am in my life, I'm where I need to be right now. I'm thinking about my future and considering possibilities. I don't have all the answers but I have some. I'm not willing to wait a few years for anyone. You're right, that person will need to be compatible with me. What's compatible? I'm figuring that out. So many people are happy with partners who are totally opposite to themselves. Nothing about this is easy. It's the most difficult thing I've ever done in my life. I leave for Kansas July 9th and return on the 22nd. I've got a week.

You can have all the doubts about me that you can find. I have some about you also. Why do I write? I write because there is a little part of me that still wonders about you. There is a little part of me that thinks you may be a fantastic woman and that you would be great to be with. There is a little part of me that thinks I could replace the name Ingrid with Halley. There is a little part of me that thinks we would be great together. There is a little part of me that thinks you are in fact "real" and that you would be so much more than anyone I have ever known. The real question is—if you're trying to work things out with your husband, why do you write to me?

I'm feeling that there is a reason that we communicate with each other the way we have. Have a nice weekend. Jon

How could he say such cruel things about me. How it couldn't be that way with me at a birthday party. What did that mean? I cried as I read the part about how he had to hold back the tears. He was right about his niece. She had been a beautiful baby. But, she was a very spoiled girl. And, to me, that made her ugly in another way. She expected everything to be handed to her and that wasn't attractive.

How could he say that I had not been there with him over the years. I had supported everything that he demanded be done and had encouraged him to reach goals he would never have reached had it not been for me. How could he think that after all this time apart that things were the same for me? And, why hadn't he ever tried to communicate with me. The question I kept asking myself was how could he spend so much time communicating with strangers and not even give me two minutes? It just wasn't fair at all.

I knew the reason he would not attempt to work anything out with me was his family. Period. That was it. He had finally gained their recognition and approval by behaving in the same manner as they and to admit that he had made a mistake would be failure in their eyes. This weakness in him frightened me.

And the locks. I did this because I couldn't let go and felt too much love for him and Jon's access to the house when I was there or wasn't there was too painful and too difficult for me. And, after the run-in with the Belly Ring Girl, I wanted to know that he would not be sneaking her into our home when I wasn't there. I needed to have even a shred of peace knowing I was allowed some privacy.

It sounded to me like he had no idea how to find the "right" person. He was looking so hard I couldn't imagine he would ever "see" her if she appeared. The truth was that I was the "right" person and he had dumped me. I thought that he should go look in the dumpster of our life together and there he would find his "perfect match," or at least his "perfect match" from before his Dr. Jekyll makeover!

The last line of his message struck me like a rock. How could he be so blind? The reason we could communicate with one another the way that we did was because we were "soul mates." But, if I revealed myself to him, would he only hate me more for deceiving him into reality?

JUNE 29

Jon, just one thing for now. What do you have to lose by having one "real" conversation with your wife. Just one. You have nothing more to lose by talking to her one last time. You've both lost everything already, right? Is it your pride that keeps you from being willing to talk to her? Or, are you afraid? We are all afraid. But, you have to go into the fear to get to the other side. Talking to her is not going back to her. It's just one conversation.

You keep thinking that things are the same. Let me tell you. They don't ever stay the same! And, they never will! How do you know who she is now? You don't. If you say that you've changed, then she has changed. I am just trying to get you to see the "new" reality of your situation, one that you are not willing to "see." How do you know that she doesn't eat junk food every day now? How do you know that she hasn't bought herself one of those "bad boys?" You just can't assume anything!

So, she had the locks changed. Maybe it's because she's hurt or trying to let go or she's upset? Who knows? But, you won't know unless you ask her. And, she probably can't tell you because it seems you don't want to talk to her? I'm just guessing. It seems from everything I remember you saying that you left and never looked back and you keep it in your mind that she is the same as the day you left and will never change. Is that fair?

I'm sure that if you have experienced all of the things you have in the last several months, she has had her own experiences and she can't be the same person that you knew. It just isn't possible. I know you are hurting and I know from my own experience that she is hurting. It's just a lot of hurt floating around and it needs to be "caught" and dealt with. It's not going to do either of you any good to end things this way. Don't you want to know if she has changed? Even if it doesn't change your mind, don't you really want to know? I would and I did and I do and I am in the process of deciding. And, I want that for you.

But, it has to be you that makes this decision on your own—just you. And, no one ever has to know. You could talk to her before you leave for Kansas and when you are away you will be able think and make an even clearer decision—even though you may think you already have a clear view. I think your view is clouded by the past and not the present.

And, when I mean talk to her—I mean talk to her like she is someone you don't know yet without condemning her. And, ask her to talk to you without condemning you and see what happens. You have nothing to lose and everything to gain, whether the gain is in the form of staying away with a clearer view or considering what you thought to be impossible, Jon. I know what I am talking about. Please believe me. I hope I hear from you before you leave and I will be thinking about you. Your friend, Halley

I was desperate. I so wanted him to give me a chance. That afternoon, I went for a walk up the road for the first time in years and no one saw me. I wondered if anyone would ever know or "see" the real me....

JULY 1

Halley: I'm listening to you and you make some good points. You're doing the same thing you used to do. You're not answering my questions and you're not talking to me. I feel like a lab rat for some classroom psychology class. It's as though you push me with your thoughts and then talk about my reply to a classroom full of students so they can evaluate my response. This must be a great experiment for you. Did the entire class just cheer because I finally figured it out? The truth is I've felt this way for a long time. You give me the most limited information and then your e-mail requires an intimate response on my part. Who are you!!!!!!!!!!!!!!!!!!!!! Or maybe the question should be, "Who do you think you are?"

THE QUESTION? We know why I write to you. I have nothing but honest, sincere motives. What is your motivation to tell me what I should and should not do with my marriage? If you are trying to work things out with your husband and it's such a good thing to do, why do you write to me? You have told me nothing about your marital situation or why you even left him. This game doesn't work anymore. I need a lot more from you before you can tell me what I should and should not be doing in regard to my "soontobeex." Jon

What had happened? How had the conversation gone wrong? Had I pushed too far?

JULY 1

Jon! You asked me to tell you like I see it and that's what I am doing. I am in the middle of trying to work things out with my husband. I told you before that we had issues in regard to children etc. In your emails, you seem confused so I am trying to help in any way that I can. And I am not sharing this with a classroom of students!! What I am trying to do is make you aware of the entire "picture." I do believe that both of us leaving the way that we did—our views were or are clouded by the past. What I am trying to do is see his present behavior and the present "reality" of my situation. In order to get to the deepest "truth" about our situations, we need to face the present, we need to find out who we really are but even more, we need to find out who they are before completely "jumping off the cliff" into an abyss of complete uncertainty. God, I hope this makes sense!

Ooooo "intimate response?" That's what you think I am looking for? No. I want that for you from your wife and I want that for your wife from you. If I were you I would want to know everything. I do. Even if in the end I decide to not go back, I want to know exactly what he is thinking if that is possible and I want him to know exactly what I am thinking and who I am NOW, not last month or last year but NOW, so I can make the best decision possible. Don't you want that?

And, I am not telling you what you should or should not do! I am only suggesting some things that might give you a VERY clear view so that in the years to come you don't have to wonder. What I am trying to do is help you. But if you don't want my help, you don't have to take it and I will understand.

And, this is not a game. This is my life and it is your life and we are in similar situations and I think we have learned a great deal from one another and I think I am in a position to help you. But, if you choose to think otherwise, that is your choice and your responsibility.

I told you about my situation. I left because he wasn't ready to have children in the beginning. So, the years go by. And, I am finally in a position where my career is taking off in the direction I want it to and he decides it is time and now I am not ready. I felt pressured so I bailed! And, that's not all. There were many other issues that needed to be dealt with such as our lack of communication with one another. My communication with you has been an unbelievable learning experience. It has helped me to work through some things with him. And, his obsession with his work, and the complaining, and the nitpicking, and family situations. It took over our life together. Our relationship became last on the list and that's where everything broke down and instead of seeing that the right thing to do was to stay and work through things, I ran away! So, this is not an experiment. It is reality. And, it is very difficult.

I am just trying to get you to look at every possible angle. If you think you can be happy with someone like Ashley because she looks the way you want someone to look, then go for it. But, it seems you are not satisfied or happy with just that. I don't think you are that kind of person. I think you want someone who is more than that. Like I said before, it is entirely your decision. It is your life to do with as you want. I am only trying to help you with the knowledge I have gained with everything that has happened with me. And, I am sorry if I have offended you.

I am going to ask you again and you don't have to answer. What if ....? What if things are not as you perceive them to be? Don't you want to know? If you think I make some good points, what do you have to lose by talking to her without condemning her and asking questions and giving answers? By not asking a few questions or giving answers, you might lose more than you ever thought possible. Or, maybe you can live with not knowing??? I can't and you don't seem like the kind of person that would want that. Or, are you? Have I missed something?

"Who do you think you are?" I think I am someone who knows what she is talking about and I consider myself your friend. I think we have been through a great deal together. All I want is for you to think about what I have said and act on it if YOU decide it is what you want to do. That is all.

If I don't hear from you before you leave, I hope your trip goes well and I hope that you really think about what I have said without the prejudice of the "past." Your friend, Halley

How could he keep ignoring the "truth?" At this point, it seemed like he was going to ignore it for the rest of his life. I had tried my hardest. There really was nothing more that I could do.

JULY 2

Halley: I don't think I have the time to respond tonight. I don't have the time right now and it might take until tomorrow for me to reply. Talk to you later. Jon

Well, the old brush off. He couldn't handle the "unknowns" and he couldn't handle hearing about them. That seemed to be the only "truth" I was going to get out of all this "messaging."

JULY 2

I wanted my marriage so badly it was eating me alive. I realized my communications through a fake persona were desperate and obsessive. So, we had something in common. I was desperate for him and he was desperate for someone else....if he could only look back and see the real truth, not the truth he had conjured in his mind....

JULY 3

As I turned to lock my car door, I saw Spencer's back. Who could mistake it. We had worked together for years. He looked good—too good... I could tell he was apprehensive toward me so I spoke up and said "Hello" and we talked for a minute about the cars we were driving. He asked me what I was doing. I met with the printing person and then he was still standing there waiting for copies. He said something to me about having a good summer and I replied that it should be interesting and he asked how. I replied with a question—did he really want to know and he replied that he did. And so I told him that Jon had left in December and it seemed to be a case of mid-life crisis. He said there was a lot of that going around and wished me good luck at least twice. I told him it was good seeing him and said goodbye. I felt that he cared.

As I walked out of the drugstore and looked up to take into view the brand new Hummer that was parked in the parking lot, Michaela, my sister-in-law by marriage came into my focus. She looked like crap. She said, "Hi, how are you" like there was nothing wrong. I was taken off guard slightly and I felt the anger creeping up my throat. I replied "good." I quickly turned and asked if she had gotten the copy of the letter I had sent her in December and she said "yes." I asked why she had not responded to it and she said she didn't know she was supposed to write back. What a stupid bitch. Any person with a shred of decency would have at least called or sent a card!!!!!!!!!! I said it would have been nice to have known that someone cared. She said she did, but I could tell she didn't. I made some remark about how they all just had Jon's side of the "story." She made some stupid remark about it not being a "story." And I said how hard it was for me knowing that everyone knew about it before I did and how her husband had supported Jon in his decision. She replied that Jon was a "big boy" and he could make his own decision. I should have said— "big boy" is right because he definitely was not a man! And I told her Jon had told me that Dave had helped him. She didn't know what to say, the bitch. I had never seen her like this to my face. Then, I told her that someday he would regret his decision and I turned and walked off.

I stopped at my sister's and she said that Michaela stayed away from her. "Your mother-in-law is dirt" she said. "She is your mother-in-law" and she couldn't even send you a note or anything. And Michaela being so obsessive with her "ex" in-laws from her first marriage, you would think she could have at least sent me a card or called or whatever.........

One thing I knew at that very moment in time was that I could never be a part of that family because they had never allowed me in. They had no class or care or feeling. It was truly pathetic. And they were all circling around Jon and saying "poor Jon" right now and did not even hold him accountable for his terrible actions of the last several months and even before. I took his crap for far too long and look where it had gotten me! They were snakes—all of them.

I wanted to be a part of family that cared and was understanding and I wanted to be loved by someone who cared and who wouldn't hold my imperfections against me.

JULY 4

July 4th. I couldn't believe he was out in the driveway digging in the grass. Rocks from the driveway had gotten shoved into the grass during the winter plowing and he was throwing them back into the driveway. Then, he changed the oil in his truck. I walked out and asked him what he was doing and he asked me for his extra truck key. I hadn't gotten to use it yet. I had been planning to play a joke like driving by and setting off the alarm. Oh well. I got the key and brought it back out. After he changed the oil, he washed the truck. He spent the entire afternoon in the driveway. I sat on the deck and wrote in my journal for a while and finally gave up the fight of waiting for him to approach me to talk to me and went inside. It seemed obvious that he had nothing to say to me or didn't have the capacity to communicate with me. It was sad. Here we were together on July 4th and we had nothing to celebrate. We were together, but alone and apart. I thought back to the previous July 4th and realized we probably had done the same thing on that day. And, this year, I definitely didn't have anything to celebrate. It was kind of funny. I kept looking for fireworks and couldn't find any in the area. It was the same for us. I couldn't even find a spark in him. I felt like the balloon that had been floating around in my house for a couple of months that had gotten caught in the spinning ceiling fan one day. It was spinning and flapping, caught in the center of the fan and its flat body whipped against the flat wings of the fan. I just couldn't get out..... I just couldn't stop the feelings....

JULY 5

Still thinking? Halley

It had been three days and he hadn't replied to my very question-
ing message. I wondered why it took such a loss to fully appreciate what
one had and I also thought that we must always look behind us because
it might be there that we might find what we had been searching for.
How I wished he could look back at me and us and see it was what he
had been seeking.....

JULY 5

Halley: So, you left because your husband wanted to start a
family and you did not. I'm sure there was more to it than that, but
that was the final big straw right? I'm trying to understand the
conversation. How must it have gone in order for you to feel so
much pressure as to move out. He must be a very different person
than I am. Looking on it now, I wish I could have done the same.
At least I would be in my home right now and not an apartment.
Is he the jealous type? I'm glad that our communication has helped
you communicate with him. Tell me, does he know about your new
blue "tool?" :)

There are things that I know and feel in my heart, but I'm not
willing to share them with you. You can continue to question me, as
well as my relationships with whomever but, until I know you better
I will not respond.

Your reasons for leaving convince me even more to the fact that
you can't have any comprehension as to what I have had to endure.
I'm sorry, Halley, but you are simply way off when it comes to my
wife. The only way you could understand is if your husband totally
controlled your entire life. If you were completely isolated from others
due to the fact that he was incapable of communicating with others
and wanted the same for you. Divorce sucks. It sucks for everyone
who is in the middle of it, but your situation sounds vastly different
than my own. It also leaves me with a question. You know how I feel
about children. Why did you ever start communicating with me in
the first place, knowing that I want to start a family?

This is probably my last e-mail before I leave for Kansas tomorrow. I'm going to try to write while I'm gone, but I'm unsure as to how I'll do that. Hopefully, I'll talk to you soon. Jon

He was not capable of comprehending what I had been trying to say in any way, shape or form. He was taking everything backwards. He was refusing to get it at all. But, I had to wonder what he knew and felt in his heart.....

JULY 5

You're trying to skip over the part about how we were supposed to have a family when we were first married and he put me off in the first place. And, you're also forgetting how I told you about how I held a baby while I was away when my grandfather was ill and knew that I had made a mistake dealing with my situation the way that I did. Everyone makes mistakes and final judgments without the thought that they should sometimes, you know? Or, are we supposed to have these things held against us for a lifetime and not forgiven for them? You are living with the prejudice of the past in your mind. There is no doubt about this in my mind. I am so glad that I am not doing this because it will allow me to think on a clearer level.

And, no, he is not necessarily the "jealous" type. He respects me and now realizes that demanding me to see his side of things the way he did was wrong. And, I know that my reaction to his demands was not necessarily the most productive way to approach the situation. However, I will say that a period of separation can be very revealing and not necessarily a bad thing when faced with "issues."

And, no, he does not know about "blue" yet? And I bet you don't know about anything your wife has either, huh?

"Things that you know and feel in your heart." About your wife or the "girlfriend?" And I am not way off when it comes to your wife. You are. If she controlled you, you must have controlled her. And no one forced you to be isolated and no one forced her to be isolated.

And my situation is not very different from your own and you fail to see that. And, I do want a family. It is just that the way he approached it made me feel so pressured that I could not deal with it. Did you do the same to your wife? Just some questions you should think about.

Like I said, it's your decision but it seems that you are confused, like the rest of us. And, I think we need to talk about this more so you understand my situation, as well as your own. Or, do you think you have it all figured out on your own or through talking to Ashley? Be careful whose counsel you keep. She's prejudiced in one direction and will go along with whatever you say because she wants to "trap" you and maybe you want to be "trapped" by her? But, again, I don't want to offend you and I hope I've helped clarify things.

I hope you have a great trip and I hope to hear about it. It sounds like a great experience. And, I hope it allows you to get some perspective on everything. Your friend, Halley

I was getting harder on him. Trying to get through by being nice wasn't working so maybe a slightly harder tactic might work? I didn't know what else to do and I was getting really tired of trying but I would not give up, not yet.

twenty

KANSAS

JULY 5

Halley: You sound more like my wife every day. Are you sure your name is Halley?

Oh well, we'll see what happens in the future won't we? I thought I would do a quick e-mail before I left tomorrow. Don't assume that I'm not listening to everything you're saying, okay? It's just that I have a different take on some things. I'm listening, though. Don't think that I don't skip around all of those thoughts at one time or another. I don't hold things over people for the past.

I want to sing. I want to find a place in Kansas where I can sing. I've gotten much better over the last few months. I think it's the "Insatiable" song. It's strengthened my voice doing all those high parts. Don't worry. I won't be trapped by anyone. Jon

I felt like I had been trying to manipulate his thoughts. I had. It was my only chance and it wasn't working. He was so damn stubborn and ignorant. How could I ever get through to someone like that? And it seemed he had gotten more dogged in this regard over the past several months. I suddenly realized that my skills of persuasion were not working and had not been effective since before he had left me. And, it almost seemed as if he was really suspicious—asking me if my name was really Halley???

JULY 6

Welcome to Kansas! How is it out there?

Now, for your last email to me. I sound like her? Do you actually talk to her? And, my name had better be Halley or I wouldn't want to be you! :) hehehe Maybe she and I should get to know one another? :) Maybe I could help!? Maybe I could tell her about "blue?" Or about you? (Scared you, didn't I?) hehe

I'm glad you're listening, but I wonder if you are saying that to get me to shut up about everything.

I hope you find a place to sing. Have you ever thought about taking voice lessons to go even further with it? I think you have great potential. Maybe you could be a professional singer??? There are so many possibilities! And, if you do I expect front row tickets! :)

Good luck with your class and I hope to hear all about it when you get back. Your friend, Halley

The only thing I could do now to save face was to lighten the mood of my messages and hope that he would respond.

JULY 6

Halley: I'm here in Kansas. What a screwed up deal it was getting here. It's a long story that I'll tell you some other time. I'm at Kinko's and it's 20 cents a minute so I want to keep it a little short. It's nice being away. It's nice knowing I have my room and I'm out just checking the place out. When I've got more to tell you, I'll write again. Talk to you later. Jon

*All I could wonder was what the hell was "Kinko's?" Was I naïve
or what?*

JULY 6

Jon: Just checking in before I go to bed and was so surprised to
get a message from you out in Kansas! It is nice being away, isn't it? I
get so much perspective from being away (when I can). I can't wait to
hear about your trip. Sleep well. Your friend, Halley

JULY 7

Halley: Last night I went bar hopping. I discovered that Manhat-
tan is a college town. All the bars in Agateville were full of young
people looking to create something new. They had little to offer in
regard to showing anyone character. Determined to find something
meaningful, I continued asking around for the place to go and discovered McGraw's. It's a country bar. As I sat at the bar, I watched people
in their fifties dance in a way that only two people who have been
together for a lifetime can dance. I hope that I can be like that one day.
Afterward, I had to go to Wal-Mart and pick up a Garth Brooks CD.
I'm not into country, but this place requires me to listen to it. I have a
newfound appreciation for it. Anyway, I've spent the morning driving
through the countryside listening to Garth's Double Live album. If you
would like to join me, all you need to do is purchase it.

Kansas is beautiful. It is clean-cut young men in cowboy hats
numbering ten to one woman. It's rolling farmland stretching on for
what seems like eternity. It gives one the same feeling as standing
before an ocean—that same sense of smallness and the vastness of
the world in which we live. Corn, wheat, round bails and stone barns
are all that you can see for miles. Kansas is straight roads climbing
up and down over gently rolling hills. Kansas is land—land that goes
on forever. My first sense of the place was how boring it must be in
such emptiness. Now I see it for what it truly is. I love it here. I've

stopped countless times on the highway to take pictures. Every time I stop, I have the desire to do my head-back spin. Perhaps, it's just my need to be here right now. I don't know. I've had a tear in my eye for the last couple of hours. Like I said, you can join me with the album. My friend I've never seen who knows so much about me. I want the chance to go back out there tonight and look at a star-filled sky and to listen to the crickets and bugs in the humid night. Talk later. Jon

What was he doing to me. He was killing me with his words. When he wanted to write, he could really write. I cried through the whole message. It was getting too emotional and I knew that I had to be careful. I didn't know how I was going to make it. The loneliness and uncertainty— I couldn't let go. I felt like my only strength was weakness.

JULY 7

Well, it sounds like I need to move to Kansas! Ten men for one woman! Your writing is beautiful and it brings tears to my eyes. I have to admit that I have been really emotional lately.

It makes me want to be there with you. Please send me a picture if you can sometime. I hope you're thinking about everything I've said even though it seems you don't want to hear it. I think you have the opportunity to think about "things" out there in a different light if you allow yourself to.

Don't you think it would be great to live someplace else? Make everything new? Take what was good out of the bad and make it better in the end? I know. I am talking in riddles, aren't I? But, you have to figure out the answers.

And, I think it would be beautiful to dance together like those people you described. The opportunity is there. You only have to figure it out for yourself.

I'll have to get the album but I can't imagine the experience can be the same unless you are in Kansas where you are and where I would like to be right now... Let me know how the experience of it all feels tonight. Thanks for the beautiful words. Your friend, Halley

I begged God to bring him back to me that night...

twenty-one

DESPERATION

JULY 8

I composed a letter to Jon that I didn't have the courage to send...I was so afraid....

Dear Jon: Someone who cares gave me this address so I could communicate with you while you are away. I will not use it again. Because of the opportunity I have been given, I am writing because there are things I need to say to you and I need to know I have done everything I possibly can. I want to show you, somehow, that I am not the same person you think I am. Seven months allows a person to change in ways they never thought possible. I understand your frustration and unwilling-ness to give me a chance. But, I hope you will listen to what I have to say and think about this in a different way than you ever have. It is possible to take experiences we have had with an open mind and an open heart and make "things" better. Things do not stay exactly the same. Everything is constantly changing. We need to grow together through experience, not apart. I want you to know how much I miss you—in every way. I regret so many things—of not being able to do enough in every area of my life and our lives together. I regret not doing things on the spur of the moment. I regret the effort I put into classes and how it caused me to neglect our relationship. I regret not sharing my innermost feelings with you. I regret not seeing the world with you. I regret being so "hard to hold" at times. I miss being with you in every way and I regret holding back in every area of our lives together. I regret all the missed opportunities. I regret my feelings toward the things that upset me and I regret voicing them to you in a way that you didn't know how to respond or that caused you resentment in your heart. I know the missed opportunities cannot be recovered but I wish that you could believe that new and better opportunities could be a reality for us, together; I wish that you would let me show you that this is true.

I have nothing to lose at this point. You, my soul mate, are out there lost to me and I want you to see that all is not lost for us. There is always hope. That is why I am telling you how I feel. I have experienced feelings and emotions in the last several months that I never knew I could have. I will not give up on our marriage without one last attempt at knocking down the walls that you have put up around your heart toward me. I have enough hope for both of us to go on "to infinity and beyond!" We have not been where we have been for no reason. We have not made it this far for nothing. When a door closes, a window opens. This is a window of opportunity for things to be better, together. If you had not left in the way that you did, I would still be in my box. I will not go back to living that way. I had no identity and it was not healthy. I wish that I could have listened to you without prejudice. I don't know what to say to get you to listen to me and really hear what I am saying. Me, speechless? Yes. Please don't close your heart and mind to what I am saying. I want so much for you to communicate with me, without tension or hurt emotions. I want to know if it is possible for you to love me and care for me, even though I am not perfect. I remember how we loved each other, do you? I need to know or I cannot go on. I want to meet you when you return from Kansas and talk to you without the past affecting our conversation or our feelings. Could you do that or would it be too hard for you or too painful? I need to know if your feelings have changed, but I want you to know that I will never give up on the love I have for you in my heart, no matter what. I want to give you everything in my heart for the rest of our lives. I am not ashamed of my feelings for you and I will never regret that I shared them with you no matter what you proclaim your feelings to be, and I am not afraid to face anyone's opinion of me because of my honesty.

I have to communicate this to you because for the rest of my life I don't want to think that I did not make every effort possible for things to be the way they were meant to be between us. I know that it is possible to work through things and make them better than before. This experience has taught me the most painful way to knowing forgiveness and letting go of resentment in every area of my life. I truly believe and know that there is a reason for everything that happens in this world. I also know that every relationship passes through various seasons of love. I made a commitment to you and I want to honor it. I hope that you will at least give me the chance to hear your feelings and for you to feel mine. Please tell me that you will talk to me. If you can't talk to me, please just tell me that you will meet me and hold me in your arms one last time.

Love, Hunter

Instead, I emailed him the following message with knots in my gut. My instincts were in shreds. I was desperate for him to know that I could really be who he wanted me to be....

JULY 8

Dear Jon: Someone who cares gave me this address so I could write to you while you are away. I will not use it again without your permission. Because of the opportunity I have been given, I am writing to tell you how I feel about you. I have learned so much over the last months about myself and how I haven't yet lived and how I have discovered a part of me that I never knew before......

I miss you so much. Every part of you. I need your warm, naked body next to mine. I miss the sexy scar on your chin. I need your warm embrace. I miss the feel of your cheek against mine. I miss your strong neck. I miss your tongue touching mine. I want your lips on my breasts. I need to have you inside of me, deep inside of me. I miss your tight buttocks.... I want to feel all of you against me and in me, naked in every way. I want you so much that I can feel you as I write. I want to take a bath with you and make it an experience of a lifetime. Then, I want to take a long, warm shower with you and touch every part of you and have you touch every part of me with your hands, your mouth........ I have something I want to show you that will "energize" your mind and the softest part of me.... I know what you want, let me give it to you. I want to love you like you have never been loved before, without reservation. I want to sleep with you and wake up next to you and begin all over again. I want to be with you for an entire weekend surrounded by flowers, candles, wine, strawberries and love. I need to be held in your arms and loved in every way.....and I want to love you in every way.....the way that we are meant to love a soul mate...... I want to be your lover and I want for you to be mine.....

My heart, mind and body are open to you..... If you want me, give me a sign.....

Love, Hunter

I received nothing back from him. My gut felt like a rock.

JULY 9

I felt like a fool and thought I had better try to make contact with him through Halley.

JULY 9

Have you turned into a cowboy yet? :) I hope your class is going well. Halley

Had I made the "fatal mistake" because I had gotten too emotionally attached? Should I have sent that all-revealing email? I had gotten no response and I was very afraid that I had blown my "cover"…but wasn't that what my heart had wanted???

JULY 10

I decided to back off and let it go. Instead of concentrating on emailing, I got to know my house as my home. I finally took a bath in the mosaic-tiled tub that he had finally grouted just before he had left. Somehow, I had gotten him to do it. I had to use pliers to turn on the hot water from the backside of the tub because of a "glitch" in his plumbing handiwork, but where there was a will there was a way. And, I found many ways to do things that I had to do or wanted to do. I named my tub the "goddess tub" because it made me feel so special to sit there, even if I had to sit on a towel. Glass tiles were sharp on the edges! As I started to really look around, I finally felt like I was home—this was the place I wanted to be. I felt lonely, but there was so much of him in that house. It was the only connection I had left to him. I decided to make a bid for my home in court when the hearing occurred. I knew I would have to have a full-time job and I knew I would have to find someone to loan me the money. I felt like the thorns and vines that had been holding me in were disappearing because I was deciding what I wanted and not doing what someone else wanted me to do—maybe the vines and thorns holding me in had been Jon himself. I wondered if Jon was the "alligator prince" who existed in my nightmare when I was six years old….. He was the person who had closed the lid of the box I had lived in for so long and the one who had gladly taken my identity and thrown it to the 'gators—only thinking of himself…..and I had allowed it to happen.

JULY 10

I kept remembering things as I soaked in the tub. I remembered the day years before when he had rushed into the emergency room of the hospital after I had rolled my vehicle over and how concerned he had been. He hadn't been ashamed of his emotions and he had held my hand the entire time. I remembered how loved I felt. It brought me to tears and my tears fell into the hot, soapy water as I sobbed uncontrollably. He was lost to me. We were lost. Everything was lost.

I remembered how he used to pull the car over to the side of the road just so he could kiss me and how hard he tried to make my birthdays something I would enjoy and how hard he tried to make me believe that I was beautiful….. I prayed that he would come home to me but deep inside I knew that once he made up his mind it would take the strength of a mountain-mover to bring him back….

JULY 21

I couldn't stand it anymore. I hadn't heard from him and it was driving me crazy and I was getting really pruney from all those baths!

JULY 22

Are you lost out there? :) Halley

July 23

I just got home late last night. What a trip! I'm tired. Jon

July 23

When you've got some sleep, I'd love to hear about your experience! Halley

July 24

I got home from my photography class and I knew I had to call him, I had to get it over with. It was 9:40 PM and I quickly pressed the numbers on the telephone.....

I had to know. I had to talk to him. There was so much silence on his end. He was so closed. There seemed to be no hope, no faith, and no belief.... He freely admitted that he had none. I knew that without belief and faith, there was no hope for our existence together.

But, the wall was finally speaking, albeit with a hopeless attitude.

I admitted to having a domineering attitude at times and how much I had come to realize and explained to him that he should have told me how he felt instead of running away. I asked him how was I supposed to know there were problems if he never could tell me? He had no reply. He knew that he hadn't been fair in this regard but would never come clean. His attitude was very pig-headed but not that of a "fighter" or that of a "survivor." He had stuck his head and his tail between his legs and run away. He told me that he was now able to do "whatever he fucking wanted to do whenever he wanted." I couldn't believe that I was conversing with someone who proclaimed to want children. His attitude was confusing and it seemed as if he wanted no responsibility in his life. He told me that he resented me and did say that he would talk to me after the final hearing. I wondered about that. I knew that there was little hope of him talking to me ever again unless I left with nothing. It was obvious to me that every time he thought of me or looked at me in any way, he saw a big "NO" in his mind.

He accused me of wanting information out of him and told me he felt that was my reason for calling him. I told him I only wanted to discuss our feelings. His answer to that was noncommittal. He told me that, in the future, his answer in regard to any relationship difficulties would be "fuck you, see you later, bye." I was really hurt by this. How could one not be? I told him I was looking for closure even though in my heart I was looking for an opening. I said so many things—things that I had wanted to say for so long. I told him that I hoped that someday he would forgive my imperfections and asked that he read the copies that I had mailed to him. I had mailed him five pages from a book that I read that summed up our relationship and illustrated that it could be saved if we were both willing. He probably burnt them. I then asked him to talk with me to my face and he said he would think about it. Translated—this meant no, again. It was obvious to me during the conversation that he would base his opinion of me only on the past and not the present nor the future. It was also obvious to me that the only way he could get through this was to only see me in the past.

There was so much anger in his voice. I knew he was angry because I was being allowed to live in the house and he was in an apartment. But, it had been his choice to leave without giving me any hope at all. What did he expect? And, it was very obvious that he was seeking a perfect life without having to work at it.

As I spoke and after I hung up the phone an hour later, I realized that I had never before been so rational in a conversation with him. In that one conversation, we communicated more than we ever had before as Hunter and Jon. I wish that I had told him that. I felt like he was holding back so much from me. I felt like he was sitting on the other side of a stone wall. Before the conversation ended, I asked him if he had meant the beautiful things he had said to me the week before he had left and he replied "at the time." How I was supposed to take that I had no idea and it broke my heart again to think that he had, perhaps, just used me. But, I knew that somewhere inside that rock was the sensitive person that I had been married to—somewhere—and, I hoped, someday, he would resurface and I would have the chance to see him as that person again.

Through the conversation, I came to realize and know that the Jon I married was gone forever and that I didn't want the Jon that had left me....but that I would gladly take back the Jon whom I had married if he could only exist again.....I believed that I would always love the Jon that I had married but knew that the person who existed now—the one who was self-destructive, self-motivated and so full of resentment could not be a part of my life.... It was as if he was caught up in a "web" of resentment. The spider was the prejudice of the past, his obsession with money and his obsession with material possessions—his house and his truck. And, to him, I was the "web."

JULY 25

Have you woken up yet? Just checking! Waiting to hear about your trip. Halley

JULY 25

I cried my out heart for the millionth time knowing I didn't want the Jon who left me and knowing that the Jon I married was never coming back....and realizing that fighting for my home was the right thing to do. I knew it would be the only way I could hang on to what was left of us. And, I couldn't survive thinking I would have nothing left of what we had had together.

JULY 26

I am feeling so incredibly creative right now. I'm feeling free, alive and ready to take on the world. That trip did wonders for me.

Have you ever wondered what you would do if you won mega-bucks? I remember thinking how I would leave my wife if I won. That was years ago, yet I continued to stay.

Did you know you're going to die someday? Don't wait to win the lottery to do what you want to do with your life, do it now. You may never win, you may never have money, but you will die anyway. I'm living like I may not live another day, starting from this point on. I'm going to say what I feel I should say and I'm going to do what I think I should do and I will be successful.

I want to keep talking, but I want more from you. Somehow, someway, you need to give me more. There are many things wrong with our communication. You are timid. For whatever reason, you do not want to reveal yourself to me which only makes me suspect that you have something to hide. I don't have room for timidness. I have no desire to deal with anyone not willing to take a little risk.

You left your husband because he wanted to start a family and I left my wife because she refused to start a family. Do you see a problem here? You screwed me over one time already and I shouldn't even be communicating with you. What do you want from me? You don't answer my questions and I don't even know why I ask them but I still do.

I want only one type of response from you in regard to this e-mail. Give me a call. 208-784-2299. I don't even need to talk to you. If you get my answering machine, leave a message. Call anytime day or night.

Remember, you're going to die some day. Do you really want to remain timid your entire life? Are you so afraid to do something so real as to place a phone call? Use a calling card and do it from a pay phone. No one needs to know and no one can find out who you are. Do you want to hide behind a keyboard for the rest of you life?

We reached the peak of our communication months ago. There is no point in going on. It's foolish of me to communicate through email and waste my time with a cyber person that I have never heard or seen. If you're not willing to even speak to me on the phone, I really see no point. Jon

JULY 27

He was definitely suspicious of me now if he hadn't been before. I had blown it with that "over-the-top" email from me, his wife, to his personal email account. He had not responded to either of us, Halley or me after that. This email said it all and I was afraid that I couldn't hide anymore....

The defining moment for me was reading that he would have left me if he had won megabucks "years ago".......and knowing that there was nothing left to hang on to as far as our marriage.........and I knew what I had to do.

JULY 27

Well, I suppose this will be my last email to you. I thought I had made a friend but you are saying if you can't have more than that you don't want anything. But, I have to ask you why you are so worried about when you die? Don't you think you need to think about this and talk to someone who can really help you understand this? You seem so obsessed by it in your email. No offense.

You've admitted that leaving your wife was based on money? Was your whole life based on money? And, I wonder how she would feel if she knew that was how you felt. I find this so cruel. Instead of thinking this way, why didn't you really try to talk to her? I am seeing parts of you that don't make sense to me.

I hope that you have success but if you keep on handling things the way you say you will, I wonder what will really happen. I mean to communicate this in a caring way even though it may sound harsh.

You keep bringing up the family issue and you keep forgetting that I had told you that I realized that I was wrong. Did your wife? And, the way that you talk communicates to me that you have no desire to be settled with a family. It sounds like you want to be free from anyone or anything. Or, have I interpreted your words in the wrong way?

And, I didn't "screw you over," Jon. Things happen.

You keep asking what I want from you and I have told you repeatedly. I don't want anything. I thought I could help. I enjoyed having a friend to communicate with about our similar situations. But, you don't want my help. You believe you are doing the right thing and someday you will realize if your decision was the right one. It is too early for you to even know if it is because of the way you made your decision. It seems you communicated with everyone but your wife about your situation and a decision made in this way cannot be the right one. I hope, for your sake, that it is but as a woman I can tell you that I don't think it has been handled the way it should have been. Most women would tell you the same thing—most. I am sure your "Belly Ring Girl" would not. She does not exist on this level. You give your opinions freely, so I am not being timid with mine.

I only hope that your wife comes out of this better than you ever imagined. And, I do hope you find a way to be happy and successful, but I think the happiness you think you feel right now is an illusion that will eventually disintegrate. I hope my email does not anger you. I only want you to see the truth of your situation and I feel I am allowed because you said you did not want to deal with "timid." So, here is the hard truth for you to think about.

I just want you to know that it is possible to work things out with someone you love. But you have to be willing. And, you clearly are not. Running away is never the answer to anything. I have discovered that. Fortunately, I listened. I wish the same for you, but it is very clear you have no intention of listening to what you don't want to hear either from me or your wife. It sounds to me from what you have told me that she never had a chance and didn't even know it because you held everything away from her. I hope you think about this even if you hate me for saying it. She never had a chance because she couldn't read your mind. Am I right?

I don't mean to anger you in any way with my comments but you didn't want timidness so I gave you the truth of what I think. If I never hear from you again, just know that I will never forget you but I will always wonder if you found what you were looking for and maybe, someday, we will be in a room together and I will see if you are truly happy or if you did make the worst mistake of your life by not listening to someone who cared. Love, Halley

I received no reply. I knew that it was the end this time. There was no chance for Jon and Hunter but for divine circumstances.

JULY 28

I wanted my home. It was all I had left. I had to stop my delusions of reconciliation. I approached my uncle who said he would help me financially. I knew, still, that I had to come up with a job in order to support the house and I kept trying.

AUGUST 1

I received the notice of the final hearing in the mail stating that it would be held on October 11. Time was running out.

I went to the mall to get some cards and couldn't believe my luck. Someone who looked vaguely like Kristan was walking across the parking lot toward a vehicle that I knew was hers. She looked unhappy and guilty. As I walked toward the store, I stared at her and she stared at me as she drove off. She had that same bitter, unhappy look as Jon wore on his face.....whenever I saw him...... I had intended to confront her but she had gotten away.... Maybe it was better that way.

AUGUST 3

I saw Jon's truck in the garage and decided to see what kind of a response I would get. I quickly got dressed and took his shirts in a storage bag out with me knowing that school would be starting soon and he would want them. He was defensive and resentful as usual. I changed the subject. With my non-committal attitude, he wasn't so defensive but there was so much anger there. After he left, I felt as if I had been talking to a ghost—a ghost who knew no truth, only lies.

AUGUST 6

Every day when I opened up the closet doors to get clothes to wear, I was forced to see his things—the things he had left behind—like me. I knew I had to get them out of my sight in order to move on somehow. I packed up everything and moved the crates down-stairs. The things that were downstairs, I moved near the door. The pile of things was incredibly small compared to what I would have to move if I were forced to leave my home. I loaded up my car and drove over to the garage and unloaded his things onto the couch from his sister's house he had left there. I made two trips. There were still things that had to be moved but they were too heavy. That after-noon, my nephew helped me move them in the rain. I had packed everything well so there was no need for him to complain. After all, I hadn't thrown everything out of the windows. As I walked through the house afterwards, I felt a sense of emptiness and freedom. I was making the house my home because it looked like he wasn't coming back. Maybe, I was even trying to punish him in some way. I didn't know. I just knew I had to breathe and I couldn't with his things in my face every day. At least for the time that I was there, if it was only temporary, I could feel as if it was mine and mine alone. Even though, at the same time, I was surrounded by him. The house was him. We had both put all of us, our blood, sweat and tears, into that house and, really, it had never been a home but only for a few moments here and there.

The photography class I was taking was like therapy to me, espe-cially the time in the darkroom. It was a time where I could see magic and creation. Slipping the exposed paper into the chemicals and seeing an image instantly emerge was magic. And, the sense of accomplishment was really what I needed. I only wished that I could slip his brain into some magic chemical and transform it to rebuilding and restructure rather than where it was—in self-destruction. The pictures that I took were all of objects in the house and of the house itself. Every assignment to me pertained to my house—shapes, textures, and landscapes. The instructor was probably sick of seeing them but they gave me comfort. And, I wondered if they would be all I had left in the end. There was no way of knowing what would happen.

AUGUST 8

I watched with fear as Jon stood in the doorway of the garage looking at his things sitting there. He stood there for what seemed like hours and finally went inside. He came back out with his bike, loaded it and left. At least, he hadn't tried to confront me. I didn't know what I would have done if he had.

AUGUST 11

I so wished for just one more hug and to feel his cheek against mine and feel his hair with my hands. But, there wasn't much hair left to feel. He was in some sort of short hair mode. Why someone with such beautiful hair would want to chop it all off I couldn't even fathom. But, I knew the answer. It was because he knew that I didn't like it so short. He was so handsome with it longer. It was as if he was trying to make himself physically ugly to match his inner feelings of ugliness—the feelings of resentment he had toward me.

AUGUST 14

I was getting dressed and was only in a t-shirt and noticed that he was out in the driveway again. That orange truck. Every time I saw it, my stomach lurched. I couldn't believe what he was doing. Taking pictures of the half-mown lawn. I opened the door in my half-dressed state and asked what he was doing. Of course, I got no reply. I was livid with rage. So I yelled at him to "Get the hell out of here or I'll call the police!." He made a comment about how the lawn looked worse than it had before. So, now I was supposed to think that any improvement was worse than no improvement? He made some idiotic comment about me thinking I could take care of "this place" and how ridiculous it was. I replied with the question, "Who said that?" I told him to leave again and he continued to take pictures. I was hoping he hadn't gotten a picture of me standing there with only a t-shirt on with nothing underneath! He finally left and I then realized that I had missed another opportunity to get a picture of him in the dooryard. The bottom line was that he had come again without calling. And, I was sure he would while I was gone. Actually, I was sure he was there especially when he noticed my car not in the yard. He was continually in contempt of court and was able to get away with it. If it had been me, I wouldn't have gotten two feet into the driveway. Unfortunately, the "princess" was always free to do as he pleased no matter what action I took to protect myself.

I had my last photography class. I knew I would miss it. It had been such a welcome distraction in such a turbulent time. After I finished printing my final picture, I took a walk through the building, the same building where Jon's classroom would be in the next week. It was easy to find. It was the only classroom with a soap dispenser, towel holder, and a sink. Mr. Clean or what. He had given me so much crap about asking him to wash his hands before eating and here he had the best set up in the town for washing your hands! I wondered why a drafting room would need a cleaning facility on its premises. It was such a joke to me. The hypocrisy of it all was amazing. I kept hearing how he was doing everything I had suggested for years—why did it take leaving me for his mind to open up? He was taking everything I had said and was using it so I had every right in reciprocating that fact. There was no doubt in my mind then.

I heard how thin he had gotten. I wondered if it was the circumstances of our situation, the lack of my cooking or the thought he might lose the house. My bet was on the last two.

twenty-two

THE LAWN

AUGUST 15

My brother-in-law tried to mow the lawn that had become a hayfield but with little success. And, I had been told I couldn't use our lawn tractor. It was evident that I needed heavy-duty equipment.

I was so lucky to find Jack, the bush hog man. He was so willing to help—so unlike my in-laws who only wanted to take and would only help for a price. I wondered how people could be so different. I was so amazed and disgusted at the same time. He was able to bush hog the entire area that needed to be done in one day. In the process, he found two underground hornet's nests. I must have gone through eight cans of hornet spray but I did it. Now, I needed a farmer to bale the hay that covered the lawn.

AUGUST 16

I couldn't believe my luck in finding a farmer who would actually mow down the rest of the lawn and bale everything and take it away. Miracle or what? Now, I wondered why couldn't I get a miracle like that with my marriage? Why?

Lonely as usual that night, I went onto "Hearts.com" to see what would come up. I couldn't believe it. There was no picture but I knew his voice. I would always know his voice and his writing. Even though it said "Littleton, New Hampshire" and that he was divorced, I knew it was him. There was no question in my mind. I wondered if he was using the same password as he had the previous time he had been on "Hearts.com," so I tried it. I couldn't believe it worked. I was able to look at the account information and know that it was Jon. It was all there in black and white and in full-blown color. I knew him better than he knew himself. I thought about how I could use this access......and wondered how I could wreak some havoc....

Using the email account name that I found in his account information—the account where any correspondence he was getting would go, I attempted to log on using the same password. I couldn't believe that the password for the email account was the same. So, on a daily basis, I was able to look at any emails he got, which seemed to be few and far between. I knew he still had the original email account, *flyinghigh@hotmail.com* where Halley had sent messages to him and I knew that was where he had gotten messages from Ashley and who knows who else by now. I knew if I wanted information, I had to get access to that account. But, how in the world was that possible?

AUGUST 18

As I stood in the hot, baking sun hand raking the area over the septic tank, Jon drove in with his father. I did the only thing I could do and stood there and smiled and waved. They turned around and I could see that Jon was, again, taking pictures. This time, of the hay rolls at the bottom of the driveway. What did he hope to gain by that? It was so stupid. Here I was killing myself raking and he was riding around in an air-conditioned truck taking pictures of his poor wife working her butt off. What kind of a husband was that? I decided I would go into the house until they left and looked out the window. They had backed back up the driveway and were taking more pictures. I quickly grabbed the digital camera and walked out onto the deck and got a picture of him. Finally, I had proof that he was violating the court order.

I found out later that he stopped at my sister Anna's house torqued out of his mind about me cleaning up the lawn. He was afraid that I had intentions of staying. And, that was my intention. I didn't want to leave. But, I didn't know how I could stay. All I knew was that I had to do what was right. And, the blisters on my hands should have told me that I couldn't keep taking care of everything. It was just getting too hard. And, I was having no luck finding a job.

AUGUST 21

I was obsessed with his "Hearts.com" account. I couldn't believe how he proclaimed himself as "mentally strong." To me, he was trying to prove it to himself by writing it to the world. And, it was so untrue. He was so unstable. The next time I checked he had changed it to "emotionally strong." Did he think that sounded more convincing? I had to laugh. But, it really wasn't funny. Anyone having to put that in their description was highly questionable as far as their state of mind.

That night, my sister's husband came by and got the lawn mower started. He had gotten a mower belt and a key for me. After my lawyer had told me I could use the lawn mower, I had found the key missing. And, the first time my brother-in-law tried got the mower started, we found that the belt was missing. I assumed Jon removed them when I had asked to use the mower back in May so no one could use it. It was so strange for me to see someone else riding Jon's lawn mower. I felt so sad that I would probably never see Jon on it ever again... It was funny how he seemed happiest when he had been riding that mower and it made me remember how he had told me many years before how the most enjoyable job he had ever had had been during the summer after he had graduated from high school when he had worked for a sheep farmer and had driven a tractor...... Who was he??? Who had I married?

August 22

Well, his picture was in place now on the dating website so I decided to change the password and name access to Jon's new "Hearts. com" account and the corresponding email account so he couldn't access it. I wanted to see what would happen and it made me feel like I had some sort of weird power over his life. He wanted nothing to do with me so I was going to have a piece of him somehow, someway..... I couldn't believe how he was getting no "hits" to his account. It was so pathetic.

I decided to try my hand at using the lawn mower. I was scared but I wanted to prove to myself that I could do it. I had memorized all the steps to starting it but still forgot that I had to push the choke switch back in after the thing started. Gray smoke filled the garage. I burned a lot of rubber that day just getting used to the thing plus the grass was so high and I didn't know that I had to leave the deck partially raised. Every time I headed down the lawn, the mower deck would shut off. I had to remember to sit as far back on the seat as I could. I thought that maybe taping the safety switch down under the seat might solve the problem but, boy, was I wrong. I burned the mower belt right off the tractor doing this and had to wait for another belt before I could mow the lawn again. The mower jumped and jerked and the smoke billowed out like a train. It wouldn't start for several minutes and I was scared to death that Jon would drive in. I prayed to God that it would start so that I could just get it back into the garage. Well, I would get a vacation from mowing until the new belt came in. But, I had mown the lawn for the first time. It was an unbelievable accomplishment for me.

August 22

I kept thinking about how Jon described himself and his "perfect" match on his "Hearts.com" account and decided to try describing myself. I was struck by depression when I realized that I couldn't do it. My entire identity was tied up in him, as well as in the house we had built together. I knew there was a real hole here that I needed to work on. I just didn't know how to say anything really positive about myself and if I couldn't how could I ever achieve my dreams?

twenty-three

TOO CLOSE

AUGUST 23

I found an email that Jon sent to his own email account which he couldn't access accusing me of being Hunter and Halley and of stealing his account and calling me a "pathetic bitch." I deleted it and pretended it never existed, so when he was again able to access his account the next week it wasn't there, as well as an email that had come back incorrectly on the account from "Hearts.com" that included mention of his new password. I tried this password out on his "flyinghigh" account and was able to gain access. It was a dream or a nightmare—I didn't know which. He didn't have a clue that I had access to his original email account.....and this is what I had been hoping for....even though I knew that I might discover information that would make me feel as though I was more in the middle of a nightmare than I had thought before.....

AUGUST 27

It was incredible and out of this world that this odd email had been sent to the wrong account and enabled me to get access to the *flyinghigh@hotmail account.* I was shocked to find so many emails from so many women including Ashley, as well as a girl who lived in Essexton and one in Newport. There was even one from an old friend of his sister's who was decidedly whacked. Her emails were so belligerent and supportive of his resentful attitude toward me and she didn't even know me!

The girl in Essexton was definitely a workaholic and was obsessed with sports, houses, dogs, ski trips, money, family and married men and especially herself—good fit or what? I couldn't believe that he had been corresponding with her since at least Spring and he still hadn't met her. It seemed his emails must have turned her off in some way because they kept getting more distant as time went on. For some reason, he had saved various emails from her including the ones with pictures. She was the spitting image of his sister but had a bigger nose. In these emails, he admitted to going to a "strip" club during the Spring, and how embarrassed he had been. I wondered if he had gone alone or with someone.

The email from his previous schoolmate who was a friend of his sister's encouraged him in regard to his divorce. There was also an email that had to do with his class reunion. It had been sent to the coordinator of the event and she had returned a reply. He had asked if she knew of any "single, sexy women" and she had replied that she would "keep him in mind." And, I knew that she had told my sister an entirely different "story." She had told her that she had been disgusted with his email. It was amazing the liars there were out there. I was so disgusted with all of them.

From the various emails, I discovered an older woman from Newport who called herself the "Princess of the NEK." She seemed far from that from what I could gather from her writings. In one of his emails to her, I found out that he had ended it for the second time with Ashley in August after he had returned from Kansas. He had actually ended it via email and told her that she was not his "soul mate." He didn't even have the guts to tell her to her face. But, he hadn't had any guts with me either.....

In the emails to the woman in Newport, he said how he was considering finishing his degree at a local college, where Kristan had received her Bachelor's Degree. I couldn't believe that he was throwing away his original idea of getting his Bachelor's Degree from the aeronautical university and just settling for whatever was easiest. He was settling for less in every area of his life. Had it only been my encouragement and support that had allowed him to reach for the top?

AUGUST 27

I kept looking over the emails I had printed from his "flying-high" account and part of one that he had written to the "Essexton chick" really struck me. What he wrote was so true in regard to his attitude of being scared and of being so aware of his mortality. "Time is a difficult thing. We want things, we do things and we mean to do things. We look back at what we have done and haven't done and there isn't a thing we can do to change it. Time continues on regardless of what we do or don't do. Before you know it, many years have gone by and those things we want, we still haven't found time for. I think of all my hopes and dreams, even the wild ones like being in the Olympics. I think of all the wonderful dreams I had as a kid and how I still feel the same way. Luckily, I feel that all the dreams that are truly important to me are still possible and I feel so grateful for that. But, one thing I've learned, the most important thing of all is that regardless of intentions, wants, desires, if you are not careful, if you don't aggressively strive to fulfill them, life, time and the wants and desires of others will give you plenty of things to do and plenty of reasons to put your own off until things are better, things are right. I notice it most in the morning when I wake up to my clock radio. The sense of mortality is the strongest then. I don't know why but, upon waking, rolling out of bed and starting a new day, I realize that I am an individual being. That's an important thing to know. We drive down the road totally separated from reality in our separate automobiles and separate lives and separate journeys but, everyone you meet on the highway is an individual, a separate living entity with their own wants and desires, goals, and every separate individual thinks they, at that moment, are the height of importance. I know I sometimes look upon others on the highway as nothing more than jam cars like the ones I used as a kid with a slot car racing set. Their sole purpose was to try to block me, get in my way, to slow my race to my goals. Of course, that is not what others are, they are the same as me. All of us will end our journey one day. One day, we will not get up to shut off the clock radio and the dreams won't matter anymore. What we have accomplished or not accomplished does not control when this will happen, only time. In the scheme of things, it doesn't even matter when one of us leaves the rest. There are many others to fill the empty slot, others with their own dreams who also feel that time means nothing in their life. I don't know where I'm going with this but, I felt like writing it.

I was upset by some of his statements because I had supported all of his dreams and even helped make some of them reality. If it were not for my support and encouragement and input, he would not have achieved what he had been able to achieve. I was also scared by some of his words. They seemed so sad and lost.

twenty-four
SWINGING

AUGUST 28

I kept staring at the oak tree just beyond the deck that Jon had transplanted from my childhood home. I had waited so long for it to be big enough to have a swing in it. I decided to go to the store and buy a swing and put it up. If there was even a chance that I would have to leave my home, I was going to experience as much of it as I could for as long as I could. And, now, I could experience it without the threat of knowing he could drive into the yard anytime he wanted. It had finally come down to that. I had had to get a letter sent from my attorney to keep him away. I had had no choice. His constant presence and behavior had me on the verge of a breakdown.

I swung from my blue swing with the leaves blowing in the darkness, a warning of an impending storm. I leaned back my head and watched the leaves straight up through to the top of the tree. I felt like I was in the movie, "Legend," with everything blowing all about. It was so wonderful, but I felt a sense of impending doom. I knew that I had better savor every moment because everything was so uncertain. I wondered if all the cheap thrills that Jon had paid so much for had made him half as happy as I felt in those few moments on my swing. I didn't think so. How could being with strangers even compare? I knew he must be mad—crazily mad. As I walked onto the deck, there was a frog and I spoke to him and told him of the story that Jon had always begun but had never finished. "Once upon a time there was a frog….." I would always ask Jon to tell me a story and he would always do the frog story. I didn't know if it was a lack of imagination that always brought him to this or if he really liked it. Whatever it was, it was always funny and endearing but he never had a good middle or end to the story and I didn't either.…

I let the frog be on his way and turned and almost stepped on another frog who jumped under my car. It was wonderful to see that life had returned since all the mowing had been done. They hadn't been able to jump up from the pond because of the long hay and now they could. The creatures were returning to the field. There had been so much turmoil with all the cleaning up of the yard and now it was becoming how it used to be. How I wished that the ducks would return. They had been at the pond during the Spring briefly but had disappeared. I wondered if it was because they knew he wasn't there anymore. I never saw any babies. Maybe no babies were ever to live there again?

AUGUST 29

I received my order from "Amazon.com." I couldn't believe that the Tina Arena CD I had bought had a song on it entitled "Sixteen Years." It was so similar to our situation it was incredible. In an email to Jon clearing up an account mix-up, I told him he should listen to it. Like he would care. But, I couldn't stop trying to get through to him. I was born with a sense of not giving up.

No ducks. I had no ducks in the pond. It made me sad. There had only been two during the Spring and they had disappeared. They were someplace else where love and life resided.

SEPTEMBER 1

The fair was tonight. Seventeen years ago, we were all there together. Jon, Don, Bob, Quinn, my sister and I. I remember how Jon included me and didn't leave me behind. And, I remember going to the Plywood Pony Bar after and then to the H&P truck stop and how much fun we had....

On the way back, Jon had ridden in the back seat with me. I sat as close to the door as I could but, really, I had wanted to sit on his lap.

SEPTEMBER 2

There was an email from the "Belly Ring Girl" in Jon's account that told him how she was moving to their mutual friend's apartment building. Somehow, in my mind, I came to the conclusion that it had been she who had set them up. All the time she was cutting my hair, she had been setting him up with someone else—while we were still married. And the joke was that she had been divorced before—but she had been the one in Jon's position. The one who threw the other out of the marriage. So, it made sense.

The constant emails from the older woman in Newport, Ashley and the "Essexton chick" were unbelievable. They all "stroked" him about his divorce and told him that life was going to be wonderful for him as soon as he got rid of me. The exception was the "Essexton chick." She was not belligerent in her replies and emails. It was as if she understood part of the situation. Of course, she had been involved with a married man.....and she seemed to have a better take on both sides of the story.....

SEPTEMBER 3

I remembered how I had always wanted twins......for years. I planned on having twins. I knew in my soul that I would have them. And, now, what were my chances of that?

SEPTEMBER 3

From one of the emails in Jon's account, he spoke of how his attorney was leaving the area as of November 15 and how this would ensure that the hearing would take place on time. He always assumed things and most of the time assumptions never worked out.

SEPTEMBER 3

I found an interesting email from the older woman in Newport where Jon acknowledged that things had not worked out with Ashley. The Newport woman felt badly about that but, at the same time, suggested one of her "hippy" friends for him to go out with to which I never saw the reply. I knew that wasn't what he was looking for.

SEPTEMBER 3

I decided I would find a way to celebrate my anniversary each year. It was over a month and a half away but I didn't want to ever forget the happiness of my wedding day. I wondered if I might send him a card but then thought again. This would definitely take some thought over the next year and I didn't have time to think about it now.

SEPTEMBER 4

The emails from the "Essexton chick" constantly put him off as far as meeting. She was working through the breakup of her "true love" and long-term relationship with a married man and it seemed she didn't want to get involved with another! How could Jon be in pursuit of someone who freely admitted to not being "free????" It seemed again to me that he was only interested in one thing or that he didn't care who was with who. All he cared about was getting something for himself no matter what the price might be for the other person.

It seemed as if he only had female friends. It was strange. He never really had had any male friends. And I had been the only one he had done anything with except for the odd meet-up at the ski area with people he worked with. I couldn't help thinking for the millionth time how if only he could see that what he'd left behind was what he was searching for..... In my mind, my marriage would always exist. For me, I felt it would never end. I knew I had to find a way to move on, even if there was still a place in my heart for him.

SEPTEMBER 6

The Newport woman got really vicious in one of her messages to Jon that I was out to screw him because I wanted to stay in my home (actually—in the physical sense, maybe I did!) and that he should buy some chocolate, eat it and go to "The Box House" and bump and grind it with all of the single, available women. As for "single, available women," I wondered at the quality of choice at this particular location. It couldn't have been that great. I was shocked that Jon would correspond with someone who would even suggest such a thing but things had changed and I had to try to get it through my head and I was clearly not grasping it.

In the same message, he admitted to thinking of returning to me and my heart fell into my gut....... I knew it was what my heart wanted but I didn't want him back because he was afraid of losing money or the house and I didn't know if I could deal with what he had done with the Belly Ring Girl. These would be for the wrong reasons. I wanted him back because I loved him and because he wanted to be with me. I'm sure he realized soon enough after he wrote these words that there would be work to do with our relationship after the destruction that had been caused and he couldn't face it because it was reality. And, clearly, reality was not what he was looking for at this point. He wanted a fantasy...

SEPTEMBER 9

Over the winter I had separated things, packed things and organized things but I had left the Christmas decorations alone. They were so special to me. Every year, we had picked out special decorations that reflected our life together. Pulling out "his" decorations from the box had to be one of the most emotionally painful things I had had to do. I couldn't help but keep the little blue airplane with the yellow stripes. As I held it from it's gold string, I remembered the day when he had flown over the house in circles in his blue airplane and tipped the wing at me to say "hi" as I stood on the deck far below in my bright yellow shirt. I took it and left behind one of my treasured decorations—a cherry pie with a mouse that sat on its edge. I remembered how many pies I had baked for him over the years and how much he had loved them. And, I hoped he would keep it and remember.

In the same box, I left behind copies of all of the letters that I had written to him over the past year that I had never sent—ones that he had refused and others that I had been afraid to send. I also left behind a letter that I had written on our first anniversary that told him how happy he had made me and how I couldn't wait to see our babies. In the closet, I left the stuffed animals I had bought for him over the years. I didn't know why I put them there because I intended to stay in the house. It was strange. I really didn't want to leave the mini "Elmo" but I had given it to him as he had given me a larger one. They belonged together—the small "Elmo" always sat on the big "Elmo's" lap. It was sort of like me sitting on his lap and being held and loved. He had given the big "Elmo" to me on a day when I had been so upset and depressed. I had been suffering with a foot injury for several months and the physical therapist had coldly told me he could do nothing more for me. I felt as though my life was over and to top it off it had been my birthday. As I sat and cried, he consoled me and told me that everything would get better—but it didn't. In the end, he ran away and left me all alone.

I taped a short recording on the video camera for him because I knew I would not take the camera with me. My voice quivered with emotion as I spoke in my spotlight of the house as I had decorated it in his absence. I also left a picture of the most beautiful sunset I had ever seen at our house, which I had taken. I placed it in the corner of a large framed picture he had taken years before I had known him. I wondered, then, if I had ever truly known him.

The letter that I had written to him on our first anniversary together kept going through my mind......

October 25, 1987

Dear Jon:

I love you more each day. You are the reason that I exist. I don't know if I can ever give you all the love that I feel inside because there is so much it is never ending; it is endless. When I look at you I see all my hopes and dreams come alive. You have made me so happy; happier than I could ever hoped for. You are so precious to me. I want to make all your dreams come true for you.

Sometimes, I look at you and I still can't believe that you are my husband. You are so caring, so understanding and so awesome. You are me. When I look at you, I see myself. And sometimes I see our babies; they will be so precious.

I want you to have and be everything you've ever dreamed of. I will make it happen for you. I love you so much, baby. I will always belong to you. You are the dearest, most precious part of my life and you are part of me forever. I want to make you truly happy all the time that we are together; forever.

I'll never forget the night when you melted my heart when you told me that I deserved to have the best and to be happy. This is what you deserve to have more than anyone else ever and I will make it come true for you.

I will love you forever, Jon.
Love, Hunter

I remembered the afternoon I had written that note as I sat in the bed in our apartment waiting for him to come home. We were planning our house and I wanted him to know that I couldn't wait until we could have babies there. We wanted to build a haven for a children where happiness and love would be the greatest things in their lives.

I couldn't help thinking back to several months before that moment when he had had to have a hernia operation and how he had lain in this bed in the third floor apartment while I waited on him. His job had caused it. When he started ripping at things, he didn't think—just like he had done with our marriage. I remembered the day I had gone back to work and left him there alone. My sister, Anna, had called me and said that she had seen "some guy" hobbling down the street near our apartment house and then realized it was Jon! The doctor had told him to get out and walk around but the staples holding the incision together had really made him have to walk funny. It was just another memory that haunted me of how much I loved him and how I would have done anything to help him.

SEPTEMBER 11

I couldn't believe the email Jon had asked for and received from his Newport girl. He had asked her to email him a picture. I hoped that it was a high school photo! She looked like an old lady with over-permed hair! And this was the chick I thought he had slept with at the Comfort Inn—desperate or what! It seemed to me he was only "doing" women who reminded him of his sister. The Comfort Inn charge had been on the discovery information and she had made comments in her emails that made me think it might be her. And, it could only have been for casual sex because she was older, divorced and had grown children and I had heard that he had told Ashley that he wanted someone younger who had no children. I had also read in an email he had sent to another babe that the Newport girl wasn't the "one" for him because it wouldn't be fair of him to ask her to start over. I never knew if I was reading truth, lies or innuendo....

SEPTEMBER 19

I couldn't believe that I was willing to overlook what he had done with other women. I didn't want divorce so badly that I pleaded with him to think about his choice. *In the next three weeks, I hope you take one more moment of time to think about your choice. And, I hope for both of our sakes, that your choice will be what is right.* I was so grateful when the hearing became postponed for an additional two weeks. But it didn't change his mind.

SEPTEMBER 19

I kept thinking about everything I done in the past year, things I had never thought myself capable of. I mowed the lawn again on this day and it went so well. I thought how sad it was that I didn't have any pictures of myself doing all the things that I had done like pushing my bike up the basement stairs, vacuuming flies in the upper windows of the peak of the house on a collapsible ladder and then off a nine foot stepladder and removing and replacing insulation in the end vents. But, especially, mowing the lawn and opening the heavy garage door by hand because he hadn't fixed the electric openers. And, then the time I drove the lawn mower over to the house and put it in the basement so he would wonder where it was if he did show up when I wasn't there! Me, going to the dump and shoveling snow and putting salt in the softener and cleaning the spring leak in the basement and changing the water in the spa and refilling it all by myself. And, me just surviving by myself—being a survivor and not running away like Jon did. It was unbelievable to me how he could have so little feeling or stifle his feelings to such an extreme that he didn't care what happened to me. What a jerk. And, me riding my bike and raking nearly an acre of lawn or more. There was so much that I had done, it was unreal to me. It was just like the entire divorce situation—it was so unreal to me and just couldn't possibly exist or be happening. I was existing on pure adrenalin.

SEPTEMBER 20

As I was leaving the most pathetic interview of my life, Jon drove by on his way out of town. There was no mistaking that truck. I knew where he was going. The only place he could be going on a Friday night. To meet a stranger for dinner at an expensive, out-of-town location. I burst into tears and realized at that moment all I wanted in my life was for him to come home to me. I cried tears of hopelessness and desperation.

SEPTEMBER 23

I found out about the "Quechee girl" through an email that somehow got incorrectly returned to the iflyinsky@hotmail account instead of his new account and I checked her out on "Hearts.com." Red nails, lipstick and bleached blonde hair. She was a virtual twin to Kristan. He was obviously still obsessed with his co-worker or at least her stereotype.

The same day I found an email from the "Belly Ring Girl" that had a prior one attached from Jon saying that "the bitch is going to fight for the house." And how he was going to "fight till the end".....
I couldn't believe how he was referring to me to these "virtual" strangers, really. It was unbelievable to me and it hurt.

I decided to look in all of the folders in his account just out of curiosity. I couldn't believe that he had saved my "hot" email from Halley and the "hot" email from me, Hunter, in the "Drafts" section of his account. I knew I couldn't leave them there so I deleted them. Hopefully, he wouldn't notice. Then, I thought that he probably wouldn't remember that he had saved them or, maybe, he would think that they were automatically deleted by the system. I just couldn't leave the evidence behind.....

SEPTEMBER 26

After reading another email from Jon's Newport "friend," I knew that she had been the one whom he had spent the night with at the Comfort Inn during Memorial Day weekend in May. I had had this information for so long via the credit card information but her comment in an email confirmed it. "I happen to think you're a very hard worker." It was a reply to him when he made a comment he had made about a joke she had forwarded to him in regard to how hard men work at sex in regard to their age. Her reply was the answer to my question of so many months. I wondered if it had been worth the $97.00!

twenty-five

LOVE AND HATE

SEPTEMBER 26

I forwarded him quotes that had been sent to me by a friend about love. They were so beautiful I wanted, stupidly, to share them with him. In response, I received an email that changed my feelings in regard to staying in the house that we had built with so much love and hope for the future. "Like a cat that tries to hang on by embedding its claws in flesh. You just don't get it. You will never get it. The deeper you dig, the more repulsive and transparent you become. I try to prepare myself for your next move, knowing in your mind it will be calculated and in mine, wildly unbelievable. Don't email me with quotes you can't begin to fathom. Don't wave to me and don't talk to me unnecessarily. You, at this moment, are my greatest enemy. Pathetic, using, disgusting. See you in court." I was so torn up by his message. His words were the cruelest I had ever heard and they didn't sound as though they had come from him. It was as if someone else had written the message for him. Intimidation? He was clearly upset in regard to my bid for the house and was attempting to use intimidation. And, it was working. I did not want to be thought of as his greatest enemy and did not want our marriage to end on such a terrible note. Even though he had treated me badly since he had left, I wondered what I was supposed to do. It was crystal clear to me that he didn't care what happened to me and I wanted so much to save him from himself.

To his message, I replied. "You made this choice and I feel so sad for both of us. You are destroying yourself with the resentment that you feel. Resentment that is not warranted because you are aiming it at the person who will always be the one who cared the most and would have done anything for you. I will not email you again at your request. I was only trying to pass along something that sounded so beautiful to me. You are so wrong about me and I hope someday that you will come to realize it. You cannot say what I can or cannot fathom because you never took the time to really know me. I apologize for trying to help." I didn't know what to do about anything and felt so confused. I wondered at his comment about being "wildly unbelievable." Was he referring to my façade as Halley? But, he didn't have the guts to come right out with it and ask just like he never had the guts to deal with any "real" situation that needed to be dealt with during our entire marriage.

OCTOBER 2

All summer, I had put up with our nephew and brother-in-law four-wheeling to the edge of the lawn repeatedly and sometimes down the lawn and the driveway. I had asked Jon to tell them to stop but it hadn't worked. So, when it continued, I emailed him again. He denied any knowledge of anyone's actions and told me to call the police. His communications were ridiculous and I was stupid to even try. I emailed him back with names and information to which he replied with more cruelty. He told me how excited he was about his future and how his life was just beginning and how wonderful the women were that he had been with. He was speaking to me as he had since the beginning of the previous November. Nothing had changed. He told me that I had warped his sense of reality. It was all blame; misdirected blame. How could I warp his sense of reality? It wasn't possible. His communication to me was so full of resentment and hate and so warped. He was right about one thing. He was warped. He went on to tell me that his resentment was based in my survival. Because I had a lawyer and was attempting to get what was fair and reasonable, I was to be resented by him. He finally accused me only of taking and not giving. All the years I had spent giving and supporting and encouraging, and he could only tell me that I had taken from him. The hurt was unbearable.

OCTOBER 3

I felt I had no choice but reply to his email of the previous day even though everyone told me I was wasting my time because no matter what I would say he would not believe. But, I had to for my own sake. "I feel sadness and grief for your actions. You still don't know me. It is easier for you to believe the negative because if you faced the fact that there is positive you would have to admit your mistake and the guilt that comes with it. After reading your message, I do know that you need help more than I do. I lived the life you wanted for fifteen years and I did the things you wanted for fifteen years. Apartments, obsession with money, etc. were not in my hopes and dreams. I remember saying to you in the first few months we were married that we could not have the life we dreamed of if we didn't get away from the apartment buildings and you ignored me. And, now you want me to leave "your" house with only what you want me to have. You ran away from our life—the life that you created and now you think you can solve everything by "starting over." I think that you will be "starting over" for the rest of your life. No one will meet your expectations. As for disgusting, I won't go there. The things that I have heard and have had to live with hearing of in the last ten months have been disgusting and shameful to me, your wife. It was the only way you knew of to deal with your pain. I have not taken anything from you. You have taken everything from yourself. I know the true reason you left me and it had nothing to do with any of the excuses you gave me. And, you don't know me because you never allowed me to be who I really was and I didn't allow myself to be who I really was. You have become whom you have hidden from me since before I met you. Someone told me the other day that the person that exists now is the real person. The person who I was married to for fifteen years was not the "real" Jon and that is very sad because the Jon that I married seemed to be a wonderful person and the Jon that exists today is a self-centered, hurting individual who things that jumping from one woman to the next is the answer. And, that is the saddest part of the story. I will always love the Jon I married no matter how much you hate that thought. But, I am horrified by the Jon that exists now. He is a complete stranger to me with a "wish list" that revolves around money. There is no reality in it. I have only tried to protect myself in the last months. With the constant threats and your constant harass-ment, I have dealt with so much pain—pain that you will not allow yourself to feel. If you don't allow yourself to feel the pain of all of this, it will get to you eventually. How is someone supposed to react to their husband who they have supported without limit—running away from their life together? I know now that you believed me to be so weak that I would leave the house within a week after you left. But, I had no place to go and I still have no place to go and you don't care about anything except for your base needs. How can you not see the sadness in this situation? I am losing everything that ever mattered to me—my marriage, my husband, the person who I gave myself to. I know that deep down there somewhere is goodness within you but there is also a terrible darkness in you that scares me. You can hide behind the façade only for so long before you have to face the reality of what you have done and continue to do. I have heard nothing but lies since before you left and expect to hear them again next week. It is sad that the only thing that matters to you is this house. And, yes, it is the only thing that I have left of you but it doesn't matter as much to me—you are what matters and I hope that someday you come out of this "place" you are in for your own sake. I can't help but think in the last few days about the little boy on Prospect Street, Pee Wee, with his salamanders in the gutter water and how moved you were by him as I was. And, I can't help but think that there is a connection to him in all of this. Maybe, you could see yourself in some way in him. I think we all have many things to think about—if only we allow ourselves to. I have no choice but to let you go—it has been forced on me. But, I will never forget the good memories. I will not focus on the bad memories as you are doing. I will not become the cold, calculating machine that you have become. I am a warm, loving person who deserves to be loved by someone who will appreciate me for who I am and for whom I can be. I don't like emailing you. All I want from you is to be able to sit down with you and talk to you but you do not want this and I believe at this point are not capable of it. It would be too hurtful as your email has been to me. Defiance? No. I just don't want this but know that I have no choice but to go along with whatever you want—just as it was during our marriage. I hope you find what you are looking for—whatever that may be but I wonder if it will be enough for you in the end.

His reply was abrupt and said that my reply to his email was why he didn't usually bother writing back to me. He accused me of refusing to listen and consider what he was saying. He said there was no point in trying to make me understand because I never would. He replied to my email a second time to tell me that he was sleeping with no one. Guilt or what? And, more lies.

I was so hurt by his response that I replied again. "What is wrong with you? I just spilled my heart out to you and this is the response that I get? I am told there is no way to understand what has happened. And, through this interchange of feelings, it is obvious you don't want to hear anything positive about me or from me. I am so sorry that you feel this way. This is no way to end what began so beautifully, but that is your choice. You want me to hate you, don't you? And, you want me to go out and do what you are doing so you don't look as badly as you really do to the people who know me more than you ever have wanted to know me. This time you don't get what you want."

OCTOBER 3

I just didn't get it. He was right about that. I felt so strongly that I sent another message. "Why didn't you experience everything you needed to experience before you decided that you should be married? You were so overwhelming to me with attention that I wanted to do everything and anything for you and wanted to do whatever you wanted me to do. Why did you wait so long to figure out that you didn't want me? Why? And, tell me please, how the fairytale ended as such a nightmare? You told me you had no doubts and I know I had no doubts. What is the answer? That "life" got in the way?" I told him that I didn't expect an answer but only wanted him to think about what I was saying.

OCTOBER 4

He didn't get it. He replied to me the next day. "You say you spilled your heart out to me. What I see is a one-sided view, lots of criticism, with no consideration of my point of view at all." At this point, I gave up and apologized once again. "I'm sorry. We are both to blame and I feel that I always have to justify myself and that is wrong. Please forgive me but it is hard when I feel that you are blaming me for everything." I received no reply. How could he?

OCTOBER 9

The hurt was bubbling out of me like a spurting volcano. Maybe because I was reading all of his messages and kept seeing how he spoke to other women and how they encouraged his decision. Maybe that was it. I emailed him yet again telling him how I knew about all the money he was spending after seeing the legal documents. I asked him how could he think of himself of as happy eating dinners with strangers. I also questioned how he could even look at himself in the mirror. I was feeling alone and lost and made sure that I told him that no one would ever take my place. I was angry. I wanted to know how he could violate our marriage so badly and mentioned the hotel charge. I knew I had to find a way to accept all he had done but it was so incredibly hard and I needed to vent. I did tell him that my message was written with sadness and pain for the tremendous loss I felt. I did not understand how he could be so disrespectful of our marriage. I bared my soul to him and told him that I didn't know why I couldn't stop missing him even though he treated me so badly in person and with his words. I even tried to make light of the situation by telling him how much I missed his head and how much we had joked about it. I told him how alone I was and how I felt that no one would ever be able to take his place in my life and asked that he not respond if he was only going to say something that would hurt me more than I already hurt. I just couldn't stop crying.

OCTOBER 10

I checked his *flyinghigh@hotmail* account constantly. He was still communicating with the "Belly Ring Girl," Ashley. She continued to tell him that all of "this" was the end of a new beginning for him for the rest of his life. And, she continually asked that she be told what happened at the courthouse. I decided that she was a gossip. And, she was right with her badly worded statement. This divorce was the end of a new beginning for him for the rest of his life! The girl had rocks for brains.

OCTOBER 11

The lawn needed to be mowed again. It seemed every time I mowed the lawn it was raining. I wasn't sure why this always happened but it was like the sky was crying as I rode for hours cutting, raising and lowering the deck as I circled the lawn as he had always done. I knew it might be the last time I would mow and I savored every minute. It had become one of the few things that I did that brought me any pleasure. I had always wondered why he liked doing it so much and now I knew. I would miss it so much that I thought about taking the mower with me. It would only start another war. As I passed by one of the trees, I got a little too close and skun the bark right off the side of it. The hit jarred the tractor and I almost fell off. If anyone had been watching, they would have had quite a laugh. I couldn't imagine what it must have looked like. It was a good thing I had a good hold on the steering wheel or the tractor would have made it to the bottom of the lawn and ran right into the trees. As I neared the top of the lawn, I decided that I would leave part of it uncut. I cut a half circle so that when I would look out from the house, their would be a crescent shape, just like a new moon. As I was finishing, an idea came into my mind that made me laugh. If I could manage the hydraulic deck, I could use that uncut section of the lawn for another purpose. If the four-wheeling fools wanted to keep harassing my peace, I would give them something to look at. I stopped and took a quick look at the space I had to work with and started with my project. I couldn't believe I was doing it. I started laughing and couldn't stop. When I was finished I drove down on to the center of the lawn and burst out laughing and felt like the Wicked Witch of the East! There, in front of my eyes, was a message for him and for anyone else who chose to look. "HI JON" spelled out in fifteen foot long letters. As I drove back the tractor back to the garage, I couldn't help but smile. I had created a work of art with his lawn tractor. Even he hadn't ever thought of doing that! I had learned well from the master. And, that was just the beginning.......

OCTOBER 12

I decided to have a gargoyle throwing party. I knew I couldn't sell them and I didn't want them so I threw them. My sister had already thrown a broken one into the pond so I thought I would have some fun. Adrenalin was flowing and I needed to get it out of my veins. I threw a few of the smaller ones into the pond. When it came to the big, 80 pound gargoyle, I had to drag it on a towel across the tiled floor of the second story of the house and then I pushed it out of the atrium door. I couldn't believe that it didn't break. But, it made a gaping hole in the lawn. I went out and rolled it over the bank where I hoped he wouldn't see it. Then, I did something I couldn't believe. Jon had welded a flower in the welding class that he taught and had given it to me. I had put it in the garage to leave it behind and decided that I didn't want any other woman to have it. So, I pitched it into the pond. After all, it had always been a dangerous thing. The tips of the petals and leaves were pointed and razor sharp. It reminded me of "Sleeping Beauty" and the spinning wheel that she had pricked her finger upon and had fallen in a long, dark sleep. Throwing the flower in the pond was my way of waking myself up to the reality of my situation. And, I had created my own archaeological dig for someone to find someday. I did feel badly about the flower after but I didn't want anything that had anything to do with that school. And, I hoped that someday he or someone else would have the pond drained or dredged and find everything and wonder what had happened. There was a story to be told in the bottom of my heart-shaped pond.

OCTOBER 13

I first noticed the crack on this day. I thought at first that it was a reflection, but it wasn't. With binoculars, I could see that the beautiful spindle that Jon had created for the top of the tower roof was cracking around the ball section. It was horrible and I was so afraid he would see it and blame it on me as he blamed me for everything else. It seemed to be a sign for me—a sign for me to go. I went into the house and packed three more crates. As I wrapped and packed, I could only think of the day the original tower had been attached to the house and of when I came home for lunch and saw it completely attached with the top on with the rampart edges. It had made me feel like a real-life princess. And, now, the crown was being ripped from my head…

OCTOBER 15

I met with my lawyer to go over everything for the final hearing. I told him that I wanted to make a "clean offer" to Jon—one where he would get the house and have to pay no alimony. I knew he didn't want to pay alimony from reading his emails and I knew that without a full-time job I could not support the house that had become my home. My heart was breaking but I didn't want to go through the torture of testifying in the courtroom. The Temporary Order Hearing had been difficult enough. I couldn't imagine what the Final Hearing could end up being like. My attorney advised me that I might be shortchanging myself but said that if I felt as strongly as I said I did that he would call Jon's lawyer and make the offer. The call was made and I was told that we would hear something by the following day.

OCTOBER 15

I felt compelled to write. I regretted that I had had no children. I wondered if it would have worked out if we had in the beginning. But, he had refused. Then, I had been afraid. I dealt with my feelings by writing a letter.

Dear Babies:

Please forgive me that you were never born. But, please know that there was so much love for you within my heart. I wanted to have you. I called you my "precious babies"—our "precious babies" in a letter that I wrote to your father on our first wedding anniversary. I wonder what you would have been like. Would you have been short like me or tall like your father? Would you have had your father's beautiful wavy dark hair or my big hazel eyes? Would you have had his million-dollar smile? If you had, I would have named you "Maximillien" if you had been a boy and "Maximilliana" if you had been a girl. Twins. I so wanted to have twins. You could have been twins.

But, I was always afraid that you would have hated me for not being enough. But, I know I would have loved you with all of my heart and soul—just as I loved your father and how I still love him. I gave him everything in my power to give— everything that he asked for and more. I would have given him you but he decided he wanted someone else who could give him other babies and not you. He didn't think that I should be your mother. So, please forgive me that I wasn't good enough for you because you were so wonderful to me in my dreams of you. I shall always dream of you and what you might have been like and what you might have become.... I am so sorry that I was not allowed to give you life but, in truth, sometimes feared that life would be so hard, as it had been for me. I begged your father to stay but he would not and he ran away from us. I know he wonders but he believes he is doing the right thing abandoning us. I would give anything to go back and do things right, but it is over. I am so sorry. Please forgive me. I love you and I love your father even though he has deserted me. And, just know that I will forever regret that I was never able to give you life.

Love, me.

I remembered the baby name book with all of the handwritten names in the back that I had and how it was packed away with my wedding dress and the baby t-shirt we had bought on our honeymoon and I couldn't help but cry again for all of the losses that had been created by his decision and his tunnel vision.

OCTOBER 17

I went into town after dark to get a video to watch because I only got two channels and one of them wasn't working. As I drove past the Laundromat, I saw Jon walking toward the front of the building–gaunt and thin and unhappy looking. I had to hold myself back from going in and seeing him. I drove past the Laundromat at least three times and turned around in the parking lot twice. I wanted to bring him home and feed him a good meal and take care of him. He looked sick. He looked desperate. And, I knew that I didn't want to take his house away from him but that I didn't want to lose my home—all I had left of him.

OCTOBER 18

The meeting with my attorney had been on Tuesday and on Friday we still had not received a response from Jon's attorney. That was when I received a call from Jon.

I couldn't believe my ears. He was telling me that my offer was made as a punishment to him for leaving me. In my heart, I had made the offer with love. It was an offer that would allow him to have the house and be free of alimony. I couldn't believe his next statement—that I was taking his life away from him because he had to pay me off and that I reneged on our marriage agreement because we had no children. I never went back on any agreement. I wanted children because with him I thought anything was possible. I wanted children because he would be their father. Were these the wrong reasons? And in the last years, his resentment about my inconsistent work had made things so difficult. And, then we were both on a path for better work environments through working on college degrees. And then at the last moment, he used this against me. He wanted me to, again, give up my life for him and have a child—with all of the responsibility for the child to be mine and I panicked. Threats and panic. A deadly combination. He used my panic in response to his month-long threats as the "fatal mistake" in order to cover for his cowardice. It gave him his way out. He knew he was going to someone else but that couldn't be used as the excuse. His reputation would be compromised. So he left me standing alone.

To his demand that my offer was made in anger and that I was taking his life away, I told him that my offer had been made in love and that the day he walked out the door he took my life with it. He had no response. He screamed his comments to me, constantly interrupting my responses. He was upset that he had not received my offer until so late. His lawyer had not called him on Tuesday as she was supposed to. He went on to say that his lawyer sucked and that my lawyer sucked and that they all sucked. I replied that my lawyer was good and he said it all again. He called me to give me his counteroffer because he thought he could intimidate me once more and put me into the box he believed I belonged in…. His offer was ludicrous. He wanted me to be responsible for half of the mortgage on the apartment building that he was responsible for according to the temporary order and for which he had not done anything toward keeping it up during the time before our divorce.

He accused me of not moving on. He told me that if I was moving on I would be out dating. I replied that moving on was not about dating, it was about dealing with the grief and the loss of our situation. And, I told him that I knew and believed that everything could have been worked out between us if he had given us a chance. He laughed and said that it could never be fixed. I told him that whatever he believed was his truth, but my beliefs were otherwise. I said that with belief and hope anything was possible. To this, he screamed at me to "take your fucking hope and shove it up your ass." I was horrified and didn't know what to say. He had no belief system. How could he say he was happy when he was acting so desperate and screaming at me? I wondered if he had been dumped by another Internet babe.

He continued on and said that at the offer amount I had made, he would tell the judge he couldn't afford it and that I could have it. I replied that at that point it might be determined that the house would be sold. He reacted violently to this and I asked if he had heard what my attorney had said at the temporary hearing. He was livid and replied that that was what my lawyer had said and I replied that it was a very real possibility. He then accused me of telling my lawyer I wanted alimony. I told him that was not true—that I had made the offer so that I would not have to go that route. He listed off all the debts that he was willing to absolve me from in exchange for me being responsible for half of the apartment building mortgage and I replied that they were not all valid. He wanted me to be penalized for the money I was forced to use to live on over the winter and the money he had borrowed so that he could take strangers out to dinner. I told him I would not be responsible for the extravagant dinners he had paid for on his dates with strangers. All this time, my tone remained calm and he yelled and carried on. He was angry about my knowledge of his credit card debt and said that I was using it against him. I told him he could do whatever he wanted to do but that I shouldn't have to be responsible for debt that was his choice.

All the time I listened to him, I realized that he hadn't changed from the beginning of this legal battle. The anger and bitterness in his voice was overwhelming and was certainly not that of a happy person. I felt so sad for him, for me, and for us. It was very clear to me at this point that he was over the edge in desperation. And, I wondered if he'd always been this person. Master of disguise?

I wondered about the outcome of the hearing. I wondered if he would lie straight through the entire thing. I wondered if I would end up with so much less. I decided that whatever happened would be what was meant to be.

OCTOBER 19

I emailed Jon to make sure that he understood that his "no" to my offer reinstated my interest in the house. To this he replied cruelly once again. "You know something? You're a complete fucking idiot. See you on Wednesday." It was just too much to take any more. I had to stop trying to communicate with him.

OCTOBER 21

The email I read from his friend in Newport was horrible to say the least. He told her of my "clean" offer and that I was threatening him with alimony. My offer waived alimony! He really didn't want to pay alimony and he referred to me as a "bitch." His friend suggested that he walk away and take whatever my payoff to him would be so he wouldn't have to pay alimony. I wondered at his intelligence. With friends like this who he sought out as advisors, where would he be in the end?

OCTOBER 22

I spent all day going back and forth with my attorney reviewing and revising paperwork. Numbers, figures, words. They were spinning by the end of the day. I made numerous trips to his office to deliver papers. During our last phone call of the day at 6:30 PM, I was told that I had to make a decision about the house. I didn't have a full-time job or income that would support the house. I knew I could get the backing to buy out Jon's half but that was it. I didn't want to let go of all I had left of him but the stakes were high and they were so uncertain. I had to make one choice. I could not say one thing and if something was decided, make another choice—in the courtroom. I realized that I had to really put my trust in this man who was representing me and who had done a great job of it so far. I went with his suggestion that we would ask that the house be sold and for alimony. I was sad but I felt some peace because a decision and a commitment to that decision had finally been made. I had gone back and forth so many times in recent months as to what I should do or could do and it was finally over. This was it. I really had no other choice. This was the moment of reckoning.

As I sat there that night, I realized how much I thought I loved Jon and was so angry with him at the same time. I wondered how many years these feelings would exist for me.

OCTOBER 22

That night, the night before the Final Hearing, I read an email on his account that made me hurt for him so badly even though he had done nothing but strike at me with words and actions since the beginning of the entire "mess." He admitted to his Newport "girl" that he had spent the night prior crying and feeling sorry for himself. But, in the next sentence he explained that he had to stop feeling sorry for himself and get pissed off so he could fight me. My emotions were so conflicting. All that mattered to me was him and all that mattered to him was the stupid house. I didn't know what to do and decided that fate would be the decision-maker. His "advisor" advised him that whatever happened, he would be better and stronger for it and that eventually he would like himself a lot better. What would there be to like about someone who had run away from his wife after so many years? What?

twenty-six

THE HEARING

OCTOBER 23

I woke up at 5:00 AM. Started my period. But my mind was very clear—much more so than it would have been if I had had PMS. I decided to wear the only one of the two shirts that were appropriate for the hearing knowing that it had been my mother-in-law who had gifted me with it at Christmas last year by absenteeism. It was funny. I was using the purse she had given me and wearing the shirt to a hearing for a divorce from her son. Weird. I went to the lawyer's office for 8:00 AM and gave him the documents he needed. We arrived at the courthouse at five of nine. Of course, I set the metal detector off. My sister and the attorney's ex-secretary were standing there. I said out loud, "Good luck to me" and my sister followed me up the stairs. I was wired. My attorney was already all the way down the hall. As I pulled the door open to go into the courtroom, my attorney was walking toward me and escorting me out of the courtroom. What I saw beyond was a shocker. My sister went into the courtroom already knowing who was in there and he shut the door. "So, who is the gang in there?" he asked with a smirk. I didn't know what to say. It was Jon's entire family. He told me to relax and I asked him where the bathroom was. It wasn't as if it was a complete surprise but I felt stronger for it and I felt that Jon had made himself look like an idiot by allowing all of them to be there. Intimidation or what? He had already intimidated me enough but I had been given a gift in all of his intimidations. I had realized what everyone was suggesting—that my offer was the right one. My offer was not made as a form of punishment or anger—it was truly an offer made in love—a release for him from any connection to me in the future if he chose and a way for him to hold on to his precious house, which was really just a pile of fancy sticks with emotions holding them together.

As I walked into the courtroom for the first time, I did not look to the right. I let my peripheral vision show me that there were many people there. My sister sat by herself to the left behind where I would be sitting. My attorney asked them if any of them were witnesses and they replied that they were not. However, my sister later told me that there was a pink list of witness names that the deputy had been holding. I wondered later who they might have had on call. I felt as though I was in the middle of a circus. My sister termed it as "being in a pack of wolves with no teeth." Here I was in the most serious moment of my life, and they sat there joking and laughing. How I held my composure I had no idea. My attorney proceeded to label all exhibits as they all carried on like fools. All I could think was "Circus City." There was no control in their conversation. It was as if they had something to celebrate. Counting their chickens before they were hatched.

Both lawyers were called into the judge's chambers. I thought this strange. I had never heard of this before. I read through the brief that Jon's lawyer had prepared and couldn't believe the lies and the information that was clearly wrong. I made notes for my attorney for when he would return. With the lawyers not present in the room, the conversation became worse. At one point, I heard my brother-in-law say to his father that if Jon didn't like the settlement that he could appeal. All this time I had been writing and remaining focused. Now, I turned my head and stared at him until he looked at me. He turned away like a coward. As I sat there and wrote and my sister sat in silence, it seemed all at once that things became quieter at least for a very short time. I knew they were wondering what we were doing, especially me. I was writing with purpose. But, it didn't last for long. The pace quickened and Jon's father became louder than ever.

It was very apparent to me that Jon was finally a "true member" of his family. He was now a doer of infidelity, which made him one of them. Every single one of them was guilty of infidelity in one way or another. The presence of his mother and father was unbelievable knowing what I did about his father's constant affair of the past two years. At one point, I almost turned around and told them that this was not a party—that this was serious. How ignorant could they be—not knowing that their conduct was inappropriate—that silence and whispering were the only forms of behavior that were appropriate in a court of law. It just wasn't the place for stories, chatting and laughing. A relationship founded in love was ending. I could see that Jon finally had the support that he had always dreamed of from his family and I felt sad for him. It took dumping me out of his life after fifteen long years to make him a part of his family and I thought how pathetic that was. They had not changed. And, I was being allowed one last look at their idiotic behaviors and seeing that it was nothing I wanted any part of. Here they were trying to turn my divorce into a joke and attempting to take away any dignity allowed by a court of law and which was something they would never understand. Their stupidity was unbelievable. This being like death to me—I was losing my husband and they saw it as some sort of sick birthday party.

All I could think was that the judge would see that Jon was a weakling having his entire family there to attempt to intimidate me. No character. My composure was severely tested as Jon's sister sat directly opposite me and discussed her new pregnancy with Jon. Jon said hardly a word. She was so loud and belligerent and obnoxious. I wanted to cry. Here I was with little chance of ever having a child and no chance of ever having Jon's child and she was clearly motivated to cause me more pain than I was already feeling. She and her father. Bitch and bastard.

I hoped that he would have to pay up today and even if he didn't, I knew he would pay someday for his actions. I thought to myself that he already was paying very dearly. He was alone essentially and living in an apartment, with his cares being limited to extravagant dinners with strangers and his precious truck and thoughts of his house. The talk went on and on and the lawyers remained behind closed doors. I thought how I had never known just how ignorant they were until now—how completely ignorant they were. I knew that if his father were present during the hearing, he would probably be asked to leave. I knew that it was impossible for him to keep his big mouth shut and I was sure his facial expressions would have irritated the judge. Clearly, it would be a mark against Jon's case to have his father there. As I sat there, I couldn't believe how they continued to carry on and laugh and joke. I couldn't understand how they could behave in such a manner when the only thing that mattered to me was Jon. What I did realize even more was that I did not want to be a part of this "family," if it could even be called such a thing. I knew that I didn't want to be a part of a family that was so cold and uncaring—despicable. It was strange but through this entire exchange, I never heard his mother speak. As his father got louder and louder, I heard loud "shhhhh's" from someone but didn't know who was responsible for them. They were clearly trying to shake my composure and intimidate me but it wasn't working. I never would have believed that Jon would be so weak that he would have allowed them to all be present. In the first few moments in the courtroom, my lawyer's face had given it all away that he thought it was a joke. I hoped that the judge would see their tactics and behavior as an indication of what I had had to put up with for over fifteen years. I realized as I sat there that I didn't want to be with someone who so easily cheated on me and treated me and our marriage with such disrespect. It amazed me as I sat there listening how they all seemed the same—extremely unintelligent, loud mouthed and stupid, except for Jon and his mother. I wanted to tell them to shut up or leave. Their behavior illustrated to me what I had been feeling for years—how unfeeling and uncaring they all were under their facades and I knew that I deserved and wanted better for myself.

I looked back at my sister and the look on her face said it all. She was clearly unbelieving of what she was witnessing. I had told her on countless occasions of their behavior and here it was all in a nutshell for her to witness. I was so glad she was sitting there.

I knew there had to be a way to have better than what I had had. I wondered how I could have been so naïve and stupid as to marry someone without knowing his family. I must have been numb with his overwhelming nature and love to have consented to such a thing and married someone who had emerged as a complete idiot—something he had called me in the previous week. In truth, he had been speaking about himself.

I felt this was a very serious moment and all they could continue to do was laugh and joke. How could they be so blatantly disrespectful? A family of idiots. But, I knew that I had done some wonderful things for their son—things I would never be remembered for or acknowledged. Only the negative would be acknowledged—borne of their own brains which were, essentially, trains. It was so hypocritical to me how they supported each other in times of crises of their own making, yet they destroyed each other behind each other's backs! I just couldn't believe I was having to put up with their antics on what was, possibly, the worst day of one's life—of my life. It was reprehensible. At this moment, I could only see what was around me. Selfishness, greed, childishness and no love existed there.

Would it have been a good thing if I had had Jon's child? Another Logan in the world? I didn't know what to think, but my heart sadly knew the answer.

He had never brought me around them. Now I knew why. I never belonged. He never belonged. Now he belonged because he had lowered himself to their behavior. I had to ask myself over and over as I had done for so many months why this had happened. I would have done anything to stay with him but he didn't want me. Why? I couldn't stand to be in the room especially with the person who had violated our marriage in every way—knowing that he was thinking and believing that what he had done and was doing was completely acceptable. I wondered what the hell was going on in the judge's chambers and what was taking so long? I was freezing cold..... His father piped up and got louder and made the comment that he was going to have to leave and he wasn't going to get to hear anything! I wanted to throw something at him as I thought that he had no business hearing anything anyway.

The lawyers finally came out of the judge's chambers and called us both out of the courtroom and into separate conference rooms. It was there that I found out that the judge felt that alimony was a good possibility for me. It was also very clear that there was a large amount of debt on Jon's part. Jon's lawyer was informed that her client should be pressed with my offer once again as the judge thought it very reasonable for both sides. We were out of the conference room in a few minutes but the door of Conference Room B remained closed as my attorney and I walked up and down the corridor. As we headed back down the corridor toward the hearing room, Jon's lawyer was filing Jon's family members into Room B. My attorney and I looked at each other humorously. So, he couldn't make the decision on his own. I returned to the hearing room where my sister sat alone and my attorney continued in and out waiting for a response from Jon's lawyer. He called me out again and said we were very close to an agreement and I thought my eyes would bug out of my head. He left again. When he returned, he began handwriting an agreement and then asked me to read through it as he left again. When I was finished, he took the agreement and left with it. My sister, the deputy and I went on forever talking and waiting for something to happen. Another deputy came to relieve the deputy on call and I left to go to the bathroom, then returned to the courtroom. Finally, My attorney appeared again with the agreement signed by Jon. I then signed it. Jon's lawyer stuck her head in the door and asked if I wanted my name to be changed and I replied that I would not at this time. She said she would have it stated that it could be changed at a point in the future so I would not have to go through probate in order to do it if I chose to do so. How nice and convenient for them all—to be rid of me in name too. Finally, they all returned except for his father and mother. I was glad to be rid of his father.

The judge then finally appeared with two side judges and we both testified to the agreement we had signed. It was at this point that I felt the most depressed. I was told that I would receive the cash values of the life insurance policies within two weeks and the balance within ninety days. I had to be out of the house within thirty days. Everyone had been right. The house was not good for me and I knew it. I had been packing for over ten months. Deep inside of me, I must have known. The memories were constantly there for me. By allowing him to have the house and waiving my rights to alimony, I was truly letting go of him. As he testified, I looked at him straight on for the first time and noticed that his eyes were clearly bloodshot and sunken. The dark bags underneath his eyes were very apparent. My sister told me afterwards that during the testimony, his brothers had looked like ghosts. Maybe they were thinking what could happen to them! His sister continued to make light of the situation and my sister did notice a very forced half-smile from Jon outside the courthouse.

There was so much sadness and all his sister could talk about was a celebration party. How could something akin to death be a celebration? As I had read so many times over the last months, "the words of another man's wife will be like poison......." Those words stuck in my brain like jelly.

The catalyst. His sister. The major thing that kept Jon going in the direction of divorce was his sister. He was convinced that her second marriage was perfect and he wanted that. But, the truth was that the only thing that held them together was their money. It was all evident later and he realized that he had made the worst mistake of his life not giving me a chance to be who I was meant to be and running away...... It was just too apparent to me that he probably would not have stayed away from me much less gone through with this if it hadn't been for all of them telling him what to do—wolves without teeth.

On the ride from the courthouse to the lawyer's office to pick up my car, my sister told me how she had gotten to the courthouse and only Jon had been sitting there and how devastated he had appeared. She had told me that he could barely utter a word to her and she couldn't believe how like a ghost he looked....probably wondering if he had made the biggest mistake of his life? No, for him it was all about the money and nothing else.

I realized that I had never thought my five minutes of fame would be in divorce court or, perhaps, it was my five minutes of infamy and the fame was to come???

OCTOBER 24

I was so relieved that it was over or at least partially over. I felt good about myself that I had made a fair and reasonable offer and that we hadn't had to go through the horrible act of testifying against one another. How could he not see the goodness in that? If the hearing had taken place, we would have wiped the floor with him. How could he not be thankful for that? But, still, he couldn't face me and he couldn't tell the truth.

I couldn't believe it. He was still trying to get things out of me. I received an email detailing various items that he wanted in the house. The first few emails were civil but then it was all downhill and I had to finally tell him the way it was going to be. After costing me an additional two grand in pre-hearing prep fees because he couldn't accept my offer before the hearing, he was trying to get the spa and the computer out of me! That was it for me. I sold the spa and decided that the computer would come with me. As for the TV, I decided to give it away rather than leave it behind. If he didn't care—what did it matter?

OCTOBER 25

Our wedding anniversary.....I felt strangely calm. The hearing was over. The document was signed. All I had to do was wait. I wasn't thinking about where I would go or what I would do. I was calm for the first time in years.

OCTOBER 26

In an email to his friend in Newport, he told her that he was going to use money from the sale of his truck to pay down on his one remaining apartment building. I couldn't believe it. What a waste and he saw it as a good thing. But, I knew that he saw it as going from one trophy to another..... I didn't know who to feel more sorry for.

twenty-seven

PUSH PULL

OCTOBER 26

Someone told me that if you wrote on a steamed mirror, it would reappear the next time the mirror was steamed up from someone taking a shower. I tried it and it worked. So, I wrote on the steamed bathroom mirror and drew hearts and messages for him that he would see the first time he took a shower and steamed up the bathroom mirrors..... I was still obsessed with getting his attention or not being forgotten. I didn't know which. I wanted to leave my mark behind. I wanted him to feel and "see" a part of me in our home when he returned.

OCTOBER 27

I was tired from reading his emails in his private account and found a message, printed and deleted it. It had been from his "Essexton chick." He was so out of it. He was telling her he was divorced and we both knew it wasn't final until January! He also admitted to feeling sorry for himself because of the amount he had to pay me. And, on top of that, said he was too nice of a guy for me. I was livid at this comment. He then went on to say that now he wasn't stuck to someone who was dragging him down by having to pay her bills. So, it was all about money, AGAIN. But, then he admitted to marriage being wonderful. All in the same email. I was so confused I wanted to hit him. So, he was saying that if I had been making a good paycheck, all would have been perfect???

OCTOBER 27

Neither of us would give in. He emailed me again in response to my email regarding the spa and the computer and again tried to intimidate me. But, enough with the intimidation. I wasn't going to take any more. His golden words were "I don't care." He accused me of taking all that he had worked for his entire life. So, where had I been for the last fifteen plus years? His email was as ludicrous as all the rest of his communications. It was just unbelievable. He even accused me of being an "incomplete" person. Did he think I would keep taking this crap? I had already given him what he wanted. No me in his life and his house and he still wanted more. I had to respond.

I told him I wouldn't take his crap any longer and that our lives were not a "game." I reminded him that my offer had been made out of love as I had told him before. He just didn't seem to get it. He refused to acknowledge the fact that it had been me that had given in to what he wanted. But, maybe he didn't know what he wanted? Yes, he wanted everything for nothing, and he wanted me to get nothing. I asked him how he could continue to be so cruel. I had to. I told him how I was trying to find a job with benefits and a place to live. But, it was hard without connections. Connections like he had had through me. I told him how in the last year he had done nothing but hurt me with his words, his actions and his choices. "Who are you?" I asked. I wanted him to answer me but how could he when he didn't know who he was. I reiterated how fair the settlement was for him—he didn't have to pay alimony. And, I stressed to him how we had achieved what we had because we had worked together. It was not his achievement alone.

I didn't understand why he had to keep thinking that it was all his. I also stated how everything had been finally coming together and that he ran away from our life together—a coward was what I called him. I called him on this. I told him that he was the one who didn't have the courage to face reality and take the time to work on our relationship, which had been neglected through his obsession with work and money. Instead of taking even one month's time to work with me, he had been floundering around for the past year "looking for love in all the wrong places." I let all of my feelings out about children and how he was the one who put it off and my fears and how horrible it was for me to hear in front of a counselor that he had decided to leave me because of a co-worker. I then called him on his relationship with Ashley and compared her to the tenants he had rented to in one of his apartment buildings. He knew the truth and I knew the truth. I told him how sorry I felt for him that he had chosen to be with the sort of person whom he had always led me to believe was so beneath the level on which he existed. I couldn't believe that he had chosen to give everything he had to give to someone who wouldn't even know how to appreciate it. I even knew that she didn't appreciate it through my email exchanges as Halley. He had even said that the "Belly Ring Girl" had no appreciation for his accomplishments and his work.

I then asked him to thank his family for turning our time in the courtroom at the Final Hearing into a circus. I wasn't letting anything go. I asked him whether or not they knew that a courtroom was a place where respect belonged. But, I told him, it made me realize the truth.

His accusations as to my "taking" everything hurt me to the core. I had only given to him the entire time we were together and even afterwards in my heart. I asked him how could he say such things to me when I had given him my heart, my soul and my life and he had thrown it back in my face and at the same time had thrown it back into the faces of my family. I asked him how was it possible for him to look at himself in the mirror every morning.

I again told him that I didn't believe in divorce and hoped that, someday, he would realize what a mistake it really was. I also reiterated that if all he thought I did throughout those years we were together was nothing, that he was completely delusional. His career was cast in cement with my connections and my support and encouragement. Truly, I gave until I was empty and I continued to give. I couldn't understand how he could continue to ignore this.

He accused me of extortion because my attorney was going to ask for alimony and the judge agreed that I would get it—not much—but I would get it. It was he who throughout the entire year had continually tried to get things from me. Even now, he was trying to get me to leave behind the computer and the spa. I wondered why on earth he would want the spa after how he had complained about it. Maybe to use it as a babe magnet? I let it all out. I told him that I finally cared about me. It had always been all about Jon and now I had to think about myself. And, his references to "complete" people were crazy. How could he think he was "complete" when he had taken off and was acting like an eighteen year old? I was the one who had come up with the offer by myself and I hadn't listened to anyone. I didn't need my entire family to tell me what to do. And, I asked him how could he keep proclaiming that he was happy. If he were truly happy, why would he have to continually harass me, scream at me, and make fun of me. Why? His attitude was terrible. I asked why he couldn't face me and talk to me face-to-face about all of this instead of through email. I knew the answer. Because he didn't have the guts.

I told him that I couldn't let myself feel sorry for him any longer. It had been long enough and he deserved what he was getting as far as not being able to find the "perfect match." I reminded him of his past mistakes because I had no choice in order to make a point. I felt that the decision he had made in regard to our divorce was a mistake. It was just the "final mistake" of his life. Or was it?

I knew I had to say what I did but I also knew that I wanted to end the communication in a positive way. "I wish the person that

I married could exist again. And, maybe he does for someone else or for everyone else other than me. I don't know. But, Jon, you have disappointed me in such a way that I will never forget. Part of me will always love you no matter how you hate that thought. No matter what you say or do, you can't take that away from me. You can take you away from me but you can't erase the good memories that I have. For some reason, you can only focus on the negative where I am concerned. Perhaps, it is the only way that you are able to cope with you decision. I don't know and probably will never know. I just want you to know that this never had to happen if you had not been afraid—afraid of how things could have been if you hadn't run away. Running away doesn't solve anything. It only creates more problems. And, what has happened is definitive proof of that. Maybe, someday, you will understand. I hope so. Right now, all I can think of is where I was sixteen years ago tonight and it really hurts me to think where we are tonight, sixteen years later. How can you live with that?"

Sixteen years ago this night we were on our honeymoon.....

OCTOBER 29

I laughed out loud when I saw the messages from his ex-girl-friend, Ashley. She had emailed him with a message asking if it was him on "Hearts.com" and asked if he had a twin because the location of the person who looked just like him was listed as having residence in a nearby town. Finally, someone had caught him! I went to "Hearts.com" and he had already hidden his profile. She had freaked him out! Then, she had emailed him telling him she had heard he was looking for a roommate! He just couldn't run far enough.

OCTOBER 30

I just couldn't resist the temptation. I emailed Jon and told him how I loved his profile and commented on all his pictures. I also reminded him that I had always told him that he belonged in Hollywood!

OCTOBER 30

In response to Ashley's question about how the whole "Hearts. com" thing worked for him, he replied how great it was and how many people he had met. I knew this would piss her off! I could tell by her reply that she was not impressed and said she would have to give it a lot of thought.......yeah, right! She was giving him a lot of thought and was thinking that he had done nothing but keep the truth from her! And, she was probably wondering if he had been doing the "Hearts.com" thing while they had been "together!" And, yeah, he had! I wondered if he would invite her to "his" house.......

twenty-eight

LEAVING

NOVEMBER 2

I didn't know how I was going to leave my home.....at some moments I knew I could do it but most of the time I thought I would go crazy......And, I kept questioning myself and kicking myself in my mind as to whether or not I should have gone for the alimony....

NOVEMBER 4

I had been falling asleep on the couch until 3:00 AM in the morning and then getting up, brushing my teeth and going to bed on a mattress that lay on the floor. My transitory existence sucked. Since he had left, I had sat on his "side" of the couch. It had been my only physical connection to him and I would never get rid of that couch just for that reason. I was surrounded by a partially dismantled house. It was so depressing. Sleeping on a mattress that had been covered with a vinyl cover for protection in the storage unit, crates stacked everywhere in clumps according to where they would go. It was just too much to deal with. The house was becoming more unwelcome every day. And, maybe that was a good thing.....but, it was so hard to deal with. I took long baths every night in the tiled tub trying to feel like a goddess of luxury. I was living in luxury, the luxury of hell. No husband, broken dreams—that's all I had left.

That afternoon, I had watched as Jon walked over to the empty spot on the deck where the spa had been and kicked at the wire stub—all that was left of it. I had had to sell it. Didn't know how I was going to go without it but had had no choice. I kept thinking about the cruel emails he had sent me the prior weekend. It was just too much to deal with. As he walked across the deck, he looked into the glass of the atrium door and I looked back. We were a reflection to each other and that is all. A reflection of the past. Me thinking of the past as something so wonderful and positive and him thinking of it as so horrible and negative. It was surreal. I didn't know how I was going to go on without my home, but especially without him whom I still thought I loved more than anything......

He kept saying to everyone he was happy but I just couldn't believe it. He didn't look happy but what was happy anyway?

It just wasn't fair. I had designed most of the interior of the house, had picked most everything out and I had to leave it all behind. Because of my love for him. I was giving up my home because I loved him so much. I felt so stupid and questioned everything. All I wanted was my marriage back. Why was that so hard? Why did I have to lose it? Why did I have to let it go? How could there be anything or anyone better out there for me? How? And where? My thoughts were beyond sad. How was I going to leave my home? But, even if I didn't, he wouldn't be there. So, what did it matter? I only wanted him. That was the bottom line. And, it became the answer to all my questions. I was scared—scared to death of being alone, of being without an identity, of being without my true love. I felt so cold, so alone.....

NOVEMBER 7

I kept hearing how he was telling everyone he "won" the house.......and reading the emails from his sister's friend who seemed so belligerent. She didn't even know me and the things that she said in reference to me were more cruel than any of the comments I had read from anyone else but, I had to admit they were on the same level as his had been and probably the rest of his family—especially his sister. I wanted to bag the bitch. She told him in her email that paying me off was better than being "stuck" with me for the rest of his life. What the hell did she know about me or our life together??? Nothing. I had never even met her. It was in this email that I discovered why he had dumped the girl from Quechee. She had been to counseling and had taken medication for a time in connection with her own divorce or who knows what. This bitch writing to Jon agreed with him that he didn't need the "baggage" of someone like that. Oh, how I wanted to tell her what I thought. And, maybe I would get the opportunity....... And, how could he dump someone for these reasons when he had taken medication before for depression and anxiety. And, how could he keep feeling the way he did about counseling when he really seemed to need it!

NOVEMBER 8

It was so hard disassembling my home. I felt disappointment, disgust and anger and sadness. It was a home built with so much love and hope for the future. What had happened? I remembered the first day we had lived in our half-finished home and how happy we had been. The tiles had only been grouted a week before, there was plywood on the floors in the bedrooms and the living room but we were "oh so happy" as he constantly referred to Halley in his emails. We were so happy. I could still feel that moment of happiness in my heart.

As I removed things from the walls, my eyes settled on the Old World map in the wooden frame and I couldn't help but cry. I remembered the day we had bought it. We had been on vacation in Maine to see a concert. The afternoon before the concert we went to the mall and shopped. He had to have the map. It was beautiful. When he finally made the decision to buy it, we were late for the concert. All

I could think of was how we had run through the mall laughing our heads off, hurrying to get out of there so we could make it back to the motel. I struggled with taking it or leaving it behind and decided I couldn't leave it behind because of the image I got every time I looked at it. The image of his happy face smiling back at me.....

NOVEMBER 8

I decided that it was time to remove the "permanent" things from the walls that had to be taken with me. The back-breaker was going to be the bookcase. I bought a tool to pound the nails through. Why he had used nails to attach the thing to the wall I didn't know. Screws would have been a better choice, especially in my current circumstances. I hammered for hours and only managed to get a few through. The top section was finally done and was loose from the wall. My sister and my nephew helped me lower it to the floor and move it out of the way. I then began working on the bottom section. It just wasn't going to work. On the bottom, there were too many levels of wood to pound through. I finally decided that the pry bar suggestion my father had made was all that might work. I went out to the garage and found one. It was amazing. The thing came away from the wall like nothing and there was no damage. I pulled and pushed the bottom level away from the wall and I couldn't believe the nails still stuck in the wall and the holes left behind. Thirty nails. The idiot had used thirty nails to fasten the thing to the wall when I hadn't been looking or when I hadn't been there. It was like everything else he had done. He always over-constructed and overdid everything— so much so that it created more problems. But, I wondered if he had come in one day when I wasn't there and put them in on purpose to make things even harder for me than they already were. He could take the time to do this but in regard to our relationship, he had done nothing....he had given it no special attention in the end. I pried the nails out of the wall and filled the holes with joint compound. I would not have him saying that I left the place in a mess. I figured he could sand and paint the wall. I had done enough. I was exhausted.

NOVEMBER 9

I was so tired of packing and taping and prying. It was a daily event and I didn't have much time left. Ten more days was all I had left to get everything ready to be moved.

I needed a break so I called a neighbor who was having her own marital problems and we went out to eat. After about an hour, Jon walked in. He was stone-faced to me, then turned and smiled at her. She smiled back. I was shocked at her return of the smile. It was awful but I handled it better than I could have imagined. My heart raced but I kept on talking as if nothing was wrong. It hurt to see my husband and to see him treat me like a stranger. It was very strange. And I was appalled at the ignorance on her part. Later, I found out she was just another slut on the market for a man no matter what she had to do.

NOVEMBER 12

I found an email that gave Jon directions to the bitch's house in Boston so he could visit and celebrate his divorce and deleted it. I felt resentful. She emailed him again. Then, I heard on the news that it was going to be a very bad weekend in regard to weather and wondered if he would still go.

NOVEMBER 16

I had a glass of wine and decided it was time to wreak more havoc. I knew he was away in Boston visiting his sister's bitch friend and I decided to have some fun. I went into his email account and deleted everything but didn't change the password. He would find an empty email account and I wondered what he would think. I decided, and even hoped, that he would change the password so I wouldn't be able to read any more of his messages so that I would have to let go even more and would not be able to know what he was doing.

NOVEMBER 18

I saw an email that had been replied to where he had told the Newport girl that all of his email messages had disappeared. I wondered why he hadn't changed the password........How could he be so blind as to what was going on?

NOVEMBER 19

Moving day. I stood in front of the atrium door and stared at the message I had created in the lawn over a month before. With the new snow, it was a real attention grabber. "Hi Jon." I thought to myself that maybe I should have written "Bye Jon." But, then, I still had been wanting to welcome him back to our home when I had carved it into the unmown section of the lawn I had decided to let grow. In my heart, I had known I would be leaving. I couldn't admit to myself back then that I couldn't take his home away from him, even though he had no second thoughts about taking it away from me. All I had wanted was him and he didn't want any part of me.

The movers came and loaded my things, our things, into the moving van. I don't know how I managed it all. I had no choice. The house was empty. We went to the storage unit first and unloaded everything but the furniture. But, I did leave the bookcase in the storage unit. I didn't want to have to see it. Then, we went to my uncle's where we left all of the furniture in hopes that I would be able to sell some of it by Spring. I was completely washed out. When I got home, I decided there were still more things to be moved to the storage unit and to my uncle's. For hours, I moved things with my father and by myself.

I got home late that afternoon after taking my bike up to the storage unit by myself. Before I could even breathe, I saw Jon backing around to the back of the house with his truck. I couldn't believe it.

One of the worst days of my life and here he was to gloat. I opened the window and told him he wasn't supposed to be around for another three days and he said he needed to unload the salt in his truck. I yelled at him and, of course, eventually gave up the ghost and told him the basement door would unlock with his old house key, but then remembered the board under the doorknob. I opened the basement door and proceeded to let him have it. I called him a "Bimbo." He told me I would never see the inside of the house again. I was so pissed. I told him to go fuck himself and he returned the comment. He then proceeded to tell me to go get some batteries and have some fun. I thought I would die. He really was suspicious of my true "fake" identity. I yelled at him from upstairs asking him to explain what he meant but he gave no reply. He finally left and I yelled out the window that the house was half mine until he paid me off. And, I told him not to come back until Saturday.

NOVEMBER 21

I couldn't believe it. He was ordering a "spycam." I had discovered this when I accessed his email account again. Was he so afraid I would be around the house that he needed one of these? Or, was he simply afraid of being there by himself? Or, was he going to make porn flicks??? I was grateful for my secret link to know what he was doing even though it was painful to read most of the messages.

NOVEMBER 22

My last day. I loaded up my car with the rest of my stuff, all except for what I would need to take a bath and my precious cactus. I had grown it from the time it was a baby and now it was like a giant spider reaching out in all directions. When it flowered, it was truly beautiful—like our love had been. I went into town and got a meatball grinder, a scone and a chocolate cookie. I decided I would do my bills and organize papers. There certainly was a lot of room to do this on the carpet because nothing was left in the house. I walked around the house feeling the curves of the wood and the woodwork that he had made. It felt silky smooth to my touch. So many of the designs had been my idea and he had come up with the construction methods. We were better together than alone. How I wished he could have remembered that. In the back of his mind, I knew that he did. But his mind was clouded by the comments of other men's wives and ex-wives—what was I to do? I kept looking at the logs and the paper I had placed in the fireplace during the winter in case of a power outage. Why not? I went into the basement and got some more wood and opened the damper. I couldn't believe it. I lit my first fire in the fireplace on the last day I could be there! So, I sat in front of the fireplace, ate, did bills and drank what was left in a bottle of wine I had opened the previous week.

I threw some paper into the fireplace and instead of burning and falling beneath the logs it shot up the chimney. I quickly went outside and saw streams of charred, black paper bits shoot out of the chimney with some landing on the roof! It would figure that I would burn the house down on my last day there! It was funny. I turned and looked at the spindle on the top of the tower roof that looked like it would fall over at any moment. Lightning strike my ass! It was the combination of materials he had used to construct it that had made it burst open. Or, maybe not? I remember the night I swung on my blue swing and the storm that followed. Maybe he was right?

As I sat in front of the fireplace, I remembered the first time I had sat in front of it and written a poem while Jon had slept on the floor. I had written about how it looked and felt and knew that I wanted to write, just as I had known when I was in high school. I felt so alone and wondered what would become of me. No husband. No real job. A partially finished manuscript. A few children's stories. I knew in my heart that these were my only hope for the future. I was getting a good settlement but not enough to live on. What I wanted was my husband back in my life away from our old home in an idyllic life—whatever that was—the one we had hoped for when we had become engaged and when we were first married.

I wondered just why he was so pissed at me. Was it more his suspicions of my fake identity or was it the money? I still couldn't get out of my mind how he had slept with other women—especially the bimbo, the "Belly Ring Girl." I had no clue how he could do this. I truly didn't know him. And, I didn't think he knew himself.

I remembered how he told me when "this" was "over" how he would talk to me and I wondered when I was supposed to approach him on this or if I should.....

As I sat there feeling warmer and warmer inside, I noticed a colored dot in the corner of the room. It was one of those candied Vitamin C drops and I couldn't help remembering how he would open all of them and separate the orange ones from the pink ones. He would eat the orange and would save the pink ones for me. I missed that. Having someone to share with.

The wine went to my head and I achieved a "genius" or "craziness" of mind. I decided that there had to be a way to leave even more of myself behind than I had thought previously. He had always left his mark on everything he had built by writing his name and dating it—underneath tiles, underneath counters, everywhere. And, I decided to use his idea. I laid on the floor on my back and reached up under the sink that he had built for me in the master bedroom and wrote, "This sink was built for Hunter Logan by her loving husband Jon Logan." I found numerous other places where I believed he would never find my messages. But, the way he was it was possible he would be as clever as I was. Hadn't I learned this from him??? In the little hiding place he had built off from the storage room within the upper part of the fireplace that was encased in cedar, I left a broken heart in pen on the side wall with a message to him of how grateful I was for the time and effort he had put into building the house with me and for the tower he had built for me. I then drew a picture of a plane crossing the sea, thinking of how I had always dreamed of going to Europe and how we had talked about it over the years. I hoped he wouldn't be mad, but what the hell did I expect his reaction to be? I knew that it was a real possibility that I would be slandered for it and for the first time I didn't care.

As the fire burned down in the fireplace, I went back downstairs and looked outside and watched as the oak leaves stuck in the snow waved "goodbye" to me in the wind. My oak tree. The oak tree that had come from my home—not his. How would he stand to look at a tree that had been from my home? How could he be so ignorant and cold to that fact? And, I was leaving my blue swing behind. My ghost. My gift to him.

I took a long, hot bath for the last time in my beautiful custom built, tiled tub that I had designed and he had built. It was so difficult for me knowing it would be my last. But, then, I would not say "never" as there would be another tub in another place. "Never" in my life had always come back to slap me in the face and I wasn't going to say it now even if maybe in this circumstance it was true. Then, I took a shower in the tub with the seat that I loved so much and knew that for an unknown time I would not have the opportunity to have such a relaxing bath and shower. But, I knew that I would someday—I would just have to work very hard AGAIN and I could have something even better.... I got dressed and finished loading up the car and went out to the garage to leave the keys on the bulletin board as I said I would. Hopefully, he wouldn't show up as he had three previous times that day to see if I was still there. As I was getting ready to go out to the garage a thought crossed my mind and I laughed out loud.

I pinned the keys to the board and proceeded to write him a note on the white board. "Once upon a time there was a frog. One day a princess came into his life and turned him into a prince. Then, fifteen years later he ran away and turned into a frog once more.....

In my mind, I wanted to add more to the story but knew that he would hate me even more for it. "The princess' heart broke into pieces and she lay so very still. The frog returned to his home and kissed the pieces of her broken heart until they became welded as one once more. The princess awoke and saw her frog had turned back into a prince and smiled. She would be alone no more." This part I could not write on his board. It only stayed etched in my mind. I shut the lights off and walked out of the garage for the last time or would it be? I couldn't believe it even though I knew in my heart it was true.

As I walked across the yard toward the house, I looked again at the spindle on the top of the tower roof. It looked as though it would fall over backward and roll off the roof at any moment. The ball portion of the spindle was so wide open it looked like a mouth; it looked like the pointed hat in the popular wizard movie that I had just rented a few months before. It was as if it was a sign to me, to him, to everyone—a strange sign that destruction had taken place here in our beautiful wooden castle that had been built with so much hope and love. He had destroyed our marriage. It seemed everything he touched became damaged. It wasn't because he didn't try—it was because he didn't know how to approach or deal with any situation in the right way. I thought of how he had explained to me how he had constructed the spindle. I wondered, again, if he had used too many types of materials and it had proven to be true. The elements of nature had determined that they didn't fit together and couldn't work with one another so they had split apart….. With us, he had taken it upon himself to split himself away from me after being motivated and affected by the outside elements that surrounded him away from our home. He didn't know how to approach me with what he thought he needed and had run away from our life together. And, the elements of human nature had driven him toward his own destruction in the process……

I went back into the house and looked around one last time hoping still. I walked out and locked the door and got into my car and drove out of the yard in the dark and I didn't look back……I was really alone, even more alone than I had been before him, and I wondered if I would ever not be alone…..

NOVEMBER 24

He had written to the Newport girl and with her return email, his original message was attached. He told her how he was back in his house but that "something" was missing. I thought to myself— Love, maybe??? He talked about how "scary" it was being there alone and how I had been there all the time and how every time he came home, it was empty. He placated himself by saying that he would make it a place where people would be all the time. I wondered, really, if that were possible.....

NOVEMBER 26

I went to the movies with a friend I had met in a class I had been taking. She was already divorced. I wanted to see the new James Bond movie so badly. It was great to get out and feel free and not boxed up like where I was living. I had been forced to move in with my parents because I only had a part-time job and only a down payment on the pay-off. When I got home from the movie, I was actually feeling better than I had after having to move out of my home. Moving out of my home had been like losing Jon all over again. I couldn't believe the waves of depression that I had had to deal with in the previous two weeks. Within five minutes of returning from the movie, my parents phone rang. It was for me. It was Jon. He screamed at me wanting to know where the vacuum attachment was. I told him that it was in the closet but he said it was not. He said that I had stolen it or the movers had taken it. I replied that it was in the closet and that I had helped the movers and had watched everything they had taken. I reiterated that they had not taken the attachment. He then told me he wanted the original knobs for the bathroom cabinets back immediately. I told him they were somewhere in storage and I had no idea which bin they could be in. I had replaced the knobs with knobs we had painted ourselves. I had done this months ago and thought they looked much better anyway. He was livid and threatened that he would deduct the cost of a new vacuum attachment along with the cost of new knobs from my pay-off. I screamed back at him and finally told him where to go and hung up the phone. It was a horrible start to a new beginning.

NOVEMBER 27

I felt compelled to follow his phone call with an email to make sure he was aware of the facts. I told him in the email that he was not to call my parents number but my own number and only if it was about something important and only if he could discuss it rationally. I also told him to review the final court document so that he would know that he couldn't "deduct" for knobs, vacuum attachments, etc. I told him I would not be intimidated any longer. I had had enough of his intimidations, harassments, and threats of the last eleven months and wouldn't take it any longer. I knew that he must be associating with the kind of people who would support this and all I could think of was the bimbo, Ashley. She was an unhappy, bitchy, gossip who hung out in bars during all of her free time with any guy who would buy her drinks and dinner.

I made sure I communicated to him that there were several things that I had left behind that I didn't have to leave such as the video camera, the new vacuum power head, etc. At this point, I couldn't take it any longer and just gave it to him. I told him to go buy a "Swiffer" if he couldn't find the vacuum attachment that he was harassing me over. That would work. I also made sure I told him for the millionth time that I had cleaned the basement and the garage at least twice.

I told him to find someone else to complain to because I wasn't going to be harassed any longer. I told him that I didn't want to deal with someone who was cruel and unkind and that I deserved better. I couldn't believe I was finally telling him these things in the manner that I was saying them. I was tired of his crap. I told him that he needed to deal with his feelings and that he should find someone to help him do so or his chances for a positive future were slim. I explained to him that anyone who would run away from someone who would do anything for them definitely had issues to deal with. I also told him that I hoped he would attempt to understand what I was trying to communicate to him but if he didn't—it wasn't my problem anymore. I only half-believed the last statement I made but I was getting there.

twenty-nine

RAGE AND SADNESS

NOVEMBER 30

I was raging inside. I still had access to his email account and I was going to use it and I was going to destroy something. I remembered that he had had a link to a resume website and I knew what I would do. I accessed the resume website via his email account and just stared at it. How could he? How dare he? He had submitted a resume advertising himself to the world. Was it because he wanted to separate himself from a job that he knew he had because of me? Or, was it simply because he wanted more money? I played with ideas in my head and finally noticed an option where you could delete. It was so easy. I clicked on "delete" and it was gone. What would he think?

I was so angry I wanted him to drop dead so I could spit on his grave and tell him what a lying bastard he was. And, at the same time, I wanted to be able to tell him I loved him. Maybe it was my fault. Maybe I had tried to make him into something he couldn't be? Or, maybe I had thought he was someone that he wasn't? I was confusing myself. I had to let go of him and of us.

DECEMBER 2

I had decided to change the password to his email account so I could no longer have access to it. When I went to do this, it had already been changed. He had finally woken up. My links were gone. And, it was better for me this way. I couldn't take the pain any longer. I just couldn't read any more of the cruel emails and I needed to let go.

DECEMBER 5

I received another screaming call from Jon. This time, it was about permits that had to be done that had not been done on our land when they should have been done. He insisted that I have a quit-claim deed ready to go within fifteen days. He insisted that he talk to the attorney who was doing the deed. I told him that I would call and find out if it could be done within that time frame. I also told him that I thought it didn't need to be done until the 23rd of January as he had told me I wouldn't get paid off until then when we had communicated in November. He was crazed with rage and anger. He explained to me that it was like everything else—how everything was always a mess. I let him have it on this statement. I told him that it was only a mess because it had to do with him—that everything he touched became a mess. I told him I would call and get back to him and I told him that I did not trust him. I was shaking. I called my attorney's office and explained the problem and they said they would communicate with Jon's attorney.

I finally lost it and cried for hours. My life was gone. When I was done crying, I called Jon's attorney's office and told the secretary what had happened and she said it would be relayed accordingly. The phone rang repeatedly throughout the day. It was him. She had told me not to answer it and I didn't. When I couldn't stand it any longer, I left to do errands and when I returned there was a message from his attorney. I called him and he explained that Jon had offered to pay for the deed so that it could be done as quickly as possible. I just didn't care. I informed his attorney that he needed to deal with Jon and make sure he didn't call me again. His behavior was just too much for me to deal with. I had lost everything. I had given him what he wanted and he was still screaming at me.

DECEMBER 6

I found two emails that morning from Jon. One told me how impossible he thought I was to deal with and that he would not pay for any more than he had to and the other said he would pay for the deed in order to make it happen sooner. I did not reply to these emails. It was the first time that I hadn't replied to him. It was a beginning for me.

DECEMBER 12

I kept looking at the watch on my wrist. He had given it to me on Christmas Eve the previous year, two weeks after he had left me. I couldn't stand to wear it any longer knowing that it had been given to me under false pretenses. I was talking to my sister about it and she asked if I still had the box. I knew that I did. She suggested that I send it back to him for Christmas. I didn't go that far but I knew that I had to get rid of it. I couldn't throw it away. So, I wrapped it in brown paper and mailed it back to him. I didn't care what he did with it but I couldn't keep it. If it had been worth anything, I would have sold it. But, it wasn't. And, as I walked out of the post office, I had a smile on my face. And, I wished I could be a bug on the wall when he opened it.

DECEMBER 13

I finally decided that I had to take my engagement ring off. I put it into the safe deposit box where I had previously put many other things that reminded me of our life together. It was just too painful to keep seeing it on my finger every day. Even after I left it there, I kept feeling it on my finger. It's image was burnt into my mind. I could not forget it and I never would. It was a diamond surrounded by leaves as a rose would be. I remembered the night he had given it to me. We had been checking on an empty apartment in his one apartment building and he just came out with it and said, "Marry me?" Of course, I said yes. He was shaking and had to sit down on the hardwood floor. I was so touched by his emotions. It seemed to me now that all of his good emotions had been clouded by angry ones since he had made his decision to leave me.

DECEMBER 23

I had made reservations to go away for a few days at the bottom of my "wave" a few weeks before. I wasn't supposed to leave until the next day but I just couldn't wait any longer so I left without saying anything to anyone. I felt so free. I had never done this by myself before and I needed to know that I could get my "independence" back. I needed to know that I could do something and have it go well and not be afraid. I checked into the hotel, which was beautiful. I had made sure that the room I reserved had a Jacuzzi tub. I had been far too long without a tub—even though it had only been about a month. I just couldn't stand it any longer. The first thing I did was to drop off my bags and go shopping. It was the first time in so long that I could feel free to buy something just for me and not feel guilty. Ever since I had been married, guilt had been attached to spending money on anything besides the damned house. I returned to my room with an armful of bags and tried everything on again. At least it was a distraction to my loss and to my pain—even if it was only for a little while. I went to dinner armed with my new book and dressed in my new sweater. It was quiet. How could it not be? Who would be staying at a hotel two days before Christmas??? The prime rib was great and the wine went down very easily. I went into the bar area and had another glass of wine and then went looking around. Back in the room, I filled the tub and couldn't believe how much more comfortable it was than my custom-built, mosaic-tiled tub, even if I couldn't get the jets to work! The faucet was so high I could wash my hair. The water was soft like I had been used to. I was in heaven if even for a few moments. I knew that all I really needed in the world to be happy was someone to love and to be loved by and a Jacuzzi tub!

The wine made me dizzy for hours but it was just what I needed. I hadn't been getting any sleep and I hadn't had any time alone and I desperately needed it. I cried for hours and then I felt better. I had been holding it in ever since I had moved and I just couldn't any longer. Those short, muffled cries in the shower at my parent's house just weren't long enough to do any good. The venting system in the room kept me awake but the trip was so worth the effort.

DECEMBER 24

I decided not to stay another night as I had woken up at 4:00 AM and I knew that I should be with my family for Christmas. So, I went shopping all morning and went home. I felt re-energized. I couldn't imagine what I would have felt like if I had gone on a week long vacation—I probably would have been a completely different person! When I returned home, my sister called me and told me that Jon had called her and harassed her about me. He wanted to know where I was. She said I was gone for a few days to which he replied that I would ruin everything and that the closing date was supposed to be on Friday. She told him I knew nothing about the closing date—which was true—and told him to call his lawyer. She gave him a piece of her mind at the same time. All that year, he had approached her several times. I had never approached his family to find out anything about him or to say things about him. What was wrong with him?

DECEMBER 25

Christmas. I had a bottle of expensive wine that I had bought months before hoping it would be for a special dinner. But, it never happened. So, I decided I would share it with everyone on Christmas. But, I ended up being the only one who drank any. I drank half of it and it was the easiest Christmas I had ever had. Easy in the sense that I had been away and I was relaxed—and the wine definitely helped to numb the pain of the day. Maybe it wasn't the right thing to do but it worked and no one ever knew I had consumed half the bottle until they saw it! I thought I would drink the rest New Year's Eve...

DECEMBER 31

New Year's Eve. I sat and watched a movie I had seen when I had last lived at home with my parents and I drank the rest of the wine. I thought to myself that it wasn't much but it was better than the previous year when I had laid in bed and watched the snowmobile lights bounce off the ceiling as the Logan's rode in the field above our house at midnight. All I had been able to do that night was cry. I had sorted papers, cried, watched TV, cried, gone to bed and cried. At least this year, there were no tears.

JANUARY 1

I was depressed on New Year's Day. I realized that my "buddy" was gone forever. Forever was a long time, but it seemed to be the way it would be. The pain just wouldn't stop. I was alone most of the day and that made it easier. But, I couldn't stop thinking about what could have been and what should have been. But, I also realized that I had to leave it behind me and figure out what could be for me in this new year—this new beginning.

JANUARY 4

I saw my sister who told me how Jon was "stalking" someone we both knew. Apparently, he had been calling this girl repeatedly who was older than me and had a grown child. She told my sister that she had no interest in him and asked her if he was my husband. She said that she didn't trust his eyes. I couldn't believe it. It was only two weeks earlier that I had been looking at the picture frame that held the wedding photographs of my mother and father, my sister and her husband and myself and Jon. When I finally looked at the picture of us, all I could see were his eyes and all I could think was that I didn't trust them....and I wondered why I hadn't seen his eyes that way before....and I didn't know what to think anymore.

That night, she called me and told me how she had spoken with an ex-friend of Jon's. He had been at a nearby restaurant where the gossipy owner of the place had mentioned "poor Jon." He replied that "poor Jon" wasn't the one who she should be sympathizing with. He told her how Jon had slandered him and lied and also mentioned that he knew about both "sides" and was inclined to think that my "side" was more truthful. I was so grateful that someone actually had something positive to say about me. I had been living for months thinking that everyone thought of me as a bad person and it wasn't true. It was like my father said—the real truth would reveal itself in time.

JANUARY 5

I kept thinking about my home. I came to the realization that I didn't want to live in a house that a liar had built. But, then, we had built it together and had he been a liar in the beginning? Every time I had looked at the beautiful woodwork, I had thought of him. It was a constant reminder to me of him and his abandonment. I realized that the right thing had happened, however difficult it was to accept.

JANUARY 6

I felt so ashamed of his actions. I couldn't believe I was married to someone who had done all of the things that he had done. I had to stop taking responsibility for the things he was doing and had done.

JANUARY 6

I got a message from the lawyer's office saying that the closing was for the next day. I stipulated to them that I would not go there if he was even in the building and that I would not sign the deed if the check was not placed in front of me. Then I received another call. There was another "mess" attached to the situation, which was typical of Jon completely. Because he had taken out a home equity loan and due to the fact that it was through an on-line "bank," the money would not be available until three days following the closing. And, for the closing to occur, I had to sign the quit-claim deed without seeing a check. The solution they came up with was for me to go to my lawyer's office to sign the deed, have a copy only faxed and I would retain the original until I received the check on Friday.......

JANUARY 7

My appointment to sign the quit-claim deed was set for 11:30 AM. I knew I didn't want to sign. I didn't like that I wouldn't receive the check but then I really didn't care. I didn't want the money. I wanted my home. I wanted my marriage. But, I didn't want the person who lived now as the distorted "being" of whom I had been married to and had loved for over sixteen years. I had never met the lawyer who was doing the land deed until now. She needed some makeup and some haircolor. That's all I could think about. It was the only way that I could stand sitting there. She went through and explained the deed and then another form that had to be signed. I didn't want to sign. I couldn't hear what she was saying. The only thoughts in my head were that I didn't want to do what I had to do. I asked if he dropped dead, would I then get the house. She seemed a little surprised. I did have nerve. That was one thing I did have on my side. She said that by signing the deed I was signing away my right to the property but that there was a remote possibility that I could fight for it in court. I asked if we could wait until the 23rd, since that was the "final" date. She was visibly getting worried. I just didn't want to sign. I wanted to make him suffer like he had made me suffer. I wanted to make him feel the pain like I had felt the pain. I wanted him to feel more pain. I think she really thought she was going to lose me there for a few minutes.

I asked if I could take the forms to his lawyer's office and sign them there if I decided to sign before 4:00 PM. She said that I could but that she had wanted to drop them off herself. I knew she was afraid that I wouldn't sign if she let me take the papers with me unsigned. I wanted to make him sweat so badly........ I asked about his loan— if there was a way to know the deadline of his loan. She called his lawyer and was told that he would have to start over again if it didn't happen as scheduled. I thought that would be stupid. Then, I thought to myself that if I didn't sign at all or waited to sign, I would be sinking to a level as low as he and I didn't want to do that. So I just hurried and signed my name. I think she was about to have a stroke waiting for me. I couldn't help but say out loud that he would "pay" for what he had done and for what he was doing and I told her that this was not my choice—that I was going to fight for my home but I didn't have the income to do so. She didn't seem to get it but at least I said what I felt like saying. So, I didn't sink to his level but I made sure I knew the facts and I made everyone hold their breath—even me...

I just wanted to cry as I left. I had signed a form that was going to make me homeless. I had given up the biggest link. Our love was nailed, sanded, grouted and sealed into that house. I was giving up my castle, my refuge from the world, as well as being my prison in reality. And, I just couldn't deal with it so I stuffed the papers in my glove box and locked it. And, wondered if I would deliver them on Friday... on time...or if I would be late...or if I wouldn't show up at all...

JANUARY 10

I checked in with Jon's attorney's office and was told to come by in the afternoon. When I arrived, the attorney who was taking care of the "deal" was out for the day and the remaining attorney was in court. I was told to come back in an hour's time. No money. The attorney told me the money wouldn't be available until the following Monday. As I stood there hearing this, I stuffed the deed back in my pocket. I told him it didn't matter because I didn't want it anyway—that I only wanted my home. He said that he knew. This was the attorney that had helped me years ago and who I had the same respect for as I did for my divorce attorney. This attorney had actually referred me to my divorce lawyer. He said that dealing with the on-line banks wasn't such a great deal when you got down to the "brass tacks." This was my opportunity to make a statement and I did without reservation. My reply was that Jon had made many bad decisions and choices in the last year and it was just one more than he had made. I will never forget the way the attorney nodded to me in the affirmative.

JANUARY 13

I called Jon's attorney's office and found out that I could pick up the check at any time. I stopped by in the afternoon. It was as if the check was for $1.00. I didn't care. I signed the letter acknowledging that I had received the check and left. At the bank, the teller conducted the transaction and gave me the balance on a white deposit ticket. It just didn't matter. I knew I had to find a way to use the money in a way that would help me for now. I just couldn't even think about buying another house—I was still too attached to my home and anything else just wouldn't be good enough. And, I only had enough money for half a house anyway......

As I stood there and put on my gloves I said to the teller that this was the end of a fairytale....

JANUARY 16

My communications with our insurance agent had been going on for over a month. The credit I was supposed to receive from the old joint policy to my new policy hadn't been made. I found out that the insurance agent never intended to make the credit. He had given me the run around for weeks. First, he had given me amounts that I should be credited and then he told me that I needed to deal directly with Jon and get my reimbursement from Jon. Next, he told me that I needed permission from Jon for the credits to be issued. Finally, he told me there was no way he could figure out the correct amount to reimburse me. He also told me he would not contact Jon. I decided to switch agents but first I would try to remedy the situation.

The night before, Jon had left forms with my mother for me to sign so he could get credits on his apartment building insurance policy. She thought he was getting me forms so I could get credits on the other personal policies. He lied to her, too, his unsuspecting godmother and his mother-in-law. What a trick he was.

JANUARY 16

I mailed a short note to Jon asking that he contact the insurance agent. I apologized for contacting him and ask that he not be offended by anything in the note. I said I would gladly sign his cancellation forms if he would give permission for my credits. I was attempting to use what leverage I had, but, stupid me, anything I did, said or wrote offended him.

JANUARY 17

I received the cruelest and most heartless e-mail from Jon because I was trying to get the insurance credit. The main content of the email wasn't about the credit—he used his contact with me to defend himself and his family and to attack me. It was worse than any email I had received over the entire year we had been separated.

It was a sure indication to me that he still hadn't dealt with any of his feelings—why was he defending his family to me—why was he saying that the "Belly Ring Girl" was better than me—why was he saying all of these things? Because he knew deep inside that the truth was the opposite and he couldn't deal with it and the only way he could deal with it was to defend his "side." He said that he had built the entire house by himself and I wondered where I had been all that time? He was clearly delusional and on the brink of a breakdown…
…I wondered when I would hear of it and I wondered how many things he had thrown that day when he returned home….I knew he had done something. His anger scared me—I wasn't scared that he would hurt me physically—I was afraid of what he might do to himself and of what all of the anger was going to do to him…..I knew he must be frustrated with not being able to find his "perfect match." He was clearly struggling and fighting with time. Time was slipping away in his mind and he wanted something he could have had with me—but maybe he never could have dealt with it. And, how could he deal with someone else if he couldn't communicate effectively. Inside his mind, he was afraid—he knew that he might have to settle for Ashley so he could have a family in a hurry—if she could even do this because was anything ever certain?

He was desperate and in a hurry to catch up to the rest of his family when he could have had all that long before with me. He didn't like Ashley's personal habits and manner; she had no class—but she could give him what he thought he wanted. But he didn't know that she was unable to—she had lied to him. He felt she was honest and up front but he didn't know the extent of her lies and he was going to pay for what he had done—the mistake he had made in leaving me—by ending up with a classless woman and someone who would not be able to give him what he said he wanted—a child. Of course, she was the equivalent of his sister so he might be able to reconcile his acceptance of her bad habits in his mind if he felt he could change her. But can anyone change anyone? He had said it months before to my alter ego—that it was impossible to change someone else and he was still going to try to do it.

His communication was so disturbing to me the first time that I read it. When I shared it with a friend, we laughed through the entire thing! It was clear to us both that he was trying to reconcile his choices in his mind and had to graphically do it on paper to me—the woman he had married and given him all she had to give and the one who had loved him more than her own life.

JANUARY 19

As I sorted through papers, I found an email that had been written by Jon to my sister over two years before. My sister and I had been discussing some issue related to religion and Jon got into the middle of it as he received duplicates of all the emails on his computer at the school. Some of all of our statements were opinionated but some of his were very disturbing as they indicated a real lack of belief in anything other than himself. But, it wasn't this part of the email that mattered to me now.....

My heart broke again for the millionth time when I read the last sentences of the message and thinking how things could have gone so wrong in such short of a time. He had loved me then and we had had a marriage then in his mind, as well as my own. What he had communicated to Halley was not the truth but a delusion in his mind to get him through the mistake he had made in leaving me. He had told her that his marriage had been over for years and it hadn't! In the email my sister had sent to me, she had accused me of being jealous of her faith. Jon had responded to her. The last three sentences of that email I would never forget...... "I do not know your abilities at understanding the workings of other peoples minds, but I can tell you one thing. Hunter is not jealous of anyone. It is not in her personality to be jealous of anyone. In fact, that is one of the things that I love about her—she is so far beyond that type of thought. Jon" Tears again. It was the first time that I could ever remember anyone ever defending me as a person.

thirty

POESY

JANUARY 20

As I looked into the mirror, I saw the ring dangling from the necklace around my neck.......and as I looked at the middle finger of my left hand I noticed the wedding band nestled between the two ruby rings. Was it okay? My sister kept giving me a hard time for wearing the hat he had given me—the hat that bore the insignia of a flying club he belonged to. I felt I had earned that hat and it was the only baseball-type hat that fit me. I loved that hat. But, maybe she was right.

The ring had been something I had given him on one of our anniversaries. It was a replica of a "Poesy Ring" from long ago and the inscription inside read "All I Refuse and Thee I Chuse." He had only worn it a few times. I had taken it from his things after I had given him back his wedding band. I wore it as a symbol of my choice to choose myself and to remind myself of the mistakes that I must have made for all of this to happen. I knew that I had to survive and somehow it reminded me of that. I felt like I was living in hell. The creaking floorboards of my childhood home had been driving me crazy. But, I didn't have a choice but to hang on. I wondered how I would ever trust any man again after what I had been through. But, there would be a moment when I would. There really would. There had to be....

JANUARY 22

I sat in bed in the darkness and watched as the final moments of my marriage ticked away as I watched the clock strike 12 midnight. It was really over, but was it? Would it ever be really over for any of us? I knew that I would wonder about this until the end of my life or until life brought me a fated muse.

thirty-one

DISCOVERY

FIVE YEARS LATER...

OCTOBER 13

My cell phone rang. It was the woman interested in my book-case. The one I had to pry off the wall five years before. She'd driven all the way to Vermont to see it. She loved it and wanted it. The tears began to fall on my keyboard in front of me. She was so nice that I knew it was going to the right place and it would be just across the State, a place I remembered fondly from my childhood. I knew it was right. It was time to let go of another memory.

NOVEMBER 6

As I drove on the interstate on my way back from the Seacoast, I made a call on my cell phone to check on the bookcase sale in Vermont. Everything had gone well. I asked the question again that had been pulling at my gut for weeks, but to someone different this time. Someone who would tell me the truth. Yes. He and his "new" wife had had a child. The knife cut through me again. A few years before I had heard she had a miscarriage and I had felt badly for her knowing what she would probably have to deal with—she might be discarded as I had been for not being perfect in his eyes.

As I spoke on the phone, the tears threatened but I held them back. I had guessed inside me but to hear it made it real. Too real. I was hurt. Then, I was angry at being denied. I wondered why I had to keep bearing the pain even five years later.

NOVEMBER 13

I had to know how long it had been that the truth had been kept from me. It only took a few minutes to pull up the school website on my computer and there it was in black and white. Faculty births. February. And, here it was November.

NOVEMBER 18

As I was listening to a song I had found when looking for another one, I felt like a lightning bolt hit me. I started to cry and couldn't stop. I had let him take the fire inside me and it had to stop. I had to find the passion and fire I had lost. Tears fell and my heart started to heal. I knew what I had to do.

NOVEMBER 19

I searched the place until I found it. The manuscript. The one I had put away five years before. I started reading and couldn't stop. I was overwhelmed that I didn't feel what I felt before. I felt as though I was reading something that a complete stranger had written. I felt relief that he had left me standing there alone to find the real me that had been lost in the darkness of marriage to him. I felt the fire coming back and I decided I wouldn't ever let anyone take it from me again. And, I started editing and decided that this story would see the light of day no matter what anyone thought. It was only what I thought that mattered.

thirty-two

THE BEGINNING

ONE YEAR LATER...

SEPTEMBER 3

As I stood on the dock looking out at the shimmering, clear water of the lake that I loved so much and one where I had found what I had been searching for my entire life, I knew he was watching me. I felt the cold metal of the ring in my fisted hand, as cold as the heart it had been given to so many years before. It was the Poesy ring, the one that said "All I Refuse and Thee I Chuse." No more did I choose him and knew that it had never been meant to be forever. I had found it when I went to my safe deposit box and it had rolled out onto the counter and I had known immediately what I wanted to do with it to seal the deal on my new life.

I lifted my hand and threw the ring high into the air and into the water beyond the boats. I chose the lake to be its final resting place. My past life was dead and gone and so was the love that had existed. He was finally gone and out of my heart. I turned and smiled at the one who watched me from a distance, the one who had claimed my heart and loved me more than I ever imagined one could love. A real love, not a fake, fairytale love.

The one who watched came toward me and hugged me close, smelling of bike leather and fresh air. It felt right like nothing had before. I put on my helmet and he roared the motor to life. A shiny, gleaming Harley and a man full of passion, with love to give without limits. Who would have thought?

I thought, again, how life could change in one moment. Seeking the truth was the key to our reality, and I realized at that moment that dreams came true and miracles happened when we expected them.

ABOUT THE AUTHOR

D. C. Legendre is a freelance writer and aspiring fundraiser and designer who lives in New England. Thunderstorms, fairytales, and castles are some of her favorite things, as well as uncovering the mysteries in life. She believes without a doubt that life is an endless journey of the heart.